To Abbey
from Mom
2001

ONE-HUNDRED-AND-ONE
READ-ALOUD CLASSICS

ONE · HUNDRED · AND · ONE

READ·ALOUD
CLASSICS

Ten-Minute Readings from
the World's Best-Loved Literature

EDITED BY PAMELA HORN

NEW YORK

Copyright ©1995 Black Dog & Leventhal Publishers, Inc.

Published by
Tess Press
an imprint of Black Dog & Leventhal Publishers, Inc
151 West 19th Street
New York, New York 10011

ISBN: 1-57912-133-0

h g f e d c b

BOOK DESIGN BY ALLEYCAT DESIGN, INC.

Manufactured in the United States

Library of Congress Cataloging-in-Publication Data
One-hundred-and-one read-aloud classics / edited by Pamela Horn.
p. cm.
Summary: Includes excerpts, able to be read in about ten minutes,
from both contemporary and traditional children's favorites.

1. Children's literature. [1. Literature--Collections.]
I. Horn. Pamela, 1966-
PZ5.059   1995
808.8'99282--dc20   95-35953
                                     CIP
                                     AC

TABLE OF CONTENTS

8 Fantastic Creatures

INTRODUCTION

O YOU REMEMBER being read to as a child? Many people consider their early experiences of bedtime storytelling to be the most cherished and valuable memories of their lives. The peacefulness, the reassurance of a parent's voice, the escape into new and exciting worlds of adventure, the drama of a story unfolding in real time, combine to form indelible memories and mold children into book-lovers. There is no more important activity for preparing your child to succeed as a reader than reading aloud together. It is an almost organic process, stimulating their imaginations and expanding their understanding of the world. Children learn to love the sound of language even before they notice the existence of printed words on a page.

One-Hundred-and-One Read-Aloud Classics is designed to play an integral part in an invaluable learning chain: you read to your children, they develop a love of stories, they want to read on their own, they practice reading, and finally they read for their own information and pleasure. Reading aloud to children helps stimulate an interest in reading and language as it helps develop listening skills and prepares children to understand the written word. And it is not an activity limited to children who cannot yet read. You can make this all-important time together enjoyable for children of all ages. The togetherness and affection that develop during read-aloud sessions should not cease because a child knows how to read on his or her own.

Between the ages of four and seven, many children begin to recognize words on a page. Reading aloud can help demystify the reading process. By reading stories that are on their interest level, but beyond their reading level, you can stretch your young readers' understanding and motivate them to improve their skills. No method better prepares children for that moment when "reading" clicks. Reading to children effectively builds and reinforces vocabulary as well. The relationship between the printed word, the spoken word, and the meaning of words moves from the abstract to the concrete. Reading aloud contextualizes words that are often taught in isolated instances. Many of the stories in this collection may be beyond your child's reading level, but not beyond his or her listening level, and they are bound to introduce a plethora of new words. Hearing the words, following the storyline, and creating a whole picture allows the child to "place" the words, and become accustomed to using complete sentences.

Studies have shown that activities engaged in at home to reinforce concepts learned in school are an important and effective supplement. Parents, of course, can give children support and guidance that classrooms cannot give. Children who are read to grow to love books. They remember stories that made them laugh or cry. They remember sharing stories with people they love, and they anticipate with joy the time when they will be able to read for themselves.

ABOUT THE SELECTIONS

THE SELECTIONS FEATURED in *One-Hundred-and-One Read-Aloud Classics* include both traditional and contemporary works, representing some of the best writers of the Western world. The pieces were chosen for both their reading and listening pleasures, and to provide a wide variety of genres, moods, and settings. The stories are divided among thematic chapters including animals, children, fantastic creatures, adventures, historical tales, fantasy, fables, folk and fairy tales. The book entices childrens' imaginations, satisfies curiosity, and encourages them to want to read further. The ten-minute duration of the readings should satisfy the attention span of both children and parents.

The children listening to the stories may themselves be at a variety of reading levels, however, listening levels encompass a wider audience, so do not worry if you are reading the same story to children of various ages. Reading and listening vocabularies are different; children can understand words they would not recognize by sight because they will have heard the words before and can understand the context in which they now hear them being used.

Brief introductions appear at the beginning of each selection. These ground the piece within a larger context or storyline. A discussion of the author has been included where appropriate, and a bibliographic note following each selection provides information on the most recent edition of the book from which the story comes, and is included to encourage further outside reading.

ADVENTUROUS KIDS

TALES OF A FOURTH GRADE NOTHING

JUDY BLUME

Peter Hatcher is being driven crazy by his two-year-old little brother, Fudge. One day, Peter and his friend Jimmy find Sheila, a know-it-all, on their special rocks. Peter's mother asks Sheila, Peter, and Jimmy to watch Fudge for 10 minutes, but as soon as she leaves, the baby-sitting troubles begin.

Chapter 4   MY BROTHER THE BIRD

ne nice sunny afternoon I called for Jimmy Fargo and we went to the park. Jimmy is the only kid on my block who's in my class at school. Unless you count Sheila. And I don't! She lives in my building, on the 10th floor. Henry, the elevator operator, is always making jokes about me and Sheila. He thinks we like each other. The truth is, I can't stand her. She's a real know-it-all. But I've discovered that most girls are!

The worst thing about Sheila is the way she's always trying to touch me. And when she does she yells, "Peter's got the cooties!" I don't believe in cooties anymore. When I was in second grade I used to examine myself to see if I had them. But I never found any. By fourth grade most kids give up on cooties. But not Sheila. She's still going strong. So I have to keep a safe distance from her.

My mother thinks Sheila is the greatest. "She's so smart," my mother says. "And some day she's going to be a real beauty." Now that's the funniest! Because Sheila looks a lot like the monkeys that Fudge is so crazy about. So maybe she'll look beautiful to some ape! But never to me.

Me and Jimmy have this special group of rocks where we like to play when we're in the park. We play secret agent up there. Jimmy can imitate all kinds of foreign accents. Probably because his father's a part-time actor. When he's not acting he teaches a class at City College.

Today, when we got to our rocks, who should be perched up there but Sheila. She was pretending to read a book. But I think she was just waiting for me and Jimmy. To find out what we'd do when we found her on our own personal rocks.

"Hey, Sheila!" I said. "Those are our rocks."

"Says who?" she asked.

2

"Come on, Sheila," Jimmy said, climbing up. "You know me and Peter hang out here."

"Too bad for you!" Sheila said.

"Oh, Sheila!" I shouted. "Go and find yourself another rock!"

"I like this one," she said, as if she owned the park. "So why don't you two go find another rock?"

Just then who should come tearing down the path but Fudge. My mother was right behind him hollering, "Fudgie . . . wait for Mommy!"

But when Fudge gets going he doesn't wait for anybody. He was after some pigeons. "Birdie . . . here birdie," he called. That brother of mine loves birds. But he can't get it through his head that the birds aren't about to let him catch them.

"Hi, Mom," I said.

My mother stopped running. "Peter! Am I glad to see you. I can't keep up with Fudge."

"Mrs. Hatcher . . . Mrs. Hatcher," Sheila called, scrambling down from our rock, "I'll watch Fudge for you. I'll take very good care of him. Can I, Mrs. Hatcher? Oh please!" Sheila jumped up and down and begged some more.

Jimmy gave me an elbow in the ribs. He thought that my mother would let Sheila watch Fudge and then we'd be rid of her. We'd be free to play secret agent. But Jimmy didn't know that my mother would never trust Sheila with her dear little boy.

Fudge, in the meantime, was screaming. "Come back, birdies . . . come back to Fudgie!"

Then my mother did a strange thing. She checked her watch and said, "You know, I do have to run back to the apartment. I forgot to turn on the oven. Do you really think you could keep an eye on Fudge for just ten minutes?"

"Of course I can, Mrs. Hatcher," Sheila said. "I know all about baby-sitting from my sister."

Sheila's sister Libby is in seventh grade. She's about as beautiful as Sheila. The only difference is, she's bigger.

My mother hesitated. "I don't know," she said. "I've never left Fudge before." She looked at me. "Peter . . ."

"What?"

"Will you and Jimmy help Sheila watch Fudge while I run home for a minute?"

"Oh, Mom! Do we have to?"

"Please, Peter. I'll be right back. I'll feel better if all three of you are watching him."

"What do you say?" I asked Jimmy.

"Sure," he answered. "Why not?"

"But I'm in charge of Fudgie, aren't I?" Sheila asked my mother.

"Well, I guess so," my mother said to Sheila. "You probably do know more about baby-sitting. Why don't you all take Fudge over to the playground? Then I'll know where to find you."

"Swell, Mrs. Hatcher!" Sheila said. "Don't you worry. Fudgie will be just fine."

My mother turned to Fudge. "Now you be a good boy for ten minutes. Mommy will be right back. Okay?"

"Good boy!" Fudge said. "Good . . . good . . . good . . ."

As soon as my mother was gone Fudge took off. "Can't catch me!" he hollered. "Can't catch Fudgie!"

"Go get him, Sheila," I said. "You're in charge, remember?"

Me and Jimmy horsed around while Sheila ran after Fudge.

When she caught him we decided we'd better go to the playground like my mother said. It was a lot easier to keep an eye on him in a smaller place. Anyway, Fudge likes to climb on the jungle gym and that way he can't get lost.

As soon as we got to the playground Sheila started chasing me. "Peter's got the cooties! Peter's got the cooties!" she yelled.

"Cut that out!" I said.

So she chased Jimmy. "Jimmy's got the cooties! Jimmy's got the cooties!"

Me and Jimmy decided to fight back. So what if she's a girl? She started it! We grabbed her by the arms. She squirmed and tried to get away from us, but we wouldn't let go. We hollered really loud. "Sheila's got the cooties! Sheila's got the cooties!"

All three of us were so busy fooling around that we didn't notice Fudge up on the jungle gym until he called. "Pee-tah . . . Pee-tah . . . " That's how he says my name.

"What?" I asked.

"See . . . see . . . " Fudge flapped his arms around. "Fudgie's a birdie! Fudgie's a birdie! Fly, birdie . . . fly . . . "

That crazy kid! I thought, running to the jungle gym with Jimmy and Sheila right behind me.

But it was too late. Fudge already found out he didn't have wings. He fell to the ground. He was screaming and crying and his face was a mess of blood. I couldn't even tell where the blood was coming from at first. Then Jimmy handed me his handkerchief. I don't know how clean it was but it was better than nothing. I mopped some blood off Fudge's face.

Sheila cried, "It wasn't my fault. Honest, it wasn't."

"Oh shut up!" I told her.

"He's really a mess," Jimmy said, inspecting Fudge. "And his teeth are gone too."

"What are you talking about?" I asked Jimmy.

"Look in his mouth," Jimmy said. "Now, while he's screaming. See . . . he's got a big space where he used to have his front teeth."

"Oh no!" Sheila screamed. "He's right! Fudgie's teeth are gone!"

Fudge stopped crying for a minute. "All gone?" he asked.

4

"Open your mouth wide," I said.

He did and I looked in. It was true. His top two front teeth were missing.

"My mother's going to kill you, Sheila!" I said. Was I glad I wasn't left in charge of my brother.

Sheila cried louder. "But it was an accident. He did it himself . . . himself . . ."

"You better find his teeth," I said.

"Where should I look?" Sheila asked.

"On the ground, stupid!"

Sheila crawled around looking for Fudge's teeth while I tried to clean him up some more. "See," Fudge said, showing me all his wounds. "Boo-boo here. And here. More boo-boo here." His knees and elbows were all scraped up.

"I'm going to get your mother," Jimmy hollered, running out of the playground.

"Good idea!" I yelled.

"Honestly, Peter, there aren't any teeth here!"

"All gone?" Fudge asked again.

"Not all," I told him. "Just two."

Fudge started to scream. "Want my teeth! Want my teeth!"

Jimmy must have met my mother on her way back to the park because it only took about two minutes for her to get there. By that time a whole crowd of kids had gathered around us. Most of them were crawling on the ground like Sheila, looking for Fudge's teeth.

My mother picked up Fudge. "Oh my baby! My precious! My little love!" She kissed him all over. "Show Mommy where it hurts."

Fudge showed her all his boo-boos. Then he said, "All gone!"

"What's all gone?" my mother asked.

"His top two front teeth," I said.

"Oh no!" my mother cried. "Oh, my poor little angel!"

Sheila sniffled and said, "I just can't find them, Mrs. Hatcher. I've looked everywhere but Fudge's teeth are gone!"

"He must have swallowed them," my mother said, looking into Fudge's mouth.

"Oh, Mrs. Hatcher! How awful. I'm sorry . . . I'm really very sorry," Sheila cried. "What will happen to him?"

"He'll be all right, Sheila," my mother said. "I'm sure it was an accident. Nobody's blaming you."

Sheila started bawling again.

My mother said, "Let's go home now."

I thought my mother was being pretty easy on Sheila. After all, she was left in charge. When we got home Mom washed Fudge's cuts and scrapes with peroxide. Then she called Dr. Cone. He told her to take Fudge to our dentist. So my mother called Dr.

Brown's office and made an appointment for the next day.

When that was done she gave Fudge some socks to play with. I went into the kitchen to have a glass of juice. My mother followed me. "Peter Warren Hatcher!" she said. "I'm sorry that I can't trust you for just ten minutes!"

"Me?" I asked. "Trust me? What's this got to do with me?"

My mother raised her voice. "I left your brother with you for ten minutes and just look at what happened. I'm disgusted with you!"

"It was Sheila's fault," I said. "You said Sheila was in charge. So how come you're mad at me and not at Sheila?"

"I just am!" my mother shouted.

I ran to my room and slammed the door. I watched Dribble walk around on his favorite rock. "My mother's the meanest mother in the whole world!" I told my turtle. "She loves Fudge more than me. She doesn't even like me. Maybe I'm not her real son. Maybe somebody left me in a basket on her doorstep. My real mother's probably a beautiful princess. I'll bet she'd like to have me back. Nobody needs me around here . . . that's for sure!"

I didn't eat much supper that night and I had a lot of trouble falling asleep.

The next morning my mother came into my room and sat down on my bed. I didn't look at her.

"Peter," she said.

I didn't answer.

"Peter, I said some things yesterday that I didn't really mean."

I looked at her. "Honest?" I asked.

"Yes . . . you see . . . I was very upset over Fudge's accident and I had to blame somebody. So I picked on you."

"Yes," I said. "You sure did."

"It wasn't your fault though. I know that. It was an accident. It could have happened even if I had been in the playground myself."

"He wanted to fly," I said. "He thought he was a bird."

"I don't think he'll try to fly again," my mother said.

"Me neither," I told her.

Then we both laughed and I knew she was my real mother after all.

Blume, Judy. *Tales of a Fourth Grade Nothing*. New York: Dell Yearling, 1991.

FROM THE MIXED-UP FILES OF MRS. BASIL E. FRANKWEILER

E. L. KONIGSBURG

Claudia and Jamie run away from home and hide in the Metropolitan Museum of Art in New York City, where anything is possible.

CHAPTER 3

o one thought it strange that a boy and a girl, each carrying a book bag and an instrument case and who would normally be in school, were visiting a museum. After all, about a thousand schoolchildren visit the museum every day. The guard at the entrance merely stopped them and told them to check their cases and book bags. A museum rule: no bags, food, or umbrellas. None that the guards can see. Rule or no rule, Claudia decided it was a good idea. A big sign in the checking room said NO TIPPING, so she knew that Jamie couldn't object. Jamie did object, however; he pulled his sister aside and asked her how she expected him to change into his pajamas. His pajamas, he explained, were rolled into a tiny ball in his trumpet case.

Claudia told him that she fully expected to check out at 4:30. They would then leave the museum by the front door and within five minutes would re-enter from the back, through the door that leads from the parking lot to the Children's Museum. After all, didn't that solve all their problems? (1) They would be seen leaving the museum. (2) They would be free of their baggage while they scouted around for a place to spend the night. And (3) it was free.

Claudia checked her coat as well as her packages. Jamie was condemned to walking around in his ski jacket. When the jacket was on and zipped, it covered up that exposed strip of skin. Besides, the orlon plush lining did a great deal to muffle his twenty-four-dollar rattle. Claudia would never have permitted herself to become so overheated, but Jamie liked perspiration, a little bit of dirt, and complications.

Right now, however, he wanted lunch. Claudia wished to eat in the restaurant on the main floor, but Jamie wished to eat in the snack bar downstairs; he thought it would be less glamorous, but cheaper, and as chancellor of the exchequer, as holder of the veto power, and as tightwad of the year, he got his wish. Claudia didn't really mind too much when she saw the snack bar. It was plain but clean.

James was dismayed at the prices. They had $28.61 when they went into the cafeteria, and only $27.11 when they came out still feeling hungry. "Claudia," he demanded, "did you know food would cost so much? Now, aren't you glad that we didn't take a bus?"

Claudia was no such thing. She was not glad that they hadn't taken a bus. She was merely furious that her parents, and Jamie's too, had been so stingy that she had been away from home for less than one whole day and was already worried about survial money. She chose not to answer Jamie. Jamie didn't notice; he was completely wrapped up in problems of finance.

"Do you think I could get one of the guards to play me a game of war?" he asked.

"That's ridiculous," Claudia said.

"Why? I brought my cards along. A whole deck."

Claudia said, "Inconspicuous is exactly the opposite of that. Even a guard at the Metropolitan who sees thousands of people every day would remember a boy who played him a game of cards."

Jamie's pride was involved. "I cheated Bruce through all second grade and through all third grade so far, and he still isn't wise."

"Jamie! Is that how you knew you'd win?"

Jamie bowed his head and answered, "Well, yeah. Besides, Brucie has trouble keeping straight the jacks, queens, and kings. He gets mixed up."

"Why do you cheat your best friend?"

"I sure don't know. I guess I like complications."

"Well, quit worrying about money now. Worry about where we're going to hide while they're locking up this place."

They took a map from the information stand for free. Claudia selected where they would hide during that dangerous time immediately after the museum was closed to the public and before all the guards and helpers left. She decided that she would go to the ladies' room, and Jamie would go to the men's room just before the museum closed. "Go to the one near the restaurant on the main floor," she told Jamie.

"I'm not spending a night in a men's room. All that tile. It's cold. And, besides, men's rooms make noises sound louder. And I rattle enough now."

Claudia explained to Jamie that he was to enter a booth in the men's room. "And then stand on it," she continued.

"Stand on it? Stand on what?" Jamie demanded.

"You know," Claudia insisted. "Stand on it!"

"You mean stand on the toilet?" Jamie needed everything spelled out.

"Well, what else would I mean? What else is there in a booth in the men's room? And keep your head down. And keep the door to the booth very slightly open," Claudia finished.

"Feet up. Head down. Door open. Why?"

"Because I'm certain that when they check the ladies' room and the men's room, they peek under the door and check only to see if there are feet. We must stay there until we're sure all the people and guards have gone home."

"How about the night watchman?" Jamie asked.

Claudia displayed a lot more confidence than she really felt. "Oh! There'll be a night watchman, I'm sure. But he mostly walks around the roof trying to keep people from breaking in. We'll already be in. They call what he walks a cat walk. We'll learn his habits soon enough. They must mostly use burglar alarms in the inside. We'll just never touch a window, a door, or a valuable painting. Now, let's find a place to spend the night."

They wandered back to the rooms of fine French and English furniture. It was here Claudia knew for sure that she had chosen the most elegant place in the world to hide. She wanted to sit on the lounge chair that had been made for Marie Antoinette or at least sit at her writing table. But signs everywhere said not to step on the platform. And some of the chairs had silken ropes strung across the arms to keep you from even trying to sit down. She would have to wait until after lights out to be Marie Antoinette.

At last she found a bed that she considered perfectly wonderful, and she told Jamie that they would spend the night there. The bed had a tall canopy, supported by an ornately carved headboard at one end and by two gigantic posts at the other.

Claudia had always known that she was meant for such fine things. Jamie, on the other hand, thought that running away from home to sleep in just another bed was really no challenge at all. He, James, would rather stoop on the bathroom floor, after all. Claudia then pulled him around to the foot of the bed and told him to read what the card said.

Jamie read, "Please do not step on the platform."

Claudia knew that he was being difficult on purpose; therefore, she read for him, "State bed—scene of the alleged murder of Amy Robsart, first wife of Lord Robert Dudley, later Earl of . . ."

Jamie couldn't control his smile. He said, "You know, Claude, for a sister and a fuss-budget, you're not too bad."

Something happened at precisely that moment. Both Claudia and Jamie tried to explain to me about it, but they couldn't quite. I know what happened, though I never told them. Having words and explanations for everything is too modern. I especially wouldn't tell Claudia. She has too many explanations already.

What happened was: They became a team, a family of two. There had been times before they ran away when they had acted like a team, but those were very different from feeling like a team. Becoming a team didn't mean the end of their arguments. But it did mean that the arguments became a part of the adventure, became discussions not threats. To an outsider the arguments would appear to be the same because feeling like part of a team is something that happens invisibly. You might call it caring. You could even call it love. And it is very rarely, indeed, that it happens to two people at the same time—especially a brother and a sister who had always spent more time with activities than they had with each other.

They followed their plan: checked out of the museum and re-entered through a back door. When the guard at that entrance told them to check their instrument cases, Claudia told him that they were just passing through on their way to meet their mother. The guard let them go, knowing that if they went very far, some other guard would stop them again. However, they managed to avoid other guards for the remaining minutes until the bell rang. The bell meant that the museum was closing in five minutes. They then entered the booths of the rest rooms.

They waited in the booths until five-thirty, when they felt certain that everyone had gone. Then they came out and met. Five-thirty in winter is dark, but nowhere seems as dark as the Metropolitan Museum of Art. The ceilings are so high that they fill up with a lot of darkness. It seemed to Jamie and Claudia that they walked through miles of corridors. Fortunately, the corridors were wide, and they were spared bumping into things.

At last they came to the hall of the English Renaissance. Jamie quickly threw himself upon the bed forgetting that it was only about six o'clock and thinking that he would be so exhausted that he would immediately fall asleep. He didn't. He was hungry. That was one reason he didn't fall asleep immediately. He was uncomfortable, too. So he got up from bed, changed into his pajamas, and got back into bed. He felt a little better. Claudia had already changed into her pajamas. She, too, was hungry, and she, too, was uncomfortable. How could so elegant and romantic a bed smell so musty? She would have liked to wash everything in a good, strong, sweet-smelling detergent.

As Jamie got into bed, he still felt uneasy, and it wasn't because he was worried about being caught. Claudia had planned everything so well that he didn't concern himself about that. The strange way he felt had little to do with the strange place in which they were sleeping. Claudia felt it, too. Jamie lay there thinking. Finally, realization came.

"You know, Claude," he whispered, "I didn't brush my teeth."

Claudia answered, "Well, Jamie, you can't always brush after every meal." They both laughed very quietly. "Tomorrow," Claudia reassured him, "we'll be even better organized."

It was much earlier than her bedtime at home, but still Claudia felt tired. She thought she might have an iron deficiency anemia: tired blood. Perhaps the pressures of everyday stress and strain had gotten her down. Maybe she was light-headed from hunger; her brain cells were being robbed of vitally needed oxygen for good growth and, and . . . yawn.

She shouldn't have worried. It had been an unusually busy day. A busy and unusual day. So she lay there in the great quiet of the museum next to the warm quiet of her brother and allowed the soft stillness to settle around them: a comforter of quiet. The silence seeped from their heads to their soles and into their souls. They stretched out and relaxed. Instead of oxygen and stress, Claudia thought now of hushed and quiet words: glide, fur, banana, peace. Even the footsteps of the night watchman added only an accented quarter-note to the silence that had become a hum, a lullaby.

Konigsberg, E.L. *From the Mixed-Up Files of Mrs. Basil E. Frankweiler.* New York: Macmillan, Macmillan Children's Group (Aladdin), 1987.

RAMONA FOREVER

BEVERLY CLEARY

Ramona is trying to be good so her mother won't make her stay at the Kemps' after school. She's trying to get along with her older sister Beezus. But Beezus won't let her go out and play with her friend Howie, who just got a new unicycle. That's the last straw. Ramona calls Beezus a "Pizzaface" and takes off.

Chapter 3 BEING GOOD

Tuesday afternoon was much the same as Monday. Beezus talked a long time on the telephone to a friend Ramona did not know. The conversation was about who said what to a new boy at school, and what was printed on someone's T-shirt, and how some girl said she had seen some boy looking at Beezus, because Beezus said, "Do you think he looked at me, really?" and on and on. When the conversation, uninteresting to Ramona, finally ended, Beezus went into the bathroom and scrubbed her face with medicated soap.

"What good girls we have," said Mrs. Quimby when she returned from work with her waistline no larger than it had been the day before. However, she did look tired, and on the way home, had bought a pizza for dinner. Since pizzas were an extravagance in the Quimby household, this meant she did not feel like cooking dinner.

By Wednesday, Ramona began to dread being good because being good was boring, so she was happy to see Howie coming down the street, wheeling his bicycle with his unicycle balanced across the seat and handlebars. She was even happier when he laid both on her driveway. Ramona met him at the door.

"Come on out, Ramona," said Howie. "Uncle Hobart helped me learn to ride my unicycle, so now you can ride my bicycle."

Ramona's wish had come true. "Hey, Beezus," she shouted, "I'm going out and ride Howie's bike."

"You're supposed to ask first," said Beezus. "You can't go out unless I say so."

Ramona felt that Beezus was showing off in front of Howie. "How come you're so bossy all of a sudden?" she demanded.

"Mom and Dad left me in charge, and you have to mind," answered Beezus.

"You talk the way you and Mary Jane used to talk when you played house and made me be the baby. Well, I'm not a baby now." Ramona grew more determined and contrary. "Mom always lets me go out and play with Howie."

"Just the same, if you get hurt, I'm responsible," said Beezus.

11

"You're just being mean," said Ramona. "So long, Pizzaface." Just before she slammed the door, she was horrified to see Beezus's face crumple, as if she were about to burst into tears.

Howie cried out, "Ramona, look at me!"

Ramona watched Howie mount his unicycle and ride it to the corner and back, but as she watched, she felt puzzled and uncomfortable. She had made Beezus unhappy, but why? She did not understand. She had called Beezus Pieface many times without upsetting her. What was so different about Pizzaface? She happened to think of it because they had eaten pizza the night before, and pizza was a sort of pie.

"Good work, Howie," said Ramona when he had ridden to the corner and back a second time. But what about me? she thought, still worrying about Beezus. I can't spend the rest of my life sitting on a couch being good.

"Come on, ride my bike," said Howie. "Let's see if we can make it around the block."

Ramona raised Howie's bicycle, made sure one pedal was high and the other low so she would have a good start, mounted, and rode wobbling down the sidewalk.

"Atta girl, Ramona," said Howie, seating himself on his unicycle and pedaling ahead of her.

Ramona wobbled along after him, and as she wobbled, she worried. What was Beezus going to say to their mother and father? Would she have to go back to the Kemps'?

By the time Ramona reached the corner, she was less wobbly. She even managed to turn the corner without tipping over. She began to pedal faster. Now she was really riding, filled with joy, as if she were flying.

Ramona passed Howie. She stood up on the pedals to go faster. Ramona's mind was on speed, not balance, and at the next corner, as she turned, she lost control. Down she went, with the bicycle on top of her. Her left knee and elbow hurt; her breath was knocked out of her.

Howie dropped his unicycle and came running to lift his bicycle from Ramona. "You okay?" he asked.

Ramona rose stiffly to her feet. "I don't think anything's broken," she said, struggling not to cry. Blood was running down her scraped elbow and soaking the knee of her jeans. Limping, she wheeled the bicycle, and Howie wheeled his unicycle, as far as her driveway.

"Come back again, Howie," said Ramona. "I love to ride your bicycle, even if I did take a spill."

"Sure, Ramona," agreed Howie. "You better go mop up all that blood."

When Ramona went to the back door so she wouldn't bleed on the living room carpet, she had to knock because the door was locked. When Beezus opened it, she ignored her sister's dripping blood and returned to her room without speaking.

Ramona limped to the bathroom. Maybe she could make Beezus speak if she let her know she had been right, that Ramona had hurt herself when she disobeyed. She said in her most pitiful voice, "Beezus, I had a bad fall. Come and help me."

"I don't care, you hateful little creep," was her sister's answer. "Serves you right. I'm not speaking to you anymore. It's not my fault my face is all red and blotchy like a pizza."

What Ramona heard left her speechless, ashamed, and angry. She had hurt her sister's feelings accidentally, Beezus had hurt hers on purpose, and she didn't even care that Ramona was dripping blood. She was probably glad. Bossy old Beezus.

Ramona washed her own knee and elbow, sprayed them with disinfectant, plastered them with Band-Aids, and changed into clean jeans and a long-sleeved blouse to hide her wounds. She then lifted Picky-picky to the couch, sat down beside him to read and be good Ramona again.

Ramona, however, found she could not read, she felt so terrible, even though she was angry, about hurting her sister's feelings in a way she had not intended. The girls often called one another names—Beezus called Ramona Dribblepuss when her ice cream melted from a cone and trickled down her chin—but they never used really unkind names. Now Beezus called her a hateful little creep and meant it. And what if Beezus told their mother and father they had quarreled? Then it would be back to the Kemps' for Ramona.

Good girl that she was, Ramona decided to set the table. She heard Beezus go into the bathroom and wash her face before coming into the kitchen. Picky-picky managed to get down from the couch and follow her, in case she decided to feed him. Beezus scrubbed four potatoes and put them in the oven to bake. Then she picked up the cat, hugged and petted him. "Nice Picky-picky," she said so Ramona could hear. This, of course, meant that Ramona was not nice.

However, when their parents came home, Beezus acted as if nothing had happened, and so did Ramona—except they both talked to their mother and father but not to one another. Ramona thought maybe the white uniform her mother wore to work in the doctor's office looked tighter at the waist. Perhaps it had shrunk, or last night's pizza had been fattening, or maybe Beezus was right—she was going to have a baby.

As the family was about to sit down to dinner, the telephone rang, and since Mrs. Quimby happened to be standing near it, she answered. "Oh, I'm fine," she said.

Ramona wanted to look at Beezus. However, they were not only not speaking, they were not looking. She listened intently to their mother's side of the telephone conversation.

Mrs. Quimby was smiling. "Yes . . . yes, of course. I think that's a great idea . . . no, it doesn't hurt to try, so go ahead . . . it sounds like fun. Let me know how it turns out."

"What sounds like fun?" demanded Ramona and Beezus at the same time.

"Oh—something," said Mrs. Quimby airily, and winked at her husband. "I can't remember exactly what."

"You winked at Daddy," Ramona accused her mother, as if winking were somehow wicked.

"Mom! You're fibbing!" cried Beezus in exasperation. "You can too remember."

"It isn't nice to talk about things in front of people and not tell them what you are talking about." Ramona suffered from curiosity as much as Beezus.

"Who called?" asked Mr. Quimby.

Ha! thought Ramona, now we've got her. She won't fib to Dad.

"Howie's mother," said Mrs. Quimby. "She needed some information."

"Oh," was all the girls' father had to say.

"Is it about a birthday party?" asked Ramona, because her mother had mentioned fun.

"Never mind, Ramona," said her mother, "Just eat your dinner."

"Well, is it?" persisted Ramona.

"No, it isn't a birthday party," said Mrs. Quimby, "and it doesn't concern you."

Ramona hoped her mother was still fibbing. She wanted fun to concern herself.

The parents did not notice that the girls were not speaking—or if they did, they chose not to mention the matter.

After dinner, Mrs. Quimby said she was a little tired and thought she would go to bed and read awhile. The girls avoided looking at one another, even though the remark was significant.

"I'll do the dishes," volunteered Mr. Quimby as the girls cleared the table. "Then I'll work on my lesson plan for tomorrow's practice teaching." He lowered his voice. "And I want to make one thing clear to you girls. You are not to do anything to worry your mother. Do you understand?"

The girls nodded, avoiding one another's eyes. From the exasperation in their father's voice, they knew he understood they had quarreled. Beezus went off to her room.

Ramona yearned to follow her sister, to say she was sorry, that she had not meant Pizzaface the way Beezus thought she meant it, to find out what Beezus thought of the mysterious telephone call, to ask when she thought her mother was going to have a baby— if she was.

However, Ramona was not used to saying she was sorry, especially to someone who was bossy and called her a hateful little creep. Little creep she could overlook, but not hateful little creep.

Cleary, Beverly. *Ramona Forever*. New York: Dell Yearling, 1993.

THE WATER-BABIES:
A FAIRY TALE
FOR A LAND-BABY

CHARLES KINGSLEY

Tom works very hard as a chimney-sweep until one day some fairies turn him into a water-baby. He enjoys his life in the water-world but drives all the water-creatures to distraction until they get quite angry with him.

CHAPTER III

om was now quite amphibious. You do not know what that means? You had better, then, ask the nearest teacher, who may possibly answer you smartly enough, thus "Amphibious. Adjective, derived from two Greek words, amphi, a fish, and bios, a beast. An animal supposed by our ignorant ancestors to be compounded of a fish and a beast; which, like the hippopotamus, can't live on the land, and dies in the water."

However that may be, Tom was amphibious and he was clean. For the first time in his life, he felt how comfortable it was to have nothing on him but himself. But he only enjoyed it: he did not know it, or think about it; just as you enjoy life and health, and yet never think about being alive and healthy; and may it be long before you have to think about it!

He did not remember ever having been dirty. Since that sweet sleep, he had forgotten all about his master, and Harthover Place, and the little white girl, and all that had happened to him when he lived before; and what was best of all, he had forgotten all the bad words which he had learned from Grimes and the rude boys with whom he used to play. That is not strange: for you know, when you came into this world, and became a land-baby, you remembered nothing. So why should he when he became a water-baby?

Then have you lived before? My dear child, who can tell? One can only tell that by remembering something which happened where we lived before; and as we remember nothing, we know nothing about it; and no book, and no man, can ever tell us certainly.

There was a wise man once, a very wise man, and a very good man, who wrote a poem about the feelings which some children have about having lived before; and this is what he said:

"Our birth is but a sleep and a forgetting;
The soul that rises with us, our life's star,
Hath elsewhere had its setting,
And cometh from afar:
Not in entire forgetfulness,
And not in utter nakedness,
But trailing clouds of glory do we come
From God, who is our home."

There, you can know no more than that. But if I were you, I would believe that. For then the great fairy Science, who is likely to be queen of all fairies for many a year to come, can only do you good, and never do you harm; and instead of fancying that your body makes your soul, as if a steam-engine could make its own coke; or, with some people, that your soul has nothing to do with your body, but is only stuck into it like a pin into a pincushion, to fall out with the first shake; you will believe the one true, orthodox, inductive, rational, deductive, philosophical, seductive, logical, productive, irrefragable, salutary, nonimalistic, realistic, and on-all-accounts-to-be-received doctrine of this wonderful fairy tale; which is, that your soul makes your body, just as a snail makes his shell for the rest, it is enough for us to be sure that whether or not we lived before, we shall live again; though not, I hope, as poor little heathen Tom did. For he went downward into the water: but we, I hope, shall go upward to a very different place.

But Tom was very happy in the water. He had been sadly overworked in the land-world; and so now, to make up for that, he had nothing but holidays in the water-world for a long time to come. He had nothing to do now but enjoy himself, and look at all the pretty things which are to be seen in the cool clear water-world, where the sun is never too hot, and the frost is never too cold.

And what did he live on? Water-cresses, perhaps; or perhaps water-gruel, and water-milk; too many land-babies do so likewise; sometimes he went along the smooth gravel water-ways, looking at the crickets which ran in and out among the stones, as rabbits do on land; or he climbed over the ledges of rock, and saw the sandpipes hanging in thousands, with every one of them a pretty little head and legs peeping out; or he went into a still corner, and watched the caddises eating deadsticks as greedily as you would eat plum-pudding, and building their houses with silk and glue. Very fanciful ladies they were; none of them would keep to the same materials for a day. One would begin with some pebbles; then she would stick on a piece of green wood; then she found a shell, and stuck it on too; and the poor shell was alive, and did

not like at all being taken to build houses with: but the caddis did not let him have any voice in the matter, being rude and selfish, as vain people are apt to be; then she stuck on a piece of rotten wood, then a very smart pink stone, and so on, till she was patched all over like an Irishman's coat. Then she found a long straw, five times as long as herself, and said, "Hurrah, my sister has a tail, and I'll have one, too;" and she stuck it on her back, and marched about with it quite proud, though it was very inconvenient indeed.

Then sometimes he came to a deep still reach; and there he saw the water-forests; they would have looked to you only little weeds; but Tom, you must remember, was so little that everything looked a hundred times as big to him as it does to you, just as things do to a minnow, who sees and catches the little water-creatures which you can only see in a microscope.

And in the water-forest he saw the water-monkeys and water-squirrels (they had all six legs, though; everything almost has six legs in the water, except efts and water-babies); and nimbly enough they ran among the branches. There were water-flowers there, too, in thousands; and Tom tried to pick them: but as soon as he touched them, they drew themselves in and turned into knots of jelly; and then Tom saw that they were all alive—bells, and stars, and wheels, and flowers, of all beautiful shapes and colors; and all alive and busy, just as Tom was. He found that there was a deal more in the world than he had fancied at first sight.

There was one wonderful little fellow, too, who peeped out of the top of a house built of round bricks. He had two big wheels, and one little one, all over teeth, spinning round and round like the wheels in a threshing machine; and Tom stood and stared at him, to see what he was going to make with his machinery. And what do you think he was doing?

Brick-making. With his two big wheels he swept together all the mud which floated in the water: all that was nice in it he put into his stomach and ate; and all the mud he put into the little wheel on his breast, which really was a round hole set with teeth; and there he spun it into a neat hard round brick; and then he took it and stuck it on the top of his house-wall, and set to work to make another. Now was not he a clever little fellow?

Tom thought so: but when he wanted to talk to him the brick-maker was much too busy to notice him.

Now you must know that all the things under the water talk; only not such a language as ours; but such as horses, and dogs, and cows, and birds talk to each other; and Tom soon learned to understand them and talk to them; so that he might have had very company if he had only been a good boy. But I am sorry to say, he was too like some other little boys, very fond of tormenting creatures for mere sport. Some people say that boys cannot help it; that it is nature, and only a proof that we are all originally descended from beasts of prey. But whether it is nature or not, little boys can help it, and must help it. For if they have naughty, mischievous tricks in their nature, as monkeys have, that is no reason why they should give way to those tricks like monkeys, who know no better. And therefore they must not torment dumb creatures; for if they do, a certain old lady who is coming will surely give them exactly what they deserve.

But Tom did not know that; and he pecked and howked the poor water-things about sadly, till they were all afraid of him, and got out of his way, or crept into their shell; so he had no one to speak to or play with. The water-fairies were sorry to see him so unhappy, and longed to take him, and tell him how naughty he was, and teach him to be good, and to play and romp with him too: but they had been forbidden to do that. Tom had to learn his lesson for himself by sound and sharp experience, as many another foolish person has to do, though there may be many a kind heart yearning over them all the while, and long-ing to teach them what they can only teach themselves.

At last one day he found a caddis, And wanted it to peep out of its house: but its house-door was shut. He had never seen a caddis with a house-door before: so what must he do, the meddlesome little fellow, but pull it open, to see what the poor lady was doing inside. What a shame!

How should you like to have any one breaking your bedroom door in, to see how you looked when you were in bed? So Tom broke to pieces the door, which was the prettiest little grating of silk, stuck all over with shining bits of crystal; and when he looked in, the caddis poked out her head, and it had turned into just the shape of a bird's. But when Tom spoke to her she could not answer; for her mouth and face were tight tied up in a new night-cap of neat pink skin. However, if she didn't answer, all the other caddises did; for they held up their hands and shrieked like the cats in Sturwelpeter: "Oh, you nasty, horrid boy; there you are at it again! And she had just laid herself up for a fortnight's sleep, and then she would have come out with such beautiful wings, and flown about, and laid such lots of eggs: and now you have broken her door, and she can't mend it because her mouth is tied up for a fortnight, and she will die. Who sent you here to worry us out of our lives?"

So Tom swam away. He was very much ashamed of himself, and felt all the naughtier; as little boys do when they have done wrong and won't say so.

Kingsley, Charles. *The Water-Babies*. New York: Oxford University Press, 1995.

HARRIS AND ME

GARY PAULSEN

Harris is a nine-year-old Tom Sawyer and Huck Finn rolled into one, living on a farm somewhere in the Midwest in the 1950s. You will find joining this adventure hilariously funny.

WHERE I MEET BUZZER AND LEARN
THE VALUE AND SAFETY OF TEAMWORK

arris led me down to the barn and we had only been there a few moments when Knute came inside. He went to the back double-opening door and said quietly, "Bill, Bob, come on in now."

We were next to him and for a second I couldn't see who he was talking to. Then, from a stand of poplars close to the river, two huge gray horses walked out into the open.

I had seen horses in the Philippines, and in every western movie I went to, and knew about riding them. But Bill and Bob would have made two Triggers each.

They weren't just big, they were almost prehistoric—like two hair-covered dinosaurs walking slowly up from the river—and when they moved closer I could see that very little of their bulk was fat. Bunched beneath the skin on their rear ends and in their shoulders were great bulges of muscles.

Everything about them was massive. Huge heads that lowered to nuzzle Knute's hand while he stood in the back door of the barn; enormous round feet that sunk forever into the mud in back of the barn; great, soulful brown eyes that somehow made me want to hug the giants.

Knute turned and walked back into the barn and the horses followed like puppies. At the end nearest the front door was a double stall, and Bill and Bob moved into it. Knute came out of the pump house with a lard pail full of oats and poured half for each of them in a small wooden feed box nailed to the side of the manger.

Hanging on nails by the door were great loops of leather and chain with round collars over them, which I had seen earlier but hadn't understood and didn't want to ask about because I was sick of looking stupid.

Knute took the collars down and put them around the horses' necks while they were eating and then began draping the leather and chain over them, and I realized it was all harness.

Harris was all over the horses while Knute worked. He crawled under them, over them, handing ends of straps to Knute—who was back to silence—and the horses stood

20

peacefully even when Harris stooped to walk between their back legs and out into the aisle to stand next to me.

Knute stood quietly until they had finished their oats. He then held their bridles loosely and, standing between their heads, backed them out into the aisle and walked them out of the barn to the row of machinery by the granary.

I got the impression that he didn't really need to lead them. They knew exactly where to go and what to do. When they came to what I learned was the mower they turned themselves around and backed, one on either side of a long wooden tongue, into position for pulling.

Knute hooked their trace chains into a big crosspiece of wood hooked to the mower and brought the tongue up to attach to a crosspiece from one horse to the next.

"Come on," Harris said, and I was surprised to see he was carrying an empty feed sack he'd picked up somewhere. "We got to get on."

"Get on what?"

"The horses . . ."

Harris jumped into the space between the horses by climbing on the mower and hopping along the tongue until he was even with their shoulders. Then he grabbed two horns that stuck up on top of the collar and climbed up until he was sitting on the right horse.

"Come on," he said. "Get up on Bill. You want to be left behind?"

As a matter of fact I was thinking that exact thing just then—that rather than climb up onto a horse as big as most trucks, I would definitely rather be left behind. But pride won out and I hesitantly made my way onto the mower in back of the left horse, Bill, and took one careful step after another to climb the tongue until I could pull myself up on his shoulders. He was so wide my legs seemed to go straight out to either side and I could feel him breathing beneath me like warm bellows, great drafts of air as his shoulders worked slowly.

The ground seemed miles away and when I heard a sudden mechanical clanking and the horses moved slightly, I grabbed desperately for the horned things around the collar.

"Let go the hames," Harris said. "And raise your leg and put it under the reins. Pa can't drive with you sitting on the reins."

I turned and Knute had raised the sickle bar so it stood almost straight up and worked a lever to disengage it and was waiting patiently for me to do what Harris said.

"We want to hurry," Harris told me while I sorted my legs out from all the lines and straps and rings. "We want to get out of the yard before Buzzer knows we're going . . . . Oh shoot. Now it's too late."

I had just gotten squared away and was about to ask who Buzzer was when out of the corner of my eye I saw the cat come to the barn door and sit watching us. "You mean the cat?"

Harris nodded. "It's better if we get out without him seeing us."

I had seen the cat briefly earlier, during milking when Louie squirted milk into his mouth, but I hadn't appreciated just how large he was; he was the size of a collie, maybe just a bit bigger, with large forelegs and huge, round pads on his feet. On the end of each ear there was a bedraggled tuft and his coat was spotted, almost dappled.

Knute steered the team toward a gate in a pasture fence that led us directly past the front door of the barn and Harris leaned across the space between the horses to talk quietly.

"You don't want to touch Buzzer."

I nodded. "You're right. I don't want to touch him." It seemed an odd thing to say since Buzzer was sitting down on the ground and I was what felt like eight feet in the air.

"He ain't normal or nothing," Harris continued. "Louie found him in the woods one spring when he was looking for wood to cut. Buzzer was just a kitten then and Louie brought him back in his pocket. He grew some."

"I guess . . ."

I was going to say more but we were right next to the door and the cat suddenly bounced up—it seemed without effort—and landed on the rear end of the horse I was riding on.

I started, expecting the horse to react, but nothing happened. Bill just kept plodding on with Buzzer sitting on his butt, leaning out a bit to look ahead around me.

"No matter what he does, don't you touch him," Harris repeated. "Only Louie can touch him. Buzzer can be a little edgy about being touched if it ain't Louie."

I nodded and whispered to him, "Why is he riding on the horse with me?"

"He likes it when Pa mows because he can get the mice. That's why I wanted to sneak out. He makes it hard to catch the mice because he's so fast. Just watch what I do and do the same. Sometimes we can get out without him if he's sleeping, but if he sees the mower he knows what's going to happen and he comes along and ruins it for everybody."

I wasn't sure what Buzzer was going to ruin—I couldn't, for instance, understand why we were going to get mice. As far as I was concerned Buzzer could have them all. I was ready to get off and let him have the horse as well.

Knute had stopped at the gate and Harris jumped down, opened it, closed it after we were through, and scrambled back up on Bob while we were still moving.

Once through the gate Knute turned the team and we walked slowly along the fence that went next to the driveway back out toward the main road. I kept a leery eye over my shoulder, watching Buzzer, but the big cat just sat there, looking at the sky and flying birds while the horses walked.

In a quarter mile or less we came to a stand of densely packed alfalfa almost waist high, and Knute stopped the horses at the corner of the field and lowered the sickle bar. He took a can of oil from a little holder beneath the seat on the mower and squirted oil all along the sickle bar, then sat once more and worked a lever to engage the clutch.

Harris got down and motioned for me to do the same. "We got to walk in back of the mower now and catch mice."

It was finally, too much. "Harris, why do we want the mice?"

"For the money."

"What money?"

"Louie. He pays us a penny for each two mice we get him. Except for Buzzer, of course. Louie don't pay Buzzer nothing because Buzzer he just ruins 'em all to pieces and won't give them up anyway. Last summer I tried to take one away from him and get the money for it and he like to killed me. That's why I say don't you touch him nor take none of his mice."

"I won't."

Paulsen, Gary. *Harris and Me*. New York: Harcourt Brace, 1993.

ENCYCLOPEDIA BROWN SHOWS THE WAY

DONALD J. SOBOL

Ten-year-old Encyclopedia Brown is the son of Idaville's chief of police, and a brilliant detective in his own right. In the case of the headless runner, Encyclopedia comes up with an ingenious but logical solution to who might be causing serious mischief on a dark and stormy night. Is it a headless vampire?

Chapter 4 THE CASE OF THE HEADLESS RUNNER

iding the bus home from the Globe Theater, Encyclopedia wondered why he had done it. Why had he let Charlie Stewart talk him into seeing the triple-feature horror show?

He wished he had stayed home and read a book. He could have learned something useful.

Through the window of the bus he peered at the night sky. Clouds were gathering to the north.

"I'm going to be scared enough walking home in the dark without a rainstorm beating down," he thought nervously.

On the seat beside him, Charlie Stewart gave a shudder.

"I was fine through *The Headless Vampire* and *The Killer Gorilla*," said Charlie. "But those floating hands in *The Torture Chamber of Dr. LeFarge*—brrrrr!"

They were nearing their stop. Encyclopedia hoped some other passengers would get off with them.

"Pine Needle Lane," called the driver.

The two boys moved stiffly to the door. They were the only ones getting off. In a moment, they were standing alone in the dark night.

"It's spooky," moaned Charlie. "I know something terrible is going to happen."

"They were just movies," said Encyclopedia. "Nothing in them was real."

"Gorillas are real," insisted Charlie. "They can kill you."

"The nearest gorilla was in the Crandon Zoo, and he died last year," said Encyclopedia. "Now cut it out. There are no such things as headless vampires and hands that go around by themselves strangling people."

They began to walk.

"What about all the door lights that have been mysteriously broken in the neighborhood lately?" said Charlie. "Those floating hands—they always put the lights out before they attacked, remember?"

"Did you have to bring that up?" mumbled Encyclopedia.

The boys walked faster.

The night was growing darker. Storm clouds had blotted out the moonlight behind them.

They had to walk eight blocks on Pine Needle Lane and then four blocks on Rover Avenue to Encyclopedia's house. Charlie lived two blocks farther down Rover.

"Would you like to stay over at my house tonight?" Encyclopedia invited. "I'll use my sleeping bag."

"Thanks, but I'll make it home," said Charlie bravely. "Besides, there's not a light out."

It was true. Every house along Pine Needle Lane had a friendly door light burning. But the street and the spaces between the houses lay blanketed in shadows.

The boys had covered six blocks in record time when a bolt of lightning turned the night into bright day. As the lightning faded, a sharp tinkling noise sounded, followed by a might clap of thunder.

Charlie shot into the air as if he were practicing to be a human cannonball.

"D-did you hear that?" he whimpered. "It sounded like glass breaking." Suddenly he pointed and screeched, "Yiiiiii! I knew it!"

The door light in front of a house half-way down the block had gone out.

Encyclopedia stared at the blacked-out house. His eyes strained, searching the night-covered street for a pair of hands, or the ghost of the Crandon Zoo gorilla, or a headless vampire.

"Save yourself," squeaked Charlie, "I can't move."

"Try to run," urged Encyclopedia. "Try!"

"T-too late," chattered Charlie.

Something was hurrying toward them from the direction of the blacked-out house. As it drew closer, Encyclopedia made out a person—almost.

The person seemed to be waving his arms wildly above his head . . . only he had no head!

"P-please, feet," wailed Charlie. "Do your thing!"

His legs started going like sixty. Not running, knocking.

Encyclopedia was looking for a soft spot to collapse when the runner stopped and a head popped out. It belonged to Duke Kelly. Duke lived on the block and was one of Bugs Meany's Tigers. He had been pulling a shirt over his head while running.

Charlie gave a yowl of relief. "What are you doing out here?" he demanded.

"I was reading by the window," said Duke, "I must have dozed off. That clap of thunder woke me."

"So you ran down the street like a headless vampire," said Charlie. "If I didn't have so much nerve, I'd have been scared sick."

"What's this vampire jazz?" said Duke. "I woke up and looked out the window. A bolt of lightning lit the street, and I saw two kids throwing rocks at Mr. Taft's door light. They broke it. I grabbed a shirt and tried to catch them."

"You chased them while putting on your shirt?" said Encyclopedia. "Most kids take off their shirts when they fight."

"Us Tigers fight like gentlemen," said Duke.

"You'll lose to a tree someday if you keep putting on your shirt while you run," warned Encyclopedia.

"Not this shirt," replied Duke, laughing. "It's a loose knit. I can see through it."

He tucked the shirt into his jeans and regarded Encyclopedia and Charlie suspiciously.

"What are you two meatballs doing out at night?" he said. "Breaking door lights, maybe?"

"Good try, Duke," said Encyclopedia. "But you have to do a lot better. You're afraid we saw you break the light."

HOW DID ENCYCLOPEDIA KNOW?
Solution to The Case of the Headless Runner

From behind some bushes, Duke had thrown a rock at the door light—just as the lightning flashed.

The street lit up, and he saw Encyclopedia and Charlie approaching. He was afraid they might see him hiding or running back to his house.

So he made up a story. He had been awakened by the thunder. Then, in the flash of lightning, he had seen two boys break the door light. He had grabbed his shirt and given chase.

Impossible! Thunder comes after, not before, lightning. When the thunder roared, the lightning had already passed. Duke could have seen only darkness if the thunder had awakened him.

He was taking off his shirt as he ran toward Encyclopedia and Charlie, pretending to be putting it on, to make it look as if he had left his house in a hurry.

Thanks to Encyclopedia, Duke quit breaking lights in the neighborhood.

Sobol, Donald, J. *Encyclopedia Brown Shows the Way*, New York: Bantam, 1981.

PIPPI LONGSTOCKING

ASTRID LINDGREN

Pippi is a nine-year-old girl living in a large house, with only a horse for company. One day two policemen visit her and bring her some alarming news.

Chapter 3 PIPPI PLAYS TAG WITH SOME POLICEMEN

It soon became known throughout the little town that a nine-year-old girl was living all by herself in Villa Villekulla, and all the ladies and gentlemen in the town thought this would never do.

All children must have someone to advise them, and all children must go to school to learn the multiplication tables. So the ladies and gentlemen decided that the little girl in Villa Villekulla must immediately be placed in a children's home.

One lovely afternoon Pippi had invited Tommy and Annika over for afternoon coffee and pepparkakor. She had spread the party out on the front steps. It was so sunny and beautiful there, and the air was filled with the fragrance of the flowers in Pippi's garden. Mr. Nilsson climbed around on the porch railing, and every now and then the horse stuck out his head so that he'd be invited to have a cookie.

"Oh, isn't it glorious to be alive?" said Pippi, stretching out her legs as far as she could reach.

Just at that moment two police officers in full uniform came in through the gate.

"Hurray!" said Pippi. "This must be my lucky day too! Policemen are the very best things I know. Next to rhubarb pudding." And with her face beaming she went to meet them.

"Is this the girl who has moved into Villa Villekulla?" asked one of the policemen.

"Quite the contrary," said Pippi. "This is a tiny little auntie who lives on the third floor at the other end of town."

She said that only because she wanted to have a little fun with the policemen, but they didn't think it was funny at all.

They said she shouldn't be such a smarty. And then they went on to tell her that some nice people in the town were arranging for her to get into a children's home.

"I already have a place in a children's home," said Pippi.

"What?" asked one of the policemen. "Has it been arranged already then? What children's home?"

"This one," said Pippi haughtily. "I am a child and this is my home; therefore it is a children's home, and I have room enough here, plenty of room."

"Dear child," said the policeman, smiling, "you don't understand. You must get into a real children's home and have someone look after you."

"Is one allowed to bring horses to your children's home?" asked Pippi.

"No, of course not," said the policeman.

"That's what I thought," said Pippi. "You'll have to get kids for your children's home somewhere else. I certainly don't intend to move there."

"But don't you understand that you must go to school?"

"Why?"

"To learn things, of course."

"What sort of things?" asked Pippi.

"All sorts," said the policeman. "Lots of useful things—the multiplication tables, for instance."

"I have got along fine without any pluttifikation tables for nine years," said Pippi, "and I guess I'll get along without it from now on, too."

"Yes, but just think how embarrassing it will be for you to be so ignorant. Imagine when you grow up and somebody asks you what the capital of Portugal is and you can't answer!"

"Oh, I can answer all right," said Pippi. "I'll answer like this: 'If you are so bound and determined to find out what the capital of Portugal is, then, for goodness' sakes, write directly to Portugal and ask.' "

"Yes, but don't you think that you would be sorry not to know it yourself?"

"Oh, probably," said Pippi. "No doubt I should lie awake nights and wonder and wonder, 'What in the world is the capital of Portugal?' But one can't be having fun all the time," she continued, bending over and standing on her hands for a change. "For that matter, I've been in Lisbon with my papa," she added, still standing upside down, for she could talk that way too.

But then one of the policemen said that Pippi certainly didn't need to think she could do just as she pleased. She must come to the children's home, and immediately. He went up to her and took hold of her arm, but Pippi freed herself quickly, touched him lightly, and said, "Tag!" Before he could wink an eye she had climbed up on the porch railing and from there onto the balcony above the porch. The policemen couldn't quite see themselves getting up the same way, and so they rushed into the house and up the stairs, but by the time they had reached the balcony Pippi was halfway up the roof. She climbed up the shingles almost as if she were a little monkey herself. In a moment she was up on the ridgepole and from there jumped easily to the chimney. Down on the balcony stood the two policemen, scratching their heads, and on the lawn stood Tommy and Annika, staring at Pippi.

"Isn't it fun to play tag?" cried Pippi. "And weren't you nice to come over. It certainly is my lucky day today too."

After the policemen had stood there awhile wondering what to do, they went and got a ladder, leaned it against one of the gables of the house and then climbed up, first one policeman and then the other, to get Pippi down. They looked a little scared when they climbed out on the ridgepole and, carefully balancing, went step by step, toward Pippi.

"Don't be scared," cried Pippi. "There's nothing to be afraid of. It's just fun."

When the policemen were a few steps away from Pippi, down she jumped from the chimney and, screeching and laughing, ran along the ridgepole to the opposite gable. A few feet from the house stood a tree.

"Now I'm going to dive," she cried and jumped right down into the green crown of the tree, caught hold of a branch, swung back and forth a while, and then let herself fall to the ground. Quick as a wink she dashed around to the other side of the house and took away the ladder.

The policemen had looked a little foolish when Pippi jumped, but they looked even more so when they had balanced themselves backward along the ridgepole and were about to climb down the ladder. At first they were very angry at Pippi, who stood on the ground looking up at them, and they told her in no uncertain terms to get the ladder and be quick about it, or she would soon get something she wasn't looking for.

"Why are you so cross at me?" asked Pippi reproachfully. "We're just playing tag, aren't we?"

The policemen thought a while, and at last one of them said, "Oh, come on, won't you be a good girl and put the ladder back so that we can get down?"

"Of course I will," said Pippi and put the ladder back instantly. "And when you get down we can all drink coffee and have a happy time."

But the policemen were certainly tricky, because the minute they were down on the ground again they pounced on Pippi and cried, "Now you'll get it, you little brat!"

"Oh, no, I'm sorry. I haven't time to play any longer," said Pippi. "But it was fun."

Then she took hold of the policemen by their belts and carried them down the garden path, out through the gate, and onto the street. There she set them down, and it was quite some time before they were ready to get up again.

"Wait a minute," she cried and ran into the kitchen and came back with two cookie hearts. "Would you like a taste?" she asked. "It doesn't matter that they are a little burned, does it?"

Then she went back to Tommy and Annika, who stood there wide-eyed and just couldn't get over what they had seen. And the policemen hurried back to the town and told all the ladies and gentlemen that Pippi wasn't quite fit for a children's home. (They didn't tell that they had been up on the roof.) And the ladies and gentlemen decided that it would be best after all to let Pippi remain in Villa Villekulla, and if she wanted to go to school she could make the arrangements herself.

But Pippi and Tommy and Annika had a very pleasant afternoon. They went back to their interrupted coffee party. Pippi stuffed herself with fourteen cookies, and then she said, "They weren't what I mean by real policemen. No sirree! Altogether too much talk about children's homes and pluttifikation and Lisbon."

Afterward she lifted the horse down on the ground and they rode on him, all three. At first Annika was afraid and didn't want to, but when she saw what fun Tommy and Pippi were having, she let Pippi lift her up on the horse's back. The horse trotted round and round in the garden, and Tommy sang, "Here come the Swedes with a clang and a bang."

When Tommy and Annika had gone to bed that night Tommy said, "Annika, don't you think it's good that Pippi moved here?"

"Oh, yes," said Annika.

"I don't even remember what we used to play before she came, do you?"

"Oh, sure, we played croquet and things like that," said Annika. "But it's lots more fun with Pippi around, I think. And with horses and things."

Lindgren, Astrid. *Pippi Longstocking*. Translated by Florence Lamborn. New York: Penguin, Puffin Books, 1977.

HOMER PRICE

Robert McCloskey

Homer Price goes to visit his uncle Ulysses at his lunchroom in Centerburg. Uncle Ulysses needs some help with his automatic doughnut machine. He asks Homer to give him a hand with it and to mix up a batch of doughnut batter. After Homer puts the machine together, he makes a lot of doughnuts!

Chapter 3 THE DOUGHNUTS

ne Friday night in November, Homer overheard his mother talking on the telephone to Aunt Agnes over in Centerburg. "I'll stop by with the car in about half an hour and we can go to the meeting together," she said, because tonight was the night the Ladies' Club was meeting to discuss plans for a box social and to knit and sew for the Red Cross.

"I think I'll come along and keep Uncle Ulysses company while you and Aunt Agnes are at the meeting," said Homer.

So after Homer had combed his hair and his mother had looked to see if she had her knitting instructions and the right size needles, they started for town.

Homer's Uncle Ulysses and Aunt Agnes have a very up-and-coming lunchroom over in Centerburg, just across from the courthouse on the town square. Uncle Ulysses is a man with advanced ideas and a weakness for labor-saving devices. He equipped the lunchroom with automatic toasters, an automatic coffee-maker, an automatic dishwasher, and an automatic doughnut-maker. All just the latest thing in labor-saving devices. Aunt Agnes would throw up her hands and sigh every time Uncle Ulysses bought a new labor-saving device. Sometimes she became unkindly disposed toward him for days and days. She was of the opinion that Uncle Ulysses just frittered away his spare time over at the barber shop with the sheriff and the boys, so what was the good of a labor-saving device that gave you more time to fritter?

When Homer and his mother got to Centerburg they stopped at the lunch room, and after Aunt Agnes had come out and said, "My, how that boy does grow!" which was what she always said, she went off with Homer's mother in the car. Homer went into the lunchroom and said, "Howdy, Uncle Ulysses!"

"Oh, hello, Homer. You're just in time," said Uncle Ulysses. "I've been going over this automatic doughnut machine, oiling the machinery and cleaning the works . . . wonderful things, these labor-saving devices."

"Opfwo-oof!!" sighed Uncle Ulysses and, "Look here, Homer, you've got a mechanical mind. See if you can find where these two pieces fit in. I'm going across to the barber shop

31

for a spell, 'cause there's somethin' I've got to talk to the sheriff about. There won't be much business here until the double feature is over, and I'll be back before then."

Then as Uncle Ulysses went out the door he said, "Uh, Homer, after you get the pieces in place, would you mind mixing up a batch of doughnut batter and putting it in the machine? You could turn the switch and make a few doughnuts to have on hand for the crowd after the movie . . . if you don't mind."

"O.K." said Homer, "I'll take care of everything."

A few minutes later a customer came in and said, "Good evening, Bud."

Homer looked up from putting the last piece in the doughnut machine and said, "Good evening, sir, what can I do for you?"

"Well, young feller, I'd like a cup o' coffee and some doughnuts," said the customer.

"I'm sorry, mister, but we won't have any doughnuts for about half an hour, until I can mix some dough and start this machine. I could give you some very fine sugar rolls instead."

"Well, Bud, I'm in no real hurry so I'll just have a cup o' coffee and wait around a bit for the doughnuts. Fresh doughnuts are always worth waiting for is what I always say."

"O.K." said Homer, and he drew a cup of coffee from Uncle Ulysses' super automatic coffeemaker.

"Nice place you've got here," said the customer.

"Oh, yes," replied Homer, "this is a very up-and-coming lunchroom with all the latest improvements."

"Yes," said the stranger, "must be a good business. I'm in business too. A traveling man in outdoor advertising. I'm a sandwich man, Mr. Gabby's my name."

"My name is Homer. I'm glad to meet you, Mr. Gabby. It must be a fine profession, traveling and advertising sandwiches."

"Oh no," said Mr. Gabby, "I don't advertise sandwiches, I just wear any kind of an ad, one sign on front and one sign on behind, this way. . . like a sandwich. Ya know what I mean?"

"Oh, I see. That must be fun, and you travel too?" asked Homer as he got out the flour and the baking powder.

"Yeah, I ride the rods between jobs, on freight trains, ya know what I mean?"

"Yes, but isn't that dangerous?" asked Homer.

"Of course there's a certain amount a risk, but you take any method a travel these days, it's all dangerous. Ya know what I mean? Now take airplanes for instance . . ."

Just then a large, shiny, black car stopped in front of the lunchroom and a chauffeur helped a lady out of the rear door. They both came inside and the lady smiled at Homer and said, "We've stopped for a light snack. Some doughnuts and coffee would be simply marvelous."

Then Homer said, "I'm sorry, ma'am, but the doughnuts won't be ready until I make this batter and start Uncle Ulysses' doughnut machine."

"Well now aren't you a clever young man to know how to make doughnuts!"

"Well," blushed Homer, "I've really never done it before but I've got a receipt to follow."

"Now, young man, you simply must allow me to help. You know, I haven't made doughnuts for years, but I know the best receipt for doughnuts. It's marvelous, and we really must use it."

"But, Ma'am . . ." said Homer.

"Now just wait till you taste these doughnuts," said the lady. "Do you have an apron?" she asked, as she took off her fur coat and her rings and her jewelry and rolled up her sleeves. "Charles," she said to the chauffeur, "hand me that baking powder, that's right, and, young man, we'll need some nutmeg."

So Homer and the chauffeur stood by and handed things and cracked the eggs while the lady mixed and stirred. Mr. Gabby sat on his stool, sipped his coffee, and looked on with great interest.

"There!" said the lady when all of the ingredients were mixed. "Just wait till you taste these doughnuts!"

"It looks like an awful lot of batter," said Homer as he stood on a chair and poured the batter into the doughnut machine with the help of the chauffeur. "It's about ten times as much as Uncle Ulysses ever makes."

"But wait till you taste them!" said the lady with an eager look and a smile.

Homer got down from the chair and pushed a button on the machine marked "Start." Rings of batter started dropping into the hot fat. After a ring of batter was cooked on one side an automatic gadget turned it over and the other side would cook. Then another automatic gadget gave the doughnut a little push and it rolled neatly down a little chute, all ready to eat.

"That's a simply fascinating machine," said the lady as she waited for the first doughnut to roll out.

"Here, young man, you must have the first one. Now isn't that just too delicious!? Isn't it simply marvelous?"

"Yes, Ma'am, it's very good," replied Homer as the lady handed doughnuts to Charles and to Mr. Gabby and asked if they didn't think they were simply divine doughnuts.

"It's an old family recipe!" said the lady with pride.

Homer poured some coffee for the lady and her chauffeur and for Mr. Gabby, and a glass of milk for himself. Then they all sat down at the lunch counter to enjoy another few doughnuts apiece.

"I'm so glad you enjoy my doughnuts," said the lady. "But now, Charles, we really must be going. If you will just take this apron, Homer, and put two dozen doughnuts in a bag to take to the young man." She rolled down her sleeves and put on her jewelry, then Charles managed to get her into her big fur coat.

"Good night, young man, I haven't had so much fun in years. I really haven't!" said the lady as she went out the door and into the big shiny car.

"You bet!" said Homer. Then he and Mr. Gabby stood and watched the automatic doughnut machine make doughnuts.

After a few dozen more doughnuts had rolled down the little chute, Homer said, "I guess that's about enough doughnuts to sell to the after-theater customers. I'd better turn the machine off for awhile."

Homer pushed the button marked "Stop" and there was a little click, but nothing happened. The rings of batter kept right on dropping into the hot fat, and an automatic gadget kept right on turning them over, and another automatic gadget kept right on giving them a little push, and the doughnuts kept right on rolling down the little chute, all ready to eat.

"That's funny," said Homer, "I'm sure that's the right button!" He pushed it again but the automatic doughnut maker kept right on making doughnuts. "Well I guess I must have put one of those pieces in backward," said Homer.

"Then it might stop if you pushed the button marked 'Start,'" said Mr. Gabby.

Homer did, and the doughnuts still kept rolling down the little chute, just as regular as a clock can tick.

"I guess we could sell a few more doughnuts," said Homer, "but I'd better telephone Uncle Ulysses over at the barber shop." Homer gave the number and while he waited for someone to answer he counted thirty-seven doughnuts roll down the little chute.

Finally someone answered, "Hello! This is the sarber bhop, I mean the barber shop."

"Oh, hello, Sheriff. This is Homer. Could I speak to Uncle Ulysses?"

"Well, he's playing pinochle right now," said the sheriff. "Anythin' I can tell 'im?"

"Yes," said Homer. "I pushed the button marked 'Stop' on the doughnut machine but the rings of batter keep right on dropping into the hot fat, and an automatic gadget keeps right on turning them over, and another automatic gadget keeps giving them a little push, and the doughnuts keep right on rolling down the little chute! It won't stop!"

"O.K. wold the hire, I mean, hold the wire and I'll tell 'im." Then Homer looked over his shoulder and counted another twenty-one doughnuts roll down the little chute, all ready to eat. Then the sheriff said, "He'll be right over. . . . Just gotta finish this hand."

"That's good," said Homer. "G'by, Sheriff."

The window was full of doughnuts by now so Homer and Mr. Gabby had to hustle around and start stacking them on plates and trays and lining them up on the counter.

"Sure are a lot of doughnuts!" said Homer.

"You bet!" said Mr. Gabby. "I lost count at 1,202 and that was quite a while back."

People had begun to gather outside the lunchroom window, and someone was saying, "There are almost as many doughnuts as there are people in Center-burg, and I wonder how in tarnation Ulysses thinks he can sell all of 'em!"

Every once in awhile somebody would come inside and buy some, but while somebody bought two to eat and a dozen to take home, the machine made three dozen more.

By the time Uncle Ulysses and the sheriff arrived and pushed through the crowd, the lunchroom was a calamity of doughnuts! Doughnuts in the window, doughnuts piled high on the shelves, doughnuts stacked on the plates, doughnuts lined up twelve deep all along the counter, and doughnuts still rolling down the little chute, just as regular as a clock can tick.

"Hello, Sheriff, hello, Uncle Ulysses, we're having a little trouble here," said Homer.

"Well, I'll be dunked!!" said Uncle Ulysses.

"Dernd ef you won't be when Aggy gits home," said the sheriff.

"Mighty fine doughnuts though. What'll you do with 'em all, Ulysses?"

Uncle Ulysses groaned and said, "What will Aggy say? We'll never sell 'em all."

Then Mr. Gabby, who hadn't said anything for a long time, stopped piling doughnuts and said, "What you need is an advertising man. Ya know what I mean? You got the doughnuts, ya gotta create a market. . . . Understand? . . . It's balancing the demand with the supply . . . that sort of thing."

"Yep!" said Homer. "Mr. Gabby's right. We have to enlarge our market. He's an advertising sandwich man, so if we hire him, he can walk up and down in front of the theater and get the customers."

"You're hired, Mr. Gabby!" said Uncle Ulysses. Then everybody pitched in to paint the signs and to get Mr. Gabby sandwiched between. They painted "SALE ON DOUGHNUTS" in big letters on the window too.

McCloskey, Robert. *Homer Price*. New York: Penguin, Puffin Books, 1976.

KIDNAPPED

Robert Louis Stevenson

David Balfour is a seventeen-year-old Scottish boy who leaves home after the death of his mother and father to claim his rightful inheritance as Lord of the House of the Shaws. But his uncle has other things in mind for him. Two chapters follow, taking you on different adventures in David's life.

Chapter 5 I GO TO THE QUEEN'S FERRY

There was no doubt about my uncle's enmity; there was no doubt I carried my life in my hand, and he would leave no stone unturned that he might compass my destruction. But I was young and spirited, and like most lads that have been country-bred, I had a great opinion of my shrewdness. I had come to his door no better than a beggar and little more than a child; he had met me with treachery and violence; it would be a fine consummation to take the upper hand, and drive him like a herd of sheep.

I sat there nursing my knee and smiling at the fire; and I saw myself in fancy smell out his secrets one after another, and grow to be that man's king and ruler. The warlock of Essendean, they say, had made a mirror in which men could read the future; it must have been of other stuff than burning coal; for in all the shapes and pictures that I sat and gazed at there was never a ship, never a seaman with a hairy cap, never a big bludgeon for my silly head, or the least sign of all those tribulations that were ripe to fall on me.

Presently, all swollen with conceit, I went upstairs and gave my prisoner his liberty. He gave me good morning civilly; and I gave the same to him, smiling down upon him from the heights of my sufficiency. Soon we were set to breakfast, as it might have been the day before.

"Well, sir," said I, with a jeering tone, "have you nothing more to say to me?" and then, as he made no articulate reply, "It will be time, I think, to understand each other," I continued. "You took me for a country Johnnie Raw, with no more mother-wit or courage than a porridge-stick. I took you for a good man, or no worse than others at the least. It seems we were both wrong. What cause you have to fear me, to cheat me, and to attempt my life—"

He murmured something about a jest, and that he liked a bit of fun; and then, seeing me smile, changed his tone, and assured me he would make all clear as soon as we had breakfasted. I saw by his face that he had no lie ready for me, though he was hard at work preparing one; and I think I was about to tell him so, when we were interrupted by a knocking at the door.

Bidding my uncle sit where he was, I went to open it, and found on the doorstep a half-grown boy in sea-clothes. He had no sooner seen me than he began to dance some steps of the sea-hornpipe (which I had never before heard of, far less seen), snapping his fingers in the air and footing it right cleverly. For all that, he was blue with the cold; and there was something in his face, a look between tears and laughter, that was highly pathetic and consisted ill with his gaiety of manner.

"What cheer, mate?" says he, with a cracked voice.

I asked him soberly to name his pleasure.

"O, pleasure!" says he; and then began to sing:

> *For it's my delight, of a shiny night,*
> *In the season of the year.*

"Well," said I, "if you have no business at all, I will even be so unmannerly as to shut you out."

"Stay, brother!" he cried. "Have you no fun about you? Or do you want to get me thrashed? I've brought a letter from old Heasy-Oasy to Mr. Belflower." He showed me a letter as he spoke. "And I say, mate," he added, "I'm mortal hungry."

"Well," said I, "come into the house, and you shall have a bite if I go empty or it."

With that I brought him in and set him down to my own place, where he fell-to greedily on the remains of breakfast, winking to me between whiles, and making many faces, which I think the poor soul considered manly. Meanwhile, my uncle had read the letter and sat thinking; then, suddenly, he got to his feet with a great air of liveliness and pulled me apart into the farthest corner of the room.

"Read that," said he, and put the letter in my hand.

Here it is, lying before me as I write:

The Hawes Inn, at the Queen's Ferry

Sir,—I lie here with my hawser up and down, and send my cabinboy to informe. If you have any further commands for over-seas, to-day will be the last occasion, as the wind will serve us well out of the firth. I will not seek to deny that I have had crosses with your doer, (agent) Mr. Rankeillor; of which, if not speedily redd up, you may looke to see some losses follow. I have drawn a bill upon you, as per margin, and am, sir, your most obedt., humble servant,

Elias Hoseason

"You see, Davie," resumed my uncle, as soon as he saw that I had done, "I have a venture with this man Hoseason, the captain of a trading brig, the Covenant, of Dysart. Now, if you and me was to walk over with yon lad, I could see the captain at the Hawes, or maybe on board the Covenant if there was papers to be signed; and so far from a loss of time, we can jog on to the lawyer, Mr. Rankeillor's. After a' that's come and gone, ye would be swear to believe me upon my naked word; but ye'll believe Rankeillor. He's factor to half the gentry in these parts; an auld man, forby: highly respeckit; and he kenned your father."

I stood awhile and thought. I was going to some place of shipping, which was doubtless populous, and where my uncle durst attempt no violence, and, indeed, even the society of the cabin-boy so far protected me. Once there, I believed I could force on the visit to the lawyer, even if my uncle were now insincere in proposing it; and, perhaps, in the bottom of my heart, I wished a nearer view of the sea and ships. You are to remember I had lived all my life in the inland hills, and just two days before had my first sight of the firth lying like a blue floor, and the sailed ships moving on the face of it, no bigger than toys. One thing with another, I made up my mind.

"Very well," says I, "let us go to the Ferry."

My uncle got into his hat and coat, and buckled an old rusty cutlass on; and then we trod the fire out, locked the door, and set forth upon our walk.

The wind, being in that cold quarter the northwest, blew nearly in our faces as we went. It was the month of June; the grass was all white with daisies and the trees with blossom; but, to judge by our blue nails and aching wrists, the time might have been winter and the whiteness a December frost.

Uncle Ebenezer trudged in the ditch, jogging from side to side like an old ploughman coming home from work. He never said a word the whole way; and I was thrown for talk on the cabin-boy. He told me his name was Ransome, and that he had followed the sea since he was nine, but could not say how old he was, as he had lost his reckoning. He showed me tattoo marks, baring his breast in the teeth of the wind and in spite of my remonstrances, for I thought it was enough to kill him; he swore horribly whenever he remembered, but more like a silly schoolboy than a man; and boasted of many wild and bad things that he had done; stealthy thefts, false accusations, ay, and even murder; but all with such a dearth of likelihood in the details, and such a weak and crazy swagger in the delivery, as disposed me rather to pity than to believe him.

I asked him of the brig (which he declared was the finest ship that sailed) and of Captain Hoseason, in whose praises he was equally loud. Heasy-Oasy (for so he still named the skipper) was a man, by his account, that minded for nothing either in heaven or earth; one that, as people said, would "crack on all sail into the day of judgement"; rough, fierce, unscrupulous, and brutal; and all this my poor cabin-boy had taught himself to admire as something seamanlike and manly. He would only admit one flaw in his idol. "He ain't no seaman," he admitted. "That's Mr. Shuan that navigates the brig; he's the finest seaman in the trade, only for drink; and I tell you I believe it! Why, look 'ere"; and turning down his stocking he showed me a great, raw, red wound that made my blood run cold. "He done that—Mr. Shuan done it," he said, with an air of pride.

"What!" I cried, "do you take such savage usage at his hands? Why, you are no slave, to be so handled!"

"No," said the poor moon-calf, changing his tune at once, "and so he'll find. See 'ere"; and he showed me a great case-knife, which he told me was stolen. "Oh," says he, "let me see him try; I dare him to; I'll do for him! Oh, he ain't the first!" And he confirmed it with a poor, silly, ugly oath.

I have never felt such pity for anyone in this wide world as I felt for that half-witted creature; and it began to come over me that the big Covenant (for all her pious name) was little better than a hell upon the seas.

Chapter 14 THE ISLET

n all the books I have read of people cast away, they had either their pockets full of tools, or a chest of things would be thrown upon the beach along with them, as if on purpose. My case was very different. I had nothing in my pockets but money and Alan's silver button; and being inland bred, I was as much short of knowledge as of means.

I knew indeed that shellfish were counted good to eat; and among the rocks of the isle I found a great plenty of limpets, which at first I could scarcely strike from their places, not knowing quickness to be needful. There were, besides, some of the little shells that we call buckies; I think periwinkle is the English name. Of these two I made my whole diet, devouring them cold and raw as I found them; and so hungry was I, that at first they seemed to me delicious.

Perhaps they were out of season, or perhaps there was something wrong in the sea about my island. But at least I had no sooner eaten my first meal than I was seized with giddiness and retching, and lay for a long time no better than dead. A second trial of the same food (indeed I had no other) did better with me, and revived my strength. But as long as I was on the island, I never knew what to expect when I had eaten; sometimes all was well, and sometimes I was thrown into a miserable sickness; nor could I ever distinguish what particular fish it was that hurt me.

All day it streamed rain; the island ran like a sop, there was no dry spot to be found; and when I lay down that night, between two boulders that made a kind of roof, my feet were in a bog.

The second day I crossed the island to all sides. There was no part if it better than another; it was all desolate and rocky; nothing living on it but game birds which I lacked the means to kill, and the gulls which haunted the outlying rocks in a prodigious number. But the creek, or straits, that cut off the isle from the mainland of the Ross, opened out on the north into a bay, and the bay again opened into the Sound of Iona; and it was the neighborhood of this place that I chose to be my home; though if I had thought upon the very name of the home in such a spot, I must have burst out weeping.

I had good reasons for my choice. There was in this part of the isle a little hut of a house like a pig's hut, where fishers used to sleep when they came there upon their business; but the turf roof of it had fallen entirely in; so that the hut was of no use to me, and gave me less shelter than my rocks. What was more important, the shellfish on which I lived grew there in great plenty; when the tide was out I could gather a peck at a time and this was doubtless a convenience. But the other reason went deeper. I had become in no way used to the horrid solitude of the isle, but still looked round me on all sides (like a man that was hunted), between fear and hope that I might see some human creature coming. Now, from a little up the hillside over the bay, I could catch a sight of the great, ancient church and the roofs of the people's houses in Iona. And on the other hand, over the low country of the Ross, I saw smoke go up, morning and evening, as if from a homestead in a hollow of the land.

I used to watch this smoke, when I was wet and cold, and had my head half turned with loneliness; and think of the fireside and the company, till my heart burned. It was the same with the roofs of Iona. Altogether, this sight I had of men's homes and comfortable lives, although it put a point on my own sufferings, yet it kept hope alive, and helped me to eat my raw shellfish (which had soon grown to be a disgust) and saved me from the sense of horror I had whenever I was quite alone with dead rocks, and fowls, and the rain, and the cold sea.

I say it kept hope alive, and indeed it seemed impossible that I should be left to die on the shores of my own country, and within view of a church tower and the smoke of men's houses. But the second day passed; and though as long as the light lasted I kept a bright lookout for boats on the Sound or men passing on the Ross, no help came near me. It still rained, and I turned in to sleep, as wet as ever, and with a cruel sore throat, but a little comforted, perhaps, by having said good night to my next neighbors, the people of Iona.

Charles the Second declared a man could stay outdoors more days in the year in the climate of England than in any other. This was very like a king, with a palace at his back and changes of dry clothes. But he must have had better luck on his flight from Worchester than I had on that miserable isle. It was the height of the summer; yet it rained for more than than twenty-four hours, and did not clear until the afternoon of the third day.

This was the day of incidents. In the morning I saw a red deer, a buck with a fine spread of antlers, standing in the rain on the top of the island; but he had scarce seen me rise from under my rock, before he trotted off upon the other side. I supposed he must have swum the straits; though what should bring any creature to Earraid was more than I could fancy.

A little after, as I was jumping about after my limpets, I was startled by a guinea-piece, which fell upon a rock in front of me and glanced off into the sea. When the sailors gave me my money again, they kept back not only about a third of the whole sum, but my father's leather purse; so that from that day out I carried my gold loose in a pocket with a button. I now saw there must be a hole, and clapped my hand to the place in a great hurry. But this was to lock the stable door after the steed was stolen. I had left the shore at Queensferry with near on fifty pounds; now I found no more than two guinea-pieces and a silver shilling.

It is true I picked up a third guinea a little after, where it lay shining on a piece of turf. That made a fortune of three pounds and four shillings, English money, for a lad, the rightful heir of an estate, and now starving on an isle at the extreme end of the wild Highlands.

This state of my affairs dashed me still further; and indeed my plight on that third morning was truly pitiful. My clothes were beginning to rot; my stockings in particular were quite worn through, so that my shanks went naked; my hands had grown quite soft with the continual soaking; my throat was very sore, my strength had much abated, and my heart so turned against the horrid stuff I was condemned to eat that the very sight of it came near to sicken me.

And yet the worst was not yet come.

There is a pretty high rock on the northwest of Erraid, which (because it had a flat top and overlooked the Sound) I was much in the habit of frequenting; not that ever I stayed in one place, save when asleep, my misery giving me no rest. Indeed I wore myself down with continual and aimless goings and comings in the rain.

As soon, however, as the sun came out, I lay down on the top of that rock to dry myself. The comfort of the sunshine is a thing I cannot tell. It set me thinking hopefully of my deliverance, of which I had begun to despair; and I scanned the sea and the Ross with a fresh interest. On the south of my rock, a part of the island jutted out and hid the open ocean, so that a bus could thus come quite near me upon that side and I be none the wiser.

Well, all of a sudden, a coble with a brown sail and a pair of fishers aboard of it came flying round that corner of the isle, bound for Iona. I shouted out, and then fell on my knees on the rock and reached my hands and prayed to them. They were near enough to hear—I could even see the color of their hair; and there was no doubt but they observed me, for they cried out in Gaelic tongue, and laughed. But the boat never turned aside, and flew on, right before my eyes, for Iona.

I could not believe such wickedness, and ran along the shore from rock to rock, crying on them piteously: even after they were out of reach of my voice, I still cried and waved to them; and when they were quite gone, I thought my heart would have burst. All the time of my troubles I wept only twice. Once, when I could not reach the yard, and now, the second time, when these fishers turned a deaf ear to my cries. But this time I wept and roared like a wicked child, tearing up the turf with my nails and grinding my face in the earth. If a wish would kill men, those two fishers would never have seen morning, and I should likely have died upon the island.

When I was a little over my anger, I must eat again, but with such loathing of the mess as I could now scarce control. Sure enough I should have done as well to fast, for my fishes poisoned me again. I had all my first pains; my throat was so sore I could scarce swallow; I had a fit of strong shuddering, which clucked my teeth together; and there came on me that dreadful sense of illness, which we have no name for either in Scotch or English. I thought I should have died, and made my peace with God, forgiving all men, even my uncle and the fishers; and as soon as I had thus made up my mind to the worst, clearness came upon me: I observed the night was falling dry; my clothes were dried a good deal, truly; I was in a better case than ever before since I had landed on the isle; and so I got to sleep at last, with a thought of gratitude.

The next day (which was the fourth of this horrible life of mine) I found my bodily strength run very low. But the sun shone, the air was sweet, and what I managed to eat of the shellfish agreed well with me and revived my courage.

I was scarce back on my rock (where I went always the first thing after I had eaten) before I observed a boat coming down from the Sound, and with her head, as I thought, in my direction.

I began at once to hope and fear exceedingly; for I thought these men might have thought better of their cruelty and be coming back to my assistance. But another disappointment, such as yesterday's, was more than I could bear. I turned my back accordingly, upon the sea, and did not look again till I had counted many hundreds. The boat was still heading for the island. The next time I counted the full thousand, as slowly as I could, my heart beating so as to hurt me. And then it was out of all question. She was coming straight to Earraid!

I could no longer hold myself back, but ran to the sea side and out, from one rock to another, as far as I could go. It is a marvel I was not drowned; for when I was brought to a stand at last, my legs shook under me, and my mouth was so dry, I must wet it with sea-water before I was able to shout.

All this time the boat was coming on; and now I was able to perceive it was the same boat and the same two men as yesterday. This I knew by their hair, which the one had of a bright yellow and the other black. But now there was a third man along with them, who looked to be of a better class.

As soon as they were come within easy speech, they let down their sail and lay quiet. In spite of my supplications, they drew no nearer in, and what frightened me most of all, the new man tee-hee'd with laughter as he talked and looked at me.

Then he stood up in the boat and addressed me a long while, speaking fast and with many wavings of his hand. I told him I had no Gaelic; and at this he became very angry, and I began to suspect he thought he was talking English. Listening very close, I caught the word "whateffer" several times; but all the rest was Gaelic and might have been Greek and Hebrew for me.

"Whatever," said I, to show him I had caught a word.

"Yes, yes—yes, yes," says he, and then he looked at the other men, as much as to say, "I told you I spoke English," and began again as hard as ever in Gaelic.

This time I picked out another word, "tide." Then I had a flash of hope. I remembered he was always waving his hand towards the mainland of the Ross.

"Do you mean when the tide is out—?" I cried, and could not finish.

"Yes, yes," said he. "Tide."

At that I turned tail upon their boat (where my adviser had once more begun to tee-hee with laughter), leaped back the way I had come, from one stone to another, and set off running across the isle as I had never run before. In about half an hour I came out upon the shores of the creek; and, sure enough, it was shrunk into a little trickle of water, through which I dashed, not above my knees, and landed with a shout on the main island.

A sea-bred boy would not have stayed a day on Earraid; which is only what they call a tidal islet, and, except in the bottom of the neaps, can be entered and left twice in every twenty-four hours, either dryshod, or at the most wading. Even I, had the tide going out and in before me in the bay, and even watched for the ebbs, the better to get my shellfish—even I (I say), if I had to sit down to think, instead of raging at my fate, must have soon guessed the secret, and got free. It was no wonder the fishers had not understood me. The wonder was rather that they had ever guessed my pitiful illusion, and taken the trouble to come back. I had starved with cold and hunger on that island for close upon one hundred hours. But for the fishers, I might have left my bones there in pure folly. And even as it was, I had paid for it pretty dear, not only in past sufferings, but in my present case; being clothed like a beggar-man, scarce able to walk, and in great pain of my sore throat.

I have seen wicked men and fools, a great many of both; and I believe they both get paid in the end; but the fools first.

Stevenson, Robert L. *Kidnapped.* Illustrated by N.C. Wyeth. New York: Random House, 1989.

LITTLE HOUSE ON THE PRAIRIE

Laura Ingalls Wilder

It's the Ingalls family's first Christmas in their new house on the prairie. The nearby creek is rising and they're afraid neither their neighbor Mr. Edwards nor Santa Claus will be able to cross it in time for Christmas dinner.

MR. EDWARDS MEETS SANTA CLAUS

a said it was too bad. She hated to think of Mr. Edwards eating his bachelor cooking all alone on Christmas day. Mr. Edwards had been asked to eat Christmas dinner with them, but Pa shook his head and said a man would risk his neck, trying to cross that creek now.

"No," he said. "That current's too strong. We'll just have to make up our minds that Edwards won't be here tomorrow."

Of course that meant that Santa Claus could not come, either.

Laura and Mary tried not to mind too much. They watched Ma dress the wild turkey, and it was a very fat turkey. They were lucky little girls, to have a good house to live in, and a warm fire to sit by, and such a turkey for their Christmas dinner. Ma said so, and it was true. Ma said it was too bad that Santa Claus couldn't come this year, but they were such good girls that he hadn't forgotten them; he would surely come next year.

Still, they were not happy.

After supper that night they washed their hands and faces, buttoned their red-flannel nightgowns, tied their night-cap strings, and soberly said their prayers. They lay down in bed and pulled the covers up. It did not seem at all like Christmas time.

Pa and Ma sat silent by the fire. After a while Ma asked why Pa didn't play the fiddle, and he said, "I don't seem to have the heart to, Caroline."

After a longer while, Ma suddenly stood up.

"I'm going to hang up your stockings, girls," she said. "Maybe something will happen."

Ma took one of Mary's clean stockings and one of Laura's, and she hung them from the mantel-shelf, on either side of the fireplace. Laura and Mary watched her over the edge of their bed-covers.

"Now go to sleep," Ma said, kissing them good night. "Morning will come quicker if you're asleep."

She sat down again by the fire and Laura almost went to sleep. She woke up a little when she heard Pa say, "You've only made it worse, Caroline." And she thought she heard Ma say: "No, Charles. There's the white sugar." But perhaps she was dreaming.

Then she heard Jack growl savagely. The door-latch rattled and someone said, "Ingalls! Ingalls!" Pa was stirring up the fire, and when he opened the door Laura saw that it was morning. The outdoors was gray.

"Great fishhooks, Edwards! Come in, man! What's happened?" Pa exclaimed.

Laura saw the stockings limply dangling, and she scrooged her shut eyes into the pillow. She heard Pa piling wood on the fire, and she heard Mr. Edwards say he had carried his clothes on his head when he swam the creek. His teeth rattled and his voice shivered. He would be all right, he said, as soon as he got warm.

"It was too big a risk, Edwards," Pa said. "We're glad you're here, but that was too big a risk for a Christmas dinner."

"Your little ones had to have a Christmas," Mr. Edwards replied. "No creek could stop me, after I fetched them their gifts from Independence."

Laura sat straight up in bed. "Did you see Santa Claus?" she shouted.

"I sure did," Mr. Edwards said.

"Where? When? What did he look like? What did he say? Did he really give you something for us?" Mary and Laura cried.

"Wait, wait a minute!" Mr. Edwards laughed. And Ma said she would put the presents in the stockings, as Santa Claus intended. She said they mustn't look.

Mr. Edwards came and sat on the floor by their bed, and he answered every question they asked him. They honestly tried not to look at Ma, and they didn't quite see what she was doing.

When he saw the creek rising, Mr. Edwards said, he had known that Santa Claus could not get across it. ("But you crossed it," Laura said. "Yes," Mr. Edwards replied, "but Santa Claus is too old and fat. He couldn't make it, where a long, lean razor-back like me could do so.") And Mr. Edwards reasoned that if Santa Claus couldn't cross the creek, likely he would come no farther south than Independence. Why should he come forty miles across the prairie, only to be turned back? Of course he wouldn't do that!

So Mr. Edwards had walked to Independence. ("In the rain?" Mary asked. Mr. Edwards said he wore his rubber coat.) And there, coming down the street in Independence, he had met Santa Claus. ("In the daytime?" Laura asked. She hadn't thought that anyone could see Santa Claus in the daytime. No, Mr. Edwards said; it was night, but light shone out across the street from the saloons.)

Well, the first thing Santa Claus said was, "Hello, Edwards!" ("Did he know you?" Mary asked, and Laura asked, "How did you know he was really Santa Claus?" Mr. Edwards said that Santa Claus knew everybody. And he had recognized Santa at once by his whiskers. Santa Claus had the longest, thickest, whitest set of whiskers west of the Mississippi.)

So Santa Claus said, "Hello, Edwards! Last time I saw you you were sleeping on a corn-shuck bed in Tennessee." And Mr. Edwards well remembered the little pair of red-yarn mittens that Santa Claus had left for him that time.

Then Santa Claus said, "I understand you're living now down along the Verdigris River. Have you ever met up, down yonder, with two little young girls named Mary and Laura?"

"I surely am acquainted with them," Mr. Edwards replied.

"It rests heavy on my mind," said Santa Claus. "They are both of them sweet, pretty, good little young things, and I know they are expecting me. I surely do hate to disappoint two good little girls like them. Yet with the water up the way it is, I can't ever make it across that creek. I can figure no way whatsoever to get to their cabin this year. "Edwards," Santa Claus said. "Would you do me the favor to fetch them their gifts this one time?"

"I'll do that, and with pleasure," Mr. Edwards told him.

Then Santa Claus and Mr. Edwards stepped across the street to the hitching-posts where the pack-mule was tied. ("Didn't he have his reindeer?" Laura asked. "You know he couldn't," Mary said. "There isn't any snow." Exactly, said Mr. Edwards. Santa Claus traveled with a pack-mule in the southwest.)

And Santa Claus uncinched the pack and looked through it, and he took out the presents for Mary and Laura.

"Oh, what are they?" Laura cried; but Mary asked, "Then what did he do?"

Then he shook hands with Mr. Edwards, and he swung up on his fine bay horse. Santa Claus rode well for a man of his weight and build. And he tucked his long, white whiskers under his bandana. "So long, Edwards," he said, and he rode away on the Fort Dodge trail, leading his pack-mule and whistling.

Laura and Mary were silent an instant, thinking of that.

Then Ma said, "You may look now, girls."

Something was shining bright in the top of Laura's stocking. She squealed and jumped out of bed. So did Mary, but Laura beat her to the fireplace. And the shining thing was a glittering new tin cup.

Mary had one exactly like it.

These new tin cups were their very own. Now they each had a cup to drink out of. Laura jumped up and down and shouted and laughed, but Mary stood still and looked with shining eyes at her own tin cup.

Then they plunged their hands into the stockings again. And they pulled out two long, long sticks of candy. It was peppermint candy, striped red and white. They looked and looked at the beautiful candy, and Laura licked her stick, just one lick. But Mary was not so greedy. She didn't take even one lick of her stick.

Those stockings weren't empty yet. Mary and Laura pulled out two small packages. They unwrapped them, and each found a little heart-shaped cake. Over their delicate brown tops was sprinkled white sugar. The sparkling grains lay like tiny drifts of snow.

The cakes were too pretty to eat. Mary and Laura just looked at them. But at last Laura turned hers over, and she nibbled a tiny nibble from underneath, where it wouldn't show. And the inside of the little cake was white!

It had been made of pure white flour, and sweetened with white sugar.

Laura and Mary never would have looked in their stockings again. The cups and the cakes and the candy were almost too much. They were too happy to speak. But Ma asked if they were sure the stockings were empty.

Then they put their hands down inside them, to make sure.

And in the very toe of each stocking was a shining, bright, new penny!

They had never even thought of such a thing as having a penny. Think of having a whole penny for your very own. Think of having a cup and a cake and a stick of candy and a penny.

There never had been such a Christmas.

Now of course, right away, Laura and Mary should have thanked Mr. Edwards for bringing those lovely presents all the way from Independence. But they had forgotten all about Mr. Edwards. They had even forgotten Santa Claus. In a minute they would have remembered, but before they did, Ma said, gently, "Aren't you going to thank Mr. Edwards?"

"Oh, thank you, Mr. Edwards! Thank you!" they said, and they meant it with all their hearts. Pa shook Mr. Edwards' hand, too, and shook it again. Pa and Ma and Mr. Edwards acted as if they were almost crying, Laura didn't know why. So she gazed again at her beautiful presents.

She looked up again when Ma gasped. And Mr. Edwards was taking sweet potatoes out of his pockets. He said they had helped to balance the package on his head when he swam across the creek. He thought Pa and Ma might like them, with the Christmas turkey.

There were nine sweet potatoes. Mr. Edwards had brought them all the way from town, too. It was just too much. Pa said so. "It's too much, Edwards," he said. They never could thank him enough.

Mary and Laura were too excited to eat breakfast. They drank the milk from their shining new cups, but they could not swallow the rabbit stew and the cornmeal mush.

"Don't make them, Charles," Ma said. "It will soon be dinner-time."

For Christmas dinner there was the tender, juicy, roasted turkey. There were the sweet potatoes, baked in the ashes and carefully wiped so that you could eat the good skins, too. There was a loaf of salt-rising bread made from the last of the white flour.

And after all that there were stewed dried blackberries and little cakes. But these little cakes were made with brown sugar and they did not have white sugar sprinkled over their tops.

Then Pa and Ma and Mr. Edwards sat by the fire and talked about Christmas times back in Tennessee and up north in the Big Woods. But Mary and Laura looked at their beautiful cakes and played with their pennies and drank their water out of their new cups. And little by little they licked and sucked their sticks of candy, till each stick was sharp-pointed on one end.

That was a happy Christmas.

Wilder, Laura Ingalls. *Little House on the Prairie*. New York: HarperCollins, 1971.

ANIMAL TALES

THE BLACK STALLION

WALTER FARLEY

In Walter Farley's The Black Stallion, *Alec Ramsey is on a ship, the* Drake, *returning from his summer in India. While the ship is temporarily docked, Alec notices a mighty, black horse—the most beautiful animal in the world! The following paragraphs are the remarkable beginning of a long, exciting relationship.*

Chapter 2 THE STORM

he Drake stopped at Alexandria, Bengasi, Tripoli, Tunis, and Algiers, passed the Rock of Gibraltar, and turned north up the coast of Portugal. Now they were off Cape Finisterre on the coast of Spain, and in a few days, Captain Watson told Alec, they would be in England.

Alec wondered why the Black was being shipped to England—perhaps for stud, perhaps to race. The slanting shoulders, the deep broad chest, the powerful legs, the knees not too high nor too low—these, his uncle had taught him, were marks of speed and endurance.

That night Alec made his customary trip to the stall, his pockets filled with lumps of sugar. The night was hot and still; heavy clouds blacked out the stars; in the distance long streaks of lightning raced through the sky. The Black had his head out the window. Again he was looking out to sea, his nostrils quivering more than ever. He turned, whistled as he saw the boy, then again faced the water.

Alec felt elated—it was the first time that the stallion hadn't drawn back into the stall at sight of him. He moved closer. He put the sugar in the palm of his hand and hesitantly held it out to the stallion. The Black turned and once again whistled—softer this time. Alec stood his ground. Neither he nor anyone else had been this close to the stallion since he came on board. But he did not care to take the chance of extending his arm any nearer the bared teeth, the curled nostrils. Instead he placed the sugar on the sill. The Black looked at it, then back at the boy. Slowly he moved over and began to eat the sugar. Alec watched him for a moment, satisfied; then as the rain began to fall, he went back to his cabin.

He was awakened with amazing suddenness in the middle of the night. The *Drake* lurched crazily and he was thrown onto the floor. Outside there were loud rolls of thunder, and streaks of lightning made his cabin as light as day.

His first storm at sea! He pushed the light switch—it was dead. Then a flash of lightning again illuminated the cabin. The top of his bureau had been swept clear and the

52

floor was covered with broken glass. Hurriedly he pulled on his pants and shirt and started for the door; then he stopped. Back he went to the bed, fell on his knees and reached under. He withdrew a life jacket and strapped it around him. He hoped that he wouldn't need it.

He opened the door and made his way, staggering, to the deck. The fury of the storm drove him back into the passageway; he hung on to the stair rail and peered into the black void. He heard the shouts of Captain Watson and the crew faintly above the roar of the winds. Huge waves swept from one end of the *Drake* to the other. Hysterical passengers crowded in to the corridor. Alec was genuinely scared now; never had he seen a storm like this!

For what seemed hours, the *Drake* plowed through wave after wave, trembling, careening on its side, yet somehow managing to stay afloat. The long streaks of lightning never diminished; zigzagging through the sky, their sharp cracks resounded on the water.

From the passageway, Alec saw one of the crew make his way along the deck in his direction, desperately fighting to hold on to the rail. The *Drake* rolled sideways and a huge wave swept over the boat. When it had passed, the sailor was gone. The boy closed his eyes and prayed.

The storm began to subside a little and Alec felt new hope. Then suddenly a bolt of fire seemed to fall from the heavens above them. A sharp crack and the boat shook. Alec was thrown flat on his face, stunned. Slowly he regained consciousness. He was lying on his stomach; his face hot and sticky. He raised his hand, and withdrew it covered with blood. Then he became conscious of feet stepping on him. The passengers, yelling and screaming, were climbing, crawling over him! The *Drake* was still—its engines dead.

Struggling, Alec pushed himself to his feet. Slowly he made his way along the deck. His startled eyes took in the scene about him. The *Drake*, struck by lightning, seemed almost cut in half! They were sinking! Strange, with what seemed the end so near, he should feel so calm. They were manning the lifeboats, and Captain Watson was there shouting directions. One boat was being lowered into the water. A large wave caught it broadside and turned it over—its occupants disappeared in the sea.

The second lifeboat was being filled and Alec waited his turn. But when it came, the boat had reached its quota.

"Wait for the next one, Alec," Captain Watson said sternly. He put his arm on the boy's shoulder, softening the harshness of his words.

As they watched the second lifeboat being lowered, the dark-skinned man appeared and rushed up to the captain, waving his arms and babbling hysterically.

"It's under the bed, under the bed!" Captain Watson shouted at him.

Then Alec saw the man had no life jacket. Terror in his eyes, he turned away from the captain toward Alec. Frantically he rushed at the boy and tried to tear the life jacket from his back. Alec struggled, but he was no match for the half-crazed man. Then Captain Watson had his hands on the man and threw him against the rail.

Alec saw the man's eyes turn to the lifeboat that was being lowered. Before the captain could stop him, he was climbing over the rail. He was going to jump into the boat! Suddenly the *Drake* lurched. The man lost his balance and, screaming, fell into the water. He never rose to the surface.

The dark-skinned man had drowned. Immediately Alec thought of the Black. What was happening to him? Was he still in his stall? Alec fought his way out of line and toward the stern of the boat. If the stallion was alive, he was going to set him free and give him his chance to fight for life.

The stall was still standing. Alec heard a shrill whistle rise above the storm. He rushed to the door, lifted the heavy bar and swung it open. For a second the mighty hoofs stopped pounding and there was silence. Alec backed slowly away.

Then he saw the Black, his head held high, his nostrils blown out with excitement. Suddenly he snorted and plunged straight for the rail and Alec. Alec was paralyzed, he couldn't move. One hand was on the rail, which was broken at this point, leaving nothing between him and the open water. The Black swerved as he came near him, and the boy realized that the stallion was making for the hole. The horse's shoulder grazed him as he swerved, and Alec went flying into space. He felt the water close over his head.

When he came up, his first thought was of the ship; then he heard an explosion, and he saw the *Drake* settling deep into the water. Frantically he looked around for a lifeboat, but there was none in sight. Then he saw the Black swimming, not more than ten yards away. Something swished by him—a rope, and it was attached to the Black's halter! The same rope that they had used to bring the stallion aboard the boat, and which they had never been able to get close enough to the horse to untie. Without stopping to think, Alec grabbed hold of it. Then he was pulled through the water, into the oncoming seas.

The waves were still large, but with the aid of his life jacket, Alec was able to stay on top. He was too tired now to give much thought to what he had done. He only knew that he had had his choice of remaining in the water alone or being pulled by the Black. If he was to die, he would rather die with the mighty stallion than alone. He took one last look behind and saw the *Drake* sink into the depths.

For hours Alec battled the waves. He had tied the rope securely around his waist. He could hardly hold his head up. Suddenly he felt the rope slacken. The Black had stopped swimming! Alec anxiously waited; peering into the darkness he could just make out the head of the stallion. The Black's whistle pierced the air! After a few minutes, the rope became taut again. The horse had changed his direction. Another hour passed, then the storm diminished to high, rolling swells. The first streaks of dawn appeared on the horizon.

The Black had stopped four times during the night, and each time he had altered his course. Alec wondered whether the stallion's wild instinct was leading him to land. The sun rose and shone down brightly on the boy's head; the salt water he had swallowed during the night made him sick to his stomach. But when Alec felt that he could hold out no longer, he looked at the struggling, fighting animal in front of him.

Suddenly he realized that they were going with the waves, instead of against them. He shook his head, trying to clear his mind. Yes, they were riding in; they must be approaching land! Eagerly he strained his salt-filled eyes and looked into the distance. And then he saw it—about a quarter of a mile away was a small island, not much more than a sandy reef in the sea. But he might find food and water there, and have a chance to survive. Faster and faster they approached the white sand. They were in the breakers. The Black's scream shattered the stillness. He was able to walk; he staggered a little and shook his black head. Then his action shifted marvelously, and he went faster through the shallow water.

Alec's head whirled as he was pulled toward the beach with ever-increasing speed. Suddenly he realized the danger of his position. He must untie this rope from around his waist, or else he would be dragged to death over the sand. Desperately his fingers flew to the knot; it was tight, he had made sure of that. Frantically he worked on it as the shore drew closer and closer.

The Black was now on the beach. Thunder began to roll from beneath his hoofs as he broke out of the water. Hours in the water had swelled the knot—Alec couldn't untie it! Then he remembered his pocketknife. Could it still be there? Alec's hand darted to his rear pants pocket. His fingers reached inside and came out with the knife.

He was now on the beach being dragged by the stallion; the sand flew in his face. Quickly he opened the knife and began to cut the rope. His body burned from the sand, his clothes were being torn off of him! His speed was increasing every second! Madly he sawed away at the rope. With one final thrust he was through! His outflung hands caressed the sand. As he closed his eyes, his parched lips murmured, "Yes—Uncle Ralph—it did—come in handy."

Farley, Walter. *The Black Stallion*. New York: Random House, 1991.

OLD YELLER

FRED GIPSON

Travis, a fourteen-year-old boy is left in charge of his family, and with the help of Old Yeller, tries to make a life for all of them in the Texas wilderness.

When it happened, I was down the creek a ways, splitting rails to fix up the yard fence where the bulls had torn it down. I'd been down there since dinner, working in a stand of tall slim post oaks. I'd chop down a tree, trim off the branches as far up as I wanted, then cut way the rest of the top. After that I'd start splitting the log.

I'd split the log by driving steel wedges into the wood. I'd start at the big end and hammer in a wedge with the back side of my axe. This would start a little split running lengthways of the log. Then I'd take a second wedge and drive it into the split. This would split the log further along and, at the same time loosen the first wedge. I'd then knock the first wedge loose and move it up in front of the second one.

Driving one wedge ahead of the other like that, I could finally split a log in two halves. Then I'd go to work on the halves, splitting them apart. That way, from each log, I'd come out with four rails.

Swinging that chopping axe was sure hard work. The sweat poured off me. My back muscles ached. The axe got so heavy I could hardly swing it. My breath got harder and harder to breathe.

An hour before sundown, I was worn down to a nub. It seemed like I couldn't hit another lick. Papa could have lasted till past sundown, but I didn't see how I could. I shouldered my axe and headed toward the cabin, trying to think up some excuse to tell Mama to keep her from knowing I was played clear out.

That's when I heard Little Arliss scream.

Well, Little Arliss was a screamer by nature. He'd scream when he was happy and scream when he was mad and a lot of times he'd scream just to hear himself make a noise. Generally, we paid no more mind to his screaming than we did to the gobble of a wild turkey.

But this time was different. The second I heard his screaming, I felt my heart flop clear over. This time I knew Little Arliss was in real trouble.

I tore out up the trail leading toward the cabin. A minute before, I'd been so tired out with my rail-splitting that I couldn't have struck a trot. But now I raced through the tall trees in that creek bottom, covering ground like a scared wolf.

56

Little Arliss's second scream, when it came, was louder and shriller and more frantic-sounding than the first. Mixed with it was a whimpering crying sound that I knew didn't come from him. It was a sound I'd heard before and seemed like I ought to know what it was, but right then I couldn't place it.

Then, from way off to one side came a sound that I would have recognized anywhere. It was the coughing roar of a charging bear. I'd just heard it once in my life. That was the time Mama had shot and wounded a hog-killing bear and Papa had to finish it off with a knife to keep it from getting her.

My heart went to pushing up into my throat, nearly choking off my wind. I strained for every lick of speed I could get out of my running legs. I didn't know what sort of fix Little Arliss had got himself into, but I knew that it had to do with a mad bear, which was enough.

The way the late sun slanted through the trees had the trail and cross-banded with streaks of bright light and dark shade. I ran through these bright and dark patches so fast that the changing light nearly blinded me. Then suddenly, I raced out into the open where I could see ahead. And what I saw sent a chill clear through to the marrow of my bones.

There was Little Arliss, down in that spring hole again. He was lying half in and half out of the water, holding onto the hind leg of a little bear cub no bigger than a small coon. The bear cub was out on the bank whimpering and crying and clawing the rocks with all three of his other feet, trying to pull away. But Little Arliss was holding on for all he was worth, scared now and screaming his head off. Too scared to let go.

But all of that didn't matter now. What mattered was the bear cub's mama. She'd heard the cries of her baby and was coming to save him. She was coming so fast that she had the brush popping and breaking as she crashed through and over it. I could see her black heavy figure piling off down the slant on the far side of Birdsong Creek. She was roaring mad and ready to kill.

And worst of all, I could see that I'd never get there in time!

Mama couldn't either. She'd heard Arliss, too, and here she came from the cabin, running down the slant toward the spring, screaming at Arliss, telling him to turn the bear cub loose. But Little Arliss wouldn't do it. All he'd do was hang with that hind leg and let out one shrill shriek after another as fast as he could suck in a breath.

Now the bear was charging across the shallows in the creek. She was knocking sheets of water high in the bright sun, charging with her fur up and her long teeth bared, filling the canyon with that awful coughing roar. And no matter how fast Mama ran or how fast I ran, the she bear was going to get there first!

I think I nearly went blind then, picturing what was going to happen to Little Arliss. I know that I opened my mouth to scream and not any sound came out.

Then just as the bear went lunging up the creek bank toward Little Arliss and her cub, a flash of yellow came streaking out of the brush.

It was that big yeller dog. He was roaring like a mad bull. He wasn't one third as big and heavy as the she-bear, but when he piled into her from one side, he rolled her clear off her feet. They went down in a wild, roaring tangle of twisting bodies and scrambling feet and slashing fangs.

As I raced past them, I saw the bear lunge up to stand on her hind feet like a man while she clawed at the body of the yeller dog hanging on to her throat. I didn't wait to see more. Without ever checking my stride I ran in and jerked Little Arliss loose from the cub. I grabbed him by the wrist and yanked him up out of that water and slung him toward Mama like he was a half-empty sack of corn. I screamed at Mama. "Grab him, Mama! Grab him and run!" Then I swung my chopping axe high and wheeled, aiming to cave in the she-bear's head with the first lick.

But I never did strike, I didn't need to. Old Yeller hadn't let the bear get close enough. He couldn't handle her; she was too big and strong for that. She'd stand there on her hind feet, hunched over, and take a roaring swing at him with one of those big front claws. She'd slap him head over heels. She'd knock him so far that it didn't look like he could possibly get back there before she charged again, but he always did. He'd hit the ground roaring rolling, yelling his head off with the pain of the blow; but somehow he'd always roll to his feet. And here he'd come again, ready to tie into her for another round.

I stood there with my axe raised, watching them for a long moment. Then from up toward the house, I heard Mama calling: "Come away from there, Travis. Hurry, son! Run."

That spooked me. Up till then, I'd been ready to tie into that bear myself. Now, suddenly, I was scared out of my wits again. I ran toward the cabin.

But like it was, Old Yeller nearly beat me there. I didn't see it, of course; but Mama said that the minute Old Yeller saw we were all in the clear and out of danger, he threw the fight to that she-bear and lit out for the house. The bear chased him for a little piece, but at the rate Old Yeller was leaving her behind, Mama said it looked like the bear was backing up.

But if the big yeller dog was scared or hurt in any way when he came down dashing into the house he didn't show it. He sure didn't show it like we all did. Little Arliss had hushed his screaming, but he was trembling all over and clinging to Mama like he'd never let her go. And Mama was sitting in the middle of the floor, holding him up close and crying like she'd never stop. And me, I was close to crying, myself.

Old Yeller, though, all he did was come bounding in to jump on us and lick us in the face and bark so loud that there, inside the cabin, the noise nearly made us deaf.

The way he acted, you might have thought that bear fight hadn't been anything more than a rowdy romp that we'd all taken part in for the fun of it.

Gipson, Fred. *Old Yeller*. New York: HarperCollins, 1989.

THE JUNGLE BOOK

RUDYARD KIPLING

Mowgli, the "manchild," son of a woodcutter, takes us through the rigors of the jungle when he is abandoned by his parents and left to fend for himself. Mowgli's parents fled when their camp was attacked by Shere Khan, a bengal tiger. Mowgli finds safety in the cave of a wolf pack where Mother Wolf and Father Wolf take him in to raise him as one of their cubs.

MOWGLI'S BROTHERS

The Law of the Jungle, which never orders anything without reason, forbids every beast to eat Man except when he is killing to show his children how to kill, and then he must hunt outside the hunting-grounds of his pack or tribe. The real reason for this is that man-killing means, sooner or later, the arrival of white men on elephants, with guns, and hundreds of brown men with gongs and rockets and torches. Then everybody in the jungle suffers. The reason the beasts give among themselves is that Man is the weakest and most defenseless of all living things, and it is unsportsmanlike to touch him. They say too—and it is true—that man-eaters become mangy, and lose their teeth.

The purr grew louder, and ended in the fullthroated "*Aaarh!*" of the tiger's charge.

Then there was a howl—an untigerish howl—from Shere Khan. "He has missed," said Mother Wolf. "What is it?"

Father Wolf ran out a few paces and heard Shere Kahn muttering and mumbling savagely, as he tumbled about in the scrub.

"The fool has had no more sense than to jump a wood-cutter's camp-fire, so he has burned his feet," said Father Wolf, with a grunt. "Tabaqui is with him."

"Something is coming uphill," said Mother Wolf, twitching one ear. "Get ready."

The bushes rustled a little in the thicket, and Father Wolf dropped with his haunches under him, ready for his leap. Then, if you had been watching, you would have seen the most wonderful thing in the world—the wolf checked in midspring. He made his bound before he saw what it was he was jumping at, and then he tried to stop himself. The result was that he shot up straight into the air for four or five feet, landing almost where he left the ground.

"Man!" he snapped. "A man's cub. Look!"

Directly in front of him, holding on by a low branch, stood a naked brown baby who could just walk—as soft and as dimpled a little thing as ever came to a wolf's cave at night. He looked up into Father Wolf's face and laughed.

THE TIGER'S ROAR FILLED THE CAVE WITH THUNDER.

"Is that a man's cub?" said Mother Wolf. "I have never seen one. Bring it here."

A wolf accustomed to moving his own cubs can, if necessary, mouth an egg without breaking it, and though Father Wolf's jaws closed right on the child's back, not a tooth even scratched the skin as he laid it down among the cubs.

"How little! How naked, and—how bold!" said Mother Wolf, softly. The baby was pushing his way between the cubs to get close to the warm hide. "Ahai! He is taking his meal with the others. And so this is a man's cub. Now, was there ever a wolf that could boast of a man's cub among her children?"

"I have heard now and again of such a thing, but never in our pack or in my time," said Father Wolf. "He is altogether without hair, and I could kill him with a touch of my foot. But see, he looks up and is not afraid."

The moonlight was blocked out of the mouth of the cave, for Shere Kahn's great square head and shoulders were thrust into the entrance. Tabaqui, behind him, was squeaking: "My Lord, my Lord, it went in here!"

"Shere Khan does us great honor," said Father Wolf, but his eyes were very angry. "What does Shere Khan need?"

"My quarry. A man's cub went this way," said Shere Khan. "Its parents have run off. Give it to me."

Shere Khan had jumped at a wood-cutter's camp-fire, as Father Wolf had said, and was furious from the pain of his burned feet. But Father Wolf knew that the mouth of the cave was too narrow for a tiger to come in by. Even where he was, Shere Khan's shoulders and forepaws were cramped for want of room, as a man's would be if he tried to fight in a barrel.

"The Wolves are a free people," said Father Wolf. "They take orders from the Head of the Pack, and not from any striped cattle-killer. The man's cub is ours—to kill if we choose."

"Ye choose and ye do not choose! What talk is this of choosing? By the bull that I killed, am I to stand nosing into your dog's den for my fair dues? It is I, Shere Khan, who speaks!"

The tiger's roar filled the cave with thunder. Mother Wolf shook herself clear of the cubs and sprang forward, her eyes, like two green moons in the darkness, facing the blazing eyes of Shere Kahn.

"And it is I, Raksha [the Demon], who answers. The man's cub is mine, Lungri—mine to me! He shall not be killed. He shall live to run with the Pack and to hunt with the Pack; and in the end, look you, hunter of little naked cubs—frog-eater—fish-killer, he shall hunt thee! Now get hence, or by the Sambhur that I killed (I eat no starved cattle), back thou goest to thy mother, burned beast of the jungle, lamer than ever thou camest into the world! Go!"

Father Wolf looked on, amazed. He had almost forgotten the days when he won Mother Wolf in a fair fight from five other wolves, when she ran in the Pack and was not called Demon for compliment's sake. Shere Khan might have faced Father Wolf, but he could not stand up against Mother Wolf, for he knew that where he was she had all the advantage of the ground, and would fight to the death. So he backed out of the cave-mouth growling, and when he was clear he shouted:

"Each dog barks in his own yard! We will see what the Pack will say to this fostering of man-cubs. The cub is mine, and to my teeth he will come in the end, O bush-tailed thieves!"

Mother Wolf threw herself down panting among the cubs, and Father Wolf said to her gravely: "Shere Khan speaks this much truth. The cub must be shown to the Pack. Wilt thou still keep him, Mother?"

"Keep him!" she gasped. "He came naked, by night, alone and very hungry; yet he was not afraid! Look, he has pushed one of my babes to one side already. And that lame butcher would have killed him, and he would have run off to the Waingunga while the villagers here hunted through all of our lairs in revenge! Keep him? Assuredly I will keep him. Lie still, little frog. O thou Mowgli—for Mowgli, the Frog I will call thee—the time will come when thou wilt hunt Shere Khan as he hunted thee!"

"But what will our Pack say?" said Father Wolf.

Kipling, Rudyard. *The Jungle Book*. Stamford: Longmeadow Press, 1990.
Other Editions:
——. *The Jungle Book*, New York: Penguin, Puffin Books, 1987.
——. *The Jungle Book and Just So Stories*, New York: Bantam, 1986.

THE STORY OF DOCTOR DOLITTLE

HUGH LOFTING

Dr. John Dolittle lives in Puddleby-on-the Marsh. His house is filled with animals in every nook and cranny. He likes animals more than people! An old woman with rheumatism once came to see the doctor, sat on a hedgehog sleeping on the sofa, and never came to see him again. Soon he lost almost all of his people patients. Then one day, the cat's-meat man gave him some very valuable advice—why not take care of animals?

ANIMAL LANGUAGE

t happened one day that the Doctor was sitting in his kitchen talking with the cat's-meat man, who had come to see him with a stomach ache.

"Why don't you give up being a people's doctor, and be an animal doctor?" asked the cat's-meat man.

The parrot, Polynesia, was sitting in the window looking out at the rain and singing a sailor song to herself. She stopped singing and started to listen.

"You see, Doctor," the cat's-meat man went on, "you know all about animals—much more than what these here vets do. That book you wrote about cats—why, it's wonderful! I can't read or write myself, or maybe I'd write some books. But my wife, Theodosia, she's a scholar, she is. And she read your book to me. Well, it's wonderful—that's all can be said—wonderful. You might have been a cat yourself. You know the way they think. And listen: You can make a lot of money doctoring animals. Do you know what? You see, I'd send all the old women who had sick cats or dogs to you. And if they didn't get sick fast enough, I could put something in the meat I sell 'em to make 'em sick, see?"

"Oh, no," said the Doctor quickly. "You mustn't do that. That wouldn't be right."

"Oh, I didn't mean real sick," answered the cat's-meat man. "Just a little something to make them droopylike was what I had reference to. But as you say, maybe it ain't quite fair on the animals. But they'll get sick anyway because the old women always give 'em too much to eat. And look, all the farmers round about who had lame horses and weak lambs—they'd come. Be an animal doctor."

When the cat's-meat man had gone the parrot flew off the window onto the Doctor's table and said, "That man's got sense. That's what you ought to do. Be an animal doctor.

Give the silly people up if they haven't brains enough to see you're the best doctor in the world. Take care of animals instead. They'll soon find it out. Be an animal doctor."

"Oh, there are plenty of animal doctors," said John Dolittle, putting the flower pots outside on the windowsill to get the rain.

"Yes, there are plenty," said Polynesia. "But none of them are any good at all. Now listen, Doctor, and I'll tell you something. Did you know that animals can talk?"

"I know that parrots can talk," said the Doctor.

"Oh, we parrots can talk in two languages—people's language and bird language," said Polynesia proudly. "If I say 'Polly wants a cracker,' you understand me. But hear this: Ka-ka oi-ee, fee-fee?"

"Good gracious!" cried the Doctor. "What does that mean?"

"That means 'is the porridge hot yet?' in bird language."

"My! You don't say so!" said the Doctor. "You never talked that way to me before."

"What would have been the good?" said Polynesia, dusting some cracker crumbs off her left wing. "You wouldn't have understood me if I had."

"Tell me some more," said the Doctor, all excited, and he rushed over to the dresser drawer and came back with the butcher's book and a pencil. "Now, don't go too fast and I'll write it down. This is interesting, very interesting—something quite new. Give me the Birds' ABC first—slowly, now."

So that was the way the Doctor came to know that animals had a language of their own and could talk to one another. And all that afternoon, while it was raining, Polynesia sat on the kitchen table giving him bird words to put down in the book.

At teatime, when the dog, Jip, came in, the parrot said to the Doctor, "See, he's talking to you."

"Looks to me as though he were scratching his ear," said the Doctor.

"But animals don't always speak with their mouths," said the parrot in a high voice, raising her eyebrows. "They talk with their ears, with their feet, with their tails—with everything. Sometimes they don't want to make a noise. Do you see now the way he's twitching up one side of his nose?"

"What's that mean?" asked the Doctor.

"That means 'Can't you see that it has stopped raining?'" Polynesia answered. "He is asking you a question. Dogs nearly always use their noses for asking questions."

After a while, with the parrot's help, the Doctor got to learn the language of the animals so well that he could talk to them himself and understand everything they said. Then he gave up being a people's doctor altogether.

As soon as the cat's-meat man had told everyone that John Dolittle was going to become an animal doctor, old ladies began to bring him their pet pugs and poodles who had eaten too much cake, and farmers came many miles to show him sick cows and sheep.

One day a plow horse was brought to him, and the poor thing was terribly glad to find a man who could talk in horse language.

"You know, Doctor," said the horse, "that vet over the hill knows nothing at all. He has been treating me six weeks now—for spavins. What I need is spectacles. I am going blind in one eye. There's no reason why horses shouldn't wear glasses the same as people. But that stupid man over the hill never even looked at my eyes. He kept on giving me big pills. I tried to tell him, but he couldn't understand a word of horse language. What I need is spectacles."

"Of course, of course," said the Doctor. "I'll get you some at once."

"I would like a pair like yours," said the horse, "only green. They'll keep the sun out of my eyes while I'm plowing the 50-acre field."

"Certainly," said the Doctor. "Green ones you shall have."

"You know, the trouble is, sir," said the plow horse as the Doctor opened the front door to let him out, "the trouble is that anybody thinks he can doctor animals, just because the animals don't complain. As a matter of fact, it takes a much cleverer man to be a really good animal doctor than it does to be a good people's doctor. My farmer's boy thinks he knows all about horses. I wish you could see him. His face is so fat he looks as though he had no eyes, and he has got as much brain as a potato bug. He tried to put a mustard plaster on me last week."

"Where did he put it?" asked the Doctor.

"Oh, he didn't put it anywhere—on me," said the horse. "He only tried to. I kicked him into the duck pond."

"Well, well!" said the Doctor.

"I'm a pretty quiet creature as a rule," said the horse, "very patient with people, don't make much fuss. But it was bad enough to have that vet giving me the wrong medicine. And when that red-faced booby started to monkey with me, I just couldn't bear it anymore."

"Did you hurt the boy much?" asked the Doctor.

"Oh, no," said the horse. "I kicked him in the right place. The vet's looking after him now. When will my glasses be ready?"

"I'll have them for you next week," said the Doctor. "Come in again Tuesday. Good morning!"

Then John Dolittle got a fine big pair of green spectacles, and the plow horse stopped going blind in one eye and could see as well as ever.

And soon it became a common sight to see farm animals wearing glasses in the country around Puddleby, and a blind horse was a thing unknown.

And so it was with all the other animals that were brought to him. As soon as they found that he could talk their language, they told him where the pain was and how they felt, and of course it was easy for him to cure them.

Now all these animals went back and told their brothers and friends that there was a doctor in the little house with the big garden who really was a doctor. And whenever any creatures got sick—not only horses and cows and dogs, but all the little things of the fields, like harvest mice and water voles, badgers and bats—they came at once to his house on the edge of the town, so that his big garden was nearly always crowded with animals trying to get in to see him.

There were so many that came that he had to have special doors made for the different kinds. He wrote HORSES over the front door, COWS over the side door, and SHEEP on the kitchen door. Each kind of animal had a separate door—even the mice had a tiny tunnel made for them into the cellar, where they waited patiently in rows for the Doctor to come around to them.

And so, in a few years' time, every living thing for miles and miles got to know about John Dolittle, M.D. And the birds who flew to other countries in the winter told the animals in foreign lands of the wonderful doctor of Puddleby-on-the-Marsh, who could understand their talk and help them in their troubles. In this way he became famous among the animals all over the world, better known even than he had been among the folks of the West Country. And he was happy and liked his life very much.

One afternoon when the Doctor was busy writing in a book, Polynesia sat in the window, as she nearly always did, looking out at the leaves blowing about in the garden. Presently she laughed aloud.

"What is it, Polynesia?" asked the Doctor, looking up from his book.

"I was just thinking," said the parrot, and she went on looking at the leaves.

"What were you thinking?"

"I was thinking about people," said Polynesia. "People make me sick. They think they're so wonderful. The world has been going on now for thousands of years, hasn't it? And the only thing in animal language that people have learned to understand is that when a dog wags his tail he means 'I'm glad!' It's funny, isn't it? You are the very first man to talk like us. Oh, sometimes people annoy me dreadfully—such airs they put on talking about 'the dumb animals.' Dumb! Huh! Why, I knew a macaw once who could say good morning in seven different ways without once opening his mouth. He could talk every language—and Greek. An old professor with a gray beard bought him. But he didn't stay. He said the old man didn't talk Greek right, and he couldn't stand listening to him teach the language wrong. I often wonder what's become of him. That bird knew more geography than people will ever know. People! Golly! I suppose if people ever learn to fly—like any common hedge sparrow—we shall never hear the end of it!"

"You're a wise old bird," said the Doctor. "How old are you really? I know that parrots and elephants sometimes live to be very, very old."

"I can never be quite sure of my age," said Polynesia. "It's either 183 or 182. But I know that when I first came here from Africa, King Charles was still hiding in the oak tree—because I saw him. He looked scared to death."

Lofting, Hugh. *Doctor Dolittle*. New York: Dell, 1988.

THE CALL OF THE WILD

JACK LONDON

Buck is a sled dog who has been kidnapped from his home in California, taken to the Canadian Arctic, and sold to men who are searching for wealth in the days of the gold rush. He learns to survive in the wild and becomes the leader of a team of dogs. Jack London gives us a harsh and brutal look into the existence of animals and humans at their most primitive level—fighting for their lives and existence.

Chapter 2 THE LAW OF CLUB AND FANG

uck's first day on the Dyea beach was like a nightmare. Every hour was filled with shock and surprise. He had been suddenly jerked from the heart of civilization and flung into the heart of things primordial. No lazy, sunkissed life was this, with nothing to do but loaf and get bored. Here was neither peace, nor rest, nor a moment's safety. All was confusion and action, and every moment life and limb were in peril. There was imperative need to be constantly alert; for these dogs and men were not town dogs and men. They were savages, all of them, who knew no law but the law of club and fang.

It was the wolf manner of fighting, to strike and leap away; but there was more to it than this. Thirty or forty huskies ran to the spot and surrounded the combatants in an intent and silent circle. Buck did not comprehend that silent intentness, nor the eager way with which they were licking their chops. Curly rushed her antagonist, who struck again and leaped aside. He met her next rush with his chest, in a peculiar fashion that tumbled her off her feet. She never regained them. This was what the onlooking huskies had waited for. They closed in upon her, snarling and yelping, and she was buried, screaming with agony, beneath the bristling mass of bodies.

So sudden was it, and so unexpected, that Buck was taken aback. He saw Spitz run out his scarlet tongue in a way he had of laughing; and he saw Francois, swinging an axe, spring into the mess of dogs. Three men with clubs were helping him to scattter them. It did not take long. Two minutes from the time Curly went down, the last of her assailants were clubbed off. But she lay there limp and lifeless in the bloody, trampled snow, almost literally torn to pieces, the swart half-breed standing over her and cursing horribly. The scene often came back to Buck to trouble him in his sleep. So that was the way. No fair play. Once down, that was the end of you. Well, he would see to it that he never went down. Spitz ran out his tongue and laughed again, and from that moment Buck hated him with a bitter and deathless hatred.

Before he had recovered from the shock caused by the tragic passing of Curly, he received another shock. Francois fastened upon him an arrangement of straps and buckles. It was a harness, such as he had seen the grooms put on the horses at home. And as he had seen horses work, so he was set to work, hauling Francois on a sled to the forest that fringed the valley, and returning with a load of firewood. Buck learned easily, and under the combined tuition of his two mates and Francois made remarkable progress. Ere they returned to camp he knew enough to stop at "ho," to go ahead at "mush," to swing wide on the bends, and to keep clear of the wheeler when the loaded sled shot downhill at their heels.

"T'ree vair' good dogs," Francois told Perrault. "Dat Buck, heem pool lak hell. I tich heem queek as anyt'ing."

By afternoon, Perrault, who was in a hurry to be on the trail with his dispatches, returned with two more dogs. "Billee" and "Joe" he called them, two brothers, and true huskies both. Sons of the one mother though they were, they were as different as day and night. Billee's one fault was his excessive good nature, while Joe was the very opposite, sour and introspective, with a perpetual snarl and a malignant eye. Buck received them in comradely fashion, Dave ignored them, while Spitz proceeded to thrash first one and then the other. Billee wagged his tail appeasingly, turned to run when he saw that appeasement was of no avail, and cried (still appeasingly) when Spitz's sharp teeth scored his flank. But no matter how Spitz circled, Joe whirled around on his heels to face him, mane bristling, ears laid back, lips writhing and snarling, jaws clipping together as fast as he could snap, and eyes

diabolically gleaming—the incarnation of belligerent fear. So terrible was his appearance that Spitz was forced to forego disciplining him; but to cover his own discomfiture he turned upon the inoffensive and wailing Billee and drove him to the confines of the camp.

By evening Perrault secured another dog, an old husky, long and lean and gaunt, with a battle-scarred face and a single eye which flashed a warning of prowess that commanded respect. He was called Sol-leks, which means the Angry One. Like Dave, he asked nothing, gave nothing, expected nothing; and when he marched slowly and deliberately into their midst, even Spitz left him alone. He had one peculiarity which Buck was unlucky enough to discover. He did not like to be approached on his blind side. Of this offense Buck was unwittingly guilty, and the first knowledge he had of his indiscretion was when Sol-leks whirled upon him and slashed his shoulder to the bone for three inches up and down. Forever after Buck avoided his blind side, and to the last of their comradeship had no more trouble. His only apparent ambition, like Dave's, was to be left alone; though, as Buck was afterward to learn, each of them possessed one other and even more vital ambition.

That night Buck faced the great problem of sleeping. The tent, illumined by a candle, glowed warmly in the midst of the white plain; and when he, as a matter of course, entered it, both Perrault and Francois bombarded him with curses and cooking utensils, till he recovered from his consternation and fled ignominiously into the outer cold. A chill wind was blowing that nipped him sharply and bit with especial venom into his wounded shoulder. He lay down on the snow and attempted to sleep, but the frost soon drove him shivering to his feet. Miserable and disconsolate, he wandered about among the many tents, only to find that one place was as cold as another. Here and there savage dogs rushed upon him, but he bristled his neck-hair and snarled (for he was learning fast), and they let him go his way unmolested.

Finally an idea came to him. He would return and see how his own teammates were making out. To his astonishment, they had disappeared. Again he wandered about through the great camp, looking for them, and again he returned. Were they in the tent? No, that could not be, else he would not have been driven out. Then where could they possibly be? With drooping tail and shivering body, very forlorn indeed, he aimlessly circled the tent. Suddenly the snow gave way beneath his fore legs and he sank down. Something wriggled under his feet. He sprang back, bristling and snarling, fearful of the unseen and unknown. But a friendly little yelp reassured him, and he went back to investigate. A whiff of warm air ascended to his nostrils, and there, curled up under the snow in a snug ball, lay Billee. He whined placatingly, squirmed and wriggled to show his good will and intentions, and even ventured, as a bribe for peace, to lick Buck's face with his warm wet tongue.

Another lesson. So that was the way they did it, eh? Buck confidently selected a spot, and with much fuss and wasted effort proceeded to dig a hole for himself. In a trice the heat from his body filled the confined space and he was asleep. The day had been long and arduous, and he slept soundly and comfortably, though he growled and barked and wrestled with bad dreams.

Nor did he open his eyes till roused by the noises of the waking camp. At first he did not know where he was. It had snowed during the night and he was completely buried. The snow walls pressed him on every side, and a great surge of fear swept through him—the fear of the wild thing for the trap. It was a token that he was harking back through his own life to the lives of his forebears; for he was a civilized dog, an unduly civilized dog, and of his own experience knew no trap and so could not of himself fear it. The muscles of his whole body contracted spasmodically and instinctively, the hair on his neck and shoulders stood on end, and with a ferocious snarl he bounded straight up into the blinding day, the snow flying about him in a flashing cloud. Ere he landed on his feet, he saw the white camp spread out before him and knew where he was and remembered all that had passed from the time he went for a stroll with Manuel to the hole he had dug for himself the night before.

A shout from Francois hailed his appearance. "Wot I say?" the dog-driver cried to Perrault. "Dat Buck for sure learn queek as anyt'ing."

Perrault nodded gravely. As courier for the Canadian government, bearing important dispatches, he was anxious to secure the best dogs, and he was particularly gladdened by the possession of Buck.

London, Jack. *The Call of the Wild*. New York: Portland House Illustrated Classics, 1987.
  Other Editions:
    ——. *Call of the Wild, White Fang & Other Stories*. ed. by Andrew Sinclair, New York: Oxford University Press, 1990.
    ——. *Call of the Wild & Other Stories*. New York: Silver, 1985.

SUMMER OF THE MONKEYS

WILSON RAWLS

This is the story of fourteen-year-old Jay Berry, growing up in Oklahoma's Cherokee Ozarks, and a summer adventure that changes his life. Jay learns from his grandfather that thirty monkeys have escaped from a circus, and there is a big reward for anyone who finds them. Jay's first efforts to catch the monkeys result in a chilling meeting.

CHAPTER 4

I was still admiring my work when, from the corner of my eye, I thought I saw a movement in the branches of a sycamore tree. It was just a flash and I didn't see it again, but I was pretty sure that I had seen something.

Picking up my gunny sack, I whispered to Rowdy, "I'm not sure, boy, but I think I saw something. It could have been a monkey. Come on, let's hide and see what happens."

About thirty-five yards away, but still in view of my traps, I found a small opening in a thick stand of elders. It was a dandy hiding place, and I proceeded to make myself comfortable. Taking my lunch and apples from the gunny sack, I laid them to one side and sat down on the empty sack.

Now, I never did like to wait for anything. It seemed that half of my life had been wasted away waiting for things. I had to wait for Christmas, and Thanksgiving. Then there was a long spell of waiting for spring and fishing time. Now I was waiting for a monkey.

The longer I sat there, the more uncomfortable I became. First I got hungry, then I got thirsty. The sack I was sitting on got hard as a rock and my tail bone started hurting. I got hot and began to sweat. Deer flies and mosquitoes came and started gnawing on me. Just about the time that I had convinced myself that there wasn't a living thing within a hundred miles of me, up popped a monkey, and out popped my eyes.

I never did know where the monkey came from. One instant there wasn't as much as a jaybird around my traps; then as quick as Mama was with a peach-tree switch, there was a monkey. I could have sworn that he just popped up out of the ground. Anyhow, there he was, standing on his spindly legs, staring at those big red apples.

I held my breath, watched, and waited.

70

For several seconds, the monkey just stood, staring at the apples and twisting his head, as if he were trying to make up his mind about something. Then he started jumping around and squealing and making all kinds of noises.

The next thing that happened all but caused me to have a jerking spell. It started raining monkeys. They seemed to come from everywhere; down from the branches of the bur oak tree, from out of the underbrush, and everywhere else. There were big monkeys and little monkeys, fat monkeys and skinny monkeys.

I was paralyzed. It looked like ten jillion monkeys, leaping and squealing. They bunched up about ten feet from my traps and started chattering as if they were talking something over.

Before the monkeys showed up, Rowdy had been lying at my side. Growling and showing his teeth, he started getting to his feet. He was getting ready to tie into those monkeys and I knew it. I laid my hand on his back and I could feel his rock-hard muscles knotting and quivering.

"Rowdy," I whispered, "for heaven's sake, don't do anything now. Those monkeys are worth more money than we'll ever see the rest of our lives. If you make any noise and scare them away, I'll tie you in the corn crib for a year, and I won't ever give you a drink of water."

Of course, I didn't mean that, but Rowdy thought I did. He lay down again and kept his mouth shut.

One little monkey, bolder than the others, left the bunch and started over toward my traps. I reached for my gunny sack and got ready.

Just when I thought for sure that the monkey was going to walk right into my trap, the same loud cry that I had heard before rang out through the bottoms. As if the cry were some kind of signal, the monkeys stopped chattering and stood still. The one that I had thought was going to get in my trap hurried back to the bunch.

I could tell that whatever had made the cry was much closer now that it had been before, and I didn't feel too good about it.

"Rowdy," I whispered, "you keep your eyes open and whatever it is that's squalling like that, don't let it get too close to us."

The way Old Rowdy was sniffing and looking, I couldn't tell whether he was mad or scared. This didn't help me at all. I put a lot of confidence in Old Rowdy; and if he was scared, then it was time for me to be getting away from there.

I was trying to make up my mind what to do, when I heard the cry again. This time it was so close it made my eardrums ring. My hair flew straight up and felt as if it was pushing the top out of of my old straw hat.

The noise was coming from above me. I started looking around in the treetops. On the limb of a big sycamore, I saw something. At first I thought it was a boy. It looked just like a small boy, standing there on a limb. I wondered what he was doing up in a tree, screaming his head off. Maybe he had climbed the tree and couldn't get down. I had done that several times and Papa had had to come and help me down. Then again he might be a crazy boy. Daisy had told me that crazy people did all kinds of things like that.

I forgot about being scared and got kind of mad.

"Rowdy," I whispered, "I don't know if that's a boy or not, but if it is, he's sure messing things up for us. If he keeps on screaming like that, and scares the monkeys away, I'm going to wear him out."

Just than the thing moved out on the limb into some sunlight and I got a better look at it. I could see then that it wasn't a boy but was some kind of black, hairy animal. It had short stubby legs, and long arms that hung down almost to the limb it was standing on. When I discovered that it didn't have a tail, I didn't know what to think. I had never seen an animal that didn't have a tail of some kind.

It was too far away to tell what color its eyes were, but I could have sworn that they were as red as our old red rooster. Anything that had red eyes always did scare me. Goose pimples jumped out all over me. My old heart started running around inside me like a scared lizard.

"Rowdy," I whispered, in a shaky voice, "that's an animal all right, but I've never laid eyes on anything that looked like that before, and I don't like the looks of it."

I had just about decided that my monkey-catching days were over and was getting ready to get away from there, when I remembered what my grandpa had told me about that hundred-dollar monkey. He had said that it was different than the other monkeys, and that thing I was looking at sure didn't look like those other monkeys.

Just then the big monkey let out another cry, and running to the end of the limb, he leaped high in the air. I was so startled by this I stood up. I thought sure that he had sprouted wings and was flying away. Instead, he lit in the branches of the bur oak tree; and using those long arms, he started dropping down from limb to limb and landed on the ground between the little monkeys and my traps.

This all happened so fast it left me a little bit breathless. I thought squirrels could move around in the timber, but they couldn't do anything that monkeys couldn't do. Every move he made was as sure as Daniel Boone's musket and as smooth as the dasher in Mama's old churn.

All the time this had been going on, the little monkeys hadn't made a sound. They just stood there in a bunch, watching every move the big monkey made.

About that time one of them decided that as long as there were some apples around, he may as well have one. He left the bunch and with his skinny tail sticking straight in the air, he started toward my traps.

The big monkey saw this and went all to pieces. He started jumping up and down, and making deep grunting noises as if he were talking to the little monkey. The little monkey seemed to understand what the big monkey was saying. He squealed like someone had stepped on his tail and scurried back to the others. It was hard for me to believe what

I had seen. Yet it was as plain as the stripes in a rainbow. That big monkey had known that the little monkey was in danger, and in his monkey talk, he had simply told him so.

"Rowdy," I whispered, "did you see what the monkey was doing? He was talking to that little monkey, that's what he was doing. Grandpa didn't tell me that they could talk to each other."

As if he were proud of the fact that he had knocked me out of a two-dollar reward, the big monkey then did something that all but caused me to swallow my Adam's apple. Looking straight at my hiding place, he pealed his lips back, opened his mouth, and let out another one of those squalls. When he did, I got a good look at his fighting tools.

I had thought that our old mules had big mouths and teeth, but they were nothing compared to what that monkey had. To me, it looked as if you could have thrown a pumpkin straight down his throat and never scratched the peeling on one of his long teeth.

"Holy smokes, Rowdy," I whispered, "did you see those teeth? You'd better think twice before you jump on him. He could eat you up—collar and all."

Old Rowdy didn't seem to be the least bit scared. If I had said "Sic 'em!" he would have torn out of those elders like a cyclone. He may have taken a whipping, but there would have been a lot of monkey hair flying around while it was going on.

I didn't have to worry about the big monkey jumping on us. Instead, he turned, and still making those deep grunting noises, he walked up within two feet of a trap and stopped. For several seconds, he just stood there, looking at the apple and all around at the ground. He kept making funny little noises, as if he were talking to himself.

The strain was almost more than I could stand. My insides got all knotted up and I felt like I was going to bust wide open. If the monkey hadn't done something about then, I think I would have. Instead of stepping in my trap, he just reached out with one of those long arms, took hold of the apple, and pulled on it until the nail came out.

Holding the apple in his paw about like I would if I were eating one, he opened his huge mouth, took one bite, and tossed what was left to the little monkeys.

This caused a loud commotion. The little monkeys started fighting over the apple. I never heard so much squealing and chattering. In no time there wasn't as much as a seed left.

I sat there as if I were frozen to the ground and watched that big monkey walk all around the bur oak, taking the apples and never stepping in a trap. One bite from each apple seemed to be all he wanted. What was left was tossed to the little monkeys.

When the last apple had disappeared, the big monkey did something that made me wonder if I wasn't seeing things. He started turning somersaults and rolling around on the ground. At the same time, he was making the bottoms ring with a peculiar noise that he hadn't made before.

Now I had never heard a monkey laugh and didn't even know they could; but as I sat there watching the capers of that big monkey, it didn't take me long to figure out what he was doing. He was laughing at me. I was sure of it. I even remembered the dream I had about the hundred-dollar monkey—how every time he came leaping by, he would stop and laugh at me.

The little monkeys seemed to know that something funny was going on. They started screeching and chattering like a bunch of squirrels in a hickory tree.

My neck and face got all hot. I knew I was blushing, but I couldn't help it. That was the first time I had ever had a monkey laugh at me. I looked at Old Rowdy. The way I was feeling, if he had been laughing, I would have taken a stick to him. But Rowdy wasn't laughing. He was just as serious about catching those monkeys as I was.

All at once the big monkey stopped making a fool out of himself and turned to the little monkeys. Uttering a couple of those deep grunts, he just seemed to rise up in the air like fog off the river and disappeared in the branches of the bur oak tree. The little monkeys followed him—zip, zip, zip—one behind the other.

Rawls, Wilson. *Summer of the Monkeys*. New York: Bantam, 1992.

BLACK BEAUTY

ANNA SEWELL

In the nineteenth century Anna Sewell explored a horse's thoughts and emotions by having Black Beauty narrate his own tale. The following two excerpted chapters from the novel Black Beauty *provide a view into Black Beauty's impressions of life as a young colt, and then as an old horse, seasoned through the years.*

Chapter 1 MY EARLY HOME

The first place that I can well remember was a large pleasant meadow with a pond of clear water in it. Some shady trees leaned over it, and rushes and water-lilies grew at the deep end. Over the hedge on one side we looked into a ploughed field, and on the other we looked over a gate at our master's house, which stood by the roadside; at the top of the meadow was a grove of fir trees, and at the bottom a running brook overhung by a steep bank.

Whilst I was young, I lived upon my mother's milk, as I could not eat grass. In the daytime I ran by her side, and at night I lay down close by her. When it was hot, we used to stand by the pond in the shade of the trees, and when it was cold, we had a nice warm shed near the grove.

As soon as I was old enough to eat grass, my mother used to go out to work in the daytime, and come back in the evening.

There were six young colts in the meadow besides me; they were older than I was: some were nearly as large as grown-up horses. I used to run with them, and had great fun; we used to gallop all together round and round the field as hard as we could go. Sometimes we had rather rough play, for they would frequently bite and kick as well as gallop.

One day, when there was a good deal of kicking, my mother whinnied to me to come to her, and then she said, "I wish you to pay attention to what I am going to say to you. The colts who live here are very good colts, but they are cart-horse colts, and of course they have not learned manners. You have been well-bred and well-born; your father has a great name in these parts, and your grandfather won the cup two years at the Newmarket races; your grandmother had the sweetest temper of any horse I ever knew, and I think you have never seen me kick or bite. I hope you will grow up gentle and good, and never learn bad ways; do your work with a good will, lift your feet up well when you trot, and never bite or kick, even in play."

I have never forgotten my mother's advice; I knew she was a wise old horse, and our master thought a great deal of her. Her name was Duchess, but he often called her Pet.

Our master was a good, kind man. He gave us good food, good lodging, and kind words; he spoke as kindly to us as he did to his little children. We were all fond of him, and my mother loved him very much. When she saw him at the gate, she would neigh with joy, and trot up to him. He would pat and stroke her and say, "Well, old Pet, and how is your little Darkie?" I was a dull black, so he called me Darkie; then he would give me a piece of bread, which was very good, and sometimes he brought me a carrot for my mother. All the horses would come to him, but I think we were his favorites. My mother always took him to town on a market day in a light gig.

There was a ploughboy, Dick, who sometimes came into our field to pluck blackberries from the hedge. When he had eaten all he wanted, he would have what he called fun with the colts, throwing stones and sticks at them to make them gallop. We did not much mind him, for we could gallop off; but sometimes a stone would hit and hurt us.

One day he was at this game, and did not know that the master was in the next field; but he was there, watching what was going on; over the hedge he jumped in a snap, and catching Dick by the arm, he gave such a box on the ear as made him roar with the pain and surprise. As soon as we saw the master, we trotted up nearer to see what went on.

"Bad boy!" he said, "Bad boy! To chase the colts. This is not the first time, nor the second, but it shall be the last. There—take your money and go home; I shall not want you on my farm again." So we never saw Dick any more. Old Daniel, the man who looked after the horses, was just as gentle as our master, so we were well off.

Chapter 5 A FAIR START

he name of the coachman was John Manly; he had a wife and one little child, and they lived in the coachman's cottage, very near the stables.

The next morning he took me into the yard and gave me a good grooming, and just as I was going into my box, with my coat soft and bright, the Squire came in to look at me, and seemed pleased. "John," he said, "I meant to have tried the new horse this morning, but I have other business. You may as well take him around after breakfast; go by the common and the Highwood, and back by the watermill and the river; that will show his paces."

"I will, sir," said John. After breakfast he came and fitted me with a bridle. He was very particular in letting out and taking in the straps, to fit my head comfortably; then he brought a saddle, but it was not broad enough for my back; he saw it in a minute and went for another, which fitted nicely. He rode me first slowly, then a trot, then a canter, and when we were on the common he gave me a light touch with his whip, and we had a splendid gallop.

"Ho, ho! my boy," he said, as he pulled me up, "you would like to follow the hounds, I think."

As we came back through the park we met the Squire and Mrs. Gordon walking; they stopped, and John jumped off.

"Well, John, how does he go?"

"First-rate, sir," answered John; "he is as fleet as a deer, and has a fine spirit too; but the lightest touch of the rein will guide him. Down at the end of the common we met one of those traveling carts hung all over with baskets, rugs, and such like; you know, sir, many horses will not pass those carts quietly; he just took a good look at it, and then went on as quiet and pleasant as could be. The were shooting rabbits near the Highwood, and a gun went off close by; he pulled up a little and looked, but did not stir a step to right or left. I just held the rein steady but did not hurry him, and it's my opinion he has not been frightened or ill-used while he was young."

"That's well," said the Squire, "I will try him myself tomorrow."

The next day I was brought up for my master. I remembered my mother's counsel and my good old master's, and I tried to do exactly what he wanted me to do. I found he was a very good rider, and thoughtful for his horse too. When he came home, the lady was at the hall door as he rode up.

"Well, my dear," she said, "how do you like him?"

"He is exactly what John said," he replied; "a pleasanter creature I never wish to mount. What shall we call him?"

"Would you like Ebony?" said she; "he is as black as ebony."

"No, not Ebony."

"Will you call him Blackbird, like your uncle's old horse?"

"No, he is far handsomer than old Blackbird ever was."

"Yes," she said, "he is really quite a beauty, and he has such a sweet, good-tempered face and such a fine intelligent eye—what do you say to calling him Black Beauty?"

"Black Beauty—why, yes, I think that is a very good name. If you like it, it shall be his name"; and so it was.

When John went into the stable, he told James that master and mistress had chosen a good, sensible English name for me, that meant something; not like Marengo, or Pegasus, or Abdullah. They both laughed, and James said, "If it was not for bringing back the past, I should have named him Rob Roy, for I never saw two horses more alike."

"That's no wonder," said John; "didn't you know that farmer Grey's old Duchess was the mother of them both?"

I had never heard that before; and so poor Rob Roy who was killed at the last hunt was my brother! I did not wonder that my mother was so troubled. It seems that horses have no relations; at least they never know each other after they are sold.

John seemed very proud of me; he used to make my mane and tail almost as smooth as a lady's hair, and he would talk to me a great deal; of course I did not understand all he said, but I learned more and more to know what he meant, and what he wanted me to do.

I grew very fond of him, he was so gentle and kind; he seemed to know just how a horse feels, and when he cleaned me he knew the tender places and the ticklish places; when he brushed my head, he went as carefully over my eyes as if they were his own, and never stirred up any ill-temper.

James Howard, the stable boy, was just as gentle and pleasant in his way, so I thought myself well off. There was another man who helped in the yard, but he had very little to do with Ginger and me.

A few days after this I had to go out with Ginger in the carriage. I wondered how we should get on together; but except laying her ears back when I was led up to her, she behaved very well. She did her work honestly, and did her full share, and I never wish to have a better partner in double harness. When we came to a hill, instead of slackening her pace, she would throw her weight right into the collar, and pull away straight up. We had both the same sort of courage at our work, and John had oftener to hold us in than to urge us forward; he never had to use the whip with either of us; then our paces were much the same, and I found it easy to keep step with her when trotting, which made it pleasant, and master always liked it when we kept step well, and so did John. After we had been out two or three times together we grew quite friendly and sociable, which made me feel very much at home.

As for Merrylegs, he and I soon became great friends; he was such a cheerful, plucky, good-tempered little fellow that he was a favorite with everyone, especially with Miss Jessie and Flora, who used to ride him about in the orchard, and have fine games with him and their little dog Frisky.

Our master had two other horses that stood in another stable. One was Justice, a roan cob, used for riding, or for the luggage cart; the other was an old brown hunter named Sir Oliver; he was past work now, but was a great favorite with the master, who gave him the run of the park; he sometimes did a little light carting on the estate, or carried one of the young ladies when they rode out with her father; for he was very gentle, and could be trusted with a child as well as Merrylegs. The cob was a strong, well-made, good-tempered horse, and we sometimes had a little chat in the paddock, but of course I could not be so intimate with him as with Ginger, who stood in the same stable.

Sewell, Anna. *Black Beauty*. New York: Crown Publishers, 1982.
    Other Editions:
    ——. *Black Beauty*. New York: Knopf, 1993.
    ——. *Black Beauty*. New York: Scholastic, 1994.
    Owens, L., ed. *Black Beauty & Other Horse Stories*. New York: Crown Publishers, 1983.

THE RED PONY

JOHN STEINBECK

John Steinbeck, the Nobel prize–winning novelist, lived and wrote in the first-half of the twentieth century. He used America and its land as the backdrop for his stories. In The Red Pony, *we get a glimpse into life on a ranch in northern California. Jody lives on the ranch and takes care of Gabilan, a pony his father has given him. Billy Buck helps Jody take care of and train Gabilan. Then the pony becomes sick.*

Chapter 1   THE GIFT

Jody's mother looked up when he got back to the house. "You're late up from bed," she said. She held his chin in her hard hand and brushed the tangled hair out of his eyes and she said, "Don't worry about the pony. He'll be all right. Billy's as good as any horse doctor in the country."

Jody hadn't known she could see his worry. He pulled gently away from her and knelt down in front of the fireplace until it burned his stomach. He scorched himself through and then went in to bed, but it was a hard thing to go to sleep. He awakened after what seemed a long time. The room was dark but there was a grayness in the window like that which precedes the dawn. He got up and found his overalls and searched for the legs, and then the clock in the other room struck two. He laid his clothes down and got back into bed. It was broad daylight when he awakened again. For the first time he had slept through the ringing of the triangle. He leaped up, flung on his clothes and went out of the door still buttoning his shirt. His mother looked after him for a moment and then went quietly back to her work. Her eyes were brooding and kind. Now and then her mouth smiled a little but without changing her eyes at all.

Jody ran on toward the barn. Halfway there he heard the sound he dreaded, the hollow rasping cough of a horse. He broke into a sprint then. In the barn he found Billy Buck with the pony. Billy was rubbing its legs with his strong thick hands. He looked up and smiled gaily. "He just took a little cold," Billy said. "We'll have him out of it in a couple of days."

Jody looked at the pony's face. The eyes were half closed and the lids thick and dry. In the eye corners a crust of hard mucus stuck. Gabilan's ears hung loosely sideways and his head was low. Jody put out his hand, but the pony did not move close to it. He coughed again and his whole body constricted with the effort. A little stream of thin fluid ran from his nostrils.

Jody looked back at Billy Buck. "He's awful sick, Billy."

"Just a little cold, like I said," Billy insisted. "You go get some breakfast and then go back to school. I'll take care of him."

"But you might have to do something else. You might leave him."

"No, I won't. I won't leave him at all. Tomorrow's Saturday. Then you can stay with him all day." Billy had failed again, and he felt badly about it. He had to cure the pony now.

Jody walked up to the house and took his place listlessly at the table. The eggs and bacon were cold and greasy, but he didn't notice it. He ate his usual amount. He didn't even ask to stay home from school. His mother pushed his hair back when she took his plate. "Billy'll take care of the pony," she assured him.

He moped through the whole day at school. He couldn't answer any questions nor read any words. He couldn't even tell anyone the pony was sick, for that might make him sicker. And when school was finally out he started home in dread. He walked slowly and let the other boys leave him. He wished he might continue walking and never arrive at the ranch.

Billy was in the barn, as he had promised, and the pony was worse. His eyes were almost closed now, and his breath whistled shrilly past an obstruction in his nose. A film covered that part of the eyes that was visible at all. It was doubtful whether the pony could see any more. Now and then he snorted, to clear his nose, and by the action seemed to plug it tighter. Jody looked dispiritedly at the pony's coat. The hair lay rough and unkempt and seemed to have lost all of its old luster. Billy stood quietly beside the stall. Jody hated to ask, but he had to know.

"Billy, is he—is he going to get well?"

Billy put his fingers between the bars under the pony's jaw and felt about. "Feel here," he said and he guided Jody's fingers to a large lump under the jaw. "When that gets bigger, I'll open it up and then he'll get better."

Jody looked quickly away, for he had heard about that lump. "What is it the matter with him?"

Billy didn't want to answer, but he had to. He couldn't be wrong three times. "Strangles," he said shortly, "but don't you worry about that. I'll pull him out of it. I've seen them get well when they were worse than Gabilan is. I'm going to steam him now. You can help."

"Yes," Jody said miserably. He followed Billy into the grain room and watched him make the steaming bag ready. It was a long canvas nose bag with straps to go over a horse's ears. Billy filled it one-third full of bran and then he added a couple of handfuls of dried hops. On top of the dry substance he poured a little carbolic acid and a little turpentine. "I'll be mixing it all up while you run to the house for a kettle of boiling water," Billy said.

When Jody came back with the steaming kettle, Billy buckled the straps over Gabilan's head and fitted the bag tightly around his nose. Then through a little hole in the side of the bag he poured the boiling water on the mixture. The pony started away as a cloud of strong steam rose up, but then the soothing fumes crept through his nose and into his lungs, and the sharp steam began to clear out the nasal passages. He breathed loudly. His legs trembled in an ague, and his eyes closed against the biting cloud. Billy poured in more water and kept the steam rising for fifteen minutes. At last he set down the kettle and took the bag from Gabilan's nose. The pony looked better. He breathed freely and his eyes were open wider than they had been.

"See how good it makes him feel," Billy said. "Now we'll wrap him up in the blanket again. Maybe he'll be nearly well by morning."

"I'll stay with him tonight," Jody suggested.

"No. Don't you do it. I'll bring my blankets down here and put them in the hay. You can stay tomorrow and steam him if he needs it."

The evening was falling when they went to the house for their supper. Jody didn't even realize that some one else had fed the chickens and filled the wood-box. He walked up past the house to the dark brush line and took a drink of water from the tub. The spring water was so cold that it stung his mouth and drove a shiver through him. The sky above the hills was still light. He saw a hawk flying so high that it caught the sun on its breast and shone like a spark. Two blackbirds were driving him down the sky, glittering as they attacked their enemy. In the west, the clouds were moving in to rain again.

Jody's father didn't speak at all while the family ate supper, but after Billy Buck had taken his blankets and gone to sleep in the barn, Carl Tiflin built a high fire in the fireplace and told stories. He told about the wild man who ran naked through the country and had a tail and ears like a horse, and he told about the rabbit-cats of Moro Cojo that hopped into the trees for birds. He revived the famous Maxwell brothers who found a vein of gold and hid the traces of it so carefully that they could never find it again.

Jody sat with his chin in his hands; his mouth worked nervously, and his father gradually became aware that he wasn't listening very carefully. "Isn't that funny?" he asked.

Jody laughed politely and said, "Yes, sir." His father was angry and hurt, then. He didn't tell any more stories. After a while, Jody took a lantern and went down to the barn. Billy Buck was asleep in the hay, and, except that his breath rasped a little in his lungs, the pony seemed to be much better. Jody stayed a little while, running his fingers over the red rough coat, and then he took up the lantern and went back to the house. When he was in bed, his mother came into the room.

"Have you enough covers on? It's getting winter."

"Yes, ma'am."

"Well, get some rest tonight." She hesitated to go out, stood uncertainly. "The pony will be all right," she said.

Jody was tired. He went to sleep quickly and didn't awaken until dawn. The triangle sounded, and Billy Buck came up from the barn before Jody could get out of the house.

"How is he?" Jody demanded.

Billy always wolfed his breakfast. "Pretty good. I'm going to open that lump this morning. Then he'll be better maybe."

After breakfast, Billy got out his best knife, one with a needle point. He whetted the shining blade a long time on little carborundum stone. He tried the point and the blade again and again on his callused thumb-all, and at last he tried it on his upper lip.

On the way to the barn, Jody noticed how the young grass was up and how the stubble was melting day by day into the new green crop of volunteer. It was a cold sunny morning.

As soon as he saw the pony, Jody knew he was worse. His eyes were closed and sealed shut with dried mucus. His head hung so low that his nose almost touched the straw of his bed. There was a little groan in each breath, a deep-seated, patient groan.

Billy lifted the weak head and made a quick slash with the knife. Jody saw the yellow pus run out. He held up the head while Billy swabbed out the wound with weak carbolic acid salve.

"Now he'll feel better," Billy assured him. "That yellow poison is what made him sick."

Jody looked unbelieving at Billy Buck. "He's awful sick."

Billy thought a long time what to say. He nearly tossed off a careless assurance, but he saved himself in time. "Yes, he's pretty sick," he said at last. "I've seen worse ones get well. If he doesn't get pneumonia, we'll pull him through. You stay with him. If he gets worse, you can come and get me."

For a long time after Billy went away, Jody stood beside the pony, stroking him behind the ears. The pony didn't flip his head the way he had done when he was well. The groaning in his breathing was becoming more hollow.

Steinbeck, John. *The Red Pony.* New York: Viking Penguin, 1993.
    Other Editions:
    ——. *The Red Pony.* New York: Bantam, 1986.
    ——. *Black Beauty.* New York: Scholastic, 1994.
    Owens, L., ed. *Black Beauty & Other Horse Stories.* New York: Crown Publishers, 1983.

FABLES AND MYTHS

O. HENRY

O. HENRY, whose real name was William Sydney Porter, was born in 1862 in North Carolina. After attending school there and working in a drugstore, he moved to Texas where he wrote for a humor magazine, and a newspaper, and worked in a bank. But when the bank found that it was short of funds, Porter was the prime suspect. Porter fled, first to New Orleans and then to Honduras, leaving behind his wife.

Porter returned to the United States upon hearing that his wife was very ill, and was promptly arrested. He spent three years in prison, where he had ample time to reflect on his experiences. There was little else to do except think and trade stories. This period transformed him into a writer. He even borrowed the pseudonym O. Henry from a guard at the prison named Orrin Henry.

Soon after his release, O. Henry moved to New York. For eight years he wrote prodigiously, weaving together all the strands of his life and others', continually inspired by the bustling vitality of New York. At the time of his death from tuberculosis at age forty-eight, O. Henry had written more than six hundred stories.

The stories printed here exhibit the crisp style and deftly rendered sketches of life in the big city for which O. Henry is famous: a possible romance arises from a chance encounter in a store, a working girl barely makes ends meet, a romance is threatened by separation. In simple, shimmering vignettes, O. Henry reveals the fragile fabric of urban life, with its sometimes frightening anonymity and always refreshing possibility.

Henry, O. *The Best Short Stories of O. Henry.* New York: The Modern Library, 1994.

THE COUNT AND THE WEDDING GUEST

O. HENRY

Maggie Conway and Andy Donovan live in the same boardinghouse. One day she leaves the house dressed all in black. She is in mourning because the Italian count she was engaged to has died. She tells Andy the whole story.

ne evening when Andy Donovan went to dinner at his Second Avenue boarding-house, Mrs. Scott introduced him to a new boarder, a young lady, Miss Conway. Miss Conway was small and unobtrusive. She wore a plain, snuffy-brown dress, and bestowed her interest, which seemed languid, upon her plate. She lifted her diffident eyelids and shot one perspicuous, judicial glance at Mr. Donovan, politely murmured his name, and returned to her mutton. Mr. Donovan bowed with the grace and beaming smile that were rapidly winning for him social, business, and political advancement, and erased the snuffy-brown one from the tablets of his consideration.

Two weeks later Andy was sitting on the front steps enjoying his cigar. There was a soft rustle behind and above him and Andy turned his head—and had his head turned.

Just coming out of the door was Miss Conway. She wore a night-black dress of crêpe de—crêpe de—oh, this thin black goods. Her hat was black, and from it drooped and fluttered an ebony veil, filmy as a spider's web. She stood on the top step and drew on black silk gloves. Not a speck of white or a spot of color about her dress anywhere. Her rich golden hair was drawn, with scarcely a ripple, into a shining, smooth knot low on her neck. Her face was plain rather than pretty, but it was now illuminated and made almost beautiful by her large gray eyes that gazed above the houses across the street into the sky with an expression of the most appealing sadness and melancholy.

Gather the idea, girls—all black, you know, with the preference for crêpe de—crêpe de Chine—that's it. All black, and that sad, faraway look, and the hair shining under the black veil (you have to be blonde, of course), and try to look as if, although your young life had been blighted just as it was about to give a hop-skip-and-a-jump over the threshold of life, a walk in the park might do you good, and be sure to happen out the door at the right moment, and—oh, it'll fetch 'em every time. But it's fierce, now, how cynical I am, ain't it?—to talk about mourning costumes this way.

Mr. Donovan suddenly reinscribed Miss Conway upon the tablets of his consideration. He threw away the remaining inch-and-a-quarter of his cigar, that would have been good for eight minutes yet, and quickly shifted his center of gravity to his low-cut patent leathers.

"It's a fine, clear evening, Miss Conway," he said; and if the Weather Bureau could have heard the confident emphasis of his tones it would have hoisted the square white signal, and nailed it to the mast.

"To them that has the heart to enjoy it, it is, Mr. Donovan," said Miss Conway, with a sigh.

Mr. Donovan, in his heart, cursed fair weather. Heartless weather! It should hail and blow and snow to be consonant with the mood of Miss Conway.

"I hope none of your relatives—I hope you haven't sustained a loss?" ventured Mr. Donovan.

"Death has claimed," said Miss Conway, hesitating—"not a relative, but one who— but I will not intrude my grief upon you, Mr. Donovan."

"Intrude?" protested Mr. Donovan. "Why, say, Miss Conway, I'd be delighted, that is, I'd be sorry—I mean I'm sure nobody could sympathize with you truer than I would."

Miss Conway smiled a little smile. And oh, it was sadder than her expression in repose.

"'Laugh, and the world laughs with you; weep, and they give you the laugh,'" she quoted. "I have learned that, Mr. Donovan. I have no friends or acquaintances in this city. But you have been kind to me. I appreciate it highly."

He had passed her the pepper twice at the table.

"It's tough to be alone in New York—that's a cinch," said Mr. Donovan. "But, say— whenever this little old town does loosen up and get friendly it goes the limit. Say you took a little stroll in the park, Miss Conway—don't you think it might chase away some of your mullygrubs? And if you'd allow me—"

"Thanks, Mr. Donovan. I'd be pleased to accept of your escort if you think the company of one whose heart is filled with gloom could be anyways agreeable to you."

Through the open gates of the iron-railed, old, downtown park, where the elect once took the air, they strolled, and found a quiet bench.

There is this difference between the grief of youth and that of old age; youth's burden is lightened by as much of it as another shares; old age may give and give, but the sorrow remains the same.

"He was my fiancé," confided Miss Conway, at the end of an hour. "We were going to be married next spring. I don't want you to think that I am stringing you, Mr. Donovan, but he was a real count. He had an estate and a castle in Italy. Count Fernando Mazzini was his name. I never saw the beat of him for elegance. Papa objected, of course, and once we eloped, but Papa overtook us, and took us back. I thought sure Papa and Fernando would fight a duel. Papa has a very lively business—in P'kipsee, you know.

"Finally, papa came 'round, all right, and said we might be married next spring. Fernando showed him proofs of his title and wealth, and then went over to Italy to get the

86

castle fixed up for us. Papa's very proud and, when Fernando wanted to give me several thousand dollars for my trousseau, he called him something awful. He wouldn't even let me take a ring or any presents from him. And when Fernando sailed I came to the city and got a position as cashier in a candy store.

"Three days ago I got a letter from Italy, forwarded from P'kipsee, saying that Fernando had been killed in a gondola accident.

"That is why I am in mourning. My heart, Mr. Donovan, will remain forever in his grave. I guess I am poor company, Mr. Donovan, but I cannot take any interest in no one. I should not care to keep you from gaiety and your friends who can smile and entertain you. Perhaps you would prefer to walk back to the house?"

Now, girls, if you want to observe a young man hustle out after a pick and shovel, just tell him that your heart is in some other fellow's grave. Young men are grave-robbers by nature. Ask any widow. Something must be done to restore that missing organ to weeping angels in crêpe de Chine. Dead men certainly get the worst of it from all sides.

"I'm awfully sorry," said Mr. Donovan, gently. "No, we won't walk back to the house just yet. And don't say you haven't no friends in this city, Miss Conway. I'm awful sorry, and I want you to believe I'm your friend, and that I'm awful sorry."

"I've got his picture here in my locket," said Miss Conway, after wiping her eyes with her handkerchief. "I never showed it to anybody; but I will to you, Mr. Donovan, because I believe you to be a true friend."

Mr. Donovan gazed long and with much interest at the photograph in the locket that Miss Conway opened for him. The face of Count Mazzini was one to command interest. It was a smooth, intelligent, bright, almost handsome face—the face of a strong, cheerful man who might well be a leader among his fellows.

"I have a larger one, framed, in my room," said Miss Conway. "When we return I will show you that. They are all I have to remind me of Fernando. But he ever will be present in my heart, that's a sure thing."

A subtle task confronted Mr. Donovan—that of supplanting the unfortunate Count in the heart of Miss Conway. This his admiration for her determined him to do. But the magnitude of the undertaking did not seem to weigh upon his spirits. The sympathetic but cheerful friend was the role he essayed; and he played it so successfully that the next half-hour found them conversing pensively across two plates of ice-cream, though yet there was no diminution of the sadness in Miss Conway's large gray eyes.

Before they parted in the hall that evening, she ran upstairs and brought down the framed photograph wrapped lovingly in a white silk scarf. Mr. Donovan surveyed it with inscrutable eyes.

"He gave me this the night he left for Italy," said Miss Conway. "I had the one for the locket made from this."

"A fine-looking man," said Mr. Donovan, heartily. "How would it suit you Miss Conway, to give me the pleasure of your company to Coney next Sunday afternoon?"

A month later they announced their engagement to Mrs. Scott and the other boarders. Miss Conway continued to wear black.

A week after the announcement the two sat on the same bench in the downtown park, while the fluttering leaves of the trees made a dim kinetoscopic picture of them in the moonlight. But Donovan had worn a look of abstracted gloom all day. He was so silent tonight that love's lips could not keep back any longer the question that love's heart propounded.

"What's the matter, Andy, you are so solemn and grouchy to-night?"

"Nothing, Maggie."

"I know better. Can't I tell? You never acted this way before. What is it?"

"It's nothing much, Maggie."

"Yes it is; and I want to know. I'll bet it's some other girl you are thinking about. All right. Why don't you go get her if you want her? Take your arm away, if you please."

"I'll tell you then," said Andy, wisely, "but I guess you won't understand it exactly. You've heard of Mike Sullivan, haven't you? 'Big Mike' Sullivan, everybody calls him."

"No, I haven't," said Maggie. "And I don't want to, if he makes you act like this. Who is he?"

"He's the biggest man in New York," said Andy, almost reverently. "He can about do anything he wants to with Tammany or any other old thing in the political line. He's a mile high and as broad as East River. You say anything against Big Mike, and you'll have a million men on your collarbone in about two seconds. Why, he made a visit over to the old country awhile back, and the kings took to their holes like rabbits.

"Well, Big Mike's a friend of mine. I ain't more than deuce-high in the district as far as influence goes, but Mike's as good a friend to a little man, or a poor man as he is to a big one. I met him today on the Bowery, and what do you think he does? Comes up and shakes hands. 'Andy,' says he, 'I've been keeping cases on you. You've been putting in some good licks over on your side of the street, and I'm proud of you. What'll you take to drink?' He takes a cigar and I take a highball. I told him I was going to get married in two weeks. 'Andy,' says he, 'send me an invitation, so I'll keep in mind of it, and I'll come to the wedding.' That's what Big Mike says to me; and he always does what he says."

"You don't understand it, Maggie, but I'd have one of my hands cut off to have Big Mike Sullivan at our wedding. It would be the proudest day of my life. When he goes to a man's wedding, there's a guy being married that's made for life. Now, that's why I'm looking sore tonight."

"Why don't you invite him, then, if he's so much to the mustard?" said Maggie, lightly.

"There's a reason why I can't," said Andy, sadly. "There's a reason why he mustn't be there. Don't ask me what it is, for I can't tell you."

"Oh, I don't care," said Maggie. "It's something about politics, of course. But it's no reason why you can't smile at me."

"Maggie," said Andy, presently, "do you think as much of me as you did of your— as you did of the Count Mazzini?"

He waited a long time, but Maggie did not reply. And then, suddenly she leaned against his shoulder and began to cry—to cry and shake with sobs, holding his arm tightly, and wetting the crêpe de Chine with tears.

"There, there, there!" soothed Andy, putting aside his own trouble. "And what is it, now?"

"Andy," sobbed Maggie, "I've lied to you, and you'll never marry me, or love me any more. But I feel that I've got to tell. Andy, there never was so much as the little finger of a count. I never had a beau in my life. But all the other girls had; and they talked about 'em; and that seemed to make the fellows like 'em more. And, Andy, I look swell in black—you know I do. So I went out to a photograph store and bought that picture, and had a little one made for my locket, and made up all that story about the Count and about his being killed, so I could wear black. And nobody can love a liar, and you'll shake me, Andy, and I'll die of shame. Oh, there never was anybody I liked but you—and that's all."

But instead of being pushed away, she found Andy's arm folding her closer. She looked up and saw his face cleared and smiling.

"Could you—could you forgive me, Andy?"

"Sure," said Andy. "It's all right about that. Back to the cemetery for the Count. You've straightened everything out, Maggie. I was in hopes you would before the wedding-day. Bully girl!"

"Andy," said Maggie, with a somewhat shy smile, after she had been thoroughly assured of forgiveness, "did you believe all that story about the Count?"

"Well, not to any large extent," said Andy, reaching for his cigar case; "because it's Big Mike Sullivan's picture you've got in that locket of

THE GIFT OF THE MAGI

O. HENRY

Della and Jim are young and married and they love each other very much. But they don't have very much money. What can they get each other for Christmas?

ne dollar and eighty-seven cents. That was all. And sixty cents of it was in pennies. Pennies saved one and two at a time by bulldozing the grocer and the vegetable man and the butcher until one's cheeks burned with the silent imputation of parsimony that such close dealing implied. Three times Della counted it. One dollar and eighty-seven cents. And the next day would be Christmas.

There was clearly nothing to do but flop down on the shabby little couch and howl. So Della did it. Which instigates the moral reflection that life is made up of sobs, sniffles, and smiles, with sniffles predominating.

While the mistress of the home is gradually subsiding from the first stage to the second, take a look at the home. A furnished flat at eight dollars per week. It did not exactly beggar description, but it certainly had that word on the lookout for the mendicancy squad.

In the vestibule below was a letter-box into which no letter would go, and an electric button from which no mortal finger could coax a ring. Also appertaining thereunto was a card bearing the name "Mr. James Dillingham Young."

The "Dillingham" had been flung to the breeze during a former period of prosperity when its possessor was paid thirty dollars per week. Now, when the income was shrunk to twenty dollars, the letters of "Dillingham" looked blurred, as though they were thinking seriously of contracting to a modest and unassuming D. But whenever Mr. James Dillingham Young came home and reached his flat above he was called "Jim" and greatly hugged by Mrs. James Dillingham Young, already introduced to you as Della. Which is all very good.

Della finished her cry and attended to her cheeks with the powder rag. She stood by the window and looked out dully at a gray cat walking a gray fence in a gray backyard. Tomorrow would be Christmas Day and she had only $1.87 to buy a present for Jim. Her Jim. Many a happy hour she had spent planning for something nice for him. Something fine and rare and sterling—something just a little bit near to being worthy of the honor of being owned by Jim.

There was a pier-glass between the windows of the room. Perhaps you have seen a pier-glass in an eight-dollar flat. A very thin and very agile person may, by observing his reflection in a rapid sequence of longitudinal strips, obtain a fairly accurate conception of his looks. Della, being slender, had mastered the art.

Suddenly she whirled from the window and stood before the glass. Her eyes were shining brilliantly, but her face had lost its color within twenty seconds. Rapidly she pulled down her hair and let it fall to its full length.

Now, there were two possessions of the James Dillingham Youngs in which they both took a mighty pride. One was Jim's gold watch that had been his father's and his grandfather's. The other was Della's hair. Had the Queen of Sheba lived in the flat across the airshaft, Della would have let her hair hang out the window some day to dry just to depreciate Her Majesty's jewels and gifts. Had King Solomon been the janitor, with all his treasures piled up in the basement, Jim would have pulled out his watch every time he passed, just to see him pluck at his beard from envy.

So now Della's beautiful hair fell about her rippling and shining like a cascade of brown waters. It reached below her knee and made itself almost a garment for her. And then she did it up again nervously and quickly. Once she faltered for a minute and stood still while a tear or two splashed on the worn red carpet.

On went her old brown jacket; on went her old brown hat. With a whirl of skirts and with the brilliant sparkle still in her eyes, she fluttered out the door and down the stairs to the street.

Where she stopped the sign read: "Mme. Sofronie. Hair Goods of All Kinds." One flight up Della ran, and collected herself, panting. Madame, large, too white, chilly, hardly looked the "Sofronie."

"Will you buy my hair?" asked Della.

"I buy hair," said Madame. "Take yer hat off and let's have a sight at the looks of it."

Down rippled the brown cascade.

"Twenty dollars," said Madame, lifting the mass with a practiced hand.

"Give it to me quick," said Della.

Oh, and the next two hours tripped by on rosy wings. Forget the hashed metaphor. She was ransacking the stores for Jim's present.

She found it at last. It surely had been made for Jim and no one else. There was no other like it in any of the stores, and she had turned all of them inside out. It was a platinum fob chain simple and chaste in design, properly proclaiming its value by substance alone and not by meretricious ornamentation—as all good things should do. It was even worthy of The Watch. As soon as she saw it she knew that it must be Jim's. It was like him. Quietness and value—the description applied to both. Twenty-one dollars they took from her for it, and she hurried home with the eighty-seven cents. With that chain on his watch Jim might be properly anxious about the time in any company. Grand as the watch was, he sometimes looked at it on the sly on account of the old leather strap that he used in place of a chain.

When Della reached home her intoxication gave way a little to prudence and reason. She got out her curling irons and lighted the gas and went to work repairing the ravages made by generosity added to love. Which is always a tremendous task, dear friends—a mammoth task.

Within forty minutes her head was covered with tiny, close-lying curls that made her look wonderfully like a truant schoolboy. She looked at her reflection in the mirror long, carefully, and critically.

"If Jim doesn't kill me," she said to herself, "before he takes a second look at me, he'll say I look like a Coney Island chorus girl. But what could I do—oh! what could I do with a dollar and eighty-seven cents?"

At seven o'clock the coffee was made and the frying pan was on the back of the stove hot and ready to cook the chops.

Jim was never late. Della doubled the fob chain in her hand and sat on the corner of the table near the door that he always entered. Then she heard his step on the stair away down on the first flight, and she turned white for just a moment. She had a habit of saying little silent prayers about the simplest everyday things, and now she whispered: "Please God, make him think I am still pretty."

The door opened and Jim stepped in and closed it. He looked thin and serious. Poor fellow, he was only twenty-two—and to be burdened with a family! He needed a new overcoat and he was without gloves.

Jim stepped inside the door, as immovable as a setter at the scent of quail. His eyes were fixed upon Della, and there was an expression in them that she could not read, and it terrified her. It was not anger, nor surprise, nor disapproval, nor horror, nor any of the sentiments that she had been prepared for. He simply stared at her fixedly with that peculiar expression on his face.

Della wriggled off the table and went for him.

"Jim darling," she cried, "don't look at me that way. I had my hair cut off and sold it because I couldn't have lived through Christmas without giving you a present. It'll grow out again—you won't mind, will you? I just had to do it. My hair grows awfully fast. Say 'Merry Christmas!' Jim, and let's be happy. You don't know what a nice—what a beautiful, nice gift I've got for you."

"You've cut off your hair?" asked Jim, laboriously, as if he had not arrived at that patent fact yet even after the hardest mental labor.

"Cut it off and sold it," said Della. "Don't you like me just as well, anyhow? I'm me without my hair, ain't I?"

Jim looked about the room curiously.

"You say your hair is gone?" he said, with an air almost of idiocy.

"You needn't look for it," said Della. "It's sold, I tell you—sold and gone, too. It's Christmas Eve, boy. Be good to me, for it went for you. Maybe the hairs on my head were numbered," she went on with a sudden serious sweetness, "but nobody could ever count my love for you. Shall I put the chops on, Jim?"

Out of his trance Jim seemed quickly to wake. He enfolded his Della. For ten seconds let us regard with discreet scrutiny some inconsequential object in the other direction. Eight dollars a week or a million a year—what is the difference? A mathematician or a wit would give you the wrong answer. The magi brought valuable gifts, but that was not among them. This dark assertion will be illuminated later on.

Jim drew a package from his overcoat pocket and threw it upon the table.

"Don't make any mistake, Dell," he said, "about me. I don't think there's anything in the way of a haircut or a shave or a shampoo that could make me like my girl any less. But if you'll unwrap that package you may see why you had me going a while at first."

White fingers and nimble tore at the string and paper. And then an ecstatic scream of joy; and then, alas! a quick feminine change to hysterical tears and wails, necessitating the immediate employment of all the comforting powers of the lord of the flat.

For there lay The Combs—the set of combs, side and back, that Della had worshipped for long in a Broadway window. Beautiful combs, pure tortoise shell, with jewelled rims—just the shade to wear in the beautiful vanished hair. They were expensive combs, she knew, and her heart had simply craved and yearned over them without the least hope of possession. And now, they were hers, but the tresses that should have adorned the coveted adornments were gone.

But she hugged them to her bosom, and at length she was able to look up at him with dim eyes and a smile and say, "My hair grows so fast, Jim!"

And then Della leaped up like a little singed cat and cried, "Oh, oh!"

Jim had not yet seen his beautiful present. She held it out to him eagerly upon her open palm. The dull precious metal seemed to flash with a reflection of her bright and ardent spirit.

"Isn't it dandy, Jim? I hunted all over town to find it. You'll have to look at the time a hundred times a day now. Give me your watch. I want to see how it looks on it."

Instead of obeying, Jim tumbled down on the couch and put his hands under the back of his head and smiled.

"Dell," said he, "let's put our Christmas presents away and keep 'em a while. They're too nice to use just at present. I sold the watch to get the money to buy your combs. And now suppose you put the chops on."

The magi, as you know, were wise men—wonderfully wise men—who brought gifts to the Babe in the manger. They invented the art of giving Christmas presents. Being wise, their gifts were no doubt wise ones, possibly bearing the privilege of exchange in case of duplication. And here I have lamely related to you the uneventful chronicle of two foolish children in a flat who most unwisely sacrificed for each other the greatest treasures of their house. But in a last word to the wise of these days let it be said that of all who give gifts these two were the kindest. Of all who give and receive gifts, such as they are wisest. Everywhere they are wisest. They are the magi.

TWO THANKSGIVING DAY GENTLEMEN

O. HENRY

Stuffy Pete is homeless. Every Thanksgiving for the last nine years, he has been taken out for a holiday feast by an old gentleman. This year, before the old gentleman gets there, someone else takes him in and feeds him a huge dinner. Then the old gentleman shows up.

There is one day that is ours. There is one day when all we Americans who are not self-made go back to the old home to eat saleratus biscuits and marvel how much nearer to the porch the old pump looks than it used to. Bless the day. President Roosevelt gives it to us. We hear some talk of the Puritans, but don't just remember who they were. Bet we can lick 'em, anyhow, if they try to land again. Plymouth Rocks? Well, that sounds more familiar. Lots of us have had to come down to hens since the Turkey Trust got its work in. But somebody in Washington is leaking out advance information to 'em about these Thanksgiving proclamations.

The big city east of the cranberry bogs has made Thanksgiving Day an institution. The last Thursday in November is the only day in the year on which it recognizes the part of America lying across the ferries. It is the one day that is purely American. Yes, a day of celebration, exclusively American.

And now for the story which is to prove to you that we have traditions on this side of the ocean that are becoming older at a much rapider rate than those of England are—thanks to our git-up and enterprise.

Stuffy Pete took his seat on the third bench to the right as you enter Union Square from the east, at the walk opposite the fountain. Every Thanksgiving Day for nine years he had taken his seat there promptly at one o'clock. For every time he had done so things had happened to him—Charles Dickensy things that swelled his waistcoat above his heart, and equally on the other side.

But today Stuffy Pete's appearance at the annual trysting place seemed to have been rather the result of habit than of the yearly hunger which, as the philanthropists seem to think, afflicts the poor at such extended intervals.

Certainly Pete was not hungry. He had just come from a feast that had left him of his powers barely those of respiration and locomotion. His eyes were like two pale gooseberries firmly imbedded in a swollen and gravy-smeared mask of putty. His breath came in short wheezes; a senatorial roll of adipose tissue denied a fashionable set to this upturned coat collar. Buttons that had been sewed upon his clothes by kind Salvation fingers a week before flew like popcorn, strewing the earth around him. Ragged he was, with a split shirt front open to the wishbone; but the November breeze, carrying fine snowflakes, brought him only a grateful coolness. For Stuffy Pete was overcharged with the caloric produced by a super-bountiful dinner, beginning with oysters and ending with plum pudding, and including (it seemed to him) all the roast turkey and baked potatoes and chicken salad and squash pie and ice cream in the world. Wherefore he sat, gorged, and gazed upon the world with after-dinner contempt.

The meal had been an unexpected one. He was passing a red-brick mansion near the beginning of Fifth Avenue, in which lived two old ladies of ancient family and a reverence for traditions. They even denied the existence of New York and believed that Thanksgiving Day was declared solely for Washington Square. One of their traditional habits was to station a servant at the postern gate with orders to admit the first hungry wayfarer that came along after the hour of noon had struck, and banquet him to a finish. Stuffy Pete happened to pass by on his way to the park, and the seneschals gathered him in and upheld the custom of the castle.

After Stuffy Pete had gazed straight before him for ten minutes he was conscious of a desire for a more varied field of vision. With a tremendous effort he moved his head slowly to the left. And then his eyes bulged out fearfully, and his breath ceased, and the rough-shod ends of his short legs wriggled and rustled on the gravel.

For the Old Gentleman was coming across Fourth Avenue toward his bench.

Every Thanksgiving Day for nine years the Old Gentleman had come there and found Stuffy Pete on his bench. That was a thing that the Old Gentleman was trying to make a tradition of. Every Thanksgiving Day for nine years he had found Stuffy there, and had led him to a restaurant and watched him eat a big dinner. They do those things in England unconsciously. But this is a young country, and nine years is not so bad. The Old Gentleman was a staunch American patriot, and considered himself a pioneer in American tradition. In order to become picturesque we must keep on doing one thing for a long time without ever letting it get away from us. Something like collecting the weekly dimes in industrial insurance. Or cleaning the streets.

The Old Gentleman moved, straight and stately, toward the Institution that he was rearing. Truly, the annual feeding of Stuffy Pete was nothing national in its character, such as the Magna Carta or jam for breakfast was in England. But it was a step. It was almost feudal. It showed, at least, that a Custom was not impossible to New Y— ahem!—America.

The Old Gentleman was thin and tall and sixty. He was dressed all in black, and wore the old-fashioned kind of glasses that won't stay on our nose. His hair was whiter and thinner than it had been last year, and he seemed to make more use of his big, knobby cane with the crooked handle.

As his established benefactor came up Stuffy wheezed and shuddered like some woman's over-fat pug when a street dog bristles up at him. He would have flown, but all the skill of Santos-Dumont could not have separated him from his bench. Well had the myrmidons of the two old ladies done their work.

"Good morning," said the Old Gentleman. "I am glad to perceive that the vicissitudes of another year have spared you to move in health about the beautiful world. For that blessing alone this day of thanksgiving is well proclaimed to each of us. If you will come with me, my man, I will provide you with a dinner that should make your physical being accord with the mental."

That is what the Old Gentleman said every time. Every Thanksgiving Day for nine years. The words themselves almost formed an Institution. Nothing could be compared with them except the Declaration of Independence. Always before they had been music in Stuffy's ears. But now he looked up at the Old Gentleman's face with tearful agony in his own. The fine snow almost sizzled when it fell upon his perspiring brow. But the Old Gentleman shivered a little and turned his back to the wind.

Stuffy had always wondered why the Old Gentleman spoke his speech rather sadly. He did not know that it was because he was wishing every time that he had a son to succeed him. A son who would come there after he was gone—a son who would stand proud and strong before some subsequent Stuffy, and say, "In memory of my father." Then it would be an institution.

But the Old Gentleman had no relatives. He lived in rented rooms in one of the decayed old family brownstone mansions in one of the quiet streets east of the park. In the winter he raised fuchsias in a little conservatory the size of a steamer trunk. In the spring he walked in the Easter parade. In the summer he lived at a farmhouse in the New Jersey hills, and sat in a wicker armchair, speaking of a butterfly, the ornithoptera amphrisius, that he hoped to find some day. In the autumn he fed Stuffy a dinner. These were the Old Gentleman's occupations.

Stuffy Pete looked up at him for a half minute, stewing and helpless in his own self-pity. The Old Gentleman's eyes were bright with the giving-pleasure. His face was getting more lined each year, but his little black necktie was in as jaunty a bow as ever, and his linen was beautiful and white, and his gray mustache was curled gracefully at the ends. And then Stuffy made a noise that sounded like peas bubbling in a pot. Speech was not intended; and as the Old Gentleman had heard the sounds nine times before, he rightly construed them into Stuffy's old formula of acceptance.

"Thankee, sir. I'll go with ye, and much obliged. I'm very hungry, sir."

The coma of repletion had not prevented from entering Stuffy's mind the conviction that he was the basis of an Institution. His Thanks-giving appetite was not his own; it belonged by all the sacred rights of established custom, if not by the actual Statute of Limitations, to this kind old gentleman who had preempted it. True, America is free; but in order to establish tradition some one must be a repetend—a repeating decimal. The heroes are not all heroes of steel and gold. See one here that wielded only weapons of iron, badly silvered, and tin.

The Old Gentleman led his annual protégé southward to the restaurant, and to the table where the feast had always occurred. They were recognized.

"Here comes de old guy," said a waiter, "dat blows dat same bum to a meal every Thanksgiving."

The Old Gentleman sat across the table glowing like a smoked pearl at his corner-stone of future ancient Tradition. The waiters heaped the table with holiday food—and Stuffy, with a sigh that was mistaken for hunger's expression, raised knife and fork and carved for himself a crown of imperishable bay.

No more valiant hero ever fought his way through the ranks of an enemy. Turkey, chops, soups, vegetables, pies, disappeared before him as fast as they could be served. Gorged nearly to the uttermost when he entered the restaurant, the smell of food had almost caused him to lose his honor as a gentleman, but he rallied like a true knight. He saw the look of beneficent happiness on the Old Gentleman's face—a happier look than even the fuchsias and the ornithoptera amphrisius had ever brought to it—and he had not the heart to see it wane.

In an hour Stuffy leaned back with a battle won.

"Thankee kindly, sir," he puffed like a leaky steam pipe; "thankee kindly for a hearty meal."

Then he arose heavily with glazed eyes and started toward the kitchen. A waiter turned him about like a top, and pointed him toward the door. The Old Gentleman carefully counted out $1.30 in silver change, leaving three nickels for the waiter.

They parted as they did each year at the door, the Old Gentleman going south, Stuffy north.

Around the first corner Stuffy turned, and stood for one minute. Then he seemed to puff out his rags as an owl puffs out his feathers, and fell to the sidewalk like a sunstricken horse.

When the ambulance came the young surgeon and the driver cursed softly at his weight. There was no smell of whiskey to justify a transfer to the patrol wagon, so Stuffy and his two dinners went to the hospital. There they stretched him on a bed and began to test him for strange diseases, with the hope of getting a chance at some problem with the bare steel.

And lo! an hour later another ambulance brought the Old Gentleman. And they laid him on another bed and spoke of appendicitis, for he looked good for the bill.

But pretty soon one of the young doctors met one of the young nurses whose eyes he liked, and stopped to chat with her about the cases.

"That nice old gentleman over there, now," he said, "you wouldn't think that was a case of almost starvation. Proud old family, I guess. He told me he hadn't eaten a thing for three days."

A LICKPENNY LOVER

O. HENRY

Masie works in the glove department of the "Biggest Store." One day a "painter, millionaire, traveler, poet, automobilist" comes in and asks her out on a date. Could he be the man she's been waiting for?

here were 3,000 girls in the Biggest Store. Masie was one of them. She was eighteen and a saleslady in the gent's gloves. Here she became versed in two varieties of human beings—the kind of gents who buy their gloves in department stores and the kind of women who buy gloves for unfortunate gents. Besides this wide knowledge of the human species, Masie had acquired other information. She had listened to the promulgated wisdom of the 2,999 other girls and had stored it in a brain that was as secretive and wary as that of a Maltese cat. Perhaps nature, foreseeing that she would lack wise counselors, had mingled the saving ingredient of shrewdness along with her beauty, as she has endowed the silver fox of the priceless fur above the other animals with cunning.

For Masie was beautiful. She was a deep-tinted blonde, with the calm poise of a lady who cooks butter cakes in a window. She stood behind her counter in the Biggest Store; and as you closed your hand over the tape-line for your glove measure you thought of Hebe; and as you looked again you wondered how she had come by Minerva's eyes.

When the floorwalker was not looking, Masie chewed tutti frutti; when he was looking she gazed up as if at the clouds and smiled wistfully.

That is the shopgirl smile, and I enjoin you to shun it unless you are well fortified with callosity of the heart, caramels, and a congeniality for the capers of Cupid. This smile belonged to Masie's recreation hours and not to the store; but the floorwalker must have his own. He is the Shylock of the stores. When he comes nosing around the bridge of his nose is a toll-bridge. It is goo-goo eyes or "git" when he looks toward a pretty girl. Of course not all floorwalkers are thus. Only a few days ago the papers printed news of one over eighty years of age.

One day Irving Carter, painter, millionaire, traveller, poet, automobilist, happened to enter the Biggest Store. It is due to him to add that his visit was not voluntary. Filial duty took him by the collar and dragged him inside, while his mother philandered among the bronze and terra-cotta statuettes.

Carter strolled across to the glove counter in order to shoot a few minutes on the wing. His need for gloves was genuine; he had forgotten to bring a pair with him. But his action hardly calls for an apology, because he had never heard of glove-counter flirtations.

As he neared the vicinity of his fate he hesitated, suddenly conscious of this unknown phase of Cupid's less worthy profession.

Three or four cheap fellows, sonorously garbed, were leaning over the counters, wrestling with the mediatorial hand-coverings, while giggling girls played vivacious seconds to their lead upon the strident string of coquetry. Carter would have retreated, but he had gone too far. Masie confronted him behind her counter with a questioning look in eyes as coldly, beautifully, warmly blue as the glint of summer sunshine on an iceberg drifting in southern seas.

And then Irving Carter, painter, millionaire, etc., felt a warm flush rise to his aristocratically pale face. But not from diffidence. The blush was intellectual in origin. He knew in a moment that he stood in the ranks of the ready-made youths who wooed the giggling girls at other counters. Himself leaned against the oaken trysting place of a cockney Cupid with a desire in his heart for the favor of a glove salesgirl. He was no more than Bill and Jack and Mickey. And then he felt a sudden tolerance for them, and an elating, courageous contempt for the conventions upon which he had fed, and an unhesitating determination to have this perfect creature for his own.

When the gloves were paid for and wrapped, Carter lingered for a moment. The dimples at the corners of Masie's damask mouth deepened. All gentlemen who bought gloves lingered in just that way. She curved an arm, showing like Psyche's through her shirt-waist sleeve, and rested an elbow upon the show-case edge.

Carter had never before encountered a situation of which he had not been perfect master. But now he stood far more awkward than Bill or Jack or Mickey. He had no chance of meeting this beautiful girl socially. His mind struggled to recall the nature and habits of shopgirls as he had read or heard of them. Somehow he had received the idea that they sometimes did not insist too strictly upon the regular channels of introduction. His heart beat loudly at the thought of proposing an unconventional meeting with this lovely and virginal being. But the tumult in his heart gave him courage.

After a few friendly and well-received remarks on general subjects, he laid his card by her hand on the counter.

"Will you please pardon me," he said, "if I seem too bold; but I earnestly hope you will allow me the pleasure of seeing you again. There is my name; I assure you that it is with the greatest respect that I ask the favor of becoming one of your fr—acquaintances. May I not hope for the privilege?"

Masie knew men—especially men who buy gloves. Without hesitation she looked him frankly and smilingly in the eyes, and said, "Sure. I guess you're all right. I don't usually go out with strange gentlemen, though. It ain't quite ladylike. When should you want to see me again?"

"As soon as I may," said Carter. "If you would allow me to call at your home, I—"

Masie laughed musically. "Oh, gee, no!" she said, emphatically. "If you could see our flat once! There's five of us in three rooms. I'd just like to see ma's face if I was to bring a gentleman friend there!"

"Anywhere, then," said the enamored Carter, "that will be convenient to you."

"Say," suggested Masie, with a bright-idea look in her peach-blow face; "I guess Thursday night will about suit me. Suppose you come to the corner of Eighth Avenue and Forty-eighth Street at 7:30. I live right near the corner. But I've got to be back home by eleven. Ma never lets me stay out after eleven."

Carter promised gratefully to keep the tryst, and then hastened to his mother, who was looking about for him to ratify her purchase of a bronze Diana.

A salesgirl, with small eyes and an obtuse nose, strolled near Masie, with a friendly leer.

"Did you make a hit with his nobs, Masie?" she asked, familiarly.

"The gentleman asked permission to call," answered Maisie, with the grand air, as she slipped Carter's card into the bosom of her waist.

"Permission to call!" echoed small eyes, with a snigger. "Did he say anything about dinner in the Waldorf and a spin in his auto afterward?"

"Oh, cheese it!" said Masie, wearily. "You've been used to swell things, I don't think. You've had a swelled head ever since that hose-cart driver took you out to a chop suey joint. No, he never mentioned the Waldorf; but there's a Fifth Avenue address on his card, and if he buys the supper you can bet your life there won't be no pigtail on the waiter what takes the order."

As Carter glided away from the Biggest Store with his mother in his electric runabout, he bit his lip with a dull pain at his heart. He knew that love had come to him for the first time in all the twenty-nine years of his life. And that the object of it should make so readily an appointment with him at a street corner, though it was a step toward his desires, tortured him with misgivings.

Carter did not know the shopgirl. He did not know that her home is often either a scarcely habitable tiny room or a domicile filled to overflowing with kith and kin. The street corner is her parlor, the park is her drawing room; the avenue is her garden walk; yet for the most part she is as inviolate mistress of herself in them as is my lady inside her tapestried chamber.

One evening at dusk, two weeks after their first meeting, Carter and Masie strolled arm-in-arm into a little, dimly-lit park. They found a bench, tree-shadowed and secluded, and sat there.

For the first time his arm stole gently around her. Her golden-bronze head slid restfully against his shoulder.

"Gee!" sighed Masie, thankfully. "Why didn't you ever think of that before?"

"Masie," said Carter, earnestly, "you surely know that I love you. I ask you sincerely to marry me. You know me well enough by this time to have no doubts of me. I want you, and I must have you. I care nothing for the difference in our stations."

"What is the difference?" asked Masie, curiously.

"Well, there isn't any," said Carter, quickly, "except in the minds of foolish people. It is in my power to give you a life of luxury. My social position is beyond dispute, and my means are ample."

"They all say that," remarked Masie. "It's the kid they all give you. I suppose you really work in a delicatessen or follow the races. I ain't as green as I look."

"I can furnish you all the proofs you want," said Carter, gently. "And I want you, Masie. I loved you the first day I saw you."

"They all do," said Masie, with an amused laugh, "to hear 'em talk. If I could meet a man that got stuck on me the third time he'd seen me I think I'd get mashed on him."

"Please don't say such things," pleaded Carter. "Listen to me, dear. Ever since I first looked into your eyes you have been the only woman in the world for me."

"Oh, ain't you the kidder!" smiled Masie. "How many other girls did you ever tell that?"

But Carter persisted. And at length he reached the flimsy, fluttering little soul of the shopgirl that existed somewhere deep down in her lovely bosom. His words penetrated the heart whose very lightness was its safest armor. She looked up at him with eyes that saw. And a warm glow visited her cool cheeks. Tremblingly, awfully, her moth wings closed, and she seemed about to settle upon the flower of love. Some faint glimmer of life and its possibilities on the other side of her glove counter dawned upon her. Carter felt the change and crowded the opportunity.

"Marry me, Masie," he whispered, softly, "and we will go away from this ugly city to beautiful ones. We will forget work and business, and life will be one long holiday. I know where I should take you—I have been there often. Just think of a shore where summer is eternal, where the waves are always rippling on the lovely beach and the people are happy and free as children. We will sail to those shores and remain there as long as you please. In one of those far-away cities there are grand and lovely palaces and towers full of beautiful pictures and statues. The streets of the city are water, and one travels about in—"

"I know," said Masie, sitting up suddenly. "Gondolas."

"Yes," smiled Carter.

"I thought so," said Masie.

"And then," continued Carter, "we will travel on and see whatever we wish in the world. After the European cities we will visit India and the ancient cities there, and ride on elephants and see the wonderful temples of the Hindoos and the Brahmins and the Japanese gardens and the camel trains and chariot races in Persia, and all the queer sights of foreign countries. Don't you think you would like it, Masie?"

Masie rose to her feet.

"I think we had better be going home," she said, coolly. "It's getting late."

Carter humored her. He had come to know her varying, thistle-down moods, and that it was useless to combat them. But he felt a certain happy triumph. He had held for a moment, though but by a silken thread, the soul of his wild Psyche, and hope was stronger within him. Once she had folded her wings and her cool hand had closed about his own.

At the Biggest Store the next day Masie's chum, Lulu, waylaid her in an angle of the counter.

"How are you and your swell friend making it?" she asked.

"Oh, him?" said Masie, patting her side curls. "He ain't in it anymore. Say, Lu, what do you think that fellow wanted me to do?"

"Go on stage?" guessed Lulu, breathlessly.

"Nit; he's too cheap a guy for that. He wanted me to marry him and go down to Coney Island for a wedding tour!"

RUDYARD KIPLING

RUDYARD KIPLING was born in 1865 in Bombay, the child of English parents living in British-ruled India. When he was six years old, his parents sent him to England to be educated. His youthful experiences in England were not happy ones: he hated the old couple his parents sent him to live with and, later, equally despised the military school where he finished his studies.

Eager to return to India, Kipling took a job as a journalist for a paper in northwest India. His career as a reporter took him to remote parts of the land and the culture, and it was this experience that formed the basis for his literary endeavors. He published his first collection of stories at age twenty-two and enjoyed almost immediate success. His stories about unknown corners of India were popular in England and would eventually find acclaim all over the world.

In 1902 Kipling wrote a book of children's stories called the *Just So Stories*. In his elegant and simple prose, Kipling offers explanations for the mysteries of the natural universe. Here we reprint his tales of how the armadillo came to be, how the camel got his hump, how the whale got his throat, and stories about elephants and kangaroos. We also reprint in the Chapter "Animal Tales," part of Kipling's most famous work, *The Jungle Book*, a favorite of children—and adults—for generations.

Kipling, Rudyard. *Rudyard Kipling Illustrated*. New York: Crown Publishers,1982.
  Other Editions:
  ——. *Just So Stories.*(Illustrated); New York: Viking, 1993.
  ——. *Collected Stories of Rudyard Kipling*. New York: Knopf, 1994.
  ——. *The Best Fiction of Rudyard Kipling*. New York: Doubleday, 1989.
  ——. *The Jungle Book & Just So Stories*. New York: Bantam, 1986.

JUST SO STORIES

Rudyard Kipling

HOW THE CAMEL GOT HIS HUMP

Now this is the next tale, and it tells how the Camel got his big hump.

In the beginning of years, when the world was so new-and-all, and the Animals were just beginning to work for Man, there was a Camel, and he lived in the middle of a Howling Desert because he did not want to work; and besides, he was a Howler himself. So he ate sticks and thorns and tamarisks and milkweed and prickles, most 'scruciating idle; and when anybody spoke to him he said "Humph!" Just "Humph!" and no more.

Presently the Horse came to him on Monday morning, with a saddle on his back and a bit in his mouth, and said, "Camel, O Camel, come out and trot like the rest of us."

"Humph!" said the Camel; and the Horse went away and told the Man.

Presently the Dog came to him, with a stick in his mouth, and said, "Camel, O Camel, come and fetch and carry like the rest of us."

"Humph!" said the Camel; and the Horse went away and told the man.

Presently the Ox came to him, with the yoke on his neck, and said, "Camel, O Camel; come and plough like the rest of us."

"Humph!" said the Camel; and the Ox went away and told the Man.

At the end of the day the Man called the Horse and the dog and the Ox together, and said, "Three, O Three, I'm very sorry for you (with the world so new-and-all); but that Humph-thing in the Desert can't work, or he would have been here by now, so I am going to leave him alone, and you must work double-time to make up for it."

That made the Three very angry (with the world so new-and-all), and they held a palaver, and an indaba, and a punchayet, and a pow-wow on the edge of the Desert; and the Camel came chewing milkweed most 'scruciating idle, and laughed at them. Then he said "Humph!" and went away again.

Presently there came along the Djinn in charge of All Deserts, rolling in a cloud of dust (Djinns always travel that way because it is Magic), and he stopped to palavar and pow-wow with the Tree.

"Djinn of All Deserts," said the Horse, "is it right for any one to be idle, with the world so new-and-all!?"

"Certainly not," said the Djinn.

"Well," said the Horse, "there's a thing in the middle of your Howling Desert (and he's a Howler himself) with a long neck and long legs, and he hasn't done a stroke of work since Monday morning. He won't trot."

"Whew!" said the Djinn, whistling, "that's my Camel, for all the gold in Arabia! What does he say about it?"

"He says, 'Humph!'" said the Dog; "and he won't fetch and carry."

"Does he say anything else?"

"Only 'Humph!'; and he won't plough," said the Ox.

"Very good," said the Djinn. "I'll humph him if you will kindly wait a minute."

The Djinn rolled himself up in his dust-cloak, and took a bearing across the desert, and found the Camel most 'scruciatingly idle, looking at his own reflection in a pool of water.

"My long and bubbling friend," said the Djinn, "what's this I hear of your doing no work, with the world so new-and-all?"

"Humph!" said the Camel.

The Djinn sat down, with his chin in his hand, and began to think a Great Magic, while the Camel looked at his own reflection in the pool of water.

"You've given the Three extra work ever since Monday morning, all on account of your 'scruciating idleness," said the Djinn; and he went on thinking Magics, with his chin in his hand.

"Humph!" said the Camel.

"I shouldn't say that again if I were you," said the Djinn; " you might say it once too often. Bubbles, I want you to work."

And the Camel said "Humph!" again; but no sooner had he said it than he saw his back, that he was so proud of, puffing up and puffing up into a great big lolloping humph.

"Do you see that?" said the Djinn. "That's your very own humph that you've brought upon your very own self by not working. To-day is Thursday, and you've done no work since Monday, when the work began. Now you are going to work."

"How can I," said the Camel, "with this humph on my back?"

"That's made a-purpose," said the Djinn, "all because you missed those three days. You will be able to work now for three days without eating, because you can live on your humph; and don't you ever say I never did anything for you. Come out of the Desert and go to the Three, and behave. Humph yourself!"

And the Camel humphed himself, humph and all, and went away to join the Three. And from that day to this the Camel always wears a humph (we call it "hump" now, not to hurt his feelings); but he has never yet caught up with the three days that he missed at the beginning of the world, and he has never yet learned how to behave.

The Camel's hump is an ugly lump
Which well you may see at the Zoo;
But uglier yet is the hump we get
From having too little to do.

Kiddies and grown-ups too-oo-oo,
If we haven't enough to do-oo-oo,
   We get the hump—
   Cameelious hump—
The hump that is black and blue!

We climb out of bed with a frouzly head
And a snarly-yarly voice.
We shiver and scowl and we grunt and we growl
At our bath and our boots and our toys;

And there ought to be a corner for me
(And I know there is one for you)
   When we get the hump—
   Cameelious hump—
The hump that is black and blue!

The cure for this ill is not to sit still,
Or frowst with a book by the fire;
But to take a large hoe and a shovel also,
And dig till you gently perspire;

And then you will find that the sun and the wind,
And the Djinn of the Garden too,
   Have lifted the hump—
   The horrible hump—
The hump that is black and blue!

I get it as well as you-oo-oo—
If I haven't enough to do-oo-oo!
   We all get the hump—
   Cameelious hump—
Kiddies and grown-ups too!

THE BEGINNING OF THE ARMADILLOES

This, Oh Best Beloved, is another story of the High and Far-Off Times. In the very middle of those times was a Stickly-Prickly Hedgehog, and he lived on the banks of the turbid Amazon, eating shelly snails and things. And he had a friend, a Slow-Solid Tortoise, who lived on the banks of the turbid Amazon, eating green lettuces and things. And so that was all right, Best Beloved. Do you see?

But also, and at the same time, in those High and Far-Off Times, there was a Painted Jaguar, and he lived on the banks of the turbid Amazon too; and he ate everything that he could catch. When he could not catch deer or monkeys he would eat frogs and beetles; and when he could not catch frogs and beetles he went to his Mother Jaguar, and she told him how to eat hedgehogs and tortoises.

She said to him ever so many times, graciously waving her tail, "My son, when you find a Hedgehog you must drop him into the water and then he will uncoil, and when you catch a Tortoise you must scoop him out of his shell with your paw." And so that was all right, Best Beloved.

One beautiful night on the banks of the turbid Amazon, Painted Jaguar found Stickly-Prickly Hedgehog and Slow-Solid Tortoise sitting under the trunk of a fallen tree. They could not run away, and so Stickly-Prickly curled himself up into a ball, because he was a Hedgehog, and Slow-Solid Tortoise drew in his head and feet into his shell as fast as they would go, because he was a tortoise; and so that was all right, Best Beloved. Do you see?

"Now attend to me," said Painted Jaguar, "because this is very important. My mother said that when I meet a Hedgehog I am to drop him into the water and then he will uncoil, and when I meet a Tortoise I am to scoop him out of his shell with my paw. Now which of you is a Hedgehog and which is a Tortoise? Because, to save my spots, I can't tell."

"Are you sure of what your Mummy told you?" said Stickly-Prickly Hedgehog. "Are you quite sure? Perhaps she said that when you uncoil a Tortoise you must shell him out of the water with a scoop, and when you paw a Hedgehog you must drop him on the shell."

"Are you sure of what your Mummy told you?" said Slow-and-Solid Tortoise. "Are you quite sure? Perhaps she said that when you water a Hedgehog you must drop him into your paw, and when you meet a Tortoise you must shell him till he uncoils."

"I don't think it was at all like that," said Painted Jaguar, but he felt a little puzzled; "but, please, say it again more distinctly."

"When you scoop water with your paw you uncoil it with a Hedgehog," said Stickly-Prickly. "Remember that, because it's important."

"But," said the Tortoise, "when you paw your meat you drop it into a Tortoise with a scoop. Why can't you understand?"

"You are making my spots ache," said Painted Jaguar; "and besides, I didn't want your advice at all. I only wanted to know which of you is Hedgehog and which is Tortoise."

"I shan't tell you," said Stickly-Prickly. "But you can scoop me out of my shell if you like."

"Aha!" said Painted Jaguar. "Now I know you're Tortoise. You thought I wouldn't! Now I will." Painted Jaguar darted out his paddy-paw just as Stickly-Prickly curled himself up, and of course Jaguar's paddy-paw was just filled with prickles. Worse than that, he knocked Stickly-Prickly away and away into the woods and the bushes, where it was too dark to find him. Then he put his paddy-paw into his mouth, and of course the prickles hurt him worse than ever. As soon as he could speak he said, "Now I know he isn't Tortoise at all. But"—and then he scratched his head with his un-prickly paw—"how do I know that this other is Tortoise?"

"But I am Tortoise," said Slow-and-Solid. "Your mother was quite right. She said that you were to scoop me out of my shell with your paw. Begin."

"You didn't say she said that a minute ago," said Painted Jaguar, sucking the prickles out of his paddy-paw. "You said she said something quite different."

"Well, suppose you say that I said that she said something quite different, I don't see that it makes any difference; because if she said what you said I said she said, it's just the same as if I said what she said she said. On the other hand, if you think she said that you were to uncoil me with a scoop, instead of pawing me into drops with a shell, I can't help that, can I?"

"But you said you wanted to be scooped out of your shell with my paw," said Painted Jaguar.

"If you'll think again you'll find that I didn't say anything of the kind. I said that your mother said that you were to scoop me out of my shell," said Slow-and-Solid.

"What will happen if I do?" said the Jaguar most sniffily and most cautious.

"I don't know, because I've never been scooped out of my shell before; but I tell you truly, if you want to see me swim away you've only got to drop me into the water."

"I don't believe it," said Painted Jaguar. "You've mixed up all the things my mother told me to do with the things that you asked me whether I was sure that she didn't say, till I don't know whether I'm on my head or my painted tail; and now you come and tell me something I can understand, and it makes me more mixy than before. My mother told me that I was to drop one of you two into the water, and as you seem so anxious to be dropped I think you don't want to be dropped. So jump into the turbid Amazon and be quick about it."

"I warn you that your Mummy won't be pleased. Don't tell her I didn't tell you," said Slow-and-Solid.

"If you say another word about what my mother said—" the Jaguar answered, but he had not finished the sentence before Slow-and-Solid quietly dived into the turbid Amazon, swam under water for a long way, and came out on the bank where Stickly-Prickly was waiting for him.

"That was a very narrow escape," said Stickly-Prickly. "I don't like Painted Jaguar. What did you tell him that you were?"

"I told him truthfully that I was a truthful Tortoise, but he wouldn't believe it, and he made me jump into the river to see if I was, and I was, and he is surprised. Now he's gone to tell his Mummy. Listen to him!"

They could hear Painted Jaguar roaring up and down among the trees and the bushes by the side of the turbid Amazon, till his Mummy came.

"Son, son!" said his mother ever so many times, graciously waving her tail, "what have you been doing that you shouldn't have done?"

"I tried to scoop something that said it wanted to be scooped out of its shell with my paw, and my paw is full of per-ickles," said Painted Jaguar.

"Son, son!" said his mother ever so many times graciously waving her tail, "by the prickles in your paddy-paw I see that that must have been a hedgehog. You should have dropped him into the water."

"I did that to the other thing; and he said he was a Tortoise, and I didn't believe him, and it was quite true, and I haven't anything at all to eat, and I think we had better find lodgings somewhere else. They are too clever on the turbid Amazon for poor me!"

"Son, son!" said his mother ever so many times, graciously waving her tail, "now attend to me and remember what I say. A Hedgehog curls himself up into a ball and his prickles stick out every which way at once. By this you may know the Hedgehog."

"I don't like this old lady one little bit," said Stickly-Prickly, under the shadow of a large leaf. "I wonder what else she knows?"

"A Tortoise can't curl himself up," Mother Jaguar went on, ever so many times, graciously waving her tail. "He only draws his head and legs into his shell. By this you may know the Tortoise."

"I don't like this old lady at all—at all," said Slow-and-Solid Tortoise. "Even Painted Jaguar can't forget those directions. It's a great pity that you can't swim, Stickly-Prickly."

"Don't talk to me," said Stickly-Prickly. "Just think how much better it would be if you could curl up. This is a mess! Listen to Painted Jaguar."

Painted Jaguar was sitting on the banks of the turbid Amazon sucking prickles out of his paws and saying to himself—

Can't curl, but can swim—
Slow-Solid, that's him!
Curls up, but can't swim—
Stickly-Prickly, that's him!

110

"He'll never forget that this month of Sundays," said Stickly-Prickly. "Hold up my chin, Slow-and-Solid. I'm going to try to learn to swim. It may be useful."

"Excellent!" said Slow-and-Solid; and he held up Stickly-Prickly's chin, while Stickly-Prickly kicked in the waters of the turbid Amazon.

"You'll make a fine swimmer yet," said Slow-and-Solid. "Now, if you can unlace my backplates a little, I'll see what I can do toward curling up. It may be useful."

Stickly-Prickly helped to unlace Tortoise's back-plates, so that by twisting and straining Slow-and-Solid actually managed to curl up a tiddy wee bit.

"Excellent!" said Stickly-Prickly; "but I shouldn't do any more just now. It's making you black in the face. Kindly lead me into the water once again and I'll practice that side-stroke which you say is so easy." And so Stickly-Prickly practiced, and Slow-and-Solid swam alongside.

"Excellent!" said Slow-and-Solid. "A little more practice will make you a regular whale. Now, if I may trouble you to unlace my back and front plates two holes more, I'll try that fascinating bend that you say is so easy. Won't Painted Jaguar be surprised!"

"Excellent!" said Stickly-Prickly, all wet from the turbid Amazon. "I declare, I shouldn't know you from one of my own family. Two holes, I think you said? A little more expression, please, and don't grunt quite so much, or Painted Jaguar may hear us. When you've finished, I want to try that long dive which you say is so easy. Won't Painted Jaguar be surprised!"

And so Stickly-Prickly dived, and Slow-and-Solid dived alongside.

"Excellent!" said Slow-and-Solid. "A leetle more attention to holding your breath and you will be able to keep house at the bottom of the turbid Amazon. Now I'll try that exercise of wrapping my hind legs round my ears which you say is so peculiarly comfortable. Won't Painted Jaguar be surprised!"

"Excellent!" said Stickly-Prickly. "But it's straining your back-plates a little. They are all overlapping now, instead of lying side by side."

"Oh, that's the result of exercise," said Slow-and-Solid. "I've noticed that your prickles seem to be melting into one another, and that you're growing to look rather more like a pine-cone, and less like a chestnut-bur, than you used to."

"Am I?" said Stickly-Prickly. "That comes from my soaking in the water. Oh, won't Painted Jaguar be surprised!"

They went on with their exercises, each helping the other, till morning came; and when the sun was high they rested and dried themselves. Then they saw that they were both of them quite different from what they had been.

"Stickly-Prickly," said Tortoise after breakfast, "I am not what I was yesterday; but I think that I may yet amuse the Painted Jaguar."

"That was the very thing I was thinking just now," said Stickly-Prickly. "I think scales are a tremendous improvement on prickles—to say nothing of being able to swim. Oh, won't Painted Jaguar be surprised! Let's go and find him."

By and by they found Painted Jaguar, still nursing his paddy-paw that had been hurt the night before. He was so astonished that he fell three times backward over his own painted tail without stopping.

"Good morning!" said Stickly-Prickly. "And how is your dear gracious Mummy this morning?"

"She is quite well, thank you," said Painted Jaguar; "but you must forgive me if I do not at this precise moment recall your name."

"That's unkind of you," said Stickly-Prickly, "seeing that this time yesterday you tried to scoop me out of my shell with your paw."

"But you hadn't any shell. It was all prickles," said Painted Jaguar. "I know it was. Just look at my paw!"

"You told me to drop into the turbid Amazon to be drowned," said Slow-and-Solid. "Why are you so rude and forgetful today?"

"Don't you remember what your mother told you?" said Stickly-Prickly—

> *Can't curl, but can swim—*
> *Slow-Solid, that's him!*
> *Curls up, but can't swim—*
> *Stickly-Prickly, that's him!*

Then they both curled themselves up and rolled around and around Painted Jaguar till his eyes turned truly cart-wheels in his head.

Then he went to fetch his mother.

"Mother," he said, "there are two new animals in the woods today, and the one that you said couldn't swim, swims, and the one that you said couldn't curl up, curls; and they've gone shares in their prickles, I think, because both of them are scaly all over, instead of one being smooth and the other very prickly. And, besides that, they are rolling around and around in circles, and I don't feel comfy."

"Son, son!" said Mother Jaguar ever so many times, graciously waving her tail, "a Hedgehog is a Hedgehog, and can't be anything but a Hedgehog; and a Tortoise is a Tortoise, and can never be anything else."

"But it isn't a Hedgehog, and it isn't a Tortoise. It's a little bit of both, and I don't know its proper name."

"Nonsense!" said Mother Jaguar. "Everything has its proper name. I should call it 'Armadillo' till I found out the real one. And I should leave it alone."

So Painted Jaguar did as he was told, especially about leaving them alone; but the curious thing is that from that day to this, O Best Beloved, no one on the banks of the turbid Amazon has ever called Stickly-Prickly and Slow-Solid anything except Armadillo. There are Hedgehogs and Tortoises in other places, of course (there are some in my garden); but the real old and clever kind, with their scales lying lippety-lappety one over the other, like pine-cone scales, that lived on the banks of the turbid Amazon in the High and Far-Off Days, are always called Armadilloes, because they were so clever.

So that's all right, Best Beloved. Do you see?

> *I've never sailed the Amazon,*
> *I've never reached Brazil;*
> *But the Don and Magdalena,*
> *They can go there when they will!*
>
> *Yes, weekly from Southampton,*
> *Great steamers, white and gold,*
> *Go rolling down to Rio*
>
> *(Roll down—roll down to Rio!)*
> *And I'd like to roll to Rio*
> *Some day before I'm old!*
>
> *I've never seen a Jaguar,*
> *Nor yet an Armadill—*
> *O dilloing in his armor,*
> *And I s'pose I never will,*
>
> *Unless I go to Rio*
> *These wonders to behold—*
> *Roll down—roll down to Rio—*
> *Roll really down to Rio!*
> *Oh, I'd love to roll to Rio*
> *Some day before I'm old!*

HOW THE WHALE GOT HIS THROAT

I n the sea, once upon a time, O my Best Beloved, there was a whale, and he ate fishes. He ate the starfish and the garfish, and the crab and the dab, and the plaice and the dace, and the skate and his mate, and the mackereel and the pickereel, and the really truly twirly-whirly eel. All the fishes he could find in all the sea he ate with his mouth—so! Till at last there was only one small fish left in all the sea, and he was a small 'Stute Fish, and he swam a little behind the Whale's right ear, so as to be out of harm's way. Then the Whale stood up on his tail and said, "I'm hungry." And the small 'Stute Fish said in a small 'stute voice, "Noble and generous Cetacean, have you ever tasted Man?"

"No," said the Whale. "What is it like?"

"Nice," said the small 'Stute Fish. "Nice but nubbly."

"Then fetch me some," said the Whale, and he made the sea froth up with his tail.

"One at a time is enough," said the 'Stute Fish. "If you swim to latitude Fifty North, longitude Forty West (that is Magic), you will find, sitting on a raft, in the middle of the sea, with nothing to wear except a pair of blue canvas breeches, a pair of suspenders (you must not forget the suspenders, Best Beloved), and a jack-knife, one shipwrecked Mariner, who, it is only fair to tell you, is a man of infinite-resource-and-sagacity."

So the Whale swam and swam to latitude 50 North, longitude 40 West, as fast as he could swim, and on a raft, in the middle of the sea, with nothing to wear except a pair of blue canvas breeches, a pair of suspenders (you must particularly remember the suspenders, Best Beloved), and a jack-knife, he found one single, solitary shipwrecked Mariner, trailing his toes in the water. (He had his Mummy's leave to paddle, or else he would never have done it, because he was a man of infinite-resource-and-sagacity.)

Then the Whale opened his mouth back and back and back till it nearly touched his tail, and he swallowed the shipwrecked Mariner, and the raft he was sitting on, and his blue canvas breeches, and the suspenders (which you must not forget), and the jack-knife—He swallowed them all down into his warm, dark, inside cupboards, and then he smacked his lips—so, and turned round three times on his tail.

But as soon as the Mariner, who was a man of infinite-resource-and-sagacity, found himself truly inside the Whale's warm, dark, inside cupboards, he stumped and he jumped and he thumped and he bumped, and he pranced and he danced, and he banged and he clanged, and he hit and he bit, and he leaped and he creeped, and he prowled and he howled, and he hopped and he dropped, and he cried and he sighed, and he crawled and he bawled, and he stepped and he leapt, and he danced hornpipes where he shouldn't, and the Whale felt most unhappy indeed. (Have you forgotten the suspenders?)

So he said to the 'Stute Fish, "This man is very nubbly, and besides he is making me hiccup. What shall I do?"

"Tell him to come out," said the 'Stute Fish.

So the Whale called down his throat to the shipwrecked Mariner, "Come out and behave yourself. I've got the hiccups."

"Nay, nay!" said the Mariner. "Not so, but far otherwise. Take me to my natal-shore and the white-cliffs-of-Albion, and I'll think about it." And he began to dance more than ever.

So the Whale swam and swam, with both flippers and his tail, as hard as he could for the hiccups; and at last he saw the Mariner's natal-shore and the white-cliffs-of-Albion, and he rushed half-way up the beach, and opened his mouth wide and wide and wide, and said, "Change here for Winchester, Ashuelot, Nashua, Keene, and stations on the Fitchburg Road"; and just as he said "Fitch" the Mariner walked out of his mouth. But while the Whale had been swimming, the Mariner, who was indeed a person of infinite-resource-and-sagacity, had taken his jack-knife and cut up the raft into a little square grating all running criss-cross, and he had tied it firm with his suspenders (now you know why you were not to forget the suspenders!), and he dragged that grating good and tight into the Whale's throat, and there it stuck! Then he recited the following Sloka, which, as you have not heard it, I will now proceed to relate—

> *By means of a grating*
> *I have stopped your ating.*

For the Mariner he was also an Hi-ber-ni-an. And he stepped out on the shingle, and went home to his Mother, who had given him leave to trail his toes in the water; and he married and lived happily ever afterward. So did the Whale. But from that day on, the grating in his throat, which he could neither cough up nor swallow down, prevented him eating anything except very, very small fish; and that is the reason why whales nowadays never eat men or boys or little girls.

The small 'Stute Fish went and hid himself in the mud under the Doorsills of the Equator. He was afraid that the Whale might be angry with him.

The Sailor took the jack-knife home. He was wearing the blue canvas breeches when he walked out on the shingle. The suspenders were left behind, you see, to tie the grating with; and that is the end of that tale.

> *When the cabin port-holes are dark and green*
> *   Because of the seas outside;*
> *When the ship goes wop (with a wiggle between)*
> *   And the trunks begin to slide;*
> *When the Nursey lies on the floor in a heap,*
> *And the Mummy tells you to let her sleep,*
> *And you aren't waked or washed or dressed,*
> *Why, then you will know (if you haven't guessed)*
> *You're "Fifty North and Forty West"!*

THE ELEPHANT'S CHILD

 n the High and Far-Off Times the Elephant, O Best Beloved, had no trunk. He had only a blackish, bulgy nose, as big as a boot, that he could wriggle about from side to side; but he couln't pick up things with it. But there was one Elephant— a new Elephant—an Elephant's Child—who was full of 'satiable curiosity, and that means he asked ever so may questions. And he lived in Africa, and he filled all Africa with his 'satiable curiosities. He asked his tall aunt, the Ostrich, why her tail-feathers grew just so, and his tall aunt the Ostrich spanked him with her hard, hard claw. He asked his tall uncle, the Giraffe, what made his skin spotty, and his tall uncle, the Giraffe, spanked him with his hard, hard hoof. And still he was full of 'satiable curiosity! He asked his broad aunt, the Hippopotamus, why her eyes were red, and his broad aunt, the Hippopotamus, spanked him with her broad, broad hoof; and he asked his hairy uncle, the Baboon, why melons tasted just so, and his hairy uncle, the Baboon, spanked him with his hairy, hairy paw. And still he was full of 'satiable curiosity! He asked questions about everything that he saw, or heard, or felt, or smelt, or touched, and all his uncles and his aunts spanked him. And still he was full of 'satiable curiosity!

One fine morning in the middle of the Precession of the Equinoxes this 'satiable Elephant's Child asked a new fine question that he had never asked before. He asked, "What does the Crocodile have for dinner?" Then everybody said, "Hush!" in a loud and dretful tone, and they spanked him immediately and directly, without stopping, for a long time.

By and by, when that was finished, he came upon Kolokolo Bird sitting in the middle of a wait-a-bit thorn-bush, and he said, "My father has spanked me, and my mother has spanked; all my aunts and uncles have spanked me for my 'satiable curiosity; and still I want to know what the Crocodile has for dinner!"

Then Kolokolo Bird said, with a mournful cry, "Go to the banks of the great gray-green, greasy Limpopo River, all set about with fever-trees, and find out."

That very next morning, when there was nothing left of the Equinoxes, because the Precession had preceded according to precedent, this 'satiable Elephant's Child took a hundred pounds of bananas (the little short red kind), and a hundred pounds of sugar-cane (the long purple kind), and seventeen melons (the greeny-crackly kinds), and said to all his dear families, "Good-bye. I am going to the great gray-green, greasy Limpopo River, all set about with fever-trees, to find out what the Crocodile has for dinner." And they all spanked him once more for luck, though he asked them most politely to stop.

Then he went away, a little warm, but not at all astonished, eating melons, and throwing the rind about, because he could not pick it up.

He went from Graham's Town to Kimberley, and from Kimberley to Khama's Country, and from Khama's Country he went east by north, eating melons all the time, till at last he came to the banks of the great gray-green, greasy Limpopo River, all set about with fever-trees, precisely as Kolokolo Bird had said.

Now you must know and understand, O Best Beloved, that till that very week, and day, and hour, and minute, this 'satiable Elephant's Child had never seen a Crocodile, and did not know what one was like. It was all his 'satiable curiosity.

The first thing that he found was a Bi-Colored-Python-Rock-Snake curled round a rock.

"'Scuse me," said the Elephant's Child most politely, "but have you seen such a thing as a Crococile in these promiscous parts?"

"Have I seen a Crocodile?" said the Bi-Colored-Python-Rock-Snake, in a voice of dretful scorn. "What will you ask me next?"

"'Scuse me," said the Elephant's Child, "but could you kindly tell me what he has for dinner?"

Then the Bi-Colored-Python-Rock-Snake uncoiled himself very quickly from the rock, and spanked the Elephant's Child with his scalesome, flailsome tail.

"That is odd," said the Elephant's Child, "because my father and my mother, and my uncle and my aunt, not to mention my other aunt, the Hippopotamus, and my other uncle, the Baboon, have all spanked me for my 'satiable curiosity—and I suppose this is the same thing."

So he said good-bye very politely to the Bi-Colored-Python-Rock-Snake, and helped to coil him up on the rock again, and went on, a little warm, but not at all astonished, eating melons, and throwing the rind about, because he could not pick it up, till he trod on what he thought was a log of wood at the very edge of the great gray-green Limpopo River, all set about with fever-trees.

But it was really the Crocodile, O Best Beloved, and the Crocodile winked one eye— like this!

"'Scuse me," said the Elephant's Child most politely, "but do you happen to have seen a crocodile in these promiscuous parts?"

Then the Crocodile winked the other eye, and lifted half his tail out of the mud; and the Elephant's Child stepped back most politely, because he did not wish to be spanked again.

"Come hither, Little One," said the Crocodile. "Why do you ask such things?"

"'Scuse me," said the Elephant's Child most politely, "but my father has spanked me, my mother has spanked me, not to mention my tall aunt, the Ostrich, and my tall uncle, the Giraffe, who can kick ever so hard, as well as my broad aunt the Hippopotamus, and my hairy uncle, the Baboon, and including the Bi-Colored-Python-Rock-Snake, with the scalesome, flailsome tail, just up the bank, who spanks harder than any of them; and so, if it's quite all the same to you, I don't want to be spanked any more."

"Come hither, Little One," said the Crocodile, "for I am the Crocodile," and he wept crocodile-tears to show it was quite true.

Then the Elephant's Child grew all breathless, and panted, and kneeled down on the banks and said, "You are the very person I have been looking for all these long days. Will you please tell me what you have for dinner?"

"Come hither, Little One," said the Crocodile, "and I'll whisper."

Then the Elephant's Child put his head down close to the Crocodile's musky, tusky mouth, and the Crocodile caught him by his little nose, which up to that very week, day, hour, and minute, had been no bigger than a boot, though much more useful.

"I think," said the Crocodile—and he said it between his teeth, like this—"I think today I will begin with Elephant's Child!"

At this, O Best Beloved, the Elephant's Child was much annoyed, and he said speaking through this nose, like this: "Led go! You are hurtig be!"

Then the Bi-Colored-Python-Rock-Snake scuffled down from the bank and said, "My young friend, if you do not now, immediately and instantly, pull as hard as ever you can, it is my opinion that your acquaintance in the large-pattern leather ulster"—and by this he meant the Crocodile—"will jerk you into yonder limpid stream before you can say Jack Robinson."

This is the way Bi-Colored-Python-Rock-Snakes always talk.

Then the Elephant's Child sat back on his little haunches, and pulled, and pulled, and pulled, and his nose began to stretch. And the Crocodile floundered into the water, making it all creamy with great sweeps of his tail, and he pulled, and pulled, and pulled.

And the Elephant's Child's nose kept on stretching; and the Elephant's Child spread all his little four legs and pulled, and pulled, and pulled, and his nose kept on stretching; and the Crocodile threshed his tail like an oar, and he pulled, and pulled, and pulled, and at each pull the Elephant's Child's nose grew longer and longer—and it hurt him hijjus!

Then the Elephant's Child felt his legs slipping, and he said through his nose, which was now nearly five feet long, "This is too butch for be!"

Then the Bi-Colored-Python-Rock-Snake came down from the bank, and knotted himself in a double-clove hitch round the Elephant's Child's hind-legs, and said, "Rash and inexperienced traveler, we will now seriously devote ourselves to a little high tension, because if we do not, it is my impression that yonder self-propelling man-of-war with the armour-plated upper deck"—and by this, O Best Beloved, he meant the Crocodile—"will permanently vitiate your future career."

That is the way all Bi-Colored-Python-Rock-Snakes always talk.

So he pulled, and the Elephant's Child pulled, and the Crocodile pulled; but the Elephant's Child and the Bi-Colored-Python-Rock-Snake pulled hardest; and at last the Crocodile let go of the Elephant's Child's nose with a plop that you could hear all up and down the Limpopo.

Then the Elephant's Child sat down most hard and sudden; but first he was careful to say "Thank you" to the Bi-Colored-Python-Rock-Snake; and next he was kind to his poor pulled nose, and wrapped it all up in cool banana leaves, and hung it in the great gray-green, greasy Limpopo to cool.

THE SING-SONG OF
OLD MAN KANGAROO

ot always was the Kangaroo as now we do behold him, but a Different Animal with four short legs. He was gray and he was woolly, and his pride was inordinate: he danced on an outcrop in the middle of Australia, and he went to the Little God Nqua.

He went to Nqua at six before breakfast, saying, "Make me different from all other animals by five this afternoon."

Up jumped Nqua from his seat on the sand-flat and shouted, "Go away!"

He was gray and he was woolly, and his pride was inordinate: he danced on a rock ledge in the middle of Australia, and he went to the Middle God Nquing.

He went to Nquing at eight before breakfast, saying, "Make me different from all other animals; make me, also, wonderfully popular by five this afternoon."

Up jumped Nquing from his burrow in the spinifex and shouted, "Go away!"

He was gray and he was woolly, and his pride was inordinate: he danced on a sand-bank in the middle of Australia, and he went to the Big God Nquong.

He went to Nquong at ten before dinner-time saying, "Make me different from all other animals; make me popular and wonderfully run after by five this afternoon."

Up jumped Nquong from his bath in the salt-pan and shouted, "Yes, I will!"

Nquong called Dingo—Yellow-Dog Dingo—always hungry, dusty in the sunshine, and showed him Kangaroo. Nquong said, "Dingo! Wake up, Dingo! Do you see that gentleman dancing on an ashpit? He wants to be popular and very truly run after. Dingo, make him so!"

Up jumped Dingo—Yellow-Dog Dingo—and said, "What, that cat-rabbit?"

Off rang Dingo—Yellow-Dog Dingo—hungry and grinning—ran after Kangaroo.

Off went the proud Kangaroo on his four little legs like a bunny.

This, O Beloved of mine, ends the first part of the tale!

He ran through the desert; he ran through the mountains; he ran through the salt-pans; he ran through the reed-beds; he ran till his front legs ached.

He had to!

Still ran Dingo—Yellow-Dog Dingo—always hungry, grinning like a rat-trap, never getting nearer, never getting farther,—ran after Kangaroo.

He had to!

Still ran Kangaroo—Old Man Kangaroo. He ran through the ti-trees; he ran through the mulga; he ran through the long grass; he ran through the short grass; he ran through the Tropics of Capricorn and Cancer; he ran till his hind legs ached.

He had to!

Still ran Dingo—Yellow-Dog Dingo—hungrier and hungrier, grinning like a horse-collar, never getting nearer, never getting farther; and they came to the Wollgong River.

Now, there wasn't any bridge, and there wasn't any ferry-boat, and Kangaroo didn't know how to get over; so he stood on his legs and hopped.

He had to!

He hopped through the Flinders; he hopped through the Cinders; he hopped through the deserts in the middle of Australia. He hopped like a Kangaroo.

First he hopped one yard; then he hopped three yards; then he hopped five yards; his legs growing stronger; his legs growing longer. He hadn't any time for rest or refreshment, and he wanted them very much.

Still ran Dingo—Yellow-Dog Dingo—very much bewildered, very much hungry, and wondering what in the world or out of it made Old Man Kangaroo hop.

For he hopped like a cricket; like a pea in a saucepan; or a new rubber ball on a nursery floor.

He had to!

He tucked up his front legs; he hopped on his hind legs; he stuck out his tail for a balance-weight behind him; and he hopped through the Darling Downs.

He had to!

Still ran Dingo—Tired-Dog Dingo—hungrier and hungrier, very much bewildered, and wondering when in the world or out of it would Old Man Kangaroo stop.

Then came Nquong from his bath in the salt-pans, and said, "It's five o'clock."

Down sat Dingo—Poor-Dog Dingo—always hungry, dusty in the sunshine; hung out his tongue and howled.

Down sat Kangaroo—Old Man Kangaroo—stuck out his tail like a milking-stool behind him, and said, "Thank goodness that's finished!"

Then said Nquong, who is always a gentleman, "Why aren't you grateful to Yellow-Dog Dingo? Why don't you thank him for all he has done for you?"

Then said the Kangaroo—Tired Old Kangarooo—"He's chased me out of the homes of my childhood; he's chased me out of my regular meal-times; he's altered my shape so I'll never get it back; and he's played Old Scratch with my legs."

Then said Nquong, "Perhaps I'm mistaken, but didn't you ask me to make you different from all other animals, as well as to make you very truly sought after? And now it is five o'clock."

"Yes," said Kangaroo. "I wish that I hadn't. I thought you would do it by charms and incantations, but this is a practical joke."

"Joke!" said Nquong, from his bath in the blue gums. "Say that again and I'll whistle up Dingo and run your hind legs off."

"No," said the Kangaroo. "I must apologize. Legs are legs, and you needn't alter 'em so far as I am concerned. I only meant to explain to your Lordliness that I've had nothing to eat since morning, and I'm very empty indeed."

"Yes," said Dingo—Yellow-Dog Dingo—"I am just in the same situation. I've made him different from all other animals; but what may I have for my tea?"

Then said Nquong from this bath in the salt-pan, "Come and ask me about it tomorrow, because I'm going to wash."

So they were left in the middle of Australia, Old Man Kangaroo and Yellow-Dog Dingo, and each said, "That's your fault."

This is the mouth-filling song:

Of the race that was run by a Boomer,
Run in a single burst—only event of its kind—
Started by Big God Nquong from Warrigaborrigarooma,
Old Man Kangaroo first: Yellow-Dog Dingo behind.

Kangaroo bounded away,
His back-legs working like pistons—
Bounded from morning till dark,
Twenty-five feet to a bound.
Yellow-Dog Dingo lay
Like a yellow cloud in the distance—
Much too busy to bark.
My! but they covered the ground!

Nobody knows where they went,
Or followed the track that they flew in,
For that Continent
Hadn't been given a name.
They ran thirty degrees,
From Torres Straits to the Leeuwin
(Look at the Atlas, please),
And they ran back as they came.

S'posing you could trot
From Adelaide to the Pacific,
For an afternoon's run—
Half what these gentlemen did—
You would feel rather hot,
But your legs would develop terrific—
Yes, my importunate son,
You'd be a Marvelous Kid!

MYTHOLOGY

RETOLD BY THOMAS BULFINCH

The myths created by the ancient Greeks and Romans, stories of gods and goddesses, monsters and magic spells, helped them understand the numerous mysteries of the physical and spiritual world. These tales reflect all of man's enduring emotions—jealousy, fear, compassion, devotion—and they still resonate for us today, although science now provides us with many answers. Most of all, they are rich and fascinating stories, pitting good against evil with lots of suspense along the way. Here are a few tales of mythical beings, and the gods and humans who interact with them.

THESEUS

heseus was the son of Aegeus, king of Athens, and Aethra, daughter of the king of Troezen. He was brought up at Troezen, and when he arrived at manhood he was to proceed to Athens and present himself to his father. Aegeus on parting from Aethra, before the birth of his son, placed his sword and shoes under a large stone and directed her to send his son to him when he became strong enough to roll away the stone and take them from under it. When she thought the time had come, his mother led Theseus to the stone, and he removed it with ease and took the sword and shoes. As the roads were infested with robbers, his grandfather pressed him earnestly to take the shorter and safer way to his father's country—by sea; but the youth, feeling in himself the spirit and the soul of a hero, and eager to signalize himself like Hercules, with whose fame all Greece then rang, by destroying the evil-doers and monsters that oppressed the country, determined on the more perilous and adventurous journey by land.

His first day's journey brought him to Epidaurus, where dwelt a man named Periphetes, a son of Vulcan. This ferocious savage always went armed with a club of iron, and all travellers stood in terror of his violence. When he saw Theseus approach he assailed him, but speedily fell beneath the blows of the young hero, who took possession of his club and bore it afterwards as a memorial of his first victory.

Several similar contests with the petty tyrants and marauders of the country followed, in all of which Theseus was victorious. One of these evil-doers was called Procrustes, or the Stretcher. He had an iron bedstead, on which he used to tie all travelers who fell into his hands. If they were shorter than the bed, he stretched their limbs to make them fit it; if they were longer than the bed, he lopped off a portion. Theseus served him as he had served others.

Having overcome all the perils of the road, Theseus at length reached Athens, where new dangers awaited him. Medea, the sorceress, who had fled from Corinth after her separation from Jason, had become the wife of Aegeus, the father of Theseus. Knowing by her arts who he was, and fearing the loss of her influence with her husband if Theseus should be acknowledged as his son, she filled the mind of Aegeus with suspicions of the young stranger, and induced him to present him a cup of poison; but at the moment when Theseus stepped forward to take it, the sight of the sword which he wore revealed to his father who he was, and prevented the fatal draught. Medea, detected in her arts, fled once more from the deserved punishment, and arrived in Asia, where the country afterwards called Medea received its name from her. Theseus was acknowledged by his father, and declared his successor.

The Athenians were at that time in deep affliction, on account of the tribute which they were forced to pay to Minos, king of Crete. This tribute consisted of seven youths and seven maidens, who were sent every year to be devoured by the Minotaur, a monster with a bull's body and a human head. It was exceedingly strong and fierce, and was kept in a labyrinth constructed by Daedalus, so artfully contrived that whoever was enclosed in it could by no means find his way out unassisted. Here the Minotaur roamed, and was fed with human victims.

Theseus resolved to deliver his countrymen from this calamity, or to die in the attempt. Accordingly, when the time of sending off the tribute came, and the youths and the maidens were, according to custom, drawn by lot to be sent, he offered himself as one of the victims, in spite of the entreaties by his father.

THE GOLDEN FLEECE

In very ancient times there lived in Thessaly a king and queen named Athamas and Nephele. They had two children, a boy and a girl. After a time, Athamas grew indifferent to his wife, put her away, and took another. Nephele suspected danger to her children from the influence of the step-mother, and took measures to send them out of her reach. Mercury assisted her, and gave her a ram with a golden fleece, on which she set the two children, trusting that the ram would convey them to a place of safety.

The ram vaulted into the air with the children on his back, taking his course to the East, until he got to the strait that divides Europe and Asia. At that moment, the girl, whose name was Helle, fell from his back into the sea, which then became known as the Hellespont in her memory. The ram continued his journey until he reached the kingdom of Colchis, on the eastern shore of the Black Sea, where he safely landed the boy, Phryxus, who was hospitably received by Aetes, king of the country. Phryxus sacrificed the ram to

Jupiter and gave the golden fleece to Aetes, who placed it in a consecrated grove under the care of a sleepless dragon.

There was another kingdom in Thessaly near to that of Athamas and ruled over by a relative of his. The king Aeson, being tired of the cares of government, surrendered his crown to his brother Pelias on condition that he should hold it only until Aeson's son, Jason, grew up. When Jason reached adulthood and came to demand the crown from his uncle, Pelias pretended to be willing to yield it, but at the same time suggested to the young man the glorious adventure of going in quest of the Golden Fleece, which was known to be in the kingdom of Colchis, and was, said Pelias, the rightful property of their family. Jason was pleased with the thought and began preparing for the expedition.

He asked that a vessel be built for him large enough to contain 50 men—a huge undertaking at the time. When this was done, it was named "Argo," after Argus who built it. Jason sent an invitation to all the adventurous young men of Greece, and soon found himself at the head of a band of bold youths, many of whom afterwards were renowned among the heroes of Greece. They called themselves "Argonauts."

The Argo, with her crew, left the shores of Thessaly and having touched the Island of Lemnos, crossed to Mysia and then to Thrace. Here they found the sage Phineus, and from him received instruction as to their future course. It seems the entrance of the Euxine Sea was impeded by two small, rocky islands, which floated on the surface, and in their tossings and heavings, occasionally came together, crushing and grinding to bits any object that might be caught between them. Phineus instructed the Argonauts how to pass this dangerous strait. When they reached the islands they let go a dove, which took her way between the rocks, and passed in safety, only losing some feathers of her tail as the islands slammed together. Jason and his men seized the moment that the islands parted again, plied their oars with vigor, and passed safely through, though the islands closed behind them, grazing their stern. Soon they reached Colchis.

Jason made known his message to the Colchian king, Aetes, who consented to give up the Golden Fleece if Jason would yoke to the plough two fire-breathing bulls and sow the teeth of a dragon that Cadmus had slain. It was well known that from the teeth, a crop of armed men would spring up, who would turn their weapons against their producer. Jason accepted the conditions. Luckily, he possessed a charm from Medea, his fiancee and a powerful sorceress, to help him withstand danger to come.

At the appointed time, the people assembled at the grove of Mars, and the king assumed his royal seat, while the multitude covered the hillsides. The brazen-footed bulls rushed in, breathing fire from their nostrils that burned the grass and trees as they passed. The sound was like the roar of a furnace, and the smoke billowed forth. Jason advanced boldly to meet them. His friends, the chosen heroes of Greece, trembled to behold him. Regardless of the burning breath, he soothed the bulls' rage with his voice, patted their necks with a fearless hand, and adroitly slipped over them the yoke, compelling them to drag the plough. The Colchians were amazed; the Greeks shouted for joy.

Jason proceeded to sow the dragon's teeth and plough them in. And soon the crop of armed men sprang up. No sooner had they reached the surface than they brandished their weapons and rushed upon Jason. The Greeks trembled for their hero, and even she who had provided him a way of safety and taught him how to use it, Medea herself, grew pale with fear. Jason for a time kept his assailants at bay with his sword and shield, until, finding their numbers overwhelming, he resorted to the charm which Medea had taught him. He seized a stone and threw it in the midst of his foes. They immediately turned the arms against one another, and soon there was not one of the dragon's brood left alive. The Greeks embraced their hero, and Medea, if she had dared, would have embraced him too.

It remained to lull to sleep the dragon that guarded the fleece, and this was done by scattering over him a few drops of a preparation which Medea had supplied. At the smell, he relaxed his rage, stood for a moment motionless, then shut his great, round eyes and turned over on his side, fast asleep.

Jason seized the Golden Fleece and, with his friends and Medea, hastened to the vessel before Aetes could stop them. They made their way back to Thessaly, and Jason delivered the fleece to Pelias, and dedicated the Argo to Neptune, the god of the sea. What became of the Fleece afterward we do not know, but perhaps it was found after all, like many other golden prizes, not worth the trouble it had caused to procure it.

ECHO AND NARCISSUS

E cho was a beautiful nymph, fond of the woods and hills, where she devoted herself to woodland sports. She was a favorite of Diana, and attended her in the chase. But Echo had one failing; she was fond of talking, and whether in chat or argument, would have the last word. One day Juno was seeking her husband, who, she had reason to fear, was amusing himself among the nymphs. Echo by her talk contrived to detain the goddess till the nymphs made their escape. When Juno discovered the trick, she passed sentence upon Echo in these words: "You shall forfeit the use of that tongue with which you have cheated me, except for that one purpose you are so fond of—reply. You shall still have the last word, but no power to speak the first."

Later, the nymph saw Narcissus, a beautiful youth, as he pursued deer upon the mountains. She fell in love with him instantly, and followed him. Oh, how she longed to address him, converse with him, and win his love! But it was not in her power. She waited with impatience for him to speak first, and she had her answer ready.

Being separated from his companions, the youth shouted aloud, "Who's here?" Echo replied, "Here."

Narcissus looked around, but seeing no one called out, "Come." Echo answered, "Come."

As no one came, Narcissus called again, "Why do you shun me?" Echo asked the same question.

"Let us join one another," said the youth. The maid answered with all her heart in the same words, and hastened to the spot, ready to throw her arms about his neck. He started back, exclaiming, "Hands off! I would rather die than you should have me!"

"Have me!" she said, but it was all in vain. He left her, and she went to hide her blushes in the recesses of the woods. From that time forth she lived in caves and among mountain cliffs. Her form faded with grief, till at last all her flesh shrank away. Her bones were changed into rocks and there was nothing left of her but her voice. With that, she is still ready to reply to anyone who calls her, and she keeps up her old habit of having the last word.

Narcissus's cruelty to Echo was matched by his cruelty to all of the nymphs. One day a maiden who had in vain endeavored to attract him uttered a prayer that he might some time feel what it was to love someone and receive no love in return. The avenging goddess Diana heard and granted her prayer.

There was a clear fountain, with water like silver, to which the shepherds never drove their flocks. No mountain goats, no beasts of the forest ever disturbed it; nor was it defaced with fallen leaves or branches. The grass grew fresh around it, and the rocks sheltered it from the sun. Hither came one day the youth, fatigued with hunting, heated and thirsty. He stooped down to drink, and saw his own image in the water; he thought it was some beautiful water spirit living in the fountain. He stood gazing with admiration at those bright eyes, those locks curled like the locks of Bacchus or Apollo, the rounded cheeks, the ivory neck, the parted lips, and the glow of health and exercise over all. He fell in love with himself. He brought his lips near to take a kiss; he plunged his arms in to embrace the beloved object. It fled at the touch, but returned again after a moment and renewed the fascination. He couldn't tear himself away; he lost all thought of food or rest, while he hovered over the brink of he fountain gazing upon his own image.

He talked with the supposed spirit: "Why, beautiful being, do you shun me? Sure my face is not one to repel you. The nymphs love me, and you yourself look not indifferent upon me. When I stretch forth my arms you do the same; and you smile upon me and answer my beckonings with the like." His tears fell into the water and disturbed the image. As he saw it depart, he exclaimed, "Stay, I entreat you! Let me at least gaze upon you, if I may not touch you."

With this, and much more of the same kind, he cherished the flame that consumed him, so that by degrees he lost his color, his vigor, and the beauty which formerly had so charmed the nymph Echo. She kept near him, however, and when he exclaimed, "Alas! Alas!" she answered him with the same words. He pined away and died; and when his shade passed the Stygian river, it leaned over the boat to catch a look at itself in the waters. The nymphs mourned for Narcissus, especially the water nymphs. They prepared a funeral pile and would have burned the body, but it was nowhere to be found. In its place there was a flower, purple within and surrounded by white leaves, which bears the name and preserves the memory of Narcissus.

DAEDALUS

aedalus was a clever inventor, but he and his son were prisoners of King Minos, detained on the island of Crete. Daedalus contrived to make his escape, but could not leave the island by sea, as the king kept strict watch on all the vessels, and permitted none to sail without being thoroughly searched.

"Minos may control the land and sea," said Daedalus, "but not the regions of the air. I will try that way." So he set to work to make wings for himself and his young son, Icarus. He wrought feathers together, beginning with the smallest and adding larger, so as to form an increasing surface. The larger ones he secured with thread and the smaller with wax, and gave the whole a gentle curvature like the wings of a bird. Icarus, the boy, stood and looked on, sometimes running to gather up the feathers which the wind had blown away, and then handling the wax and working it over with his fingers, by his play impeding his father in his labors.

When at last the work was done, the artists, waving his wings, found himself buoyed upward, and hung suspended, poising himself on the beaten air. He next equipped his son in the same manner, and taught him how to fly, as a bird tempts her young ones from the lofty nest into the air.

When all was prepared for flight he said, "Icarus, my son, I charge you to keep at a moderate height, for if you fly too low the damp will clog your wings, and if too high the heat will melt them. Keep near me and you will be safe." While he gave these instructions and fitted the wings to his shoulders, the face of the father was wet with tears and his hands trembled. He kissed the boy, not knowing that it was for the last time. Then rising on his wings, he flew off, encouraging Icarus to follow, and looking back from his own flight to see how his son managed his wings.

As they flew, the ploughman stopped his work to gaze, and the shepherd leaned on his staff and watched them, astonished at the sight and thinking they were gods who could thus conquer the air.

They passed the islands of Samos and Delos on the left and Lebynthos on the right, when the boy, exulting in his flight, began to leave the guidance of his father and soar upward as if to reach heaven. The nearness of the blazing sun softened the wax which held the feathers together, and they came off. He fluttered with his arms, but no feathers remained to hold him in the air. With cries to his father, he plunged into the blue waters of the sea, now known as the Sea of Icarus. His father cried, "Icarus, Icarus, where are you?" At last he saw the feathers floating on the water and, bitterly lamenting his own arts, he buried the body and called the land Icaria in memory of his child. Daedalus arrived safely in Sicily, where he built a temple to Apollo, and hung up his wings, an offering to the gods.

Daedalus was so proud of his inventions that he could not bear the idea of a rival. His sister had placed her son Perdix under his charge, to be taught the mechanical arts. Perdix was an apt scholar: Walking on the beach he picked up the spine of a fish. Imitating it, he took a piece of iron and notched its edge, and thus invented the saw. He put two pieces of iron together, connecting them at one end with a rivet, and sharpening the other ends, and made a compass.

Daedalus was so envious of his nephew's cleverness that one day, when they were on top of a high tower, he pushed Perdix off. But the goddess Minerva, who favored ingenuity, saw him falling and arrested his fate by changing him into a bird called the Partridge. This bird does not build its nest in the trees, nor take lofty flights, but nestles in the hedges and, mindful of Perdix's fall, avoids high places.

Bulfinch's Mythology. New York: Crown Publishers, 1979.
    Other Editions:
    Bulfinch's Mythology. New York: Random House, 1993.

FOLK TALES AND FANTASIES

THE TALES OF
THE ARABIAN NIGHTS

AS RETOLD BY ANDREW LANG

The Tales of the Arabian Nights *is a collection of fairy tales from Middle and Far Eastern countries. These stories were told through the years by people from Persia, Asia, and Arabia. Some of the tales are now collected here for you to enjoy.*

THE STORY OF ALI COGIA, MERCHANT OF BAGDAD

Ali Cogia is a merchant in Bagdad. He decides to make a pilgrimmage to Mecca one day, and decides to hide a thousand pieces of gold in a vase under some olives and leaves the vase with a friend for safekeeping while he is gone.

fter some thought, Ali Cogia hit upon a plan which seemed a safe one. He took a large vase, and placing the money in the bottom of it, filled up the rest with olives. After corking the vase tightly down, he carried it to one of his friends, a merchant like himself, and said to him: "My brother, you have probably heard that I am starting with a caravan in a few days for Mecca. I have come to ask whether you would do me the favor to keep this vase of olives for me until I come back?"

The merchant replied readily, "Look, this is the key of my shop: take it, and put the vase wherever you like. I promise that you shall find it in the same place on your return."

A few days later, Ali Cogia mounted the camel that he had laden with merchandise, joined the caravan, and arrived in due time at Mecca. Like the other pilgrims he visited the sacred Mosque, and after all his religious duties were performed, he set out his goods to the best advantage, hoping to gain some customers among the passers-by.

Very soon two merchants stopped before the pile, and when they had turned it over, one said to the other: "If this man was wise he would take these things to Cairo, where he would get a much better price than he is likely to do here."

Ali Cogia heard the words, and lost no time in following the advice. He packed up his wares, and instead of returning to Bagdad, joined a caravan that was going to Cairo. The results of the journey gladdened his heart. He sold off everything almost directly, and bought a stock of Egyptian curiosities, which he intended selling at Damascus; but as the caravan with which he would have to travel would not be starting for another six weeks, he took advantage of the delay to visit the Pyramids, and some of the cities along the banks of the Nile.

Now the attractions of Damascus so fascinated the worthy Ali, that he could hardly tear himself away, but at length he remembered that he had a home in Bagdad, meaning to return by way of Aleppo, and after he had crossed the Euphrates, to follow the course of the Tigris.

But when he reached Mossoul, Ali had made such friends with some Persian merchants, that they persuaded him to accompany them to their native land, and even as far as India, and as it came to passs that seven years had slipped by since he had left Bagdad, and during all that time the friend with whom he had left the vase of olives had never once thought of him or of it. In fact, it was only a month before Ali Cogia's actual return that the affair came into his head at all, owing to his wife's remarking one day, that it was a long time since she had eaten any olives, and would like some.

"That reminds me," said the husband, "that before Ali Cogia went to Mecca seven years ago, he left a vase of olives in my care. But really by this time he must be dead, and there is no reason we should not eat the olives if we like. Give me a light, and I will fetch them and see how they taste."

"My husband," answered the wife, "beware, I pray, of your doing anything so base! Supposing seven years have passed without any news of Ali Cogia, he need not be dead for all that, and may come back any day. How shameful it would be to have to confess that you had betrayed your trust and broken the seal of the vase! Pay no attention to my idle words, I really have no desire for olives now. And probably after all this while they are no longer good. I have a presentiment that Ali Cogia will return, and what will he think of you? Give it up, I entreat."

The merchant, however, refused to listen to her advice, sensible though it was. He took a light and a dish and went into his shop.

"If you will be so obstinate," said his wife, "I cannot help it; but do not blame me if it turns out ill."

When the merchant opened the vase he found the topmost olives were rotten, and in order to see if the under ones were in better condition he shook some out into the dish. As they fell out a few gold pieces fell out too.

The sight of the money roused all the merchant's greed. He looked into the vase, and saw that all the bottom was filled with gold. He then replaced the olives and returned to his wife.

"My wife," he said, as he entered the room, "you were quite right; the olives are rotten, and I have recorked the vase so well that Ali Cogia will never know it has been touched."

"You would have done better to believe me," replied the wife. "I trust that no harm will come of it."

These words made no more impression on the merchant than the others had done; and he spent the whole night in wondering how he could manage to keep the gold if Ali Cogia should come back and claim his vase. Very early next morning he went out and bought fresh new olives; he then threw away the old ones, took out the gold and hid it, and filled up the vase with the olives he had bought. This done he recorked the vase and put it in the same place where it had been left by Ali Cogia.

A month later Ali Cogia re-entered Bagdad, and as his house was still let he went to an inn; and the following day set out to see his friend the merchant, who received him with open arms and many expressions of surprise. After a few moments given to inquiries Ali Cogia begged the merchant to hand him over the vase that he had taken care of for so long.

"Oh certainly," said he, "I am only glad I could be of use to you in the matter. Here is the key to my shop; you will find the vase in the place where you put it."

Ali Cogia fetched his vase and carried it to his room at the inn, where he opened it. He thrust down his hand, but could feel no money; still he was persuaded it must be there. So he got some plates and vessels from his travelling kit and emptied out the olives. To no purpose. The gold was not there. The poor man was dumb with horror, then, lifting up his hands, he exclaimed, "Can my old friend really have committed such a crime?"

In great haste he went back to the house of the merchant. "My friend," he cried, "you will be astonished to see me again, but I can find nowhere in this vase a thousand pieces of gold that I placed in the bottom under the olives. Perhaps you may have taken a loan of them for your business purposes; if that is so you are most welcome. I will only ask you to give me a receipt, and you can pay the money at your leisure."

The merchant, who had expected something of the sort, had his reply all ready. "Ali Cogia," he said, "when you brought me the vase of olives did I ever touch it? I gave you the key to my shop and you put it yourself where you liked, and did you not find it in exactly the same spot and in the same state? If you placed any gold in it, it must be there still. I know nothing about that; you only told me there were olives. You can believe me or not, but I have not laid a finger on the vase."

Ali Cogia still tried every means to persuade the merchant to admit the truth. "I love peace," he said, "and shall deeply regret having to resort to harsh measures. Once more, think of your reputation. I shall be in despair if you oblige me to call in the aid of the law."

"Ali Cogia," answered the merchant, "you allow that it was a vase of olives you placed in my charge. You fetched it and removed it yourself, and now you tell me it contained a thousand pieces of gold, and that I must restore them to you! Did you ever say anything about them before? Why, I did not even know that the vase had olives in it! You never showed them to me. I wonder you have not demanded pearls or diamonds. Retire, I pray you, lest a crowd should gather in front of my shop."

By this time not only the casual passers-by, but also the neighboring merchants, were standing round, listening to the dispute, and trying every now and then to smoothe matters between them. But at the merchant's last words Ali Cogia resolved to lay the cause of the quarrel before them, and told them the whole story. They heard him to the end, and inquired of the merchant what he had to say.

The accused man admitted that he had kept Ali Cogia's vase in his shop; but he denied having touched it, and swore that as to what it contained he only knew what Ali Cogia had told him, and called them all to witness the insult that had been put upon him.

"You have brought it on yourself," said Ali Cogia, taking him by the arm, "and as you appeal to the law, the law you shall have it! Let us see if you will dare to repeat your story before the Cadi."

Now as a good Mussulman the merchant was forbidden to refuse this choice of a judge, so he accepted the test, and said to Ali Cogia, "Very well; I should like nothing better. We shall soon see which of us is in the right."

So the two men presented themselves before the Cadi, and Ali Cogia again repeated his tale. The Cadi asked what witnesses he had. Ali Cogia replied that he had not taken this precaution, as he had considered the man his friend, and up to that time had always found him honest.

The merchant, on his side, stuck to his story, and offered to swear solemnly that not only had he never stolen the thousand gold pieces, but that he did not even know they were there. The Cadi allowed him to take the oath, and pronounced him innocent.

Ali Cogia, furious at having to suffer such a loss, protested against the verdict, declaring that he would appeal to the Caliph, Haroun-al-Raschid, himself. But the Cadi paid no attention to his threats, and was quite satisfied that he had done what was right.

Judgment being given the merchant returned home triumphant, and Ali Cogia went back to his inn to draw up a petition to the Caliph. The next morning he placed himself on the road along which the Caliph must pass after midday prayer, and stretched out his petition to the officer who walked before the Caliph, whose duty it was to collect such things, and on entering the palace to hand them to his master. There Haroun-al-Raschid studied them carefully.

Knowing this custom, Ali Cogia followed the Caliph into the public hall of the palace, and waited the result. After some time the officer appeared, and told him that the Caliph had read his petition, and had appointed an hour the next morning to give him audience. He then inquired the merchant's address, so that he might be summoned to attend also.

That very evening, the Caliph, with his grand-vizir Giafar, and Mesrour, chief of the eunuchs, all three disguised, as was their habit, went out to take a stroll through the town.

Going down one street, the Caliph's attention was attracted by a noise, and looking through a door which opened into a court he perceived 10 or 12 children, playing in the moonlight. He hid himself in a dark corner, and watched them.

"Let us play at being the Cadi," said the brightest and quickest of them all; "I will be the Cadi. Bring before me Ali Cogia, and the merchant who robbed him of the thousand pieces of gold."

The boy's words recalled to the Caliph the petition he had read that morning, and he waited with interest to see what the children would do.

The proposal was hailed with joy by the other children, who had heard a great deal of talk about the matter, and they quickly settled the part each one was to play. The Cadi took his seat gravely, and an officer introduced first Ali Cogia, the plaintiff, and then the merchant who was the defendant.

Ali Cogia made a low bow, and pleaded his cause point by point; concluding by imploring the Cadi not to inflict on him such a heavy loss.

The Cadi having heard his case, turned to the merchant, and inquired why he had not repaid Ali Cogia the sum in question.

The false merchant repeated the reasons that the real merchant had given to the Cadi of Bagdad, and also offered to swear that he had told the truth.

"Stop a moment!" said the little Cadi, "before we come to oaths, I should like to examine the vase with the olives. Ali Cogia," he added, "have you got the vase with you?" and finding he had not, the Cadi continued, "go and get it and bring it to me."

So Ali Cogia disappeared for an instant, and then pretended to lay a vase at the feet of the Cadi, declaring it was his vase, which he had given to the accused for safe custody; and in order to be quite correct, the Cadi asked the merchant if he recognized it as the same vase. By his silence the merchant admitted the fact, and the Cadi then commanded to have the vase opened. Ali Cogia made a movement as if he was taking off the lid, and the little Cadi on his part made a pretense of peering into the vase.

"What beautiful olives!" he said, "I should like to taste one," and pretending to put one in his mouth, he added, "they are excellent!"

"But," he went on, "it seems to me odd that olives seven years old should be as good as that! Send for some dealers in olives, and let us hear what they say!"

Two children were presented to him as olive merchants, and the Cadi addressed them. "Tell me," he said, "how long can olives be kept so as to be pleasant eating?"

"My lord," replied the merchants, "however much care is taken to preserve them, they never last beyond the third year. They lose both taste and color, and are only fit to be thrown away."

"If that is so," answered the little Cadi, "examine this vase, and tell me how long the olives have been in it."

The olive merchants pretended to examine the olives and taste them; then reported to the Cadi that they were fresh and good.

"You are mistaken," said he, "Ali Cogia declares he put them in that vase seven years ago."

"My lord," returned the olive merchants, "we can assure you that the olives are those of the present year. And if you consult all the merchants in Bagdad you will not find one to give a contrary opinion."

The accused merchant opened his mouth as if to protest, but the Cadi gave him no time. "Be silent," he said, "you are a thief. Take him away and hang him." So the game ended, the children clapping their hands in applause, and leading the criminal away to be hanged.

THE STORY OF THE FIRST CALENDER, SON OF A KING

A young prince, an exile in Bagdad, relates the misfortunes of his family and kingdom. His narrow escape from death has turned him into a peaceful wanderer.

n order, madam, to explain how I came to lose my right eye, and to wear the dress of a Calender, you must first know that I am the son of a king. My father's only brother reigned over the neighboring country, and had two children, a daughter and a son, who were of the same age as myself.

As I grew up, and was allowed more liberty, I went every year to pay a visit to my uncle's court, and usually stayed there about two months. In his way my cousin and I became very intimate, and were much attached to each other. The very last time I saw him he seemed more delighted to see me than ever, and gave a great feast in my honor. When we had finished eating, he said to me, "My cousin, you would never guess what I have been doing since your last visit to us! Directly after your departure I set a number of men to work on a building after my own design. It is now completed, and ready to be lived in. I should like to show it to you, but you must first swear two things: to be faithful to me, and to keep my secret."

Of course I did not dream of refusing him anything he asked, and gave the promise without the least hesitation. He then bade me wait an instant, and vanished, returning in a few moments with a richly dressed lady of great beauty, but as he did not tell me her name, I thought it was better not to inquire. We all three sat down to table and amused ourselves with talking of all sorts of indifferent things, and with drinking to each other's health. Suddenly the prince said to me, "Cousin, we have no time to lose; be so kind as to conduct this lady to a certain spot, where you will find a dome-like tomb, newly built. You cannot mistake it. Go in, both of you, and wait till I come. I shall not be long."

As I had promised I prepared to do as I was told, and giving my hand to the lady, I escorted her, by the light of the moon, to the place of which the prince had spoken. We had barely reached it when he joined us himself, carrying a small vessel of water, a pickax, and a little bag containing plaster.

With the pickax he at once began to destroy the empty sepulchre in the middle of the tomb. One by one he took the stones and piled them up in a corner. When he had knocked down the whole sepulchre he proceeded to dig at the earth, and beneath where the sepulchre had been I saw a trap door. He raised the door and I caught sight of the top of a spiral staircase; then he said, turning to the lady, "Madam, this is the way that will lead you down to the spot that I told you of."

The lady did not answer, but silently descended the staircase, the prince following her. At the top, however, he looked at me. "My cousin," he exclaimed, "I do not know how to thank you for your kindness. Farewell."

"What do you mean?" I cried. "I don't understand."

"No matter," he replied, "go back by the path that you came."

He would say no more, and, greatly puzzled, I returned to my room in the palace and went to bed. When I woke, and considered my adventure, I thought that I must have been dreaming, and sent a servant to ask if the prince was dressed and could see me. But on hearing that he had not slept at home I was much alarmed, and hastened to the cemetery, where, unluckily, the tombs were all so alike that I could not discover which was the one I was in search of, though I spent four days in looking for it.

You must know that all this time the king, my uncle, was absent on a hunting expedition, and as no one knew when he would be back, I at last decided to return home, leaving the ministers to make my excuses. I longed to tell them what had become of the prince, about whose fate they felt the most dreadful anxiety, but the oath I had sworn kept me silent.

On my arrival at my father's capital, I was astonished to find a large detachment of guards drawn up before the gate of the palace; they surrounded me directly as I entered. I asked the officers in command the reason of this strange behavior, and was horrified to learn that the army had mutinied and put to death the king, my father, and had placed the grand vizir on the throne. Further, that by his orders I was placed under arrest.

Now this rebel vizir had hated me from my boyhood, because once, when shooting at a bird with a bow, I had shot out his eye by accident. Of course I not only sent a servant at once to offer him my regrets and apologies, but I made them in person. It was all of no use. He cherished an undying hatred toward me, and lost no occasion of showing it. Having once got me in his power I felt he could show no mercy, and I was right. Mad with triumph and fury he came to me in my prison and tore out my right eye. That is how I lost it.

My persecutor, however, did not stop here. He shut me up in a large case and ordered his executioner to carry me into a desert place, to cut off my head, and then to abandon my body to the birds of prey. The case, with me inside it, was accordingly placed on a horse, and the executioner, accompanied by another man, rode into the country until they found a spot suitable for the purpose. But their hearts were not so hard as they seemed, and my tears and prayers made them waver.

"Forsake the kingdom instantly," said the executioner at last, "and take care never to come back, for you will not only lose your head, but make us lose ours." I thanked him gratefully, and tried to console myself for the loss of my eye by thinking of the other misfortunes I had escaped.

After all I had gone through, and my fear of being recognized by some enemy, I could only travel very slowly and cautiously, generally resting in some out-of-the-way place by day, and walking as far as I was able by night, but at length I arrived in the kingdom of my uncle, of whose protection I was sure.

I found him in great trouble about the disappearance of his son, who had, he said, vanished without leaving a trace; but his own grief did not prevent his sharing mine. We mingled our tears, for the loss of one was the loss of the other, and then I made up my mind that it was my duty to break the solemn oath I had sworn to the prince. I therefore lost no time in telling my uncle everything I knew, and I observed that even before I had ended his sorrow appeared to be lightened a little.

"My dear nephew," he said, "your story gives me some hope. I was aware that my son was building a tomb, and I think I can find the spot. But as he wished to keep the matter secret, let us go alone and seek the place ourselves."

He then bade me disguise myself, and we both slipped out of a garden door which opened on to the cemetery. It did not take long for us to arrive at the scene of the prince's disappearance, or to discover the tomb I had sought so vainly before. We entered it, and found the trap door which led to the staircase, but we had difficulty in raising it, because the prince had fastened it down underneath with the plaster he had brought with him.

My uncle went first, and I followed him. When we reached the bottom of the stairs we stepped into a sort of ante-room, filled with such a dense smoke that it was hardly possible to see anything. However, we passed through the smoke into a large chamber, which at first seemed quite empty. The room was brilliantly lighted, and in another moment we perceived a sort of platform at one end, on which were the bodies of the prince and a lady, both half-burned, as if they had been dragged out of a fire before it had quite consumed them.

This horrible sight turned me faint, but, to my surprise, my uncle did not show so much surprise as anger.

"I knew," he said, "that my son was tenderly attached to this lady, whom it was impossible he should ever marry. I tried to turn his thoughts, and presented to him the most beautiful princesses, but he cared for none of them, and, as you see, they have now been united by a horrible death in an underground tomb." But as he spoke, his anger melted into tears, and again I wept with him.

When he recovered himself he drew me to him. "My dear nephew," he said, embracing me, "you have come to me to take his place, and I will do my best to forget that I ever had a son who could act in so wicked a manner." Then he turned and went up the stairs.

We reached the palace without anyone having noticed our absence, when, shortly after, a clashing of drums, and cymbals, and the blare of trumpets burst upon our astonished ears. At the same time a thick cloud of dust on the horizon told of the approach of a great army. My heart sank when I perceived that the commander was the vizir who had dethroned my father, and was come to seize the kingdom from my uncle.

The capital was utterly unprepared to stand a siege, and seeing that resistance was useless, at once opened its gates. My uncle fought hard for his life, but was soon overpowered, and when he fell I managed to escape through a secret passage, and took refuge with an officer whom I knew I could trust.

Persecuted by ill-fortune and stricken by grief, there seemed to be only one means of safety left to me. I shaved my beard and my eyebrows, and put on the dress of a calender, in which it was easy for me to travel without being known. I avoided the towns till I reached the kingdom of the famous and powerful Caliph, Haroun-al-Raschid, when I had no further reason to fear my enemies. It was my intention to come to Bagdad and to throw myself at the feet of his Highness, who would, I felt certain, be touched by my sad story, and would grant me, besides, his help and protection.

After a journey which lasted some months I arrived at length at the gates of this city. It was sunset, and I paused for a little to look about me, and to decide which way to turn my steps. I was still debating on this subject when I was joined by this other calender, who stopped to greet me. "You, like me, appear to be a stranger," I said. He replied that I was right, and before he could say more the third calender came up. He, also, was newly arrived in Bagdad, and being brothers in misfortune, we resolved to cast in our lots together, and to share whatever fate might have in store.

By this time it had grown late, and we did not know where to spend the night. But our lucky star having guided us to this door, we took the liberty of knocking and of asking for shelter, which was given to us at once with the best grace in the world.

This, madam, is my story.

ALADDIN AND THE WONDERFUL LAMP

The story of Aladdin's many adventures with his magic lamp begins when he is a foolish and idle boy, tricked by a magician. But Aladdin, with the help of a powerful genie, outsmarts the magician and takes possession of the miraculous lamp.

There once lived a poor tailor who had a son called Aladdin, a careless, idle boy who would do nothing but play all day long in the streets with little idle boys like himself. This so grieved the father that he died; yet, in spite of his mother's tears and prayers, Aladdin did not mend his ways. One day, when he was playing in the streets as usual, a stranger asked him his age, and if he were not the son of Mustapha the tailor.

"I am, sir," replied Aladdin; "but he died a long while ago."

On this the stranger, who was a famous African magician, fell on his neck and kissed him, saying: "I am your uncle, and knew you from your likeness to my brother. Go to your mother and tell her I am coming."

Aladdin ran home and told his mother of his newly found uncle.

"Indeed, child," she said, "your father had a brother, but I always thought he was dead."

However, she prepared supper, and bade Aladdin seek his uncle, who came laden with wine and fruit. He presently fell down and kissed the place where Mustapha used to sit, bidding Aladdin's mother not to be surprised at not having seen him before, as he had been 40 years out of the country. He then turned to Aladdin, and asked him his trade, at which the boy hung his head, while his mother burst into tears. On learning that Aladdin was idle and would learn no trade, he offered to take a shop for him and stock it with merchandise. Next day he bought Aladdin a fine suit of clothes, and took him all over the city, showing him the sights, and brought him home at nightfall to his mother, who was overjoyed to see her son so fine.

Next day the magician led Aladdin into some beautiful gardens a long way outside the city gates. They sat down by a fountain, and the magician pulled a cake from his girdle, which he divided between them. They then journeyed onward till they almost reached the mountains. Aladdin was so tired that he begged to go back, but the magician beguiled him with pleasant stories, and led him on in spite of himself.

At last they came to two mountains divided by a narrow valley.

"We will go no farther," said the false uncle. "I will show you something wonderful; only do you gather up sticks while I kindle a fire."

When it was lit the magician threw on it a powder he had about him, at the same time saying some magical words. The earth trembled a little and opened in front of them, disclosing a square, flat stone with a brass ring in the middle to raise it by. Aladdin tried to run away, but the magician caught him and gave him a blow that knocked him down.

"What have I done, uncle?" he said piteously; whereupon the magician said more kindly: "Fear nothing, but obey me. Beneath this stone lies a treasure which is to be yours, and no one else may touch it, so you must do exactly as I tell you."

At the word treasure, Aladdin forgot his fears, and grasped the ring as he was told, saying the names of his father and grandfather. The stone came up quite easily and some steps appeared.

"Go down," said the magician; "at the foot of those steps you will find an open door leading into three large halls. Tuck up your gown and go through them without touching anything, or you will die instantly. These halls lead into a garden of fine fruit trees. Walk on till you come to a niche in a terrace where stands a lighted lamp. Pour out the oil it contains and bring it to me."

He drew a ring from his finger and gave it to Aladdin, bidding him prosper.

Aladdin found everything as the magician had said, gathered some fruit off the trees, and, having got the lamp, arrived at the mouth of the cave. The magician cried out in a great hurry:

"Make haste and give me the lamp." This Aladdin refused to do until he was out of the cave. The magician flew into a terrible passion, and throwing some more powder on the fire, he said something, and the stone rolled back into its place, trapping Aladdin inside.

The magician left Persia forever, which plainly showed that he was no uncle of Aladdin's, but a cunning magician who had read in his magic books of a wonderful lamp, which would make him the most powerful man in the world. Though he alone knew where to find it, he could only receive it from the hand of another. He had picked out the foolish

Aladdin for the purpose, intending to get the lamp and kill him afterward.

For two days Aladdin remained in the dark, crying and lamenting. At last he clasped his hands in prayer, and in so doing rubbed the ring, which the magician had forgotten to take from him. Immediately an enormous and frightful genie rose out of the earth, saying: "What wouldst thou with me? I am the Slave of the Ring, and will obey thee in all things."

Aladdin fearlessly replied: "Deliver me from this place!" Whereupon the earth opened, and he found himself outside. As soon as his eyes could bear the light he went home, but fainted on the threshold. When he came to himself he told his mother what had passed, and showed her the lamp and the fruits he had gathered in the garden, which were in reality precious stone. He then asked for some food.

"Alas! child," she said, "I have nothing in the house, but I have spun a little cotton and will go and sell it."

Aladdin bade her keep her cotton, for he would sell the lamp instead. As it was very dirty she began to rub it, that it might fetch a higher price. Instantly a hideous genie appeared, and asked what she would have. She fainted away, but Aladdin, snatching the lamp, said boldly: "Fetch me something to eat!"

The genie returned with a silver bowl, twelve silver plates containing rich meats, two silver cups, and two bottles of wine. Aladdin's mother, when she came to herself, said: "Whence comes this splendid feast?"

"Ask not, but eat," replied Aladdin.

So they sat at breakfast till it was dinner-time, and Aladdin told his mother about the lamp. She begged him to sell it, and have nothing to do with devils.

"No," said Aladdin, "since chance has made us aware of its virtues, we will use it and the ring likewise, which I shall always wear on my finger." When they had eaten all the genie had brought, Aladdin sold one of the silver plates, and so on till none were left. He then had recourse to the genie, who gave him another set of plates, and thus they lived for many years.

One day Aladdin heard an order from the Sultan, proclaiming that everyone was to stay at home and close his shutters while the princess, his daughter, went to and from the bath. Aladdin was seized by a desire to see her face, which was very difficult, as she always went veiled. He hid himself behind the door of the bath, and peeped through a chink. The princess lifted her veil as she went in, and looked so beautiful that Aladdin fell in love with her at first sight. He went home so changed that his mother was frightened. He told her he loved the princess so deeply that he could not live without her, and meant to ask her in marriage of her father. His mother, on hearing this, burst out laughing, but Aladdin at last prevailed upon her to go before the Sultan and carry his request. She fetched a napkin and laid in it the magic fruits from the enchanted garden, which sparkled and shone like the most beautiful jewels. She took these with her to please the Sultan, and set out, trusting in the lamp. The grand-vizir and the lords of council had just gone in as she entered the hall and placed herself in front of the Sultan. He, however, took no notice of her. She went every day for a week, and stood in the same place.

When the council broke up on the sixth day, the Sultan said to his vizir: "I see a certain woman in the audience-chamber every day carrying something in a napkin. Call her next time, that I may find out what she wants."

Next day, at a sign form the vizir, she went up to the foot of the throne, and remained kneeling till the Sultan said to her: "Rise, good woman, and tell me what you want."

She hesitated, so the Sultan sent away all but the vizir, and bade her speak freely, promising to forgive her beforehand for anything she might say. She then told him of her son's violent love for the princess.

"I prayed him to forget her," she said, "but in vain; he threatened to do some desperate deed if I refused to go and ask your Majesty for the hand of the princess. Now I pray you to forgive not me alone, but my son Aladdin."

The sultan asked her kindly what she had in the napkin, whereupon she unfolded the jewels and presented them.

He was thunderstruck, and turning to the vizir said: "What sayest thou? Ought I not to bestow the princess on one who values her at such a price?"

The vizir, who wanted her for his own son, begged the Sultan to withold her for three months, in the course of which he hoped his son would contrive to make him a richer present. The Sultan granted this, and told Aladdin's mother that, though he consented to the marriage, she must not appear before him again for three months.

Aladdin waited patiently for nearly three months, but after two had elapsed, his mother, going into the city to buy oil, found everyone rejoicing, and asked what was going on.

"Do you not know," was the answer, "that the son of the grand-vizir is to marry the Sultan's daughter tonight?"

Breathless, she ran and told Aladdin, who was overwhelmed at first, but presently bethought him of the lamp. He rubbed it, and the genie appeared, saying: "What is thy will?"

Aladdin replied: "The Sultan, as thou knowest, has broken his promise to me, and the vizir's son is to have the princess. My command is that tonight you bring hither the bride and bridegroom."

"Master, I obey," said the genie.

Aladdin then went to his chamber, where, sure enough, at midnight the genie transported the bed containing the vizir's son and the princess.

"Take this new-married man," he said, "and put him outside in the cold, and return at daybreak."

Whereupon the genie took the vizir's son out of bed, leaving Aladdin with the princess.

"Fear nothing," Aladdin said to her; "you are my wife, promised to me by your unjust father, and no harm shall come to you."

THE SEVEN VOYAGES OF SINDBAD THE SAILOR

Sindbad is a young man who decides to join a crew on a ship of merchants and seek his fortune. In the process he has many fanciful and exciting adventures, two of which are told here.

FIRST VOYAGE

I had inherited considerable wealth from my parents, and being young and foolish I at first squandered it recklessly upon every kind of pleasure, but presently, finding that riches speedily take to themselves wings if managed as badly as I was managing mine, and remembering also that to be old and poor is misery indeed, I began to bethink me of how I could make the best of what still remained to me. I sold all my household goods by public auction, and joined a company of merchants who traded by sea, embarking with them at Balsora in a ship which we had fitted out between us.

We set sail and took our course towards the East Indies by the Persian Gulf, having the coast of Persia upon our left hand and upon our right the shore of Arabia Felix. I was at first much troubled by the uneasy motion of the vessel, but speedily recovered my health, and since that hour have been no more plagued by sea-sickness.

From time to time we landed at various islands, where we sold or exchanged our merchandise, and one day, when the wind dropped suddenly, we found ourselves becalmed close to a small island like a green meadow, which only rose slightly above the surface of the water. Our sails were furled, and the captain gave permission to all who wished to land for awhile and amuse themselves. I was among the number, but when, after strolling about for some time, we lighted a fire and sat down to enjoy the repast which we had brought with us, we were startled by a sudden and violent trembling of the island, while at the same moment those left upon the ship set up an outcry bidding us come on board for our lives, since what we had taken for an island was nothing but the back of a sleeping whale. Those who were nearest to the boat threw themselves into it, others sprang into the sea, but before I could save myself the whale plunged suddenly into the depths of the ocean, leaving me clinging to a piece of the wood which we had brought to make our fire. Meanwhile a breeze had sprung up, and in the confusion that ensued on board our vessel in hoisting the sails and taking up those who were in the boat and clinging to its sides, no one missed me and I was left at the mercy of the waves. All that day I floated up and down, now beaten this way, now that, and when night fell I despaired for my life; but, weary and spent as I was, I clung to my frail support, and great was my joy when the morning light showed me that I had drifted against an island.

The cliffs were high and steep, but luckily for me some tree-roots protruded in places, and by their aid I climbed up at last, and stretched myself upon the turf at the top, where I lay, more dead than alive, till the sun was high in the heavens. By that time I was very hungry, but after some searching I came upon some edible herbs and a spring of clear water, and much refreshed I set out to explore the island. Presently I reached a great plain where a grazing horse was tethered, and as I stood looking at it I heard voices talking apparently underground, and in a moment a man appeared who asked me how I came upon the island. I told him my adventures, and heard in return that he was one of the grooms of Mihrage, the king of the island, and that each year they came to feed their master's horses in this plain. He took me to a cave where his companions were assembled, and when I had eaten of the food they set before me, they bade me think myself fortunate to have come upon them when I did, since they were going back to their master on the morrow, and without their aid I could certainly never have found my way to the inhabited part of the island.

Early the next morning we accordingly set out, and when we reached the capital I was graciously received by the king, to whom I related my adventures, upon which he ordered that I should be well cared for and provided with such things as I needed. Being a merchant I sought out men of my own profession, and particularly those who came from foreign countries, as I hoped in this way to hear news from Bagdad, and find out some means of returning thither, for the capital was situated upon the sea-shore, and visited by vessels from all parts of the world. In the meantime I heard many curious things, and

146

answered many questions concerning my own country, for I talked willingly with all who came to me. Also to while away the time of waiting I explored a little island named Cassel, which belonged to King Mihrage, and which was supposed to be inhabited by a spirit name Deggial. Indeed, the sailors assured me that often at night the playing of timbals could be heard upon it. However, I saw nothing strange upon my voyage saving some fish that were full two hundred cubits long, but were fortunately more in dread of us than even we were of them, and fled from us if we did but strike upon a board to frighten them. Other fishes there were only a cubit long and had heads like owls.

One day after my return, as I went down to the quay, I saw a ship which had just cast anchor and was discharging her cargo, while the merchants to whom it belonged were busily directing the removal of it to their warehouses. Drawing nearer I presently noticed that my own name was marked upon some of the packages, and after having carefully examined them, I felt sure that they were indeed those which I had put on board our ship at Balsora. I then recognized the captain of the vessel, but as I was certain that he believed me to be dead, I went up to him and asked who owned the packages that I was looking at.

"There was on board my ship," he replied, "a merchant of Bagdad named Sindbad. One day he and several of my other passengers landed upon what we supposed to be an island, but which was really an enormous whale floating asleep upon the waves. No sooner did it feel upon its back the heat of the fire which had been kindled than it plunged into the depths of the sea. Several of the people who were upon it perished in the waters, and among others this unlucky Sindbad. This merchandise is his, but I have resolved to dispose of it for the benefit of his family if I should ever chance to meet with them."

"Captain," said I, "I am that Sindbad whom you believe to be dead, and these are my possessions!"

When the captain heard these words he cried out in amazement, "Lackaday! and what is the world coming to? In these days there is not an honest man to be met with. Did I not with my own eyes see Sindbad drown, and now you have the audacity to tell me that you are he! I should have taken you to be a just man, and yet for the sake of obtaining that which does not belong to you, you are ready to invent this horrible falsehood."

"Have patience, and do me the favor to hear my story," said I.

"Speak then," replied the captain, "I'm all attention."

So I told him of my escape and of my fortunate meeting with the king's grooms, and how kindly I had been received at the palace. Very soon I began to see that I had made some impression upon him, and after the arrival of some of the other merchants, who showed great joy at once more seeing me alive, he declared that he also recognized me.

Throwing himself upon my neck, he exclaimed, "Heaven be praised that you have escaped from so great a danger. As to your goods, I pray you take them, and dispose of them as you please." I thanked him, and praised his honesty, begging him to accept several bales of merchandise in token of my gratitude, but he would take nothing. Of the choicest of my goods I prepared a present for King Mihrage, who was at first amazed, having known that I had lost my all. However, when I had explained to him how my bales had been miraculously restored to me, he graciously accepted my gifts, and in return gave me many valuable things. I then took leave of him, and exchanging my merchandise for sandal and aloes wood, camphor, nutmegs, cloves, pepper, and ginger, I embarked upon the same vessel and traded so successfully upon our homeward voyage that I arrived in Balsora with about 100,000 sequins. My family received me with as much joy as I felt upon seeing them once more. I bought land and slaves, and built a great house in which I resolved to live happily, and in the enjoyment of all the pleasures of life to forget my past sufferings.

Here Sindbad paused, and commanded the musicians to play again, while the feasting continued until evening. When the time came for the porter to depart, Sindbad gave him a purse containing one hundred sequins, saying, "Take this, Hindbad, and go home, but tomorrow come again and you shall hear more of my adventures."

The porter retired quite overcome by so much generosity, and you may imagine that he was well received at home, where his wife and children thanked their lucky stars that he had found such a benefactor.

SEVENTH AND LAST VOYAGE

fter my sixth voyage I was quite determined that I would go to sea no more. I was now of an age to appreciate a quiet life, and I had run risks enough. I only wished to end my days in peace. One day, however, when I was entertaining a number of my friends, I was told that an officer of the Caliph wished to speak to me, and when he was admitted he bade me follow him into the presence of Haroun al Raschid, which I accordingly did. After I had saluted him, the Caliph said: "I have sent for you, Sindbad, because I need your services. I have chosen you to bear a letter and a gift to the King of Serendib in return for his message of friendship."

The Caliph's commandment fell upon me like a thunderbolt.

"Commander of the Faithful," I answered, "I am ready to do all that your Majesty commands, but I humbly pray you to remember that I am utterly disheartened by the unheard of sufferings I have undergone. Indeed, I have made a vow never again to leave Bagdad."

With this I gave him a long account of some of my strangest adventures, to which he listened patiently.

"I admit," said he, "that you have indeed had some extraordinary experiences, but I do not see why they should hinder you from doing as I wish. You have only to go straight to Serendib and give my message, then you are free to come back and do as you will. But go you must; my honor and dignity demand it."

Seeing that there was no help for it, I declared myself willing to obey; and the Caliph, delighted at having got his own way, gave me a thousand sequins for the expenses of the voyage. I was soon ready to start, and taking the letter and the present I embarked at Balsora, and sailed quickly and safely to Serendib. Here, when I had disclosed my errand, I was well received, and brought into the presence of the king, who greeted me with joy.

"Welcome, Sindbad," he cried. "I have thought of you often, and rejoice to see you once more."

After thanking him for the honor that he did me, I displayed the Caliph's gifts. First a bed with complete hangings all cloth gold, which cost a thousand sequins, and another like to it of crimson stuff. Fifty robes of rich embroidery, a hundred of the finest white linen from Cairo, Suez, Cufa, and Alexandria. Then more beds of different fashion, and an agate vase carved with the figure of a man aiming an arrow at a lion, and finally a costly table, which had once belonged to King Solomon. The King of Serendib received with satisfaction the assurance of the Caliph's friendliness toward him, and now my task being accomplished I was anxious to depart, but it was some time before the king would think of letting me go. At last, however, he dismissed me with many presents, and I lost no time in going on board a ship, which sailed at once, and for four days all went well. On the fifth day we had the misfortune to fall in with pirates, who seized our vessel, killing all who resisted, and making prisoners of those who were prudent enough to submit at once, of whom I was one. When they had despoiled us of all we possessed, they forced us to put on vile raiment, and sailing to a distant island there sold us for slaves. I fell into the hands of a rich merchant, who took me home with him, and clothed and fed me well, and after some days sent for me and questioned me as to what I could do.

I answered that I was a rich merchant who had been captured by pirates, and therefore I knew no trade.

"Tell me," said he, "can you shoot with a bow?"

I replied that this had been one of the pastimes of my youth, and that doubtless with practice my skill would come back to me.

Upon his he provided me with a bow and arrows, and mounting me with him upon his own elephant took the way to a vast forest which lay far from the town. When we had reached the wildest part of it we stopped, and my master said to me: "This forest swarms with elephants. Hide yourself in this great tree, and shoot at all that pass you. When you have succeeded in killing one come and tell me."

So saying he gave me a supply of food and returned to the town, and I perched myself high up in the tree and kept watch. That night I saw nothing, but just after sunrise the next morning a large herd of elephants came crashing and trampling by. I lost no time in letting fly several arrows, and at last one of the great animals fell to the ground dead, and the others retreated, leaving me free to come down from my hiding place and run back to tell my master of my success, for which I was praised and regaled with good things. Then we went

149

back to the forest together and dug a mighty trench in which we buried the elephant I had killed, in order that when it became a skeleton my master might return and secure its tusks.

For two months I hunted thus, and no day passed without my securing an elephant. Of course I did not always station myself in the same tree, but sometimes in one place, sometimes in another. One morning as I watched the coming of the elephants I was surprised to see that, instead of passing the tree I was in, as they usually did, they paused, and completely surrounded it, trumpeting horribly, and shaking the very ground with their heavy tread, and when I saw that their eyes were fixed upon me I was terrified, and my arrows dropped from my trembling hand. I had indeed good reason for my terror when, an instant later, the largest of the animals wound his trunk round the stem of my tree, and with one mighty effort tore it up by the roots, bringing me to the ground entangled in its branches. I thought now that my last hour was surely come; but the huge creature, picking me up gently enough, set me upon its back, where I clung more dead than alive, and followed by the whole herd turned and crashed off into the dense forest. It seemed to me a long time before I was once more set upon my feet by the elephant, and I stood as if in a dream watching the herd, which turned and trampled of in another direction, and were soon hidden in the dense underwood. Then, recovering myself, I looked about me, and found that I was standing upon the side of a great hill, strewn as far as I could see on either hand with bones and tusks of elephants. "This then must be the elephants' burying place," I said to myself, "and they must have brought me here that I might cease to persecute them, seeing that I want nothing but their tusks, and here lie more than I could carry away in a lifetime."

Whereupon I turned and made for the city as fast as I could go, not seeing a single elephant by the way, which convinced me that they had retired deeper into the forest to leave the way open to the Ivory Hill, and I did not know how sufficiently to admire their sagacity. After a day and a night I reached my master's house, and was received by him with joyful surprise.

"Ah! poor Sindbad," he cried, "I was wondering what could have become of you. When I went to the forest I found the tree newly uprooted, and the arrows lying beside it, and I feared I should never see you again. Pray tell me how you escaped death."

I soon satisfied his curiosity, and the next day we went together to the Ivory Hill, and he was overjoyed to find that I had told him nothing but the truth. When we had loaded our elephant with as many tusks as it would carry and were back to the city, he said: "My brother—since I can no longer treat as a slave one who has enriched me thus—take your liberty and may Heaven prosper you. I will no longer conceal from you that these wild elephants have killed numbers of our slaves every year. No matter what good advice we gave them, they were caught sooner or later. You alone have escaped the wiles of these animals, therefore you must be under the special protection of Heaven. Now through you the whole town will be enriched without further loss of life, therefore you shall not only receive your liberty, but I will also bestow a fortune upon you."

To which I replied, "Master, I thank you, and wish you all prosperity. For myself I only ask liberty to return to my own country."

"It is well," he answered, "the monsoon will soon bring the ivory ships hither, then I will send you on your way with somewhat to pay your passage."

So I stayed with him till the time of the monsoon, and every day we added to our store of ivory till all his warehouses were overflowing with it. By this time the other merchants knew the secret, but there was enough and to spare for all. When the ships at last arrived my master himself chose the one in which I was to sail, and put on board for me a great store of choice provisions, also ivory in abundance, and all the costliest curiosities of the country, for which I could not thank him enough, and so we parted. I left the ship at the first port we came to, not feeling at ease upon the sea after all that had happened to me by reason of it, and having disposed of my ivory for much gold, and bought many rare and costly presents, I loaded my pack animals, and joined a caravan of merchants. Our journey was long and tedious, but I bore it patiently, reflecting that at least I had not to fear tempests, nor pirates, nor serpents, nor any of the other perils from which I had suffered before, and at length we reached Bagdad. My first care was to present myself before the Caliph, and give him an account of my embassy. He assured me that my long absence had disquieted him much, but he had nevertheless hoped for the best. As to my adventure among the elephants he heard it with amazement, declaring that he could not have believed it had not my truthfulness been well known to him.

By his orders this story and the others I had told him were written by his scribes in letters of gold, and laid up among his treasures. I took my leave of him, well satisfied with the honors and rewards he bestowed upon me; and since that time I have rested from my labors, and given myself up wholly to my family and my friends.

Lang, Andrew. *The Arabian Nights Entertainments.* New York: Dover Publications, Inc., 1969.
Other Editions:
Twain, Mark. *Arabian Nights.* New York: Putnam, 1981.
Wiggins, Kate D., and Smith, Nora A., eds. *Arabian Nights: Their Best-Known Tales.* New York: Macmillan, Macmillan Children's Group (Scribner's Young Readers), 1993.

THE LITTLE PRINCE

ANTOINE DE ST. EXUPÉRY

The Little Prince *tells the story of a pilot's encounter with a young boy who has left his planet in search of companionship. Before meeting up with a Pilot, the little prince has a series of meetings with other people and animals. Here is his meeting with a fox, who is also in search of friendship.*

t was then that the fox appeared.

"Good morning," said the fox.

"Good morning," the little prince responded politely, although when he turned around he saw nothing.

"I am right here," the voice said, "under the apple tree."

"Who are you?" asked the little prince, and added, "You are very pretty to look at."

"I am a fox," the fox said.

"Come and play with me," proposed the little prince. "I am so unhappy."

"I cannot play with you," the fox said. "I am not tamed."

"Ah! Please excuse me," said the little prince.

But, after some thought, he added: "What does that mean—'tame'?"

"You do not live here," said the fox. "What is it that you are looking for?"

"I am looking for men," said the little prince. "What does that mean—'tame'?"

"Men," said the fox. "They have guns, and they hunt. It is very disturbing. They also raise chickens. These are their only interests. Are you looking for chickens?"

"No," said the little prince. I am looking for friends. What does that mean—'tame'?"

"It is an act too often neglected," said the fox. "It means to establish ties."

"'To establish ties'?"

"Just that," said the fox. "To me, you are still nothing more than a little boy who is just like a hundred thousand other little boys. And I have no need of you. And you, on your part, have no need of me. To you I am nothing more than a fox like a hundred other foxes. But if you tame me, than we shall need each other. To me, you will be unique in all the world. To you I shall be unique in all the world…"

"I am beginning to understand," said the little prince. "There is a flower…I think that she has tamed me…"

"It is possible," said the fox. "On the Earth one sees all sorts of things."

"Oh, but this is not on the Earth!" said the little prince.

The fox seemed perplexed, and very curious.

"On another planet?"

"Yes."

"Are there hunters on that planet?"

"No."

"Ah, that is interesting! Are there chickens?"

"No."

"Nothing is perfect," sighed the fox.

But he came back to his idea.

"My life is very monotonous," he said. "I hunt chickens; men hunt me. All the chickens are just alike, and all the men are just alike. And, in consequence, I am a little bored. But if you tame me, it will be as if the sun came to shine on my life. I shall know the sound of a step that will be different from all others. Other steps send me hurrying back underneath the ground. Yours will call me, like music, out of my burrow. And then look: you see the grain fields down yonder? I do not eat bread. Wheat is of no use to me. The wheat fields have nothing to say to me. And that is sad. But you have hair that is the color of gold. Think how wonderful that will be when you have tamed me! The grain, which is golden, will bring me back to the thought of you. And I shall love to listen to the wind in the wheat..."

The fox gazed at the little prince for a long time.

"Please—tame me!" he said.

"I want to, very much," the little prince replied. "But I have not much time. I have friends to discover, and a great many things to understand."

"One only understands the things that one tames," said the fox. "Men have no more time to understand anything. They buy things all ready-made at the shops. But there is no shop anywhere where one can buy friendship and so men have no friends any more. If you want a friend, tame me...."

"What must I do, to tame you?" asked the little prince.

"You must be very patient," replied the fox. "First you will sit down at a little distance from me like that in the grass. I shall look at you out of the corner of my eye, and you will say nothing. Words are the source of misunderstandings. But you will sit a little closer to me, every day..."

The next day the little prince came back.

"It would have been better to come back at the same hour," said the fox. "If, for example, you come at four o'clock in the afternoon, then at three o'clock I shall begin to be happy. I shall feel happier and happier as the hour advances. At four o'clock, I shall already be worrying and jumping about. I shall show you how happy I am! But if you come at just any time, I shall never know at what hour my heart is to be ready to greet you…One must observe the proper rites…"

"What is a rite?" asked the little prince.

"Those also are actions too often neglected," said the fox. "They are what make one day different from other days, one hour from other hours. There is a rite, for example, among my hunters. Every Thursday they dance with the village girls. So Thursday is a wonderful day for me! I can take a walk as far as the vineyards. But if the hunters danced at just any time, every day would be like every other day and I should never have any vacation at all." So the little prince tamed the fox. And when the hour of his departure drew near—

"Ah," said the fox, "I shall cry."

"It is your own fault," said the little prince. "I never wished you any sort of harm; but you wanted me to tame you…."

"Yes, that is so," said the fox.

"But now you are going to cry!" said the little prince.

"Yes, that is so," said the fox.

"Then it has done you no good at all!"

"It has done me good," said the fox, "because of the color of the wheat fields." And then he added: "Go and look again at the roses. You will understand now that yours is unique in all the world. Then come back to say good-bye to me, and I will make a present of a secret."

The little prince went away, to look again at the roses.

"You are not at all like my rose," he said. "As yet you are nothing. No one has tamed you, and you have tamed no one. You are like my fox when I first knew him. He was only a fox, like a hundred thousand other foxes. But I have made him my friend, and now he is unique in all the world."

And the roses were very much embarrassed.

"You are beautiful, but you are empty," he went on. "One could not die for you. To be sure an ordinary passerby would think that my rose looked just like you the rose that belongs to me. But in herself alone she is more important than all the hundreds of other roses: because it is she that I have put under the glass globe; because it is for her that I have killed the caterpillar (except the two or three that we saved to become butterflies); because it is she that I have listened to, when she grumbled, or boasted, or even sometimes when she said nothing. Because she is my rose."

And he went back to meet the fox.

"Good-bye," he said.

"Good-bye," said the fox. "And now here is my secret, a very simple secret: It is only with the heart that one can see rightly; what is essential is invisible to the eye."

"What is essential is invisible to the eye," the little prince repeated, so that he would be sure to remember.

"It is the time you have wasted for your rose that makes your rose so important."

"It is the time I have wasted for my rose—" said the little prince, so that he would be sure to remember.

"Men have forgotten this truth," said the fox. "But you must not forget it. You become responsible forever, for what you have tamed. You are responsible for your rose…"

"I am responsible for my rose," the little prince repeated, so that he would be sure to remember.

Saint-Exupéry, Antoine de. *The Little Prince*. Translated by Katherine Woods. New York: Harcourt Brace & Company, HB Juvenile Books, 1982.

Other Editions:

——. *The Little Prince*. New York: Harcourt Brace & Company, HB Juvenile Books, 1993.

DAYS OF DREAMS
AND LAUGHTER

LUCY MAUD MONTGOMERY

The Story Girl suggests that the whole group should write down their dreams, so they can remember and laugh about them with each other when they are old and gray. They make a pact to get together regularly and record them. Some are plain, some are colorful—but they always make "a most interesting collection." Here, Beverley tells us about one of Peter's very interesting dreams, and what happens when they try to induce more colorful ones.

Chapter 23 SUCH STUFF AS DREAMS ARE MADE OF

eter took Dan and me aside one evening, as we were on our way to the orchard with our dream books, saying significantly that he wanted our advice. Accordingly, we went round to the spruce wood, where the girls would not see us to the rousing of their curiosity, and there Peter told us of his dilemma.

"Last night I dreamed I was in church," he said. "I thought it was full of people, and I walked up the aisle to your pew and sat down, as unconcerned as a pig on ice. And then I found that I hadn't a stitch of clothes on—not one blessed stitch. Now"—Peter dropped his voice—"what is bothering me is this—would it be proper to tell a dream like that before the girls?"

I was of the opinion that it would be rather questionable; but Dan vowed he didn't see why. He'd tell it just as quick as any other dream. There was nothing bad in it.

"But they're your own relations," said Peter. "They're no relation to me, and that makes a difference. Besides, they're all such ladylike girls. I guess I'd better not risk it. I'm pretty sure Aunt Jane wouldn't think it was proper to tell such a dream. And I don't want to offend Fel—any of them."

So Peter never told that dream, nor did he write it down. Instead, I remember seeing in his dream book; under the date of September fifteenth, an entry to this effect:

"Last nite i dremed a drem. it wasent a polit drem so i son't rite it down."

The girls saw this entry but, to their credit be it told, they never tried to find out what the "drem" was. As Peter said, they were "ladies" in the best and truest sense of that much abused appellation. Full of fun and frolic and mischief they were, with all the defects of their qualities and all the wayward faults of youth. But no indelicate thought or vulgar word could have been shaped or uttered in their presence. Had any of us boys ever been guilty of such, Cecily's pale face would have colored with the blush of outraged purity, Felicity's golden head would have lifted itself in the haughty indignation of insulted womanhood, and the Story Girl's splendid eyes would have flashed with such anger and scorn as would have shrivelled the very soul of the wretched culprit.

Dan was once guilty of swearing. Uncle Alec whipped him for it—the only time he ever so punished any of his children. But it was because Cecily cried all night that Dan was filled with saving remorse and repentance. He vowed next day to Cecily that he would never swear again, and he kept his word.

All at once the Story Girl and Peter began to forge ahead in the matter of dreaming. Their dreams suddenly became so lurid and dreadful and picturesque that it was hard for the rest of us to believe that they were not painting the lily rather freely in their accounts of them. But the Story Girl was the soul of honor; and Peter, early in life, had had his feet set in the path of truthfulness by his Aunt Jane and had never been known to stray from it. When they assured us solemnly that their dreams all happened exactly as they described them we were compelled to believe them. But there was something up, we felt sure of that. Peter and the Story Girl certainly had a secret between them, which they kept for a whole fortnight. There was no finding it out from the Story Girl. She had a knack of keeping secrets, anyhow; and moreover, all that fortnight she was strangely cranky and petulant, and we found it was not wise to tease her. She was not well, so Aunt Olivia told Aunt Janet.

"I don't know what is the matter with the child," said the former anxiously. "She hasn't seemed like herself the past two weeks. She complains of headache, and she has no appetite, and she is a dreadful color. I'll have to see a doctor about her if she doesn't get better soon."

"Give her a good dose of Mexican Tea and try that first," said Aunt Janet. "I've saved many a doctor's bill in my family by using Mexican Tea."

The Mexican Tea was duly administered, but produced no improvement in the condition of the Story Girl, who, however, went on dreaming after a fashion which soon made her dream book a veritable curiosity of literature.

"If we can't soon find out what makes Peter and the Story Girl dream like that, the rest of us might as well give up trying to write dream books," said Felix discontentedly.

Finally, we did find out. Felicity wormed the secret out of Peter by the employment of Delilah wiles, such as have been the undoing of many a miserable male creature since Samson's day. She first threatened that she would never speak to him again if he didn't tell her; and then she promised him that, if he did, she would let him walk beside her to and from Sunday School all the rest of the the summer, and carry her books for her. Peter was not proof against this double attack. He yielded and told the secret.

I expected that the Story Girl would overwhelm him with scorn and indignation. But she took it very coolly.

"I knew Felicity would get it out of him sometime," she said. "I think he has done well to hold out this long."

Peter and the Story Girl, so it appeared, had wooed wild dreams to their pillows by the simple device of eating rich, indigestible things before they went to bed. Aunt Olivia knew nothing about it, of course. She permitted them only a plain, wholesome lunch at bed-time. But during the day the Story Girl would smuggle upstairs various tidbits from the pantry, putting half in Peter's room and half in her own; and the result was these visions which had been our despair.

"Last night I ate a piece of mince pie," she said, "and a lot of pickles, and two grape jelly tarts. But I guess I overdid it, because I got real sick and couldn't sleep at all, so of course I didn't have any dreams. I should have stopped with the pie and pickles and left the tarts alone. Peter did, and he had an elegant dream that Peg Bowen caught him and put him on to boil alive in that big black pot that hangs outside her door. He woke up before the water got hot, though. Well, Miss Felicity, you're pretty smart. But how will you like to walk to Sunday School with a boy who wears patched trousers?"

"I won't have to," said Felicity triumphantly. "Peter is having a new suit made. It's to be ready by Saturday. I knew that before I promised."

Having discovered how to produce exciting dreams, we all promptly followed the example of Peter and the Story Girl.

"There is no chance for me to have any horrid dreams," lamented Sara Ray, "because ma won't let me have anything at all to eat before I go to bed. I don't think it is fair."

"Can't you hide something away through the day as we do?" asked Felicity.

"No." Sara shook her fawn-colored head mournfully. "Ma always keeps the pantry locked, for fear Judy Pineau will treat her friends."

For a week we ate unlawful lunches and dreamed dreams after our own hearts—and, I regret to say, bickered and squabbled incessantly through the daytime, for our digestions went out of order and our tempers followed suit. Even the Story Girl and I had a fight—something that had never had happened before. Peter was the only one who kept his normal poise. Nothing could upset the boy's stomach.

One night Cecily came into the pantry with a large cucumber, and proceeded to devour the greater part of it. The grown-ups were away that evening, attending a lecture in Markdale, so we ate our snacks openly, without any recourse. I remember I supped that night off a solid hunk of fat pork, topped off with a slab of cold plum pudding.

"I thought you didn't like cucumber, Cecily," Dan remarked.

"Neither I do," said Cecily with a grimace. "But Peter says they're splendid for dreaming. He ate one that night he had the dream about being caught by cannibals. I'd eat three cucumbers if I could have a dream like that."

Cecily finished her cucumber, and then drank a glass of milk, just as we heard the wheels of Uncle Alec's buggy rambling over the bridge in the hollow. Felicity quickly restored pork and pudding to their own places, and by the time Aunt Janet came in we were all in our respective beds. Soon the house was dark and silent. I was just dropping into an uneasy slumber when I heard a commotion in the girls' room across the hall.

Their door opened and through our own open door I saw Felicity's white-clad figure flit down the stairs to Aunt Janet's room. From the room she had left came moans and cries.

"Cecily's sick," said Dan, springing out of bed. "That cucumber must have disagreed with her."

In a few minutes the whole household was astir. Cecily was sick—very, very sick, there was no doubt of that. She was even worse than Dan had been when he had eaten the bad berries. Uncle Alec, tired as he was from his hard day's work and evening outing, was dispatched for the doctor. Aunt Janet and Felicity administered all the homely remedies they could think of, but to no effect. Felicity told Aunt Janet of the cucumber, but Aunt Janet did not think the cucumber alone could be responsible for Cecily's alarming condition.

"Cucumbers are indigestible, but I never knew of them making any one as sick as this," she said anxiously. "What made the child eat a cucumber before going to bed? I didn't think she liked them."

"It was that wretched Peter," sobbed Felicity indignantly. "He told her it would make her dream something extra."

"What on earth did she want to dream for?" demanded Aunt Janet in bewilderment.

"Oh, to have something worth while to write in her dream book, ma. We all have dream books, you know, and every one wants their own to be the most exciting—and we've been eating rich things to make us dream, and it does—but if Cecily—oh, I'll never forgive myself," said Felicity, incoherently, letting all kinds of cats out of the bag in her excitement and alarm.

"Well, I wonder what on earth you young ones will do next," said Aunt Janet in the helpless tone of a woman who gives it up.

Cecily was no better when the doctor came. Like Aunt Janet, he declared that cucumbers alone would not have made her so ill; but when he found out that she had drunk a glass of milk also the mystery was solved.

"Why, milk and cucumber together make a rank poison," he said. "No wonder the child is sick. There—there now—" seeing the alarmed faces around him, "don't be frightened. As old Mrs. Fraser says, 'It's no deidly.' It won't kill her, but she'll probably be a pretty miserable girl for two or three days."

She was. And we were all miserable in company. Aunt Janet investigated the whole affair and the matter of our dream books was aired in family conclave. I do not know which hurt our feelings most—the scolding we got from Aunt Janet, or the ridicule which the other grown-ups, especially Uncle Roger, showered on us. Peter received an extra "setting down," which he considered rank injustice.

"I didn't tell Cecily to drink the milk, and the cucumber alone wouldn't have hurt her," he grumbled. Cecily was able to be out with us again that day, so Peter felt that he might venture on a grumble. "'Sides, she coaxed me to tell her what would be good for dreams. I just told her as a favor. And now your Aunt Janet blames me for the whole trouble."

"And Aunt Janet says we are never to have anything to eat before we go to bed after this except plain bread and milk," said Felix sadly.

"They'd like to stop us from dreaming altogether if they could," said the Story Girl wrathfully.

"Well, anyway, they can't prevent us from growing up," consoled Dan.

Montgomery, Lucy. *Days of Dreams and Laughter: The Story Girl and Other Tales*. New York: Crown Publishers, 1990.

ANNE OF GREEN GABLES

LUCY MAUD MONTGOMERY

The heroine in this story is an orphan nobody wants. Marilla and Mathew, an elderly brother and sister, want to adopt a boy but get Anne instead. Marilla goes to talk with Mrs. Spencer about the mixup. On the drive there, Anne, who has a great big imagination, tells Marilla all about her life and what she thinks about it.

Chapter Five: ANNE'S HISTORY

o you know," said Anne confidentially, "I've made up my mind to enjoy this drive. It's been my experience that you can nearly always enjoy things if you make up your mind firmly that you will. Of course, you must make it up firmly. I am not going to think about going back to the asylum while we're having our drive. I'm just going to think about the drive. Oh, look, there's one little early wild rose out! Isn't it lovely? Don't you think it must be glad to be a rose? Wouldn't it be nice if roses could talk? I'm sure they could tell us such lovely things. And isn't pink the most bewitching color in the world? I love it, but I can't wear it. Redheaded people can't wear pink, not even in imagination. Did you ever know of anybody whose hair was red when she was young, but got to be another color when she grew up?"

"No, I don't know as I ever did," said Marilla mercilessly, "and I shouldn't think it likely to happen in your case, either."

Anne sighed.

"Well, that is another hope gone. My life is a perfect graveyard of buried hopes. That's a sentence I read in a book once, and I say it over to comfort myself whenever I'm disappointed in anything."

"I don't see where the comforting comes in myself," said Marilla.

"Why, because it sounds so nice and romantic, just as if I were a heroine in a book, you know. I am so fond of romantic things, and a graveyard full of buried hopes is about as romantic a thing as one can imagine, isn't it? I'm rather glad I have one. Are we going across the Lake of Shining Waters today?"

"We're not going over Barry's pond, if that's what you mean by your Lake of Shining Waters. We're going by the shore road."

"Shore road sounds nice," said Anne dreamily. "Is it as nice as it sounds? Just when you said 'shore road' I saw it in a picture in my mind, as quick as that! And White Sands is

162

a pretty name, too; but I don't like it as well as Avonlea. Avonlea is a lovely name. It just sounds like music. How far is it to White Sands?"

"It's five miles; and as you're evidently bent on talking you might as well talk to some purpose by telling me what you know about yourself."

"Oh, what I know about myself isn't really worth telling," said Anne eagerly. "If you'll only let me tell you what I imagine about myself you'll think it ever so much more interesting."

"No, I don't want any of your imaginings. Just you stick to bald facts. Begin at the beginning. Where were you born and how old are you?"

"I was eleven last March," said Anne, resigning herself to bald facts with a little sigh. "And I was born in Bolingbroke, Nova Scotia. My father's name was Walter Shirley, and he was a teacher in the Bolingbroke High School. My mother's name was Bertha Shirley. Aren't Walter and Bertha lovely names? I'm so glad my parents had nice names. It would be a real disgrace to have a father named—well, say Jedediah, wouldn't it?"

"I guess it doesn't matter what a person's name is as long as he behaves himself," said Marilla, feeling herself called upon to inculcate a good and useful moral.

"Well, I don't know." Anne looked thoughtful. "I read in a book once that a rose by any other name would smell as sweet, but I've never been able to believe it. I don't believe a rose would be as nice if it was called a thistle or a skunk cabbage. I suppose my father could have been a good man even if he had been called Jedediah; but I'm sure it would have been a cross. Well, my mother was a teacher in the high school, too, but when she married father she gave up teaching, of course. A husband was enough responsibility. Mrs. Thomas said that they were a pair of babies and as poor as church mice. They went to live in a weeny-teeny little yellow house in Bolingbroke. I've never seen that house, but I've imagined it thousands of times. I think it must have had honeysuckle over the parlor window and lilacs in the front yard and lilies of the valley just inside the gate. Yes, and muslin curtains in all the windows. Muslin curtains give a house such an air. I was born in that house. Mrs. Thomas said I was the homeliest baby she ever saw, I was so scrawny and tiny and nothing but eyes, but that mother thought I was perfectly beautiful. I should think a mother would be a better judge than a poor woman who came in to scrub, wouldn't you? I'm glad she was satisfied with me anyhow; I would feel so sad if I thought I was a disappointment to her—because she didn't live very long after that, you see. She died of fever when I was just three months old. I do wish she'd lived long enough for me to remember calling her mother. I think it would be so sweet to say 'mother,' don't you? And father died four days afterwards from fever, too. That left me an orphan and folks were at their wits' end, so Mrs. Thomas said, what to do with me. You see, nobody wanted me even then. It seems to be my fate. Father and mother had both come from places far away and it was well known they hadn't any relatives living. Finally Mrs. Thomas said she'd take me, though she was poor and had a drunken husband. She brought me up by hand. Do you know if there is anything in being brought up by hand that ought to make people who are brought up that way better than other people? Because whenever I was naughty Mrs. Thomas would ask me how I could be such a bad girl when she had brought me up by hand—reproachful-like.

"Mr. and Mrs. Thomas moved away form Bolingbroke to Marysville, and I lived with them until I was eight years old. I helped look after the Thomas children—there were four of them younger than me—and I can tell you they took a lot of looking after. Then Mr. Thomas was killed falling under a train and his mother offered to take Mrs. Thomas and the children, but she didn't want me. Mrs. Thomas was at her wits' end, so she said, what to do with me. Then Mrs. Hammond from up the river came down and said she'd take me, seeing I was handy with children, and I went up the river to live with her in a little clearing among the stumps. It was a very lonesome place. I'm sure I could never have lived there if I hadn't had an imagination. Mr. Hammond worked a little sawmill up there, and Mrs. Hammond had eight children. She had twins three times. I like babies in moderation, but twins three times in succession is too much. I told Mrs. Hammond so firmly, when the last pair came. I used to get so dreadfully tired carrying them about.

"I lived up river with Mrs. Hammond over two years, and then Mr. Hammond died and Mrs. Hammond broke up housekeeping. She divided her children among her relatives and went to the States. I had to go to the asylum at Hopeton, because nobody would take me. They didn't want me at the asylum, either; they said they were overcrowded as it was. But they had to take me and I was there four months until Mrs. Spencer came."

Anne finished up with another sigh, of relief this time. Evidently she did not like talking about her experiences in a world that had not wanted her.

"Did you ever go to school?" demanded Marilla, turning the sorrel mare down the shore road.

"Not a great deal. I went a little the last year I stayed with Mrs. Thomas. When I went up river we were so far from a school that I couldn't walk it in winter and there was vacation in summer, so I could only go in the spring and fall. But of course I went while I was at the asylum. I can read pretty well and I know ever so many pieces of poetry off by heart—'The Battle of Hohenlinden,' and 'Edinburgh after Flodden,' and 'Bingen on the Rhine,' and lots of the 'lady of the Lake' and most of 'The Seasons,' by James Thompson. Don't you just love poetry that gives you a crinkly feeling up and down your back? There is a piece in the Fifth Reader—'The Downfall of Poland'—that is just full of thrills. Of course, I wasn't in the Fifth Reader—I was only in the Fourth—but the big girls used to lend me theirs to read."

"Were those women—Mrs. Thomas and Mrs. Hammond—good to you?" asked Marilla, looking at Anne out of the corner of her eye.

"O-o-o-h," faltered Anne. Her sensitive little face suddenly flushed scarlet and embarrassment sat on her brow. "Oh, they meant to be—I know they meant to be just as good and kind as possible. And when people mean to be good to you, you don't mind very much when they're not quite—always. They had a good deal to worry them, you know. It's very trying to have a drunken husband, you see; and it must be very trying to have twins three times in succession, don't you think? But I feel sure they meant to be good to me."

Marilla asked no more questions. Anne gave herself up to a silent rapture over the shore road and Marilla guided the sorrel abstractedly while she pondered deeply. Pity was suddenly stirring in her heart for the child. What a starved, unloved life she had had—a life of drudgery and poverty and neglect; for Marilla was shrewd enough to read between the lines of Anne's history and divine the truth. No wonder she had been so delighted at the prospect of a real home. It was a pity she had to be sent back. What if she, Marilla, should indulge Mathew's unaccountable whim and let her stay? He was set on it; and the child seemed a nice, teachable little thing.

"She's got too much to say," thought Marilla, "but she might be trained out of that. And there's nothing rude or slangy in what she does say. She's ladylike. It's likely her people were nice folks."

The shore road was "woodsy and wild and lonesome." On the right hand, scrub firs, their spirits quite unbroken by long years of tussle with gulf winds, grew thickly. On the left were the steep red sandstone cliffs, so near the track in places that a mare of less steadiness than the sorrel might have tried the nerves of the people behind her. Down at the base of the cliffs were heaps of surf-worn rocks or little sandy coves inlaid with pebbles as with ocean jewels; beyond lay the sea, shimmering and blue, and over it soared the gulls, their pinions flashing silvery in the sunlight.

"Isn't the sea wonderful?" said Anne, rousing from a long, wide-eyed silence. "Once, when I lived in Marysville, Mr. Thomas hired an express-wagon and took us all to spend the day at the shore ten miles away. I enjoyed every moment of that day, even if I had to look after the children all the time. I lived it over in happy dreams for years. But this shore is nicer than the Marysville shore. Aren't those gulls splendid? Would you like to be a gull? I think I would—that is, if I couldn't be a human girl. Don't you think it would be nice to wake up at sunrise and swoop down over the water and away out over the lovely blue all day; and then at night to fly back to one's nest? Oh, I can just imagine myself doing it. What big house is that just ahead, please?"

"That's the White Sands Hotel. Mr. Kirke runs it, but the season hasn't begun yet. There are heaps of Americans come there for the summer. They think this shore is just about right."

"I was afraid it might be Mrs. Spencer's place," said Anne mournfully. "I don't want to get there. Somehow, it will seem like the end of everything."

Montgomery, Lucy. *Anne of Green Gables*. Stamford: Longmeadow Press, 1986.

THE SELFISH GIANT

Oscar Wilde

Once there was a Giant who had a very beautiful garden. But because he was a very selfish Giant, he did not want anyone else to enjoy it. He chased all the children away and eternal Winter descended upon his garden until a little boy taught the Giant the error of his ways.

very afternoon, as they were coming from school, the children used to go and play in the Giant's garden.

It was a lovely garden, with soft green grass. Here and there over the grass stood beautiful flowers like stars, and there were twelve peach-trees that in the springtime broke out into delicate blossoms of pink and pearl, and in the autumn bore rich fruit. The birds sat on the trees and sang so sweetly that the children used to stop their games in order to listen to them. "How happy we are here!" they cried to each other.

One day the Giant came back. He had been to visit his friend the Cornish ogre, and had stayed with him for seven years. After the seven years were over he had said all that he had to say, for his conversation was limited, and he determined to return to his own castle. When he arrived he saw the children playing in the garden.

"What are you doing there?" he cried in a very gruff voice, and the children ran away.

"My own garden is my own garden," said the Giant; "any one can understand that, and I will allow nobody to play in it but myself." So he built a high wall all round it, and put up a notice-board:

TRESPASSERS WILL BE PROSECUTED

He was a very selfish Giant.

The poor children had now nowhere to play. They tried to play on the road, but the road was very dusty and full of hard stones, and they did not like it. They used to wander round the high wall when their lessons were over, and talk about the beautiful garden inside. "How happy we were there," they said to each other.

Then the Spring came, and all over the country there were little blossoms and little birds. Only in the garden of the Selfish Giant it was still winter. The birds did not care to sing in it as there were no children, and the trees forgot to blossom. Once a beautiful flower put its head out from the grass, but when it saw the notice-board it was so sorry for the children that it slipped back into the ground again, and went off to sleep. The only people who were pleased were the Snow and the Frost. The Snow covered up the grass with her great white cloak, and the Frost painted all the trees silver. Then they invited the North Wind to stay with them, and he came. He was draped in furs, and he roared all day about the garden, and blew the chimney-pots down. "This is a delightful spot," he said, "we must ask the Hail on a visit." So the Hail came. Every day for three hours he rattled on the roof of the castle till he broke most of the slates, and then he ran round and round the garden as fast as he could go. He was dressed in grey, and his breath was like ice.

"I cannot understand why the Spring is so late in coming," said the Selfish Giant, as he sat at the window and looked out at his cold white garden; "I hope there will be a change in the weather."

But the Spring never came, nor the Summer. The Autumn gave golden fruit to every garden, but to the Giant's garden she gave none. "He is too selfish," she said. So it was always Winter there, and the North Wind and the Hail and the Frost and the Snow danced about through the trees.

One morning the Giant was lying awake in bed when he heard some lovely music. It sounded so sweet to his ears that he thought it must be the king's musicians passing by. It was really only a little linnet singing outside his window, but it was so long since he had heard a bird sing in his garden that it seemed to him to be the most beautiful music in the world. Then the Hail stopped dancing over his head, and the North Wind ceased roaring, and a delicious perfume came to him through the open casement. "I believe the Spring has come at last," said the Giant; and he jumped out of bed and looked out.

What did he see?

He saw a most wonderful sight. Through a little hole in the wall the children had crept in, and they were sitting in the branches of the trees. In every tree that he could see there was a little child. And the trees were so glad to have the children back again that they had covered themselves with blossoms, and were waving their arms gently above the children's heads. The birds were flying about and twittering with delight, and the flowers were looking up through the green grass and laughing. It was a lovely scene, only in one corner it was still winter. It was the farthest corner of the garden, and in it was standing a little boy. He was so small that he could not reach up to the branches of the tree, and he was wandering all around it, crying bitterly. The poor tree was still quite covered with frost and snow, and the North Wind was blowing and roaring above it. "Climb up, little boy!" said the Tree, and it bent its branches down as low as it could; but the boy was too tiny.

And the Giant's heart melted as he looked out. "How selfish I have been!" he said; "now I know why the Spring would not come here. I will put that poor little boy on the top of the tree, and then I will knock down the wall, and my garden shall be the children's playground for ever and ever." He was really very sorry for what he had done.

So he crept downstairs and opened the front door quite softly, and went out into the garden. But when the children saw him they were so frightened that they all ran away, and the garden became winter again. Only the little boy did not run, for his eyes were so full of tears that he did not see the Giant coming. And the Giant stole up behind him and took him gently in his hand, and put him up into the tree. And the tree broke at once into blossom, and the birds came and sang on it, and the little boy stretched out his two arms and flung them round the Giant's neck, and kissed him. And the other children, when they saw that the Giant was not wicked any longer, came running back, and with them came the Spring. "It is your garden now, little children," said the Giant, and he took a great axe and knocked down the wall. And when the people were going to market at twelve o'clock they found the Giant playing with the children in the most beautiful garden they had ever seen.

All day they played, and in the evening they came to the Giant to bid him good-bye.

"But where is your little companion?" he said: "the boy I put into the tree." The Giant loved him the best because the boy had kissed him.

"We don't know," answered the children; "he has gone away."

"You must tell him to be sure and come here tomorrow," said the Giant. But the children said that they did not know where he lived, and had never seen him before; and the Giant felt very sad.

Every afternoon, when school was over, the children came and played with the Giant. But the little boy whom the Giant loved was never to be seen again. The Giant was very kind to all the children, yet he longed for his first little friend, and often spoke of him. "How I would like to see him!" he used to say.

Years went by, and the Giant grew very old and feeble. He could not play about any more, so he sat in a huge armchair, and watched the children at their games, and admired his garden. "I have many beautiful flowers," he said; "but the children are the most beautiful flowers of all."

One winter morning he looked out of his window as he was dressing. He did not hate the Winter now, for he knew that it was merely the Spring asleep, and that the flowers were resting.

Suddenly he rubbed his eyes in wonder, and looked and looked. It certainly was a marvelous sight. In the farthest corner of the garden was a tree quite covered with lovely white blossoms. Its branches were all golden, and silver fruit hung down from them, and underneath it stood the little boy he had loved.

Downstairs ran the Giant in great joy, and out into the garden. He hastened across the grass, and came near to the child. And when he came quite close his face grew red with anger, and he said, "Who hath dared to wound thee?" For on the palms of the child's hands were the prints of two nails, and the prints of two nails were on the little feet.

"Who hath dare to wound thee?" cried the Giant; "tell me, that I may take my big sword and slay him."

"Nay!" answered the child; "but these are the wounds of Love."

"Who art thou?" said the Giant, and a strange awe fell on him, and he knelt before the little child.

And the child smiled on the Giant, and said to him, "You let me play once in your garden, today you shall come with me to my garden, which is Paradise."

And when the children ran in that afternoon, they found the Giant lying dead under the tree, all covered with white blossoms.

Wilde, Oscar. *Oscar Wilde Stories for Children*. New York: Macmillan, Macmillan Children's Group, 1990.

    Other Editions:

    ——. *The Happy Prince & Other Stories*. New York: William Morrow & Co., Morrow Junior Books, 1991.

THE NIGHTINGALE
AND THE ROSE

Oscar Wilde

In this haunting tale, a young student needs only a red rose to win the company of the young woman he loves, but there are none to be found in the garden. The Nightingale hears the Student's quandary and selflessly tries to help.

he said that she would dance with me if I brought her red roses," cried the Student; "but in all my garden there is no red rose."

From her nest in the holm-oak tree the Nightingale heard him, and she looked out through the leaves, and wondered.

"No red rose in all my garden!" he cried, and his beautiful eyes filled with tears. "Ah, on what little things does happiness depend! I have read all that the wise men have written, and all the secrets of philosophy are mine, yet for want of a red rose is my life made wretched."

"Here at last is a true lover," said the Nightingale. "Night after night have I sung of him, though I knew him not: night after night have I told his story to the stars, and now I see him. His hair is dark as the hyacinth-blossom, and his lips are red as the rose of his desire; but passion has made his face like pale ivory, and sorrow has set her seal upon his brow."

"The Prince gives a ball tomorrow night," murmured the young Student, "and my love will be of the company. If I bring her a red rose she will dance with me till dawn. If I bring her a red rose, I shall hold her in my arms, and she will lean her head upon my shoulder, and her hand will be clasped in mine. But there is no red rose in my garden, so I shall sit lonely, and she will pass me by. She will have no heed of me, and my heart will break."

"Here indeed is the true lover," said the Nightingale. "What I sing of, he suffers: what is joy to me, to him is pain. Surely Love is a wonderful thing. It is more precious than emeralds, and dearer than fine opals. Pearls and pomegranates cannot buy it, nor is it set forth in the marketplace. It may not be purchased of the merchants, nor can it be weighed out in the balance for gold."

"The musicians will sit in their gallery," said the young Student, "and play upon their stringed instruments, and my love will dance to the sound of the harp and the violin. She will dance so lightly that her feet will not touch the floor, and the courtiers in their gay dresses will throng round her. But with me she will not dance, for I have no red rose to give her;" and he flung himself down on the grass and buried his face in his hands and wept.

"Why is he weeping?" asked a little Green Lizard, as he ran past him with his tail in the air.

"Why, indeed?" said a Butterfly, who was fluttering about after a sunbeam.

"Why, indeed?" whispered a Daisy to his neighbor, in a soft, low voice.

"He is weeping for a red rose," said the Nightingale.

"For a red rose?" they cried; "how very ridiculous!" and the little Lizard, who was something of a cynic, laughed outright.

But the Nightingale understood the secret of the Student's sorrow, and she sat silent in the oak-tree, and thought about the mystery of Love.

Suddenly she spread her brown wings for flight, and soared into the air. She passed through the grove like a shadow, and like a shadow she sailed across the garden.

In the center of the grass-plot was standing a beautiful Rose-tree, and when she saw it, she flew over to it, and lit upon a spray.

"Give me a red rose," she cried, "and I will sing you my sweetest song."

But the Tree shook its head.

"My roses are white," it answered; "as white as the foam of the sea, and whiter than the snow upon the mountain. But go to my brother who grows round the old sun-dial, and perhaps he will give you what you want."

So the Nightingale flew over to the Rose-tree that was growing round the old sun-dial.

"Give me a red rose," she cried, "and I will sing you my sweetest song."

But the Tree shook its head.

"My roses are yellow," it answered; "as yellow as the hair of the mermaiden who sits upon an amber throne, and yellower than the daffodil that blooms in the meadow before the mower comes with his scythe. But go to my brother who grows beneath the Student's window, and perhaps he will give you what you want."

So the Nightingale flew over to the Rose-tree that was growing beneath the Student's window.

"Give me a red rose," she cried, "and I will sing you my sweetest song."

But the Tree shook its head.

"My roses are red," it answered, "as red as the feet of the dove, and redder than the great fans of coral that wave and wave in the ocean-cavern. But the winter has chilled my veins, and the frost has nipped my buds, and the storm has broken my branches, and I shall have no roses at all this year."

"One red rose is all I want," cried the Nightingale, "only one red rose? Is there no way by which I can get it?"

"There is a way," answered the Tree; "but it is so terrible that I care not tell it to you."

"Tell it to me," said the Nightingale, "I am not afraid."

"If you want a red rose," said the Tree, "you must build it out of music by moonlight, and stain it with your own heart's-blood. You must sing to me with your breast against a thorn. All night long you must sing to me, and the thorn must pierce your heart, and your life-blood must flow into my veins, and become mine."

"Death is a great price to pay for a red rose," cried the Nightingale, "and Life is very dear to all. It is pleasant to sit in the green wood, and to watch the Sun in his chariot of gold, and the Moon in her chariot of pearl. Sweet is the scent of the hawthorn, and sweet are the bluebells that hide in the valley, and the heather that blows on the hill. Yet Love is better than Life, and what is the heart of a bird compared to the heart of a man?"

So she spread her brown wings for flight, and soared into the air. She swept over the garden like a shadow, and like a shadow she sailed through the grove.

The young Student was still lying on the grass, where she had left him, and the tears were not yet dry in his beautiful eyes.

"Be happy," cried the Nightingale, "be happy; you shall have your red rose. I will build it out of music by moonlight, and stain it with my own heart's blood. All that I ask of you in return is that you will be a true lover, for Love is wiser than Philosophy, though she is wise, and mightier than Power, though he is mighty. Flame-colored are his wings, and colored like flame is his body. His lips are sweet as honey, and his breath is like frankincense."

The Student looked up from the grass and listened, but he could not understand what the Nightingale was saying to him, for he only knew the things that are written down in books.

But the Oak-tree understood, and he felt sad, for he was very fond of the little Nightingale who had built her nest in his branches.

Sing me one last song," he whispered; "I shall feel very lonely when you are gone."

So the Nightingale sang to the Oak-tree, and her voice was like water bubbling from a silver jar.

When she had finished her song the Student got up and pulled a notebook and a lead-pencil out of his pocket.

"She has form," he said to himself, as he walked away through the grove—"that cannot be denied to her; but has she not got feelings? I am afraid not. In fact, she is like most artists; she is all style, without any sincerity. She would not sacrifice herself for others. She thinks merely of music, and everybody knows that the arts are selfish. Still, it must be admitted that she has some beautiful notes in her voice. What a pity it is that they do not mean anything, or do any practical good." And he went into his room, and lay down on his little pallet-bed, and began to think of his love; and, after a time, he fell asleep.

And when the Moon shone in the heavens the Nightingale flew to the Rose-tree, and set her breast against the thorn. All night long she sang with her breast against the thorn, and the cold crystal Moon leaned down and listened. All night long she sang, and the thorn went deeper and deeper into her breast, and her life-blood ebbed away from her.

She sang first of the birth of love in the heart of a boy and a girl. And on the topmost spray of the Rose-tree there blossomed a marvelous rose, petal following petal, as song followed song. Pale was it, at first, as the mist that hangs over the river—pale as the feet of the morning, and silver as the wings of dawn. As the shadow of a rose in a mirror of silver, as the shadow of a rose in a water-pool, so was the rose that blossomed on the topmost spray of the Tree.

But the Tree cried to the Nightingale to press closer against the thorn. "Press closer, little Nightingale," cried the Tree, "or the Day will come before the rose is finished."

So the Nightingale pressed close against the thorn, and louder and louder grew her song, for she sang of the birth of passion in the soul of a man and a maid.

And a delicate flush of pink came into the leaves of the rose, like the flush in the face of the bridegreoom when he kisses the lips of the bride. But the thorn had not yet reached her heart, so the rose's heart remained white, for only a Nightingale's heart's-blood can crimson the heart of a rose.

And the Tree cried to the Nightingale to press closer against the thorn. "Press closer, Little Nightingale," cried the tree, "or the Day will come before the rose is finished."

So the Nightingale pressed closer against the thorn, and the thorn touched her heart, and a fierce pang of pain shot through her. Bitter, bitter was the pain, and wilder and wilder grew her song, for she sang of the Love that is perfected by Death, of the Love that dies not in the tomb.

And the marvelous rose became crimson, like the rose of the eastern sky. Crimson was the girdle of petals, and crimson as a ruby was the heart.

But the Nightingale's voice grew fainter, and her little wings began to beat, and a film came over her eyes. Fainter and fainter grew her song, and she felt something choking her in her throat.

Then she gave one last burst of music. The white Moon heard it, and she forgot the dawn, and lingered on in the sky. The red rose heard it, and it trembled all over with ectasy, and opened its petals to the cold morning air. Echo bore it to her purple cavern in the hills, and woke the sleeping shepherds from their dreams. It floated through the reeds of the river, and they carried its message to the sea.

"Look, look!" cried the Tree, "the rose is finished now;" but the Nightingale made no answer, for she was lying dead in the long grass, with the thorn in her heart.

And at noon the Student opened his window and looked out.

"Why, what a wonderful piece of luck!" he cried; "here is a red rose! I have never seen any rose like it in all my life. It is so beautiful that I am sure it has a long Latin name;" and he leaned down and plucked it.

Then he put on his hat, and ran up to the Professor's house with the rose in his hand.

The daughter of the Professor was sitting in the doorway winding blue silk on a reel, and her little dog was lying at her feet.

"You said that you would dance with me if I brought you a red rose," cried the Student.

"Here is the reddest rose in all the world. You will wear it tonight next your heart, and as we dance together it will tell you how I love you."

But the girl frowned.

"I am afraid it will not go with my dress," she answered; "and, besides, the Chamberlain's nephew has sent me some real jewels, and everybody knows that jewels cost far more than flowers."

"Well, upon my word, you are very ungrateful," said the Student angrily; and he threw the rose into the street, where it fell into the gutter, and a cart-wheel went over it.

"Ungrateful!" said the girl. "I tell you what, you are very rude; and, after all, who are you? Only a Student. Why, I don't believe you have even got silver buckles to your shoes as the Chamberlain's nephew has"; and she got up from her chair and went into the house.

"What a silly thing Love is," said the Student as he walked away. "It is not half as useful as Logic, for it does not prove anything, and it is always telling one of things that are not going to happen, and making one believe things that are not true. In fact, it is quite unpractical, and, as in this age to be practical is everything, I shall go back to Philosophy and study Metaphysics."

So he returned to his room and pulled out a great dusty book, and began to read.

Wilde, Oscar. *Oscar Wilde Stories for Children*. New York: Macmillan, Macmillan Children's Group, 1990.

    Other Editions:

    ——. *The Happy Prince & Other Stories*. New York: William Morrow & Co., Morrow Junior Books, 1991.

FAIRY TALES

HANS CHRISTIAN ANDERSEN

HANS CHRISTIAN ANDERSEN was born in 1805 in Denmark, the son of a poor but literate shoemaker who read to his son, built him toy theaters, and took him to see plays. The young Andersen had a beautiful singing voice and a natural gift for expression. He was awarded a scholarship to study at a prestigious high school in Copenhagen, where he found academic success but had trouble socially. He was teased for his strange appearance and long nose and for the fact that he was older than the other boys. He was something of "an ugly duckling" himself.

As in the story, the awkward and insecure Hans grew to become a great success. He was known as the master of the fairy tale, in addition to being recognized for his poetry and travel books. Many of his stories are based on those his father told him in his youth— old Danish and European tales passed on through families and tradition. To these he brought his own literary gifts and personality. Other stories are entirely his own, drawn from a deep well of experience and fantasy.

Like all great literature, these stories involve love, valor, greed, revenge, the folly of vanity, and the trials of growing up. But in Andersen's world these timeless themes are enmeshed in a rich tapestry of kings and queens, witches, magic dogs, mystical objects, talking trees, poor soldiers, and a host of other fantastic creatures and characters. In this selection we have included stories that are well known, and some that are not. But all of them are rich with Andersen's brilliant imagination and acute sense of the world.

Andersen, Hans C. *Andersen's Fairy Tales*. Illustrated by Troy Howell. Stamford: Longmeadow Press, 1988.
  Other Editions:
  ——. *Andersen's Fairy Tales: Classic Fairy Tales*. New York: Crown Publishers, 1989.
  ——. *Complete Hans Christian Andersen Fairy Tales*. New York: Random House, 1993.

HANSEL AND GRETTEL

HANS CHRISTIAN ANDERSEN

One of the best-known children's stories, this is a tale of two children whose stepmother contrives to lose them in the forest so that she and her husband have enough food to eat. Once lost, Hansel and Grettel stumble hungrily upon a house made of bread and cakes. But the house is really a trap set by an old witch who intends to cook and eat the children. Using ingenious ploys, the children forestall the witch's evil plans and eventually kill her. Hauling away as much of the witch's treasure as they can carry, the children find the way home to their old guilty father, who rejoices at their return.

nce upon a time there dwelt on the outskirts of a large forest a poor woodcutter with his wife and two children; the boy was called Hansel and the girl Grettel. He had always had little enough to live on, and once, when there was a great famine in the land, he couldn't even provide them with daily bread. One night, as he was tossing about in bed, full of cares and worry, he sighed and said to his wife: "What's to become of us? How are we to support our poor children, now that we have nothing for ourselves?"

"I'll tell you what, husband," answered the woman; "early tomorrow morning we'll take the children to the thickest part of the wood; there we shall light a fire for them and give tham a piece of bread; and then we'll go on to our work and leave them alone. They won't be able to find their way home, and we shall thus be rid of them."

"No, wife," said her husband, "that I won't do; how could I find it in my heart to leave my children alone in the wood? The wild beasts would soon come and tear them to pieces."

"Oh! you fool," said she, "then we must all four die of hunger, and you may just as well go and plane the boards for our coffins"; and she left him no peace till he consented.

"But I can't help feeling sorry for the poor children," added the husband.

The children, too, had not been able to sleep for hunger, and had heard what their stepmother had said to their father. Grettel wept bitterly and spoke to Hansel: "Now it's all up with us."

"No, no, Grettel," said Hansel, "don't fret yourself; I'll be able to find a way of escape, no fear."

And when the old people had fallen asleep he got up, slipped on his little coat, opened the back door, and stole out. The moon was shining clearly, and the white pebbles which lay in front of the house glittered like bits of silver. Hansel bent down and filled his pocket with as many of them as he could cram in. Then he went back and said to Grettel, "Be comforted, my dear little sister, and go to sleep: God will not desert us," and he lay down in bed again.

At daybreak, even before the sun was up, the woman came and woke the two children: "Get up, you lie-abeds, we're all going to the forest to fetch wood." She gave them each a bit of bread and spoke: "There's something for your luncheon, but don't you eat it up before, for it's all you'll get."

Grettel took the bread under her apron, as Hansel had the stones in his front pocket. Then they set out together on the way to the forest. After they had walked for a little, Hansel stood still and looked back at the house, and this maneuver he repeated again and again.

His father observed him and spoke: "Hansel, what are you gazing at there, and why do you always remain behind? Take care, and don't lose your footing."

"Oh! father," said Hansel, "I am looking at my white kitten, which is sitting on the roof, waving me a farewell."

The woman exclaimed: "What a donkey you are! That isn't your kitten, that's the morning sun sitting on the chimney."

But Hansel had not looked back at his kitten, but had always dropped one of the white pebbles out of his pocket on to the path.

When they had reached the middle of the forest the father said: "Now, children, go and fetch a lot of wood, and I'll light a fire that you mayn't feel cold." Hansel and Grettel heaped up brushwood till they had made a pile nearly the size of a small hill. The brushwood was set fire to, and when the flames leaped high the woman said: "Now lie down at the fire, children, and rest yourselves: we are going into the forest to cut down wood; when we've finished we'll come back and fetch you."

Hansel and Grettel sat down beside the fire, and at midday ate their bits of bread. They heard the strokes of the ax, so they thought their father was quite near. But it was no ax they heard, but a bough he had tied on to a dead tree, and that was blown about by the wind. And when they had sat for a long time their eyes closed with fatigue, and they fell fast asleep.

When they awoke at last it was pitch dark. Grettel began to cry and said: "How are we ever to get out of the wood?" But Hansel comforted her. "Wait a bit," he said, "till the moon is up, and then we'll find our way sure enough." And when the full moon had risen he took his sister by the hand and followed the pebbles, which shone like new threepenny bits and showed them the path. They walked all through the night, and at daybreak reached their father's house again.

They knocked at the door, and when the woman opened it she exclaimed: "You naughty children, what a time you've slept in the wood! We thought you were never going to come back."

But the father rejoiced, for his conscience had reproached him for leaving his children behind by themselves.

Not long afterward there was again great dearth in the land, and the children heard

their mother address their father thus in bed one night: "Everything is eaten up once more; we have only half a loaf in the house, and when that's done it's all up with us. The children must be got rid of; we'll lead them deeper into the wood this time, so that they won't be able to find their way out again. There is no other way of saving ourselves."

The man's heart smote heavily, and he thought, "Surely it would be better to share the last bite with one's children!" But his wife wouldn't listen to his arguments, and did nothing but scold and reproach him. If a man yields once he's done for, and so, because he had given in the first time, he was forced to do so the second.

But the children were awake and had heard the conversation. When the old people were asleep Hansel got up and wanted to go out and pick up pebbles again, as he had one for the first time; but the woman had barred the door and Hansel couldn't get out. But he consoled his little sister and said: "Don't cry, Grettel, and sleep peacefully, for God is sure to help us."

At early dawn the woman came and made the children get up. They received their bit of bread, but it was even smaller than the time before. On the way to the wood Hansel crumbled it in his pocket, and every few minutes he stood still and dropped a crumb on the ground.

"Hansel, what are you stopping and looking about you for?" said the father.

"I'm looking back at my little pigeon, which is sitting on the roof waving me a farewell," answered Hansel.

"Fool!" said the wife; "that isn't your pigeon, it's the morning sun glittering on the chimney."

But Hansel gradually threw all his crumbs on to the path. The women led the children still deeper into the forest, further than they had ever been in their lives before. Then a big fire was lit again, and the mother said: "Just sit down there, children, and if you're tired you can sleep a bit; we're going into the forest to cut down wood, and in the evening when we're finished we'll come back to fetch you."

At midday Grettel divided her bread with Hansel, for he had strewn his all along their path. Then they fell asleep, and evening passed away, but nobody came to the poor children. They didn't wake till it was pitch dark, and Hansel comforted his sister saying: "Only wait, Grettel, till the moon rises, then we shall see the breadcrumbs I scattered along the path; they will show us the way back to the house."

When the moon appeared they got up, but they found no crumbs, for thousands of birds that fly about the woods and fields had picked them up. "Never mind," said Hansel to Grettel; "you'll see we'll still find a way out"; but all the same they did not. They wandered about the whole night, and the next day, from morning till evening, but they could not find a path out of the wood. They were very hungry, too, for they had nothing to eat but a few berries they found growing on the ground. And at last they were so tired that their legs refused to carry them any longer, so they lay down under a tree and fell fast asleep.

On the third morning after they had left their father's house they set about their wandering again, but only got deeper and deeper into the wood, and now they felt that if help did not come to them soon they must perish. At midday they saw a beautiful little snow-white bird sitting on a branch, which sang so sweetly that they stopped still and listened to it. And when its song was finished it flapped its wings and flew on in front of them. They followed it and came to a little house, on the roof of which it perched; and when they came quite near they saw that the cottage was made of bread and roofed with cakes, while the window was made of transparent sugar. "Now we'll set to," said Hansel, "and have a regular blow out. I'll eat a bit of the roof, and you, Grettel, can eat some of the window, which you'll find a sweet morsel."

Hansel stretched up his hand and broke off a little bit of the roof to see what it was like, and Grettel went to the casement and began to nibble at it. Thereupon a shrill voice called out from the room inside:

Nibble, nibble, little mouse,
Who's nibbling my house?'

The children answered,

'Tis Heaven's own child,
The tempest wild,

and went on eating, without putting themselves about. Hansel, who thoroughly appreciated the roof, tore down a big bit of it, while Grettel pushed out a whole round window pane, and sat down the better to enjoy it. Suddenly the door opened and an ancient dame leaning on a staff hobbled out. Hansel and Grettel were so terrified that they let what they had in their hands fall. But the old woman shook her head and said: "Oh, ho! you dear children, who led you here? Just come in and stay with me: no ill shall befall you."

She took them both by the hand and led them in to the house, and laid a most sumptuous dinner before them—milk and sugared pancakes,

with apples and nuts. After they had finished, two beautiful little white beds were prepared for them, and when Hansel and Grettel lay down in them they felt as if they had got into heaven.

The old woman appeared to be most friendly, but she was really an old witch who had waylaid the children, and had only built the little bread house in order to lure them in. When anyone came into her power she killed, cooked, and ate him, and held a regular feast-day for the occasion. Now, witches have red eyes and cannot see far, but, like beasts, they have a keen sense of smell and know when human beings pass by. When Hansel and Grettel fell into her hands she laughed maliciously and said jeeringly: "I've got them now; they shan't escape me."

Early in the morning, before the children were awake, she arose, and when she saw them both sleeping so peacefully, with their rosy round cheeks, she muttered to herself: "That'll be a dainty bite." Then she seized Hansel with her bony hand and carried him into a little stable, and barred the door on him; he might scream as much as he liked, it did him no good.

Then she went to Grettel, shook her till she awoke, and cried: "Get up, you lazy-bones; fetch water and cook something for your brother. When he's fat I'll eat him up." Grettel began to cry bitterly, but it was of no use: she had to do what the wicked witch bade her.

So the best food was cooked for poor Hansel, but Grettel got nothing but crab-shells. Every morning the old woman hobbled out to the stable and cried: "Hansel, put out your finger, that I may feel if you are getting fat." But Hansel always stretched out a bone, and the old dame whose eyes were dim, couldn't see it, and thinking always it was Hansel's finger, wondered why he fattened so slowly. When four weeks passed and Hansel still remained thin, she lost patience and determined to wait no longer.

"Hi! Grettel," she called to the girl, "be quick and get some water. Hansel may be fat or thin, I'm going to kill him tomorrow and cook him." Oh! how the poor little sister sobbed as she carried the water, and how the tears rolled down her cheeks! "Kind Heaven help us now!" she cried; "if only the wild beasts in the wood had eaten us, then at least we should have died together."

"Just hold your peace," said the old hag; "it won't help you."

Early in the morning Grettel had to go out and hang up the kettle full of water and light the fire. "First we'll bake," said the old dame; "I've heated the oven already and kneaded the dough." She pushed Grettel out to the oven, from which fiery flames were already issuing.

"Creep in," said the witch, "and see if it's properly heated, so that we can shove in the bread." For when she had got Grettel in she meant to close the oven and let the girl bake, that she might eat her up too.

But Grettel perceived her intention and spoke: "I don't know how I'm going to do it; how do I get in?"

"You silly goose!" said the hag, "the opening is big enough; see, I could get in myself"; and she crawled toward it and poked her head into the oven. Then Grettel gave her a shove that sent her right in, shut the iron door, and drew the bolt. Gracious! how she yelled! it was quite horrible; but Grettel fled, and the wretched old woman was left to perish miserably.

Grettel flew straight to Hansel, opened the little stable door, and cried: "Hansel, we are free; the old witch is dead."

Then Hansel sprang like a bird out of the cage when the door is opened. How they rejoiced, and fell on each other's necks, and jumped for joy, and kissed one another! And as they had no longer any cause for fear, they went into the old hag's house, and there they found, in every corner of the room, boxes with pearls and precious stones.

"These are even better than pebbles," said Hansel, and crammed his pockets full of them; and Grettel said, "I too will bring something home"; and she filled her apron full.

"But now," said Hansel, "let's go and get well away from the witch's wood." When they had wandered about for some hours they came to a big lake. "We can't get over," said Hansel; "I see no bridge of any sort or kind."

Yes, and there's no ferryboat either," answered Grettel; "but look, there swims a white duck; if I ask her she'll help us over"; and she called out:

> *Here are two children, mournful very,*
> *Seeing neither bridge nor ferry;*
> *Take us upon your white back,*
> *And row us over quack, quack!*

The duck swam toward them, and Hansel got on her back and bade his little sister to sit beside him.

"No," answered Grettel, "we should be too heavy a load for the duck: she shall carry us across separately." The good bird did this, and when they were landed safely on the other side and had gone on for awhile, the wood became more and more familiar to them, and at length they saw their father's house in the distance. Then they set off to run, and bounding into the room fell on their father's neck.

The man had not passed a happy hour since he left them in the wood, but the woman had died. Grettel shook out her apron so that the pearls and precious stones rolled about the room, and Hansel threw down one handful after the other out of his pocket. Thus all their troubles were ended, and they all lived happily ever afterward.

THE UGLY DUCKLING

Hans Christian Andersen

Of the new brood of a proud mother duck, one of the ducklings stands out as particularly ugly and awkward. The other ducks and birds torment him constantly. Even his own mother, finding his ugliness shameful, comes to wish he had never been born. Before long, he runs away from his family, only to find himself rejected by everyone he encounters. Upon seeing a beautiful flock of swans, he feels both excited at their beauty and depressed that he is so ugly. When he goes to meet them, thinking they will kill him for his ugliness, he sees his reflection in the lake and realizes that he has grown up and is as beautiful as they are—that he was a swan all along.

t was lovely summer weather in the country, and the golden corn, the green oats, and the haystacks in the meadows looked beautiful. On a sunny slope stood a pleasant old farmhouse, close by a deep river. Under some big burdock leaves on the bank sat a duck on her nest, waiting for her young brood to hatch; she was beginning to get tired of her task, for the little ones were a long time coming out of their shells.

At length one shell cracked, and then another, and from each egg came a living creature that lifted its head and cried, "Peep, peep." "Quack, quack," said the mother, and then they all quacked as well as they could, and looked about them on every side at the large green leaves. Their mother allowed them to look as much as they liked, because green is good for their eyes.

"How large the world is," said the young ducks, when they found how much more room they had now than when they were inside the egg-shell.

"Do you imagine this is the whole world?" asked the mother. "Wait till you have seen the garden; it stretches far beyond that to the parson's field, but I have never ventured so far. Are you all out?" she continued, rising; "no, I declare, the largest egg lies there still. I wonder how long this is to last, I am quite tired of it"; and she seated herself again on the nest.

"Well, how are you getting on?" asked an old duck who paid her a visit.

"One egg is not hatched yet," said the duck, "it will not break. But just look at all the others, are they not the prettiest little ducklings you ever saw?"

"Let me see the egg that will not hatch," said the old duck; "I have no doubt it is a turkey's egg. I was persuaded to hatch some once and after all my care and trouble with the young ones, they were afraid of the water. I quacked and clucked, but all to no purpose. I could not get them to venture in. Let me look at the egg. Yes, that is a turkey's egg; take my advice, leave it where it is, and teach the other children to swim."

"I think I will sit on it a little while longer," said the duck. "I have sat so long already, a few days will be nothing."

"Please yourself," said the old duck and she went away.

At last the large egg hatched, and a young one crept forth crying, "Peep, peep." It was very large and ugly. The duck stared at it, and exclaimed, "It is very large and not like the others. I wonder if it really is a turkey, We shall soon find out when we go to the water. It must go in, if I have to push it in myself."

On the next day, the weather was delightful, and the sun shone brightly on the green burdock leaves. So the mother duck took her young brood down to the water, and jumped in with a splash. "Quack, quack," cried she, and one after another the little ducklings jumped in. The water closed over their heads, but they came up again in an instant, and swam about quite prettily with their legs paddling under them as easily as possible, and the ugly duckling swam with them.

"Oh," said the mother, "that is not a turkey; how well he uses his legs and how upright he holds himself! He is my own child, and he is not so ugly after all if you look at him properly. Quack, quack! come with me now, I will take you to the farmyard, but you must keep close to me, or you may be trodden upon; and, above all, beware of the cat."

The ducklings did as they were bid, and, when they came to the yard, the other ducks stared and said: "Look, here comes another brood, as if there were not enough already! And what a queer looking object one of them is; we don't want him here," and then one flew at him and bit him in the neck.

"Let him alone," said his mother; "he is not doing any harm."

"Yes, but he is too big and ugly," said the spiteful duck, "and therefore he must be turned out."

They soon got to feel at home in the farmyard; but the poor duckling that had crept out of his shell last of all and looked so ugly, was bitten and pushed and made fun of, not only by the ducks, but by all the poultry.

"He is too big," they all said, and the turkey cock, who had come into this world with spurs, and fancied himself really an emperor, puffed himself out and flew at the duckling, and became quite red in the head with passion, so that the poor little thing did not know where to go, and was quite miserable because he was so ugly and laughed at by the whole farmyard. So it went on from day to day, till it got worse and worse. The poor duckling was driven about by every one; even his brothers and sisters were unkind to him, and would say: "Ah, you ugly creature, I wish that cat would get you," and his mother said she wished he had never been born. The ducks pecked him, the chickens beat him, and the girl who fed the poultry kicked him. So at last he ran away, frightening the little birds in the hedge as he flew over the palings.

"They are afraid of me because I am so ugly," he said. So he closed his eyes and flew still farther, until he came out on a large moor, inhabited by wild ducks. Here he remained the whole night, feeling very tired and sorrowful.

In the morning, when the wild ducks rose in the air, they stared at their new comrade. "What sort of duck are you?" they all said, coming round him.

He bowed to them and was as polite to them as he could be, but he did not reply to their question. "You are exceedingly ugly," said the wild duck, "but that will not matter if you do not marry into our family."

Poor thing! All he wanted to was to stay among the rushes, and find something to eat and drink.

After he had been on the moor two days, some men came to shoot the birds there. How they terrified the poor duckling! He hid himself among the reeds and lay quite still, when suddenly a dog came running by him, and went splash into the water without touching him.

"Oh," sighed the duckling, "how thankful I am for being so ugly; even a dog will not bite me."

It was late in the day before all became quiet, but even then the poor young thing did not dare to move. He waited for several hours, and then after looking carefully around him, hastened away from the moor as fast as he could. He ran over field and meadow until a storm arose and he could hardly struggle against it. Towards evening, he reached a poor little cottage. The duckling was so tired that he could go no farther; he sat near the bottom of the door, large enough for him to slip through, which he did very quietly and got shelter for the night.

A woman, a tom-cat, and a hen lived in this cottage. The tom-cat whom his mistress called "my little son" was a great favorite; he could raise his back and purr, and could even throw out sparks from his fur if it were stroked the wrong way. The hen had very short legs, so she was called "chickie short-legs." She laid good eggs, and her mistress loved her as if she had been her own child. In the morning the strange visitor was discovered, and the tom-cat began to purr and the hen to cluck.

"What is that noise about?" said the old woman, looking round the room, but her sight was not very good; therefore, when she saw the duckling, she thought it must be a fat duck that had strayed away from home. "Oh, what a prize!" she exclaimed, "I hope it is not a drake, for then I will have some duck's eggs. I must wait and see." So the duckling was allowed to remain on trial for three weeks, but there were no eggs.

Now the tom-cat was the master of the house, and the hen was the mistress, and they always said: "We and the world," for they believed themselves to be half the world, and the better half, too. The duckling thought that the others might hold a different opinion on the subject, but the hen would not listen to such doubts. "Can you lay eggs?" she asked. "No." "Then have the goodness to hold your tongue." "Can you raise your back or purr, or throw out sparks?" said the tom-cat. "No." "Then you have no right to express an opinion when sensible people are speaking." So the duckling sat in a corner, feeling very low-spirited, till the sunshine and fresh air came into the room through the open door, and then he began to feel such a longing for a swim on the water, that he could not help telling the hen.

"What an absurd idea," said the hen, "you have nothing else to do, therefore you have foolish fancies. If you could purr or lay eggs, they would pass away."

"But it is delightful to swim on the water," said the duckling, "and so refreshing to feel it close over your head, while you dive down to the bottom."

"Delightful, indeed!" said the hen; "why, you must be crazy! Ask the cat, he is the cleverest animal I know. Ask him how he would like to swim about on the water, or to dive under it, for I will not speak of my own opinion; ask our mistress, the old woman, there is no one in the world more clever than she is. Do you think she would like to swim, or to let the water close over her head?"

"You don't understand me," said the duckling.

"We don't understand you? Who can understand you, I wonder? Do you consider your-self more clever than the cat, or the woman? I will say nothing of myself. Don't imagine such nonsense, child, and thank your good fortune that you have been received here. Are you not in a warm room, and in society from which you may learn something? But you are a chatterer, and your company is not very agreeable. Believe me, I speak only for your good. I may tell you unpleasant truths, but that is a proof of my friendship. I advise you, there-fore, to lay eggs, and learn to purr as quickly as possible."

"I believe I must go out into the world again," said the duckling.

"Yes, do," said the hen. So the duckling left the cottage, and soon found water on which he could swim and dive, but he was avoided by all other animals because he was so ugly.

Autumn came, and the leaves in the forest turned to orange and gold; then, as winter approached, the wind caught them as they fell and whirled them in the cold air. The clouds, heavy with hail and snowflakes, hung low in the sky, and the raven stood on the ferns, crying, "Croak, croak." It made one shiver with cold to look at him. All this was very sad for the poor little duckling.

One evening, just as the sun set, amid bright clouds, there came a large flock of beautiful birds out of the bushes. The duckling had never seen any like them before. They were swans, and they curved their graceful necks, while their soft plumage shone with dazzling whiteness. They uttered a singular cry as they spread their glorious wings and flew away from those cold regions to warmer countries across the sea. As they mounted higher and higher in the air, the ugly duckling felt a strange sensation as he watched them. He whirled himself in the water like a wheel, stretched out his neck toward them, and uttered a cry so strange that it frightened himself. Could he never forget those beautiful, happy birds? And when at last they were out of his sight, he dived under the water, and rose again almost besides himself with excitement. He knew not the names of these birds, nor where they had flown, but he felt toward them as he had never felt for any other bird in the world. He was not envious of these beautiful creatures, but he wished to be as lovely as they. Poor ugly creature, how gladly he would have lived even with the ducks, had they only given him encouragement. The winter grew colder and colder, he was obliged to swim about on the water to keep it from freezing, but every night the space on which he swam became smaller and smaller. At length it froze so hard that the ice in the water cracked as he moved, and the duckling had to paddle with his legs as well as he could, to keep the space from closing up. He became exhausted at last, and lay still and helpless, frozen fast in the ice.

Early in the morning, a peasant, who was passing by, saw what had happened. He broke the ice in pieces with his wooden shoe, and carried the duckling home to his wife. The warmth revived the poor little creature; but when the children wanted to play with him, the duckling thought they would do him some harm; so he started up in terror, fluttered into the milk-pan, and splashed the milk about the room. Then the woman clapped her hands, which frightened him still more. He flew first into the butter-cask, then into the meal-tub, and out again. What a condition he was in! The woman screamed, and tumbled over each other, in their efforts to catch him; but luckily he escaped. The door stood open; the poor creature could just manage to slip out among the bushes, and lie down quite exhausted in the newly fallen snow.

It would be very sad, were I to relate all the misery and privations which the poor little duckling endured during the hard winter; but when it had passed, he found himself lying one morning in a moor, amongst the rushes. He felt the warm sun shining, and heard the lark singing, and saw that all around was beautiful spring. Then the young bird felt that his wings were strong, as he flapped them against his sides, and rose high into the air. They bore him onwards, until he found himself in a large garden, before he well knew how it happened. The apple trees were in full blossom, and the fragrant elders bent their long green branches down to the stream which wound round a smooth lawn. Everything looked beautiful, in the freshness of early spring. From a thicket close by, came three beautiful white swans, rustling their feathers, and swimming lightly over the smooth water. The duckling remembered the lovely birds, and felt more strangely unhappy than ever.

"I will fly to these royal birds," he exclaimed, "and they will kill me, because I am so ugly, and dare to approach them; but it does not matter: better to be killed by them than

pecked by the ducks, beaten by the hens, pushed about by the girl who feeds the poultry, or starved with hunger in the winter."

Then he flew to the water, and swam towards the beautiful swans. The moment they espied the stranger, they rushed to meet him with outstretched wings.

"Kill me," said the poor bird; and he bent his head down to the surface of the water, and awaited death.

But what did he see in the clear stream below? His own image; no longer a dark, gray bird, ugly and disagreeable to look at, but a graceful and beautiful swan; and the great swans swam around the newcomer, and stroked his neck with their beaks as a welcome.

Into the garden presently came some little children, and threw bread and cake into the water.

"See," cried the youngest, "there is a new one"; and the rest were delighted, and ran to their father and mother, dancing and clapping their hands, and shouting joyously. "There is another swan come, a new one!"

Then they threw more bread and cake into the water, and said: "The new one is the most beautiful of all; he is so young and pretty." And the old swans bowed their heads before him.

Then he felt quite ashamed, and hid his head under his wing; for he did not know what to do, he was so happy, and yet not at all proud. He had been persecuted and despised for his ugliness, and now he heard them say he was the most beautiful of all the birds. Even the elder tree bent down its boughs into the water before him, and the sun shone warm and bright. Then he rustled his feathers, curved his slender neck, and cried joyfully, from the depths of his heart: "I never dreamed of such happiness as this, while I was an ugly duckling."

THE EMPEROR'S NEW CLOTHES

Hans Christian Andersen

The story of the vain and insecure emperor who was tricked by two swindlers into parading naked through the city is one of the world's truly timeless tales.

any years ago there was an Emperor who was so excessively fond of new clothes that he spent all his money on them. He cared nothing about his soldiers nor for the theatre, nor for driving in the woods except for the sake of showing off his new clothes. He had a costume for every hour in the day, and instead of saying, as one does about the other King or Emperor, "He is in his council chamber," here one always said, "The Emperor is in his dressing-room."

One day two swindlers came to visit the town. They gave themselves out as weavers, and said that they knew how to weave the most beautiful stuffs imaginable. Not only were the colors and patterns unusually fine, but the clothes that were made of the stuffs had the peculiar quality of becoming invisible to every person who was not fit for the office he held, or if he was impossibly dull.

"Those must be splendid clothes," thought the Emperor. "By wearing them I should be able to discover which men in my kingdom are unfitted for their posts. I shall distinguish the wise men from the fools. Yes, I certainly must order some of that stuff to be woven for me."

He paid the two swindlers a lot of money in advance, so that they might begin their work at once.

They did put up two looms and pretended to weave, but they had nothing whatever upon their shuttles. At the outset they asked for a quantity of the finest silk and the purest gold thread, all of which they put into their own bags while they worked away at the empty looms far into the night.

"I should like to know how those weavers are getting on with the stuff," thought the Emperor; but he felt a little queer when he reflected that anyone who was stupid or unfit for his post would not be able to see it. He certainly thought that he need have no fears for himself, but he still thought he would send somebody else first to see how it was getting on.

"I will send my faithful old minister to the weavers," thought the Emperor. "He will be best able to see how the stuff looks, for he is a clever man and no one fulfills his duties better than he does!"

So the good old minister went into the room where the two swindlers sat working at the empty loom.

"Heaven preserve us!" thought the old minister, opening his eyes very wide. "Why I can't see a thing!" But he took care not to say so.

Both the swindlers begged him to be good enough to step a little nearer, and asked if he did not think it a good pattern and beautiful coloring. They pointed to the empty loom, and the poor old minister stared and pretended to see cloth.

"Oh, it is beautiful! Quite charming!" said the old minister looking through his spectacles. "This pattern and these colors! I will certainly tell the Emperor that the stuff pleases me very much."

"We are delighted to hear you say so," said the swindlers, and then they named all the colors and described the peculiar pattern. The old minister paid great attention to what they said, so as to be able to repeat it when he got home to the Emperor.

Then the swindlers went on to demand more money, more silk, and more gold, to be able to proceed with the weaving; but they put it all in their own pockets—not a single strand was ever put into the loom, but they went on as before weaving into the empty loom.

The Emperor soon sent another faithful official to see the weavers, but he, too, could see nothing at all.

"Is this not a beautiful piece of stuff?" said both the swindlers, showing and explaining the beautiful patterns and colors which were not there to be seen.

"I know I am not a fool!" thought the man, "so it must be that I am unfit for my good post! It is very strange though! However one must not let it appear! So he praised the stuff he did not see, and assured him of his delight in the beautiful colors and the originality of the design. "It is absolutely charming!" he said to the Emperor. Everybody in the town was talking about this splendid stuff.

Now the Emperor thought he would like to see it while it was still on the loom. So he selected two faithful officials who had already seen the imaginary stuff, he went to visit the crafty imposters, who were working away as hard as ever they could at the empty loom.

"It is magnificent!" said both the honest officials. "Only see, your Majesty, what a design! What colors!" And they pointed to the empty loom, for they thought no doubt the others could see the stuff.

"What!" thought the Emperor; "I see nothing at all! This is terrible! Am I a fool? Am I not fit to be Emperor? Why, nothing worse could happen to me!"

"Oh, it is beautiful!" said the Emperor. "It has my highest approval!" and he nodded his satisfaction as he gazed at the empty loom. Nothing would induce him to say that he could not see anything.

The whole suite gazed, but saw nothing more than all the others. However, they all exclaimed with his Majesty, "It is very beautiful!" and they advised him to wear a suit made of this wonderful cloth on the occasion of a great procession which was just about to take place.

"It is magnificent! Gorgeous! Excellent!" went from mouth to mouth; they were all equally delighted with it. The Emperor gave each of the rogues the title of "Gentlemen weavers."

The swindlers sat up the whole night, before the day on which the procession was to take place, cutting the air with a huge pair of scissors, and they stitched away with needles without any thread in them. At last they said: "Now the Emperor's new clothes are ready!"

The Emperor, with his grandest courtiers, went to them himself, and both the swindlers raised one arm in the air, as if they were holding something, and said: "See, these are the trousers, this is the coat, and here is the mantle!" and so on. "It is as light as a spider's web. One might think one had nothing on, but that is the very beauty of it!"

"Yes!" said all the courtiers, but they could not see anything, for there was nothing to see.

"Will your imperial Majesty be graciously pleased to take off your clothes," said the imposters, "so that we may put on the new ones, along here before the great mirror."

The Emperor took off all his clothes, and the imposters pretended to give him one article of dress after the other, of the new ones which they pretended to make. They pretended to fasten something round his waist and to tie on something; this was the train, and the Emperor turned round and round in front of the mirror.

"How well his Majesty looks in his new clothes! How becoming they are! They are the most gorgeous robes!"

"The canopy is waiting outside which is to be carried over your Majesty in the procession," said the master of ceremonies.

"Well I am quite ready," said the Emperor. "Don't the clothes fit well?" And then he turned around again in front of the mirror, so that he should seem to be looking at his grand things.

The chamberlains who were to carry the train stopped and pretended to lift it from the ground with both hands, and they walked along with their hands in the air. They dared not let it appear that they could not see anything.

Then the Emperor walked along in the procession under the gorgeous canopy, and everybody in the streets and at the windows exclaimed, "How beautiful the Emperor's new clothes are! What a splendid new train! and they fit to perfection!" Nobody would let it appear that he could see nothing, for then he would not be fit for his post, or else he was a fool.

None of the Emperor's clothes had been so successful before.

"But he has got nothing on," said a little child.

"Oh, listen to the innocent," said its father; and one person whispered to the other what the child had said. "He has nothing on; a child says he has nothing on!"

"But he has nothing on!" at last cried all the people.

The Emperor writhed, for he knew it was true, but he thought, "The procession must go on now," so held himself stiffer than ever, and the chamberlains held up the invisible train.

THE SWINEHERD

Hans Christian Andersen

A handsome young prince from a small, poor kingdom, wishes to marry a princess. But the princess he desires is the emperor's daughter. In addition to being the daughter of such a powerful man, she is spoiled and haughty. Nevertheless the young prince sends her beautiful gifts of nature—a melodious nightingale and the empire's most perfect rose—which she rejects. Then, disguised as a swineherd, he comes to work in her palace and makes even more extraordinary gifts to woo her. In the end, though, the princess's greed and arrogance get the better of her.

here was once a poor Prince; he had only quite a tiny kingdom, but it was big enough to allow him to marry, and he was bent upon marrying.

Now, it certainly was rather bold of him to say to the Emperor's daughter, "Will you have me?" He did, however, venture to say so, for his name was known far and wide; and there were hundreds of Princesses who would have said "Yes," and "Thank you, kindly," but see if she would!

Just let us hear about it.

A rose tree grew on the grave of the Prince's father, it was such a beautiful rose tree; it only bloomed every fifth year and then only bore one blossom; but what a rose that was! By merely smelling it one forgot all one's cares and sorrows.

Then he had a nightingale which sang as if every lovely melody in the world dwelt in her throat. This rose and this nightingale were to be given to the Princess, so they were put into great silver caskets and sent to her.

The Emperor had them carried before him into the great Hall where the Princess was playing at "visiting" with her ladies-in-waiting; they had nothing else to do. When she saw the caskets with the gifts she clapped her hands with delight!

"If only it were a little pussy cat!" said she—but there was the lovely rose.

"Oh, how exquisitely it is made!" said all the ladies-in-waiting.

"It is more than beautiful," said the Emperor; "it is neat."

But the Princess touched it, and then she was ready to cry.

"Fie, papa!" she said; "it is not made, it is a real one!"

"Fie," said all the ladies-in-waiting; "it is a real one!"

"Well, let us see what there is in the other casket, before we get angry," said the Emperor, and out came the nightingale. It sang so beautifully that at first no one could find anything to say against it.

"*Superbe! Charmant!*" said the ladies-in-waiting, for they all had a smattering of French,

194

one spoke it worse than the other.

"How that bird reminds me of our lamented Empress's musical box," said an old courtier. "Ah, yes, they are the same tunes, and the same beautiful execution."

"So they are," said the Emperor, and he cried like a little child.

"I should hardly think it could be a real one," said the Princess.

"Yes, it is the real one," said those who brought it.

"Oh, let that bird fly away then," said the Princess, and she would not hear of allowing the Prince to come. But he was not to be crushed; he stained his face brown and black, and, pressing his cap over his eyes, he knocked at the door.

"Good morning, Emperor," said he. "Can I be taken into service in the palace?"

"Well, there are so many wishing to do that," said the Emperor; "but let me see! Yes, I need somebody to look after the pigs, for we have so many of them."

So the Prince was made imperial swineherd. A horrid little room was given him near the pig-sties, and here he had to live. He sat busily at work all day, and by the evening he had made a beautiful little cooking pot; it had bells all around it, and when the pot boiled they tinkled delightfully and played the old tune:

Ach du lieber Augustin,
Alles ist weg, weg, weg!"

(Alas! dear Augustin,
All is lost, lost, lost!)

But the greatest charm of all about it was, that by holding one's finger in the steam one could immediately smell all the dinners that were being cooked at every stove in the town. Now this was a very different matter from a rose.

The Princess came walking along with all her ladies-in-waiting, and when she heard the tune she stopped and looked pleased, for she could play "Ach du lieber Augustin" herself; it was her only tune, and she could only play it with one finger.

"Why, that is my tune," she said; "this must be a cultivated swineherd. Go and ask him what the instrument costs."

So one of the ladies-in-waiting had to go into his room, but she put patterns on first.

"How much do you want for the pot," she asked.

"I must have ten kisses from the Princess," said the swineherd.

"Heaven preserve us!" said the lady.

"I won't take less," said the swineherd.

"Well, what does he say?" asked the Princess.

"I really cannot tell you," said the lady-in-waiting, "it is so shocking."

"Then you must whisper it." And she whispered it.

"He is a wretch!" said the Princess, and went away at once. But she had only gone a little was when she heard the bells tinkling beautifully:

Ach du lieber Augustin.

"Go and ask him if he will take ten kisses from the ladies-in-waiting."

"No, thank you," said the swineherd; "ten kisses from the Princess, or I keep my pot."

"How tiresome it is," said the Princess. "Then you will have to stand round me, so that no one may see."

So the ladies-in-waiting stood round her and spread out their skirts while the swineherd took his ten kisses, and then the pot was hers.

What a delight it was to them. The pot was kept on the boil day and night. They knew what was cooking on every stove in the town, from the chamberlain's to the shoe-maker's. The ladies-in-waiting danced about and clapped their hands.

"We know who has sweet soup and pancakes for dinner, and who has cutlets; how amusing it is."

"Highly interesting," said the mistress of the robes.

"Yes, but hold your tongues, for I am the Emperor's daughter."

"Heaven preserve us!" they all said.

The swineherd—that is to say, the Prince, only nobody knew that he was not a real swineherd—did not let the day pass in idleness, and he now constructed a rattle. When it was swung round it played all the waltzes, gallops, and jig tunes which have ever been heard since the creation of the world.

"But this is superb!" said the Princess, as she walked by. I have never heard finer compositions. Go and ask him what the instrument costs, but let us have no more kissing."

"He wants a hundred kisses from the Princess!" said the lady-in-waiting.

"I think he is mad!" said the Princess, and she went away, but she had not gone far when she stopped.

"One must encourage art," she said; "I am the Emperor's daughter. Tell him he can have ten kisses, the same as yesterday, and he can take the others from the ladies-in-waiting."

"But we don't like that at all," said the ladies.

"Oh, nonsense! If I can kiss him you can do the same. Remember that I pay your wages as well as give you board and lodging." So the lady-in-waiting had to go again.

"A hundred kisses from the Princess, or let each keep his own."

"Stand in front of me," said she, and all the ladies stood round, while he kissed her.

"Whatever is the meaning of that crowd round the pig-sties?" said the Emperor as he stepped out on the veranda; he rubbed his eyes and he put on his spectacles. "Why, it is the ladies-in-waiting, what game are they up to? I must go and see!" So he pulled up the heels of his slippers for they were shoes which he had trodden down.

Bless us, what a hurry he was in! When he got into the yard he walked very softly and the ladies were so busy counting the kisses, so that there should be fair play, and neither too few nor too many kisses, that they never heard the Emperor. He stood on tiptoe.

"What is all this?" he said when he saw what was going on, and he hit them on the head with his slipper just as the swineherd was taking his eighty-sixth kiss.

"Out you go!" said the Emperor, for he was furious, and both the Princess and the Prince were put out of his realm.

There she stood crying, and the swineherd scolded, and the rain poured down in torrents.

"Oh, miserable creature that I am! if only I had accepted the handsome Prince. Oh, how unhappy I am!"

The swineherd went behind a tree and wiped the black and brown stain from his face, and threw away his ugly clothes. Then he stepped out dressed as a Prince, he was so handsome that the Princess could not help curtseying to him.

"I am come to despise thee," he said. "Thou wouldst not have an honorable prince, thou couldst not prize the rose or the nightingale, but thou wouldst kiss the swineherd for a trumpery musical box! As thou hast made thy bed, so must thou lie upon it!"

Then he went back to his own little kingdom and shut and locked the door. So she had to stand outside and sing in earnest—

> *Ach du lieber Augustin,*
> *Alles ist weg, weg, weg!*

RICKY OF THE TUFT

Hans Christian Andersen

nce upon a time there was a queen who bore a son so ugly and misshapen that for some time it was doubtful if he would have human form at all. But a fairy who was present at his birth promised that he should have plenty of brains, and added that by virtue of the gift which she had just bestowed upon him he would be able to impart to the person whom he should love best the same degree of intelligence which he possessed himself.

This somewhat consoled the poor queen, who was greatly disappointed at having brought into the world such a hideous brat. And indeed, no sooner did the child begin to speak than his child proved to be full of shrewdness, while all that he did was somehow so clever that he charmed every one.

I forgot to mention that he was born with a little tuft of hair upon his head. For this reason he was called Ricky of the Tuft, Ricky being his family name.

Some seven or eight years later, the queen of a neighboring kingdom gave birth to twin daughters. The first one to come into the world was more beautiful than the dawn, and the queen was so overjoyed that it was feared her great excitement might do her some harm. The same fairy who had assisted at the birth of Ricky of the Tuft was present, and, in order to moderate the transports of the queen she declared that this little princess would have no sense at all, and would be as stupid as she was beautiful.

The queen was deeply mortified, and a moment or two later her chagrin became greater still, for the second daughter proved to be extremely ugly.

"Do not be distressed, Madam," said the fairy; "your daughter shall be recompensed in another way. She shall have so much good sense that her lack of beauty will scarcely be noticed."

"May Heaven grant it!" said the queen; "but is there no means by which the elder, who is as beautiful, can be endowed with some intelligence?"

"In the matter of brains I can do nothing for her, Madam," said the fairy, "but as regards beauty I can do a great deal. As there is nothing I would not do to please you, I will bestow upon her the power of making beautiful any person who shall greatly please her."

As the two princesses grew up their perfections increased, and everywhere the beauty of the elder and the wit of the younger were the subject of common talk.

It is equally true that their defects also increased as they became older. The younger grew uglier every minute, and the elder daily became more stupid. Either she answered nothing at all when spoken to, or replied with some idiotic remark. At the same time she was so awkward that she could not set four china vases on the mantelpiece without breaking one of them, nor drink a glass of water without spilling half of it over her clothes.

Now although the older girl possessed the great advantage which beauty always confers upon youth, she was nevertheless outshone in almost all company by her younger sister. At first everyone gathered round the beauty to see and admire her, but very soon they were all attracted by the graceful and easy conversation of the clever one. In a very short time the elder girl would be left entirely alone, while everybody clustered round her sister.

The elder princess was not so stupid that she was not aware of this, and she would willingly have surrendered all her beauty for half her sister's cleverness. Sometimes she was ready to die of grief, for the queen, though a sensible woman, could not refrain from occasionally reproaching her for her stupidity.

The princess had retired one day to a wood to bemoan her misfortune, when she saw approaching her an ugly little man, of very disagreeable appearance, but clad in magnificent attire.

This was the young prince Ricky of the Tuft. He had fallen in love with her portrait, which was everywhere to be seen, and had left his father's kingdom in order to have the pleasure of seeing and talking to her.

Delighted to meet her thus alone, he approached with every mark of respect and politeness. But while he paid her the usual compliments he noticed that she was plunged in melancholy.

"I cannot understand, madam," he said, "how any one with your beauty can be so sad as you appear. I can boast of seeing many fair ladies, and I declare that none of them could compare in beauty with you."

"It is very kind of you to say so, sir," answered the princess; and stopped there, at a loss what to say further.

"Beauty," said Ricky, "is of such great advantage that everything else can be disregarded; and I do not see that the possessor of it can have anything to grieve about." To this the princess replied: "I would rather be as plain as you are and have some sense than be as beautiful as I am and at the same time stupid."

"Nothing more clearly displays good sense, madam, than a belief that one is not possessed of it. It follows, therefore, that the more one has, the more one fears it to be wanting."

"I am not sure about that," said the princess, "but I know only too well that I am very stupid, and this is the reason of the misery which is nearly killing me."

"If that is all that troubles you, madam, I can easily put an end to your suffering."

"How will you manage that?" said the princess.

"I am able, madam," said Ricky of the Tuft, "to bestow as much good sense as it is possible to possess on the person whom I love the most. You are that person, and it therefore rests with you to decide whether you will acquire so much intelligence. The only condition is that you shall consent to marry me."

The princess was dumbfounded, and remained silent.

"I can see," pursued Ricky, "that this suggestion perplexes you, and I am not surprised. But I will give you a whole year to make up your mind to it."

The princess had so little sense, and at the same time desired it so ardently, that she persuaded herself the end of this year would never come. So she accepted the offer which had been made to her. No sooner had she given her word to Ricky that she would marry him within one year from that very day, than she felt a complete change come over her. She found herself able to say all that she wished with the greatest ease, and to say it in an elegant, finished, and natural manner. She at once engaged Ricky in a brilliant and lengthy conversation, holding her own so well that Ricky feared he had given her a larger share of sense than he had retained for himself.

On her return to the palace, amazement reigned throughout the Court at such a sudden and extraordinary change. Whereas formerly they had been accustomed to hear her give vent to silly, pert remarks, they now heard her express herself sensibly and very wittily.

The entire Court was overjoyed. The only person not too pleased was the younger sister, for now that she had no longer the advantage over the elder in wit, she seemed nothing but a little fright in comparison.

The king himself often took her advice, and several times held his councils in her apartment.

The news of this change spread abroad, and the princes of the neighboring kingdoms made many attempts to captivate her. Almost all asked her in marriage. But she found none with enough sense, and so she listened to all without promising herself to any.

At last came one who was so powerful, so rich, so witty, and so handsome, that she could not help being somewhat attracted by him. Her father noticed this, and told her she could make her own choice of a husband: she had only to declare herself.

Now the more sense one has, the more difficult it is to make up one's mind in an affair of this kind. After thanking her father, therefore, she asked for a little time to think it over.

In order to ponder quickly what she had better do she went to walk in a wood—the very one, as it happened, where she encountered Ricky of the Tuft.

While she walked, deep in thought, she heard beneath her feet a thudding sound, as though many people were running busily to and fro. Listening more attentively she heard voices. "Bring me that boiler," said one; then another—"Put some wood on that fire!"

At that moment the ground opened, and she saw below what appeared to be a large kitchen full of cooks and scullions, and all the train of attendants which the preparation of a great banquet involves. A gang of 20 or 30 spit-turners emerged and took up their positions round a very long table in a path in the wood. They all wore their cooks' caps on one side, and with their basting implements in their hands they kept time together as they worked, to the lilt of a melodious song.

The princess was astonished by this spectacle, and asked for whom their work was being done.

"For Prince Ricky of the Tuft, madam," said the foreman of the gang; "his wedding is tomorrow."

At this the princess was more surprised than ever. In a flash she remembered that it was a year to the very day since she had promised to marry Prince Ricky of the Tuft, and was taken aback by the recollection. The reason she had forgotten was that when she made the promise she was still without sense, and with the acquisition of that intelligence which the prince had bestowed upon her, all memory of her former stupidities had been blotted out.

She had not gone another 30 paces when Ricky of the Tuft appeared before her, gallant and resplendent, like a prince upon his wedding day.

"As you see, madam," he said, "I keep my word to the minute. I do not doubt that you have come to keep yours, and by giving me your hand to make me the happiest of men."

"I will be frank with you," replied the princess. "I have not yet made up my mind to the point, and I am afraid shall never be able to take the decision you desire."

"You astonish me, madam," said Ricky of the Tuft.

"I can well believe it," said the princess, "and undoubtedly, if I had to deal with a clown, or a man who lacked good sense, I should feel myself very awkwardly situated. 'A princess must keep her word,' he would say, 'and you must marry me because you promised to!' But I am speaking to a man of the world, of the greatest good sense, and I am sure that he will listen to reason. As you are aware, I could not make up my mind to marry you even when I was entirely without sense; how can you expect that today, possessing the intelligence you bestowed on me, which makes me still more difficult to please than formerly, I should take a decision which I could not take then? If you wished so much to marry me, you were very wrong to relieve me of my stupidity, and to let me see more clearly than I did."

"If a man who lacked good sense," replied Ricky of the Tuft, "would be justified, as you would have just said, in reproaching you for breaking your word, why do you expect, madam, that I should act differently where the happiness of my whole life is at stake? Is it reasonable that people who have sense should be treated worse than those who have none? Would you maintain that for a moment—you, who so markedly have sense, and desired so ardently to have it? But, pardon me, let us get to the facts. With the exception of my ugliness, is there anything about me which displeases you? Are you dissatisfied with my breeding, my brains, my disposition, or my manners?"

"In no way," replied the princess; "I like exceedingly all that you have displayed of the qualities you mention."

"In that case," said Ricky of the Tuft, "happiness will be mine, for it lies in your power to make the most attractive of men."

"How can that be done?" asked the princess.

"It will happen of itself," replied Ricky of the Tuft, "if you love me well enough to wish that it be so. To remove your doubts, madam, let me tell you that the same fairy who on the day of my birth bestowed upon me the power of endowing with intelligence the woman of my choice, gave to you also the power of endowing with beauty the man whom you should love, and on whom you should wish to confer this favor."

"If that is so," said the princess, "I wish with all my heart that you may become the handsomest and most attractive prince in the world, and I give you without reserve the boon which it is mine to bestow."

No sooner had the princess uttered these words than Ricky of the Tuft appeared before her eyes as the handsomest, most graceful and attractive man that she had ever set eyes on.

Some people assert that this was not the work of fairy enchantment, but that love alone brought about the transformation. They say that the princess, as she mused upon her lover's constancy, upon his good sense, and his many admirable qualities of heart and head, grew blind to the deformity of his body and the ugliness of his face; that his hump back seemed no more than was natural in a man who could make the courtliest of bows, and that the dreadful limp which had formerly distressed her now betokened nothing more than a certain diffidence and charming deference of manner. They say further that she found his eyes shine all the brighter for their squint, and that this defect in them was to her but a sign of passionate love; while his great red nose she found but martial and heroic.

However that may be, the princess promised to marry him on the spot, provided that he could obtain the consent of her royal father.

The king knew Ricky of the Tuft to be a prince both wise and witty, and on learning of his daughter's regard for him, he accepted him with pleasure as a son-in-law.

The wedding took place upon the morrow, just as Ricky of the Tuft had foreseen, and in accordance with the arrangements he had long ago put in train.

THE THREE SOLDIERS

Hans Christian Andersen

Three poor soldiers who, having fought hard in the wars, set out on their road home, were reduced to begging as they went. One evening they reached a gloomy wood, where they had to rest. To make all safe, they agreed that two should sleep while the third watched. When he was tired he was to wake one of the others, and sleep in his turn, and so on. The first one had not watched long before up came a little man in a red jacket. "Who's there?" said he.

"A friend," said the soldier.

"What sort of a friend?"

"An old, broken soldier," said the other; "come, sit down and warm yourself."

"Well," said the little man, "I will do what I can for you; take this and show it to your comrades in the morning." So he took out an old cloak and gave it to the soldier, telling him that whenever he put it over his shoulders, anything that he wished for would be fulfilled; then the little man walked away.

When the second soldier's turn to watch came, the little man in the red jacket appeared again. The soldier treated him in a friendly way, and the little man gave him a purse, which was always full of gold.

Then the third soldier's turn came, and he also had the little man for his guest, who gave him a wonderful horn that made everyone dance to its beautiful music.

In the morning each told his story, then showed his treasure; and they agreed to travel together to see the world, and for awhile to make use only of the wonderful purse. Thus they spent their time joyously, till they tired of this roving life, and thought they should like to have a home of their own. So the first soldier put his cloak on, and wished for a fine castle. In a moment it stood before their eyes; gardens and green lawns spread round it, and flocks of sheep and goats, and herds of oxen were grazing about, and out of the gate came a fine coach with three dapple-grey horses to meet them and bring them home.

This was very well for a time; but it would not do to stay at home always, so they got together all the rich clothes and horses and servants, and ordered their coach with three horses, and set out to see a neighboring king. This king had an only daughter, and as he took the three soldiers for king's sons, he gave them a kind welcome. One day the second soldier was walking with the princess. Now this princess was a witch, and knew all the wonderful things that the three soldiers brought. She set to work and made a purse so like the soldier's that no one would know one from the other, and then asked him to come and see her, and made him drink some wine that she had got ready for him, till he fell asleep. Then she felt in his pocket, and took away the wonderful purse, and left the one she had made instead.

Next morning the soldiers set out home, and soon after they reached their castle, happening to want some money, they went to their purse, and found to their great sorrow, when they had emptied it, none came in place of it. Then the cheat was found out; for the second soldier knew where he had been, and how he had told the story to the Princess, and he guessed that she had betrayed him. "Oh," said the first soldier, "I will soon get the purse back!"

So he threw his cloak across his shoulders and wished himself in the Princess's chamber. There he found her sitting alone with her gold that fell around her in a shower from the purse. The soldier stood looking at her too long, for the moment she saw him she started up and cried out: "Thieves! Thieves!" so that the whole court came and tried to seize him. The poor soldier began to be dreadfully frightened; so without thinking of the ready way of traveling his cloak gave him, ran to the window, opened it and jumped out. Unluckily, in his haste, his cloak caught and was left hanging, to the great joy of the Princess who knew its worth.

The poor soldier made his way home to his comrades on foot in a very downcast mood; but the third soldier told him to keep up his heart, and took his horn and blew a merry tune. At the first blast a countless troop of foot and horse came rushing to their aid, and they set out to make war against their enemy. The king's palace was besieged, and he was told that he must give up the purse and cloak, or that not one stone would be left upon another. The king went into his daughter's chamber and talked with her; but she said: "Let me try first if I cannot beat them." So she thought of a cunning scheme, dressed herself as a poor girl, and set out by night with her maid, and went into the enemy's camp, as if she wanted to sell trinkets.

In the morning she began singing ballads so beautifully that the soldiers ran around in crowds and thought of nothing but hearing her sing. Amongst the rest came the soldier to whom the horn belonged. As soon as she saw him she winked to her maid, who slipped slyly through the crowd and went into his tent where it hung, and stole it away. This done, they both got safely back to the palace; the besieging army went away, the three wonderful gifts were left in the hands of the Princess, and the soldiers were as penniless and forlorn as when the little man with the red jacket found them in the wood.

Poor fellows! They began to think, what was now to be done. "Comrades," at last said the soldier who had had the purse, "we had better part; we cannot live together. Let each seek his bread as well as he can." So he turned to the right, and the other two to the left; for they said they would rather travel together. On he strayed till he came to a wood, and he walked on a long time, till evening began to fall, when he sat down tired beneath a tree, and soon fell asleep.

Morning dawned, and he was delighted, at opening his eyes, to see that the tree was laden with beautiful apples. He was hungry, so he plucked and ate first one, then a second, then a third apple. A strange feeling came over his nose: when he put the apple to his mouth something was in the way; he felt it; it was his nose, that grew and grew till it hung down to his breast. It did not stop there; still it grew and grew. "Heavens!" he thought; "when will it have done growing?" And will he might ask, for by this time it reached the ground as he sat on the grass, and thus it kept creeping on till he could not bear its weight, or raise himself up; and it seemed as if it would never end, for already it stretched its enormous length all through the wood.

Meantime his comrades were journeying on, till on a sudden one of them stumbled against something. "What can that be?" said the other. They looked, but could think of nothing that it was like but a nose. "We will follow and find its owner, however," said they; so they traced it till at last they found their poor comrade stretched under the apple tree. What was to be done? They tried to carry him, but in vain. They caught an ass that was passing by, and raised him upon its back; but it was soon tired of carrying such a load. So they sat down in despair, when up came the little man in the red jacket. "Why, how now, friend?" said he, laughing; "well, I must find a cure for you, I see." So he told them to gather a pear from a tree that grew close by, and the nose would come right again. No time was lost, and the nose was soon brought to its proper size, to the poor soldier's joy.

"I will do something more for you yet," said the little man; "take some of those pears and apples with you; whoever eats one of the apples you will have his nose grow like yours just now; but if you give him a pear, all will come right again. Go to the Princess and get her to eat some of your apples; her nose will grow 20 times as long as yours did; then look sharp, and you will get what you want of her."

They thanked their old friend for his kindness, and it was agreed that the poor soldier who had already tried the power of the apple should undertake the task. He dressed himself up as a gardener's boy, and went to the king's palace, and said he had apples to sell, such as were never seen there before. Everyone that saw them was delighted, and wanted to taste, but he said they were only for the princess; and she soon sent her maid to buy his stock. They were so ripe and rosy that she soon began eating, and had already eaten three when she began to wonder what ailed her nose, for it grew and grew, down to the ground,

out at the window, and over the garden.

Then the king made known to all his kingdom, that whoever would heal her of this dreadful disease should be richly rewarded. Many tried, but the princess got no relief. And now the old soldier dressed himself up very sprucely as a doctor, who said he could cure her; so he chopped up some of the apple, and to punish her a little more gave her a dose, saying he would call tomorrow and see her again. The morrow came, and of course, instead of being better, the nose had been growing all night and the Princess was in a dreadful fright. So the doctor chopped up a very little of the pear and gave her, and said he was sure that would do good, and he would call again the next day. Next day came, and it was bigger than it was when the doctor first began to meddle with it.

Then he thought to himself: "I must frighten this cunning princess a little more before I shall get what I want of her;" so he gave her another dose of the apple, and said he would call on the morrow. The morrow came, and the nose was ten times as bad as before.

"My good lady," said the doctor, "something works against my medicine, and it was too strong for it; but I know by the force of my art what it is; you have stolen goods about you, I am sure, and if you do not give them back, I can do nothing for you."

The princess denied very stoutly that she had anything of the kind.

"Very well," said the doctor, "you may do as you please, but I am sure I am right and you will die if you do not own it."

Then he went to the king, and told him how the matter stood. "Daughter," said he, "send back the cloak, the purse, and the horn that you stole from the right owners."

Then she ordered her maid to fetch them, and begged the doctor to give them back to the soldiers; and the moment he had them safe he gave her a whole pear to eat, and the nose came right. And as for the doctor, he put on the cloak, wished the king and all his court a good day, and was soon with his two brothers, who lived from that time happily at home in their palace, except when they took airings in their coach with the three dapple-grey horses.

PETER PAN

J. M. BARRIE

Wendy and her brothers, John and Michael get an unexpected visit one night from the captain of the lost boys, Peter Pan and his fairy Tinker Bell. Peter Pan tells Wendy about the Neverland and she teaches him what a kiss is.

Chapter 3 COME AWAY, COME AWAY!

moment after the fairy's entrance the window was blown open by the breathing of the little stars, and Peter dropped in. He had carried Tinker Bell part of the way, and his hand was still messy with the fairy dust.

"Tinker Bell," he called softly, after making sure that the children were asleep, "Tink, where are you?" She was in a jug for the moment, and liking it extremely; she had never been in a jug before.

"Oh, do come out of that jug, and tell me, do you know where they put my shadow?"

The loveliest tinkle as of golden bells answered him. It is the fairy language. You ordinary children can never hear it, but if you were to hear it you would know that you had heard it once before.

Tink said that the shadow was in the big box. She meant the chest of drawers, and Peter jumped at the drawers, scattering their contents to the floor with both hands, as kings toss ha'pence to the crowd. In a moment he had recovered his shadow, and in his delight he forgot that he had shut Tinker Bell up in the drawer.

If he had thought at all, but I don't believe he ever thought, it was that he and his shadow, when brought near each other, would join like drops of water; and when they did not he was appalled. He tried to stick it on with soap from the bathroom, but that also failed. A shudder passed through Peter, and he sat on the floor and cried.

His sobs woke Wendy, and she sat up in bed. She was not alarmed to see a stranger crying on the nursery floor; she was only pleasantly interested.

"Boy," she said courteously, "why are you crying?"

Peter politefully bowed and she bowed back.

"What's your name?' he asked.

"Wendy Moira Angela Darling," she replied with some satisfaction. "What is your name?"

"Peter Pan."

She was already sure that he must be Peter, but it did seem a comparatively short name.

"Is that all?"

"Yes," he said rather sharply. He felt for the first time that it was a shortish name.

"I'm so sorry," said Wendy Moira Angela.

"It doesn't matter," Peter gulped.

She asked where he lived.

"Second to the right," said Peter, "and then straight on till morning."

"What a funny address!"

Peter had a sinking feeling. For the first time he felt that perhaps it was a funny address. "No, it isn't," he said.

"I mean," Wendy said nicely, remembering that she was hostess, "is that what they put on the letters?"

He wished she had not mentioned letters.

"Don't get any letters," he said contemptuously.

"But your mother gets letters?"

"Don't have a mother," he said. Not only had he no mother, but he had not the slightest desire to have one. He thought them very overrated persons. Wendy, however, felt at once that she was in the presence of a tragedy.

"O Peter, no wonder you were crying," she said, and got out of bed and ran to him.

"I wasn't crying about mothers," he said rather indignantly. "I was crying because I can't get my shadow to stick on. Besides, I wasn't crying."

"It has come off?"

"Yes."

Then Wendy saw the shadow on the floor and felt sorry for Peter. He had been trying to stick it on with soap. How exactly like a boy!

Fortunately she knew at once what to do. "It must be sewn on," she said, just a little patronizingly.

"What's sewn?" he asked.

"You're dreadfully ignorant."

"No, I'm not."

But she was exulting in his ignorance. "I shall sew it on for you, my little man," she said, though he was as tall as herself; and she sewed the shadow on to Peter's foot.

"I daresay it will hurt a little," she warned him.

"Oh, I shan't cry," said Peter, and soon his shadow was behaving properly, though still a little creased.

"Perhaps I should have ironed it," Wendy said thoughtfully; but Peter, boylike, was indifferent to appearances, and he was now jumping about in the wildest glee. Alas, he had already forgotten that he owed his bliss to Wendy. He thought he had attached the shadow himself. "How clever I am," he crowed rapturously, "oh, the cleverness of me!"

It is humiliating to have to confess that this conceit of Peter was one of his most fascinating qualities. To put it with brutal frankness, there never was a cockier boy.

But for the moment Wendy was shocked. "You conceit," she exclaimed, with frightful sarcasm; "of course I did nothing!"

"You did a little," Peter said carelessly, and continued to dance.

"A little!" she replied with hauteur; "if I am no use I can at least withdraw"; and she sprang in the most dignified way into bed and covered her face with the blankets.

To induce her to look up he pretended to be going away, and when this failed he sat on the end of the bed and tapped her gently with his foot. "Wendy," he said, "don't withdraw. I can't help crowing, Wendy, when I'm pleased with myself." Still she would not look up, though she was listening eagerly. "Wendy," he continued in a voice that no woman has ever yet been able to resist, "Wendy, one girl is more use than twenty boys."

Now Wendy was every inch a woman, though there were not very many inches, and she peeped out of the bedclothes.

"Do you really think so, Peter?"

"Yes, I do."

"I think it's perfectly sweet of you," she declared, "and I'll get up again"; and she sat with him on the side of the bed. She also said she would give him a kiss if he liked, but Peter did not know what she meant, and he held out his hand expectantly.

"Surely you know what a kiss is?" she asked aghast.

"I shall know when you give it to me," he replied stiffly; and not to hurt his feeling she gave him a thimble.

"Now," said he, "shall I give you a kiss?" and she replied with a slight primness, "If you please." She made herself rather cheap by inclining her face toward him, but he merely dropped an acorn button into her hand; so she slowly returned her face to where it had been before, and said nicely that she would wear his kiss on the chain round her neck. It was lucky that she did put it on that chain, for it was afterward to save her life.

When people in our set are introduced, it is customary for them to ask each other's age, and so Wendy, who always liked to do the correct thing, asked Peter how old he was. It was not really a happy question to ask him; it was like an examination paper that asks grammar, when what you want to be asked is Kings of England.

"I don't know," he replied uneasily, "but I am quite young." He really knew nothing about it; he had merely suspicions, but he said at a venture, "Wendy, I ran away the day I was born."

Wendy was quite surprised, but interested; and she indicated in the charming drawing-room manner, by a touch on her night-gown, that he could sit nearer her.

"It was because I heard father and mother," he explained in a low voice, "talking about what I was to be when I became a man." He was extraordinarily agitated now. "I don't want ever to be a man," he said with passion. "I want always to be a little boy and to have fun. So I ran away to Kensington Gardens and lived a long long time among the fairies."

Wendy had lived such a home life that to know fairies struck her as quite delightful. She poured out questions about them, to his surprise, for they were rather a nuisance to him, getting in his way, and so on, and indeed he sometimes had to give them a hiding. Still, he liked them on the whole, and he told her about the beginnings of the fairies.

"You see, Wendy, when the first baby laughed for the first time, its laugh broke into a thousand pieces, and they all went skipping about, and that was the beginning of fairies."

Tedious talk this, but being a stay-at-home she liked it.

"And so," he went on good-naturedly, "there ought to be one fairy for every boy and girl."

"Ought to be? Isn't here?"

"No. You see children know such a lot now, they soon don't believe in fairies, and every time a child says, 'I don't believe in fairies,' there is a fairy somewhere that falls down dead."

Really, he thought they had now talked enough about fairies, and it struck him that Tinker Bell was keeping very quiet. "I can't think where she has gone to," he said, rising, and he called Tink by name. Wendy's heart went flutter with a sudden thrill.

"Peter," she cried, clutching him, "you don't mean to tell me that there is a fairy in this room!"

"She was here just now," he said a little impatiently. "You don't hear her, do you?" and they both listened.

"The only sound I hear," said Wendy, "is like a tinkle of bells."

"Well, that's Tink, that's the fairy language. I think I hear her too."

The sound came from the chest of drawers, and Peter made a merry face. No one could ever look quite so merry as Peter, and the loveliest of gurgles was his laugh. He had his first laugh still.

"Wendy," he whispered gleefully, "I do believe I shut her up in the drawer!"

He let poor Tink out of the drawer, and she flew about the nursery screaming with fury. "You shouldn't say such things," Peter retorted. "Of course I'm very sorry, but how could I know you were in the drawer?"

Wendy was not listening to him. "O Peter," she cried, "if she would only stand still and let me see her!"

"They hardly ever stand still," he said, but for one moment Wendy saw the romantic figure come to rest on the cuckoo clock. "O the lovely!" she cried, though Tink's face was still distorted with passion.

"Tink," said Peter amiably, "this lady says she wishes you were her fairy."

Tinker Bell answered insolently.

"What does she say, Peter?"

He had to translate. "She is not very polite. She says you are a great ugly girl, and that she is my fairy."

PETER PAN *J. M. Barrie*

He tried to argue with Tink. "You know you can't be my fairy, Tink, because I am a gentleman and you are a lady."

To this Tink replied in these words, "you silly ass," and disappeared into the bathroom. "She is quite a common fairy," Peter explained apologetically; "she is called Tinker Bell because she mends the pots and kettles."

They were together in the armchair by this time, and Wendy plied him with more questions.

"If you don't live in Kensington Gardens now—"

"Sometimes I do still."

"But where do you live mostly now?"

"With the lost boys."

"Who are they?"

"They are the children who fall out of their perambulators when the nurse is looking the other way. If they are not claimed in seven days they are sent far away to the Neverland to defray expenses. I'm captain."

"What fun it must be!"

"Yes," said cunning Peter, "but we are rather lonely. You see we have no female companionship."

"Are none of the others girls?"

"Oh no; girls, you know, are much too clever to fall out of their prams."

This flattered Wendy immensely. "I think," she said, "it is perfectly lovely the way you talk about girls; John there just despises us."

For reply Peter rose and kicked John out of bed, blankets and all; one kick. This seemed to Wendy rather forward for a first meeting, and she told him with spirit that he was not captain in her house.

However, John continued to sleep so placidly on the floor that she allowed him to remain there. "And I know you meant to be kind," she said, relenting, "so you may give me a kiss."

For the moment she had forgotten his ignorance about kisses. "I thought you would want it back," he said a little bitterly, and offered to return her the thimble.

"Oh dear," said the nice Wendy, "I don't mean a kiss, I mean a thimble."

"What's that?"

"It's like this." She kissed him.

Barrie, J. M. *Peter Pan*. New York: Dell Yearling, 1985.
    Other Editions:
    ——. *Peter Pan*. New York: Henry Holt & Co., 1987.
    ——. *Peter Pan*. New York: Penguin, Puffin Books, 1993.
    ——. *Peter Pan: The Complete Book*. New York: Tundra Books, 1988.

BLUE BEARD

CHARLES PERRAULT

Because Blue Beard was a rich man who lived in two luxurious, fine houses, most would think him a lucky man. However, he had the true misfortune of growing a blue beard—which made him frightfully ugly! Women typically fled from him in fear and disgust. Here is the classic story of Blue Beard.

ne of his neighbors, a lady of quality, had two daughters who were perfect beauties. He desired of her one of them in marriage, leaving to her choice which of the two she would bestow on him. They would neither of them have him, and sent him backward and forward from one another, not being able to bear the thoughts of marrying a man who had a blue beard, and what besides gave them disgust and aversion was his having already been married to several wives, and nobody ever knew what became of them.

Blue Beard, to engage their affection, took them, with the lady their mother and three or four ladies of their acquaintance, with other young people of the neighborhood, to one of his country seats, where they stayed a whole week.

There was nothing then to be seen but parties of pleasure, hunting, fishing, dancing, mirth, and feasting. Nobody went to bed, but all passed the night in rallying and joking with each other. In short, everything succeeded so well that the youngest daughter began to think the master of the house not to have a beard so very blue, and that he was a mighty civil gentleman.

As soon as they returned home the marriage was concluded. About a month afterward, Blue Beard told his wife that he was obliged to take a country journey for six weeks at least, about affairs of very great consequence, desiring her to divert herself in his absence, to send for her friends and acquaintances, to carry them into the country if she pleased, and to make good cheer wherever she was.

"Here," said he, "are the keys of the two great wardrobes, wherein I have my best furniture; these are of my silver and gold plate, which is not every day in use; these open my strongboxes, which hold my money, both gold and silver; these my caskets of jewels; and this is the master-key to all my apartments. But for this little one here, it is the key of the closet at the end of the great gallery on the ground-floor. Open them all; go into all and every one of them, except that little closet, which I forbid you, and forbid it in such a manner that, if you happen to open it, there's nothing but what you may expect from my just anger and resentment."

She promised to observe, very exactly, whatever he had ordered; when he, after having embraced her, got into his coach and proceeded on his journey.

Her neighbors and good friends did not stay to be sent for by the new-married lady, so great was their impatience to see all the rich furniture of her house, not daring to come while her husband was there, because of his blue beard, which frightened them. They ran through all the rooms, closets, and wardrobes, which were all so fine and rich that they seemed to surpass one another.

After that they went up into the two great rooms, where were the best and richest furniture; they could not sufficiently admire the number and beauty of the tapestry, beds, couches, cabinets, stands, tables, and looking-glasses, in which you might see yourself from head to foot; some of them were framed with glass, others with silver, plain and gilded, the finest and most magnificent ever were seen.

They ceased not to extol and envy the happiness of their friend, who in the mean time in no way diverted herself in looking upon all these rich things, because of the inpatience she had to go and open the closet on the ground-floor. She was so much pressed by her curiosity that, without considering that it was very uncivil to leave her company, she went down a little back staircase, and with such excessive haste that she had twice or thrice like to have broken her neck.

Being come to the closet door, she made a stop for some time, thinking upon her husband's orders and considering what unhappiness might attend her if she was disobedient; but the temptation was so strong she could not overcome it. She then took the little key and opened it, trembling, but could not at first see anything plainly, because the windows were shut. After some moments she began to perceive that the floor was all covered over with clotted blood, on which lay the bodies of several dead women, ranged against the walls. (These were all the wives whom Blue Beard had married and murdered, one after another.) She thought she should have died for fear, and the key, which she pulled out of the lock, fell out of her hand.

After having somewhat recovered her surprise, she took up the key, locked the door, and went upstairs into her chamber to recover herself; but she could not, so much was she frightened. Having observed that the key of the closet was stained with blood, she tried two or three times to wipe it off, but the blood would not come out; in vain did she wash it, and even rub it with soap and sand: the blood still remained, for the key was magical and she could never make it quite clean; when the blood was gone off from one side it came again as bright as ever on the other.

Blue Beard returned from his journey the same evening, and said he had received letters upon the road informing him that the affair he went about was ended to his advantage. His wife did all she could to convince him she was extremely glad of his speedy return.

Next morning he asked her for the keys, which she gave him, but with such a trembling hand that he easily guessed what had happened.

"What!" said he, "Is not the key of my closet among the rest?"

"I must certainly," said she, "have left it above upon the table."

"Fail not," said Blue Beard," to bring it to me presently."

After several goings backward and forward she was forced to bring the key. Blue Beard, having very attentively considered it, said to his wife:

"How comes this blood upon the key?"

"I do not know," cried the poor woman, paler than death.

"You do not know!" replied Blue Beard. "I very well know. You were resolved to go into the closet, were you not? Mighty well, madam; you shall go in and take your place among the ladies you saw there."

Upon this she threw herself at her husband's feet and begged his pardon with all the signs of a true repentance, vowing that she would never more be disobedient. She would have melted a rock, so beautiful and sorrowful was she; but Blue Beard had a heart harder than any rock!

"You must die, madam," said he, "and that presently."

"Since I must die," answered she, looking upon him with her eyes all bathed in tears, "give me some little time to say my prayers."

"I give you," replied Blue Beard, "half a quarter of an hour, but not one moment more."

When she was alone she called out to her sister and said to her: "Sister Anne," for that was her name, "go up, I beg you, upon the top of the tower, and look if my brothers are not coming; they promised me that they would come today, and if you see them, give them a sign to make haste."

Her sister Anne went up upon the top of the tower, and the poor afflicted wife cried out from time to time:

"Anne, sister Anne, do you see any one coming?"

And sister Anne said:

"I see nothing but the sun, which makes a dust, and the grass, which looks green."

In the mean while Blue Beard, holding a great saber in his hand, cried out as loud as he could bawl to his wife:

"One moment longer, if you please," said his wife; and then she cried out very softly: "Anne, sister Anne, dost thou see anybody coming?"

And sister Anne answered:

"I see nothing but the sun, which makes a dust, and the grass, which is green."

"Come down quickly," cried Blue Beard, "or I will come up to you."

"I am coming," answered his wife; and then she cried: "Anne, sister Anne, dost thou not see any one coming?"

"I see," replied sister Anne, "a great dust, which comes on this side here."

"Are they my brothers?"

"Alas! no, my dear sister, I see a flock of sheep."

"Will you not come down?" said his wife, and then she cried out:

"Anne, sister Anne, dost thou see nobody coming?"

"I see," said she, "two horsemen, but they are yet a great way off."

"God be praised," replied the poor wife joyfully: "they are my brothers; I will make them a sign, as well as I can, for them to make haste."

Then Blue Beard bawled out so loud that he made the whole house tremble. The distressed wife came down and threw herself at his feet, all in tears, with her hair about her shoulders.

"This signifies nothing," says Blue Beard; "you must die"; then, taking hold of her hair with one hand and lifting up the sword with the other, he was going to take off her head. The poor lady, turning about to him and looking at him with dying eyes, desired him to afford her one little moment to collect herself.

"No, no," said he, recommend thyself to God," and was just ready to strike.

At this very instant there was such a loud knocking at the gate that Blue Beard made a sudden stop. The gate was opened, and presently entered two horsemen, who, drawing their swords, ran directly to Blue Beard. He knew them to be his wife's brothers, one a dragoon, the other a musketeer, so that he ran away immediately to save himself; but the two brothers pursued so close that they overtook him before he could get to the steps of the porch, when they ran their swords through his body and left him dead. The poor wife was almost as dead as her husband, and had not strength enough to rise and welcome her brothers.

Blue Beard had no heirs, and so wife became mistress of all his estate. She made use of one part of it to marry her sister Anne to a young gentleman who had loved her a long while; another part to buy captains' commissions for her brothers; and the rest to marry herself to a very worthy gentleman, who made her forget the ill time she had passed with Blue Beard.

Perrault, Charles and d'Aulnoy, Madame, eds. *The Sleeping Beauty and Other Classic French Fairy Tales*. New York: Random House, 1991.

    Other Editions:

    Laurence, Ann., trans. *Tales from Perrault*. New York: Oxford University Press, 1989.

    Grimm, Jacob and Grimm, Wilhelm K. *Sleeping Beauty*. New York: Silver, 1985.

    Poole, Josephine, ed. *Sleeping Beauty*. New York: Barron, 1989.

    Storer, Ronald, ed. *Sleeping Beauty & Bluebeard*. Oxford: Oxford University Press, 1972.

    Perrault, Charles. *Cinderella: Fairy Tales and Other Tales from Perrault*. New York: Henry Holt, 1989.

    Grimm, Jacob and Grimm, Wilhelm K. *Cinderella* New York: William Morrow & Co., 1981.

CINDERELLA, OR, THE LITTLE GLASS SLIPPER

CHARLES PERRAULT

This is the classic story of the girl whose coach turns into a pumpkin and whose fallen glass slipper makes all her dreams come true.

nce there was a gentleman who married for his second wife the proudest and most haughty woman that was ever seen. She had by a former husband two daughters of her own humor, who were, indeed, exactly like her in all things. He had likewise, by his first wife, a young daughter, but of unparalleled goodness and sweetness of temper, which she took from her mother, who was the best creature in the world.

No sooner were the ceremonies of the wedding over but the mother-in-law began to show herself in her true colors. She could not bear the good qualities of this pretty girl, and the less because they made her own daughters appear the more odious. She employed her in the meanest work of the house: she scoured the dishes, tables, etc., and scrubbed madam's chamber and those of misses, her daughters; she lay up in a sorry garret, upon a wretched straw bed, while her sisters lay in fine rooms, with floors all inlaid, upon beds of the very newest fashion, and where they had looking-glasses so large that they might see themselves at their full length from head to foot.

The poor girl bore all patiently and dared not to tell her father, who would have rattled her off; for his wife governed him entirely. When she had done her work she used to go into the chimney-corner and sit down among cinders and ashes, which made her commonly be called a cinder wench; but the youngest, who was not so rude and uncivil as the eldest, called her Cinderella. However, Cinderella, notwithstanding her mean apparel, was a hundred times handsomer than her sisters, though they were always dressed very richly.

It happened that the king's son gave a ball and invited all persons of fashion to it. Our young misses were also invited, for they cut a very grand figure among the quality. They were mightily delighted at this invitation, and wonderfully busy in choosing out such gowns, petticoats, and head-clothes as might become them. This was a new trouble to Cinderella, for it was she who ironed her sisters' linen and plaited their ruffles. They talked all day long of nothing but how they should be dressed.

"For my part," said the eldest, "I will wear my red velvet suit with French trimming."

"And I," said the youngest, "shall have my usual petticoat; but then, to make amends for that, I will put on my gold-flowered manteau and my diamond stomacher, which is far from being the most ordinary one in the world."

They sent for the best tire-woman they could get to make up their head-dresses and adjust their double pinners, and they had their red brushes and patches from Mademoiselle de la Poche.

Cinderella was likewise called up to them to be consulted in all these matters, for she had excellent notions and advised them always for the best, and offered her services to dress their heads, which they were very willing she should do. As she was doing this they said to her:

"Cinderella, would you not be glad to go to the ball?"

"Alas!" said she, "you only jeer me. It is not for such as I am to go thither."

"Thou art in the right of it," replied they. "It would make the people laugh to see a cinder wench at a ball."

Any one but Cinderella would have dressed their heads awry, but she was very good and dressed them perfectly well. They were almost two days without eating, so much they were transported with joy. They broke above a dozen of laces in trying to be laced up close, that they might have a fine slender shape, and they were continually at their looking-glass, at last the happy day came. They went to court, and Cinderella followed them with her eyes as long as she could, and when she had lost sight of them she fell a-crying.

Her godmother, who saw her all in tears, asked her what was the matter.

"I wish I could—I wish I could—"

She was not able to speak the rest, being interrupted by her tears and sobbing.

This godmother of hers, who was a fairy, said to her: "Thou wishest thou couldst go to the ball. Is it not so?"

"Y-es," cried Cinderella, with a great sigh.

"Well," said her godmother, "be but a good girl, and I will contrive that thou shalt go." Then she took her into her chamber and said to her: "Run into the garden and bring me a pumpkin."

Cinderella went immediately to gather the finest she could get, and brought it to her godmother, not being able to imagine how this pumpkin could make her go to the ball. Her godmother scooped out all the inside of it, having left nothing but the rind; which done, she struck it with her wand, and the pumpkin was instantly turned into a fine coach, gilded all over with gold.

She then went to look into her mouse-trap, where she found six mice, all alive, and ordered Cinderella to lift up a little the trap-door, when, giving each mouse as it went out a little tap with her wand, the mouse was that moment turned into a fine horse, which altogether made a very fine set of six horses of a beautiful mouse-colored dapple-gray.

Being at a loss for a coachman, Cinderella said:"I will go and see if there is never a rat in the rat-trap—we may make a coachman of him."

"Thou art in the right," replied her godmother. "Go and look."

Cinderella brought the trap to her, and in it there were three huge rats. The fairy made choice of one of the three which had the largest beard, and having touched him with her wand he was turned into a fat, jolly coachman, who had the smartest whiskers ever beheld. After that she said "Go again into the garden, and you will find six lizards behind the watering-pot. Bring them to me."

She had no sooner done so but her godmother turned them into six footmen, who skipped up immediately behind the coach, with their liveries all bedaubed with gold and silver, and clung as close behind each other as if they had done nothing else their whole lives. The fairy then said to Cinderella:

"Well, you see here an equipage fit to go to the ball with. Are you not pleased with it?"

"Oh! yes," cried she; "but must I go thither as I am, in these nasty rags?"

Her godmother only just touched her with her wand, and at the same instant her clothes were turned into cloth-of-gold and silver, all beset with jewels. This done, she gave her a pair of glass slippers, the prettiest in the whole world. Being thus decked out, she got up into her coach; but her godmother, above all things, commanded her not to stay till after midnight, telling her at the same time that if she stayed one moment longer the coach would be a pumpkin again, her horses mice, her coachman a rat, her footmen lizards, and her clothes become just as they were before.

She promised her godmother she would not fail of leaving the ball before midnight, and then away she drives, scarce able to contain herself for joy. The king's son, who was told that a great princess, whom nobody knew, had come, ran out to receive her. He gave her his hand as she alighted out of the coach, and led her into the hall among all the company. There was immediately a profound silence, they left off dancing, and the violins ceased to play, so attentive was every one to contemplate the singular beauties of the unknown new-comer. Nothing was then heard but a confused noise of "Ha! how handsome she is! Ha! How handsome she is!"

The king himself, old as he was, could not help watching her and telling the queen softly that it was a long time since he had seen so beautiful and lovely a creature.

All the ladies were busied in considering her clothes and head-dress, that they might have some made next day after the same pattern, provided they could meet with such fine materials and as able hands to make them.

The king's son conducted her to the most honorable seat and afterward took her out to dance with him. She danced so very gracefully that they all more and more admired her. A fine collation was served up, whereof the young prince ate not a morsel, so intently was he busied in gazing on her.

She went and sat down by her sister, showing them a thousand civilities, giving them part of the oranges and citrons which the prince had presented her with, which very much surprised them, for they did not know her. While Cinderella was thus amusing her sisters, she heard the clock strike eleven and three-quarters, whereupon she immediately made a curtsey to the company and hastened away as fast as she could.

On arriving home, she ran to seek out her godmother, and after having thanked her she said she could not but heartily wish she might go next day to the ball, because the king's son had desired her to.

As she was eagerly telling her godmother what had passed at the ball her two sisters knocked at the door, which Cinderella ran and opened.

"How long you have stayed!" cried she, gaping, rubbing her eyes, and stretching herself as if she had been just waked out of her sleep. She had not, however, had any manner of inclination to sleep since they went from home. "If thou hadst been at the ball," said one of her sisters, "thou wouldst not have been tired with it. There came thither the finest princess, the most beautiful ever was seen with mortal eyes. She showed us a thousand civilities and gave us oranges and citrons."

Cinderella seemed very indifferent in the matter. Indeed, she asked them the name of that princess, but they told her they did not know it, and that the king's son was very uneasy on her account and would give all the world to know who she was. At this Cinderella, smiling, replied:

"She must, then, be very beautiful indeed. How happy you have been! Could not I see her? Ah! dear Miss Charlotte, do lend me your yellow suit of clothes which you wear every day."

"Ay, to be sure!" cried Miss Charlotte; "lend my clothes to such a dirty cinder wench as thou art! I should be a fool."

Cinderella expected well such answer and was very glad of the refusal, for she would have been sadly put to it if her sister had lent her what she asked for jestingly.

The next day the two sisters were at the ball, and so was Cinderella, but dressed more magnificently than before. The king's son was always by her and never ceased his compliments and kind speeches to her, to whom all this was so far from being tiresome that she quite forgot what her godmother had recommended to her, so that she at last counted the clock striking twelve when she took it to be no more than eleven. She then rose up and fled as nimble as a deer. The prince followed, but could not overtake her. She left behind one of her glass slippers, which the prince took up most carefully. She got home, but quite out of breath, and in her old clothes, having nothing left of all finery but one of the little slippers, fellow to that she dropped. The guards at the palace gate were asked if they had not seen a princess go out.

They said they had seen nobody go out but a young girl, very meanly dressed, and who had more of the air of a poor country wench than a gentlewoman.

When the two sisters returned from the ball Cinderella asked them if they had been well diverted and if the fine lady had been there.

They told her yes, but that she hurried away immediately when it struck twelve, and with so much haste that she dropped one of her little glass slippers, the prettiest in the world, which the king's son had taken up; that he had done nothing but look at her all the time at the ball, and that most certainly he was very much in love with the beautiful person who owned the glass slipper.

What they said was very true, for a few days after the king's son caused it to be proclaimed, by sound of trumpet, that he would marry her whose foot this slipper would just fit. They whom he employed began to try it upon the princesses, then the duchesses and all the court, but in vain. It was brought to the two sisters, who did all they possible could to thrust their foot into the slipper, but they could not make it fit. Cinderella, who saw all this and knew her slipper, said to them, laughing:

"Let me see if it will not fit me."

Her sisters burst out a-laughing and began to banter her. The gentleman who was sent to try the slipper looked earnestly at Cinderella, and finding her very handsome said it was but just that she should try, and that he had orders to let every one make trial.

He obliged Cinderella to sit down, and putting the slipper to her foot he found it went on very easily and fitted her as if it had been made of wax. The astonishment her two sisters were in was excessively great, but still abundantly greater when Cinderella pulled out of her pocket the other slipper and put it on her foot. Thereupon in came her godmother, who, having touched with her wand Cinderella's clothes, made them richer and more magnificent than any of those she had before.

And now her two sisters found her to be that fine, beautiful lady whom they had seen at the ball. They threw themselves at her feet to beg pardon for all the ill-treatment, and as she embraced them cried that she forgave them with all her heart and desired them always to love her.

She was conducted to the young prince, dressed as she was. He thought her more charming than ever and a few days after married her. Cinderella, who was no less good than beautiful, gave her two sisters lodgings in the palace, and that very same day matched them with two great lords of the court.

Fairy Tales. New York: Random House, 1991.

    Other Editions:

    Laurence, Ann., trans. *Tales from Perrault.* New York: Oxford University Press, 1989.

    Grimm, Jacob and Grimm, Wilhelm K. *Sleeping Beauty.* New York: Silver, 1985.

    Poole, Josephine, ed. *Sleeping Beauty.* New York: Barron, 1989.

    Storer, Ronald, ed. *Sleeping Beauty & Bluebeard.* Oxford: Oxford University Press, 1972.

    Perrault, Charles. *Cinderella: Fairy Tales and Other Tales from Perrault.* New York: Henry Holt, 1989.

    Grimm, Jacob and Grimm, Wilhelm K. *Cinderella* New York: William Morrow & Co., 1981.

SLEEPING BEAUTY IN THE WOOD

CHARLES PERRAULT AND MADAME D'AULNOY

This classic French tale has delighted countless generations of young people, and has taken numerous forms—including the beloved Disney film.

nce upon a time there lived a king and queen who were grieved, more grieved than words can tell, because they had no children. They tried the waters of every country, made vows and pilgrimages, and did everything that could be done, but without result. At last, however, the queen found that her wishes were fulfilled, and in due course she gave birth to a daughter.

A grand christening was held, and all the fairies that could be found in the realm (they numbered seven in all) were invited to be godmothers to the little princess. This was done so that by means of the gifts which each in turn would bestow upon her (in accordance with the fairy custom of those days) the princess might be endowed with every imaginable perfection.

When the christening was held, all the company returned to the king's palace, where a great banquet was held in honor of the fairies. Places were laid for them in magnificent style, and before each was placed a solid gold casket containing a spoon, fork, and knife of fine gold, set with diamonds and rubies. But just as all were sitting down to table an aged fairy was seen to enter, whom no one had thought to invite—the reason being that for more than 50 years she had never quitted the tower in which she lived, and people had supposed her to be dead or bewitched.

By the king's orders a place was laid for her, but it was impossible to find her a golden casket like the others, for only seven had been made for the seven fairies. The old creature believed that she was intentionally slighted, and muttered threats between her teeth.

She was overheard by one of the young fairies, who was seated nearby. The latter, guessing that some mischievous gift might be bestowed upon the little princess, hid behind the tapestry as soon as the company left the table. Her intention was to be the last to speak, and so to have the power of counteracting, as far as possible, any evil which the old fairy might do.

Presently the fairies began to bestow their gifts upon the princess. The youngest ordained that she should be the most beautiful person in the world; the next, that she should have the temper of an angel; the third, that she should do everything with wonderful grace; the fourth, that she should dance to perfection; the fifth, that she should sing like a nightingale; and the sixth, that she should play every kind of music with the utmost skill.

It was now the turn of the aged fairy. Shaking her head, in token of spite rather than of infirmity, she declared that the princess should prick her hand with a spindle, and die of it. A shudder ran through the company at this terrible gift. All eyes were filled with tears.

But at this moment a young fairy stepped forth from behind the tapestry.

"Take comfort, your Majesties," she cried in a loud voice; "your daughter shall not die. My power, it is true, is not enough to undo all that my aged kinswoman has decreed: the princess will indeed prick her hand with a spindle. But instead of dying she shall merely fall into a profound slumber that will last a hundred years. At the end of that time a king's son shall come to awaken her."

The king, in an attempt to avert the unhappy doom pronounced by the old fairy, at once published an edict forbidding all persons, under pain of death, to use a spinning-wheel or keep a spindle in the house.

At the end of 15 or 16 years the king and queen happened one day to be away, on pleasure bent. The princess was running about the castle, and going upstairs from room to room she came at length to a garret at the top of a tower, where an old serving-woman sat alone with her distaff, spinning. This good woman had never heard speak of the king's proclamation forbidding the use of spinning-wheels.

"What are you doing, my good woman?" asked the princess.

"I am spinning, my pretty child," replied the dame, not knowing who she was.

"Oh, what fun!" rejoined the princess; "how do you do it? Let me try and see if I can do it equally well."

Partly because she was too hasty, partly because she was a little heedless, but also because the fairy decree had ordained it, no sooner had she seized the spindle than she pricked her hand and and fell down in a swoon.

In great alarm the good dame cried out for help. People came running from every quarter to the princess. They threw water on her face, chafed her with their hands, and rubbed her temples with the royal essence of Hungary. But nothing would restore her.

Then the king, who had been brought upstairs by the commotion, remembered the fairy prophecy. Feeling certain that what had happened was inevitable, since the fairies had decreed it, he gave orders that the princess should be placed in the finest apartment in the palace, upon a bed embroidered in gold and silver.

You would have thought her an angel, so fair was she to behold. The trance had not taken away the lovely color of her complexion. Her cheeks were delicately flushed, her lips like coral. Her eyes, indeed, were closed, but her gentle breathing could be heard, and it was therefore plain that she was not dead. The king commanded that she should be left to sleep in peace until the hour of her awakening should come.

When the accident happened to the princess, the good fairy who had saved her life by condemning her to sleep a hundred years was in the kingdom of Mataquin, 12,000 leagues away. She was instantly warned of it, however, by a little dwarf who had a pair of seven-league boots, which are boots that enable one to cover seven leagues at a single step. The fairy set off at once, and within an hour her chariot of fire, drawn by dragons, was seen approaching.

The king handed her down from her chariot, and she approved of all that he had done. But being gifted with great powers of foresight, she bethought herself that when the princess came to be awakened, she would be much distressed to find herself all alone in the old castle. And this is what she did.

She touched with her wand everybody (except the king and queen) who was in the castle—governesses, maids of honor, ladies-in-waiting, gentlemen, officers, stewards, cooks, scullions, errand boys, guards, porters, pages, footmen. She touched likewise all the horses in the stables, with their grooms, the big mastiffs in the courtyard, and little Puff, the pet dog of the princess, who was lying on the bed beside his mistress. The moment she had touched them they all fell asleep, to awaken only at the same moment as their mistress. Thus they would always be ready with their service whenever she should require it. The very spits before the fire, loaded with partridges and pheasants, subsided into slumber, and the fire as well. All was done in a moment, for the fairies do not take long over their work.

Then the king and queen kissed their dear child, without waking her, and left the castle. Proclamations were issued, forbidding any approach to it, but these warnings were not needed, for within a quarter of an hour there grew up all round the park so vast a quantity of trees big and small, with interlacing brambles and thorns, that neither man nor beast could penetrate them. The tops alone of the castle towers could be seen, and these only from a distance. Thus did the fairy's magic contrive that the princess, during all the time of her slumber, should have nought whatever to fear from prying eyes.

At the end of a hundred years the throne had passed to another family from that of the sleeping princess. One day the king's son chanced to go a-hunting that way, and seeing in the distance some towers in the midst of a large and dense forest, he asked what they were. His attendants told him in reply the various stories which they had heard. Some said there was an old castle haunted by ghosts, others that all the witches of the neighborhood held their revels there. The favorite tale was that in the castle lived an ogre, who carried thither all the children whom he could catch. There he dispensed with them at his leisure, and since he was the only person who could force a passage through the wood nobody had been able to pursue him.

While the prince was wondering what to believe, an old peasant took up the tale.

"Your highness," said he, "more than 50 years ago I heard my father say that in this castle lies a princess, the most beautiful that has ever been seen. It is her doom to sleep there for a hundred years, and then to be awakened by a king's son, for whose coming she waits."

This story fired the young prince. He jumped immediately to the conclusion that it was for him to see so gay an adventure through, and impelled alike by the wish for love and glory, he resolved to set about it on the spot.

Hardly had he taken a step towards the wood when the tall trees, the brambles and the thorns, separated of themselves and made a path for him. He turned in the direction of the castle, and espied it at the end of a long avenue. This avenue he entered, and was surprised to notice that the trees closed up again as soon as he had passed, so that none of his retinue were able to follow him. A young and gallant prince is always brave, however; so he continued on his way, and presently reached a large fore-court.

The sight that now met his gaze was enough to fill him with an icy fear. The silence of the place was dreadful, and death seemed all about him. The recumbent figures of men and animals had all the appearance of being lifeless, until he perceived by the pimply noses and ruddy faces of the porters that they merely slept. It was plain, too, from their glasses, in which were still some dregs of wine, that they had fallen asleep while drinking.

The prince made his way into a great courtyard, paved with marble, and mounting the staircase entered the guardroom. Here the guards were lined up on either side in two ranks, their muskets on their shoulders, snoring their hardest. Through several apartments crowded with ladies and gentlemen in waiting, some seated, some standing, but all asleep, he pushed on, and so came at last to a chamber which was decked all over with gold. There he encountered the most beautiful sight he had ever seen. Reclining upon a bed, the curtains of which on every side were drawn back, was a princess of seemingly some 15 or 16 summers, whose radiant beauty had an almost unearthly luster.

Trembling in his admiration he drew near and went on his knees beside her. At the same moment, the hour of disenchantment having come, the princess awoke, and bestowed upon him a look more tender than a first glance might seem to warrant.

"Is it you, dear prince?" she said; "You have been long in coming!"

Charmed by these words, and especially by the manner in which they were said, the prince scarcely knew how to express his delight and gratification. He declared that he loved her better than he loved himself. His words were faltering, but they pleased her the more for that. The less there is of eloquence, the more there is of love.

Her embarrassment was less than his, and that is not to be wondered at, since she had had time to think of what she would say to him. It seems (although the story says nothing about it) that the good fairy had beguiled her long slumber with pleasant dreams. To be brief, after four hours of talking they had not succeeded in uttering one half of the things they had to say to each other.

Fairy Tales. New York: Random House, 1991.

Other Editions:

Laurence, Ann., trans. *Tales from Perrault.* New York: Oxford University Press, 1989.

Grimm, Jacob and Grimm, Wilhelm K. *Sleeping Beauty.* New York: Silver, 1985.

Poole, Josephine, ed. *Sleeping Beauty.* New York: Barron, 1989.

Storer, Ronald, ed. *Sleeping Beauty & Bluebeard.* Oxford: Oxford University Press, 1972.

Perrault, Charles. *Cinderella: Fairy Tales and Other Tales from Perrault.* New York: Henry Holt, 1989.

Grimm, Jacob and Grimm, Wilhelm K. *Cinderella* New York: William Morrow & Co., 1981.

ENGLISH FAIRY TALES

Joseph Jacobs

These are traditional English fairy tales that should be shared with audiences from all over.

THE BURIED MOON

ong ago, in my grandmother's time, the Carland was all in bogs, great pools of black water, and creeping trickles of green water, and squishy mools which squirted when you stepped on them.

Well, granny used to say how long before her time the Moon herself was once dead and buried in the marshes, and as she used to tell me, I'll tell you all about it.

The Moon up yonder shone and shone, just as she does now, and when she shone she lighted up the bog-pools, so that one could walk about almost as safe as in the day.

But when she didn't shine, out came the Things that dwelt in the darkness and went about seeking to do evil and harm; Bogles and Crawling Horrors, all came out when the Moon didn't shine.

Well, the Moon heard of this, and being kind and good—as she surely is, shining for us in the night instead of taking her natural rest—she was main troubled. "I'll see for myself, I will," said she, "maybe it's not so bad as folks make out."

Sure enough, at the month's end down she stept, wrapped up in a black cloak, and a black hood over her yellow shining hair. Straight she went to the bog edge and looked about her. Water here and water there; waving tussocks and trembling mool, and great black snags all twisted and bent. Before her all was dark—dark but for the glimmer of the stars in the pools, and the light that came from her own white feet, stealing out of her black cloak.

The Moon drew her cloak faster about and trembled, but she wouldn't go back without seeing all there was to be seen; so on she went, stepping as light as the wind in summer from tuft to tuft between the greedy gurgling water-holes. Just as she came near a big black pool her foot slipped and she was nigh tumbling in. She grabbed with both hands at a snag near by to steady herself with, but as she touched it, it twined itself round her wrists, like a pair of handcuffs and gripped her so that she couldn't move. She pulled and twisted and fought, but it was no good. She was fast, and must stay fast.

Presently as she stood trembling in the dark, wondering if help would come, she heard something calling in the distance; then she heard steps foundering along, squishing in the mud and slipping on the tufts, and through the darkness she saw a white face with great feared eyes.

'Twas a man strayed in the bogs. Mazed with fear, he struggled on toward the flick-ering light that looked like help and safety. And when the poor Moon saw that he was coming nigher and nigher to the deep hole, further and further from the path, she was so mad and so sorry that she struggled and fought and pulled harder than ever. And though she couldn't get loose, she twisted and turned, till her black hood fell back off her shining yellow hair, and the beautiful light that came from it drove away the darkness.

Oh, but the man cried with joy to see the light again. And at once all evil things fled back into the dark corners, for they cannot abide the light. So he could see where he was, and where the path was, and how he could get out of the marsh. And the Moon herself was so taken up with saving him, and with rejoicing that he was back on the right path, that she clean forgot that she needed help herself, and that she was held fast by the Black Snag.

So off he went; spent and gasping, and stumbling and sobbing with joy, flaying for his life out of the terrible bogs. Then it came over the Moon she would main like to go with him. So she pulled and fought as if she were mad, till she fell on her knees, spent with tugging, at the foot of the snag. And as she lay there, gasping for breath, the black hood fell forward over her head. So out went the blessed light and back came the darkness, with all its Evil Things, with a screech and a howl. They came crowding round her, mocking and snatching and beating; shrieking with rage and spite, and swearing and snarling, for they knew her for their old enemy, that drove them back into the corner, and kept them from working their wicked wills.

"Drat thee!" yelled the witch-bodies, "thou'st spoiled our spells this year agone?"

And all the Things joined in with a great "Ho, ho!" till the very tussocks shook and the water gurgled. And they began again.

"We'll poison her—poison her!" shrieked the witches.

And "Ho-ho!" howled the Things again.

"We'll smother her—smother her!" whispered the Crawling Horrors, and twined themselves round her knees.

And "Ho, ho!" mocked the rest of them.

And again they shouted with spite and ill will. And the poor Moon crouched down, and wished she was dead and done with.

And they fought and squabbled what they should do with her, till a pale grey light began to come in the sky; and it drew night the dawning. And they told two of the Will-o-the-wykes to take turns in watching on the black snag, to see that she lay safe and still, and couldn't get out to spoil their sport.

And there lay the poor Moon, dead and buried in the bog, till someone would set her loose, and who'd know where to look for her.

Well, the days passed, and 'twas the time for the new moon's coming, and the folk put pennies in their pockets and straws in their caps so as to be ready for her, and looked about, for the Moon was a good friend to the marsh folk, and they were main glad when the dark time was gone, and the paths, were safe again, and the Evil Things were driven back by the blessed Light into the darkness and the water-holes.

But days and days passed, and the new Moon never came, and the nights were aye dark, and the Evil Things were worse than ever. And still the days went on, and the new Moon never came. Naturally the poor folk were strangely feared and mazed, and a lot of them went to the Wise Woman who dwelt in the old mill, and asked if so be she could find out where the Moon was gone.

"Well," said she, after looking in the brewpot, and in the mirror, and in the Book, "it be main queer, but I can't rightly tell ye what's happened to her. If ye hear of aught, come and tell me."

So they went their ways; and as days went by, and never a Moon came, naturally they talked—my word! I recken they did talk! Their tongues wagged at home, and at the inn, and in the garth. But so came one day, as they sat on the great settle in the inn, a man from the far end of the bog lands was smoking and listening, when all at once he sat up and slapped his knee. "My faicks!" says he, "I'd forgot, but I reckon I kens where the Moon be!" and he told them of how he was lost in the bog, and how, when he was nigh dead with fright, the light shone out, and he found the path and got home safe.

So off they all went to the Wise Woman, and told her about it, and she looked long in the pot and the Book again, and then she nodded her head.

"It's dark still, childer, dark!" says she, "and I can't rightly see, but do as I tell ye, and ye'll find out for yourselves. Go all of ye, just afore the night gathers, put a stone in your mouth, and take a hazel-twig in your hands, and say never a word till you're safe home again. Then walk on and fear not, far into the midst of the marsh, till ye find a coffin, a candle, and a cross. Then ye'll not be far from your Moon; look, and m'appen ye'll find her."

So came the next night in the darklings, out they went all together, every man with a stone in his mouth, and a hazel-twig in his hand, and feeling, thou may'st reckon, main feared and creepy. And they stumbled and stottered along the paths into the midst of the bogs; they saw naught, though they heard sighings and flutterings in their ears, and felt cold wet fingers touching them; but all at once, looking around for the coffin, the candle, and the cross, while they came right to the pool beside the great snag, where the Moon lay buried. And all at once they stopped, quaking and mazed and skeery, for there was the great stone, half in, half out of the water, for all the world like a strange big coffin; and at the head was the black snag, stretching out its two arms in a dark gruesome cross, and on it a tiddy light flickered, like a dying candle. And they all knelt down in the mud, and said, "Our Lord," first forward, because of the cross, and then backward, to keep off the Bogles; but without speaking out, for they knew that the Evil Things would catch them if they didn't do as the Wise Woman told them.

Then they went nigher, and took hold of the big stone, and shoved it up and afterwards, they said that for one tiddy minute they saw a strange and beautiful face looking up at them gladlike out of the black water; but the Light came so quick and so white and shining, that they stept back mazed with it, and the very next minute, when they could see again, there was the full Moon in the sky, bright and beautiful and kind as ever, shining and smiling down at them, and making the bogs and the paths as clear as day, and stealing into the very corners, as though she'd have driven the darkness and the Bogles clean away if she could.

CAP O' RUSHES

ell, there was once a very rich gentleman, and he had three daughters, says he.
So he says he thought he'd see how fond they were of him. So he says to the first, "How much do you love me, my dear?"

"Why," says she, "as I love my life."

"That's good," says he.

So he says to the second, "How much do you love me, my dear?"

"Why," says she, "better nor all the world."

"That's good," says he.

So he says to the third, "How much do you love me, my dear?"

"Why, I love you as fresh meat loves salt," says she.

Well, but he was angry. "You don't love me at all," says he, "and in my house you stay no more." So he drove her out there and then, and shut the door in her face.

Well, she went away on and on till she came to a fen, and there she gathered a log of rushes and made them into a kind of a sort of a cloak with a hood, to cover her from head to foot, and to hide her fine clothes. And then she went on and on till she came to a great house.

"Do you want a maid?" says she.

"No, we don't," said they.

"I haven't nowhere to go," says she; "and I ask no wages, and do any sort of work," says she.

"Well," said they, "if you like to wash the pots and scrape the saucepans you may stay," said they.

So she stayed there and washed the pots and scraped the saucepans and did all the dirty work. And because she gave no name they called her "Cap o' Rushes."

Well, one day there was to be a great dance a little ways off, and the servants were allowed to go and look at the grand people. Cap o' Rushes said she was too tired to go, so she stayed home.

But when they were gone, she took off her cap o' rushes and cleaned herself, and went to the dance. And no one there was so finely dressed as she.

Well, who should be there but her master's son, and what should he do but fall in love with her the minute he set eyes on her. He wouldn't dance with anyone else.

But before the dance was done, Cap o' Rushes slipt off, and away she went home. And when the other maids came back, she was pretending to be asleep with her cap o' rushes on.

Well, next morning they said to her, "You did miss a sight, Cap o' Rushes!"

"What was that?" says she.

"Why, the beautifullest lady you ever see, dressed right gay and ga'. The young master, he never took his eyes off her."

"Well, I should have liked to have seen her," says Cap o' Rushes.

"Well, there's to be another dance this evening, and perhaps she'll be there."

But, come the evening, Cap o' Rushes said she was too tired to go with them. Howsoever, when they were gone, she took off her cap o' rushes and cleaned herself, and away she went to the dance.

The master's son had been reckoning on seeing her, and he danced with no one else, and never took his eyes off her. But, before the dance was over, she slipt off, and home she went, and when the maids came back she pretended to be asleep with her cap o' rushes on.

Next day they said to her again, "Well, Cap o' Rushes, you should ha' been there to see the lady. There she was again, and the young master he never took his eyes off her."

"Well, there," says she, "I should ha' liked to ha' seen her."

"Well," says they, "there's a dance again this evening, and you must go with us, for she's sure to be there."

Well, come this evening, Cap o' Rushes said she was too tired to go, and do what they would she stayed at home. But when they were gone, she took off her cap o' rushes and cleaned herself, and away she went to the dance.

The master's son was very glad when he saw her. He danced with none but her and never took his eyes off her. When she wouldn't tell him her name, nor where she came from, he gave her a ring and told her if he didn't see her again, he should die.

Well, before the dance was over, off she slipped, and home she went, and when the maids came home she was pretending to be asleep with her cap o' rushes on.

Well, next day they says to her, "There, Cap o' Rushes, you didn't come last night, and now you won't see the lady, for there's no more dances."

"Well, I should have liked to have seen her," says she.

The master's son tried every way to find out where the lady was gone, but go where he might, and ask whom he might he never heard anything about her. And he got worse and worse for the love of her till he had to keep his bed.

"Make some gruel for the young master," they said to the cook. "He's dying for the love of the lady." The cook set about making it when Cap o' Rushes came in.

"What are you a-doing of?" says she.

"I'm going to make some gruel for the young master," says the cook, "for he's dying for love of the lady."

"Let me make it," says Cap o' Rushes.

Well, the cook wouldn't at first, but at last she said yes, and Cap o' Rushes made the gruel. And when she had made it, she slipped the ring into it on the sly before the cook took it upstairs.

The young man he drank it and then he saw the ring at the bottom.

"Send for the cook," says he.

So up she comes.

"Who made this gruel here?" says he.

"I did," says the cook, for she was frightened.

And he looked at her.

"No, you didn't," says he. "Say who did it, and you shan't be harmed."

"Well, then, 'twas Cap o' Rushes," says she.

"Send Cap o' Rushes here," says he.

So Cap o' Rushes came.

"Did you make my gruel?" says he.

"Yes, I did," says she.

"Where did you get this ring?" says he.

"From him that gave it me," says she.

"Who are you, then?" says the young man.

"I'll show you," says she. And she took off her Cap o' Rushes, and there she was in her beautiful clothes.

Well, the master's son he got well very soon, and they were to be married in a little time. It was to be a very grand wedding, and everyone was asked far and near. And Cap o' Rushes' father was asked. But she never told anybody who she was.

But before the wedding, she went to the cook, and says she:

"I want you to dress every dish without a mite o' salt."

"That'll be rare nasty," says the cook.

"That doesn't matter," says she.

"Very well," says the cook.

Well, the wedding day came, and they were married. And after they were married, all the company sat down to the dinner. When they began to eat the meat, it was so tasteless they couldn't eat it. But Cap o' Rushes's father tried first one dish and then another, and then he burst out crying.

"What is the matter?" said the master's son to him.

"Oh!" says he, "I had a daughter. And I asked her how much she loved me. And she said. "As much as fresh meat loves salt." And I turned her from my door, for I thought she didn't love me. And now I see she loved me best of all and she may be dead for aught I know."

"No, father, here she is!" said Cap o' Rushes. And she goes up to him and puts her arms round him.

And so they were all happy ever after.

JACK THE GIANT-KILLER

When good King Arthur reigned, there lived near the Land's End of England, in the country of Cornwall, a farmer who had one only son, called Jack. He was brisk and of ready, lively wit, so that nobody or nothing could worst him.

In those days the Mount of Cornwall was kept by a huge giant named Cormoran. He was eighteen feet in height and about three yards round the waist, of a fiece and grim countenance, the terror of all the neighboring towns and villages. He lived in a cave in the midst of the Mount, and whenever he wanted food he would wade over to the mainland, where he would furnish himself with whatever came in his way. Everybody at his approach ran out of their houses, while he seized on their cattle, making nothing of carrying half a dozen oxen on his back at a time; and as for their sheep and hogs, he would tie them round his waist like a bunch of tallow-dips. He had done this for many years, so that all Cornwall was in despair.

One day Jack happened to be at the town-hall when the magistrates were sitting in council about the giant. He asked: "What reward will be given to the man who kills Cormoran?" "The giant's treasure," they said, "will be the reward." Quoth Jack: "Then let me undertake it."

So he got a horn, shovel, and pickaxe, and went over to the Mount in the beginning of a dark winter's evening, when he fell to work, and before morning had dug a pit twenty-two feet deep and nearly as broad, covering it over with long sticks and straw. Then he strewed a little mold over it, so that it appeared like plain ground. Jack then placed himself on the opposite side of the pit, farthest from the giant's lodging, and just at the break of day, he put the horn to his mouth, and blew, Tantivy, Tantivy. This noise roused the giant, who rushed from his cave, crying, "You incorrigible villain, are you come here to disturb my rest? You shall pay dearly for this. Satisfaction I will have, and this it shall be, I will take you whole and broil you for breakfast." He had no sooner uttered this, then he tumbled into the pit, and made the very foundations of the Mount to shake. "Oh, Giant," quoth Jack, "where are you now? Oh, faith, you are gotten now into Lob's Pound, where I will surely plague you for your threatening words; what do you think now of broiling me for your breakfast? Will no other diet serve you but poor Jack?" Then having tantalized the giant for a while, he gave him a most weighty knock with his pickaxe on the very crown of his head, and killed him on the spot.

Jack then filled up the pit with earth, and went to search the cave, which he found contained much treasure. When the magistrates heard of this they made a declaration he should henceforth be termed JACK THE GIANT-KILLER and presented him with a sword and a belt, on which were written these words embroidered in letters of gold:

Here's the right valiant Cornish man,
Who slew the giant Cormoran

The news of Jack's victory soon spread over all the West of England, so that another giant, named Blunderbore, hearing of it, vowed to be revenged on Jack, if ever he should light on him. The giant was the lord of an enchanted castle situated in the midst of a lonesome wood. Now Jack, about four months afterward, walking near this wood in his journey to Wales, being weary, seated himself near a pleasant fountain and fell fast asleep. While he was sleeping the giant, coming there for water, discovered him, and knew him to be the far-famed Jack the Giant-Killer by the lines written on the belt. Without ado, he took Jack on his shoulders and carried him toward his castle. Now, as they passed through a thicket, the rustling of the boughs awakened Jack, who was strangely surprised to find himself in the clutches of the giant. His terror was only begun, for, on entering the castle, he saw the ground strewed with human bones, and the giant told him his own would ere long be among them. After this the giant locked poor Jack in an immense chamber, leaving him there while he went to fetch another giant, his brother, living in the same wood, who might share in the meal on Jack.

After waiting some time, Jack, on going to the window, beheld afar off the two giants coming towards the castle. "Now," quoth Jack to himself, "my death or my deliverance is at hand." Now, there were strong cords in a corner of the room in which Jack was, and two of these he took, and made a strong noose at the end; and while the giants were unlocking the iron gate of the castle he threw the ropes over each of their heads. The he drew the other ends across a beam, and pulled with all his might, so that he throttled them. Then, when he saw they were black in the face, he slid down the rope, and drawing his sword, slew them both. Then, taking the giant's keys and unlocking the rooms, he found three fair ladies tied by the hair of their heads, almost starved to death. "Sweet ladies," quoth Jack, "I have destroyed this monster and his brutish brother, and obtained your liberties." This said he presented them with the keys, and so proceeded on his journey to Wales.

Jack made the best of his way by traveling as fast as he could, but lost his road, and was benighted, and could find no habitation until, coming into a narrow valley, he found a large house, and in order to get shelter took courage to knock at the gate. But what was his surprise when there came forth a monstrous giant with two heads; yet he did not appear so feisty as the others were, for he was a Welsh giant, and what he did was by private and secret malice under the false show of friendship. Jack, having told his condition to the giant, was shown into a bedroom, where, in the dead of night, he heard his host in another apartment muttering these words:

> *Though here you lodge with me this night,*
> *You shall not see the morning light:*
> *My club shall dash your brains outright!*

"Say'st thou so," quoth Jack; "that is like one of your Welsh tricks, yet I hope to be cunning enough for you." Then, getting out of bed, he laid a billet in this stead, and hid himself in a corner of the room. At the dead time of the night in came the Welsh giant, who struck several heavy blows on the bed with his club, thinking he had broken every bone in Jack's skin. The next morning Jack, laughing in his sleeve, gave him hearty thanks for his night's lodging. "How have you rested?" quoth the giant; "did you not feel anything in the night?" "No," quoth Jack, "nothing but a rat, which gave me two or three slaps with her tail."

With that, greatly wondering, the giant led Jack to breakfast, bringing him a bowl containing four gallons of hasty pudding. Being loathe to let the giant think it too much for him, Jack put a large leather bag under his loose coat, in such a way that he could put the pudding into it without the giant knowing. Then, telling the giant he would show him a trick, taking a knife, Jack ripped open the bag, and out came all the hasty pudding. Whereupon, saying, "Odds splutters her nails, hur can do that trick hurself," the monster took the knife, and ripping open his belly, fell down dead.

Now, it happed in these days that King Arthur's only son asked his father to give him a large sum of money, in order that he might go and seek his fortune in the principality of Wales, where lived a beautiful lady possessed with seven evil spirits. The king did his best to persuade his son from it, but in vain; so at last gave way and the prince set out with two horses, one loaded with money, the other for himself to ride upon. Now, after several days' travel, he came to a market-town in Wales, where he beheld a vast crowd of people gathered together. The prince asked the reason of it, and was told that they had arrested a corpse for several large sums of money which the deceased owed when he died. The prince replied that it was a pity creditors should be so cruel, and said, "Go bury the dead, and let his creditors come to my lodging, and there their debts shall be paid." They came, in such great numbers that before night he had only two pence left for himself.

Now Jack the Giant-Killer, coming that way, was so taken with the generosity of the prince that he desired to be his servant. This being agreed upon, the next morning they set forward on their journey together, when, as they were riding out of the town, an old woman called after the prince, saying, "He has owed me twopence these seven years; pray pay me as well as the rest." Putting his hand into his pocket, the prince gave the woman all he had left, so that after their day's food, which cost what small store Jack had by him, they were without a penny between them.

When the sun got low, the king's son said, "Jack, since we have no money, where can we lodge this night?"

But Jack replied, "Master, we'll do well enough, for I have an uncle lives within two miles of this place; he is a huge and monstrous giant with three heads; he'll fight five hundred men in armor, and make them to flay before him."

"Alas!" quoth the prince, "what shall we do there? He'll certainly chop us up at a mouthful. Nay, we are scarce enough to fill one of his hollow teeth!"

"It is no matter for that," quoth Jack; "I myself will go before and prepare the way for you; therefore stop here and wait till I return." Jack then rode away at full speed, and coming to the gate of the castle, he knocked so loud that he made the neighboring hills resound. The giant roared out at this like thunder; "Who's there?"

Jack answered, "None but your poor cousin Jack."

Quoth her, "What news with my poor cousin Jack?"

He replied, "Dear uncle, heavy news, God wot!"

"Prithee," quoth the giant, "what heavy news can come to me? I am a giant with three heads, and besides thou knowest I can fight five hundred men in armor, and make them fly like chaff before the wind."

"Oh, but," quoth Jack, "here's the king's son a-coming with a thousand men in armor to kill you and destroy all that you have!"

"Oh, cousin Jack," said the giant, "this is heavy news indeed! I will immediately run and hide myself, and thou shalt lock, bolt, and bar me in, and keep the keys until the prince is gone." Having secured the giant, Jack fetched his master, when they made themselves heartily merry whilst the poor giant lay trembling in a vault under the ground.

A POTTLE O' BRAINS

nce in these parts, and not so long gone neither, there was a fool that wanted to buy a pottle o' brains, for he was ever getting into scrapes though his foolishness, and being laughed at by everyone. Folk told him that he could get everything he liked from the wise woman that lived on the top o' the hill, and dealt in potions and herbs and spells and things, and could tell thee all as'd come to thee or thy folk. So he told his mother, and asked her if he could seek the wise woman and buy a pottle o' brains.

"That ye should," says she; "thou'st sore need o' them, my son; and if I should die, who'd take care o' a poor fool such's thou, no more fit to look after thyself than an unborn baby? But mind they manners, and speak her pretty, my lad; for they wise folk are gay and light mispleased."

So off he went after his tea, and there she was, sitting by the fire, and stirring a big pot.

"Good e'en, missis," says he, "it's a fine night."

"Aye," says she, and went on stirring.

"It'll maybe rain," says he, and fidgeted from one foot to t'other.

"Maybe," says she.

"And m'appen it won't," says he, and looked out o' the window.

"M'appen," says she.

And he scratched his head and twisted his hat.

"Well," says he, "I can't mind nothing else about the weather, but let me see; the crops are getting on fine."

"Fine," says she.

"And—and—the beasts is fattening," says he.

"They are," says she.

"And—and—" says he, and comes to a stop— "I reckon we'll tackle business now, having done the polite like. Have you any brains for to sell?"

"That depends," says she; "if thou wants king's brains, or soldier's brains, or schoolmaster's brains, I dinna keep 'em."

"Hout no," says he, "just ordinary brains—fit for any fool—same as everyone has about here; something clean commonlike."

"Aye so," says the wise woman, "I might manage that, if so be tou'lt help thyself."

"How's that for missis?" says he.

"Jest so," says she, looking in the pot: "bring me the heart of the thing thou likes best of all, and I'll tell thee where to get thy pottle o' brains."

"But," says he, scratching his hear, "how can I do that?"

"That's not for me to say," says she; "Find out for thyself, my lad! If thou doesn't want to be a fool all thy days. But thou'll have to read me a riddle so as I can see thou'st brought the right thing, and if thy brains is about thee. And I've something else to see to," says she, "so gode'en to thee," and she carried the pot away with her into the back place.

So off went the fool to his mother, and told her what the wise woman said.

"And I reckon I'll have to kill that pig," says he, "for I like fat bacon better than anything."

"Then do it, my lad," said his mother, "for certain 'twill be a strange and good thing fur thee, if thou canst buy a pottle o' brains, and be able to look after thy own self."

So he killed his pig, and next day off he went to the wise woman's cottage, and there she sat, reading in a great book.

"Gode'en, missis," says he, "I've brought thee the heart o' the thing I like the best of all; and I put it hapt in paper on the table."

"Aye so?" says she, and looked at him through her spectacles. "Tell me this then, what runs without feet?"

He scratched his head, and thought, and thought, but he couldn't tell.

"Go thy ways," she said, "thou'st not fetched me the right thing yet. I've no brains for thee today." And she clapt the book together, and turned her back.

So off the fool went to tell his mother.

But as he got nigh the house, out came folk running to tell him that his mother was dying.

And when he got in, his mother only looked at him and smiled as if to say she could leave him with a quiet mind, since he had got brains enough now to look after himself—and then she died.

So down he sat and the more he thought about it the worse he felt. He minded how she'd nursed him when he was a tiddy brat, and helped him with his lessons, and cooked his dinners, and mended his clothes, and bore with his foolishness; and he felt sorrier and sorrier, while he began to sob and greet.

"Oh, mother, mother!" says he, "who'll take care of me now? Thou shouldn't have left me alone, for I liked thee better than everything!"

And as he said that he thought of the words of the wise woman. "Hi, yi!" says he, "must I take mother's heart to her?"

"No! I can't do that," says he. "What'll I do? What'll I do to get that pottle o' brains, now I'm alone in the world?" So he thought and thought and thought, and next day he went and borrowed a sack, and bundled his mother in, and carried it on his shoulder up to the wise woman's cottage.

"Gode'en, missus," says he, "I reckon I've fetched thee the right thing this time, surely", and he plumped the sack down *kerflap!* in the doorsill.

"Maybe," says the wise women, "but read me this, now, what's yellow and shining but isn't gold?"

And he scratched his head, and thought and thought, but he couldn't tell.

"Thou'st not hit the right thing, my lad," says he. "I doubt thou'rt a bigger fool than I thought!" and shut the door in his face.

"See there!" says he, and set down by the roadside and greets.

"I've lost the only two things as I cared for, and what else can I find to buy a pottle o' brains with!" And he fair howled, till the tears ran down into his mouth. And up came a lass that lived near at hand, and looked at him.

"What's up with thee, fool?" says she.

"Oo, I've killed my pig, and lost my mother and I'm nobbut a fool myself," says he, sobbing.

"That's bad," says she; "and haven't thee anybody to look after thee?"

"No," says he, "and I canna buy my pottle o' brains, for there's nothing I like best left."

"What art talking about?" says she.

And down she sets by him, and he told her all about the wise woman and the pig, and his mother and the riddles, and that he was all alone in the world.

"Well," says she, "I wouldn't mind looking after thee myself."

"Could thee do it?" says he.

"Ou, aye!" says she; "Folks say as fools make good husbands, and I reckon I'll have thee, if thou'rt willing."

"Can'st cook?" says he.

"Aye, I can," says she.

"And scrub?" says he.

"Surely," says she.

"And mend my clothes?" says he.

"I can that," says she.

"I reckon thou'lt do then as well as anybody," says he; "but what'll I do about this wise woman?"

"Oh, wait a bit," says she, "something may turn up, and it'll not matter if thou'rt a fool, so long'st thou'st got me to look after thee."

"That's true," says he, and off they went and got married. And she kept his house so clean and neat, and cooked his dinner so fine, that one night he says to her, "Lass, I'm thinking I like thee best of everything after all."

"That's good hearing," says she, "and what then?"

"Have I got to kill thee, go with thy heart up to the wise woman for that pottle o' brains?"

"Law, no!" say she, looking skeered, "I winna have that. But see here; thou didn't cut out thy mother's heart, did thou?"

"No, but if I had, maybe I'd have got my pottle o' brains," says he.

"Not a bit of it," says she; "just thou take me as I be, heart and all, and I'll wager I'll help thee read the riddles."

"Can thee so?" says he, doubtful like; "I reckon they're too hard for women folk."

"Well," says she, "let's see now. Tell me the first."

"What runs without feet?" says he.

"Why, water!" says she.

"It do," says he, and scratched his head.

"And what's yellow and shining but isn't gold?"

"Why, the sun!" says she.

"Faith, it be!" says he. "Come, we'll go up to the wise woman at once," and off they went. And as they came up the pad, she was sitting at the door, twining straws.

"Gode'en, missus," says he.

"Gode'en, fool," says she.

"I reckon I've fetched thee the right thing at last," says he.

The wise woman looked at them both, and wiped her spectacles.

"Canst tell me what that is as has first no legs, and then two legs, and ends with four legs?"

And the fool scratched his head and thought and thought, but he couldn't tell.

And the lass whispered in his ear, "It's a tadpole."

"M'appen," say he; then, "It may be a tadpole, missis."

The wise woman nodded her head.

"That's right," says she, "and thou'st got thy pottle o' brains already."

"Where are they?" says he, looking about and feeling in his pockets.

"In thy wife's head," says she. "The only cure for a fool is a good wife to look after him, and I've got that!" And then she nodded to them and up to the house.

So they went home together, and he never wanted to buy a pottle o' brains again, for his wife had enough for both.

TITTY MOUSE AND TATTY MOUSE

itty Mouse and Tatty Mouse both lived in a house. Titty Mouse went a leasing and Tatty Mouse went a leasing, so they both went a leasing.

Titty Mouse leased an ear of corn, and Tatty Mouse leased an ear of corn, so they both leased an ear of corn.

Titty Mouse made a pudding and Tatty Mouse made a pudding, so they both made a pudding.

And Tatty Mouse put her pudding into the pot to boil, but when Titty went to put hers in, the pot tumbled over, and scalded her to death.

Then Tatty sat down and wept; then a three-legged stool said, "Tatty, why do you weep?" "Titty's dead," said Tatty, "and so I weep." "Then," said the stool, "I'll hop," so the stool hopped.

Then a broom in the corner of the room said, "Stool, why do you hop?" "Oh!" said the stool, 'Titty's dead, and Tatty weeps, and do I hop." "Then," said the broom, "I'll sweep," so the broom began to sweep.

Then said the door, "Broom, why do you sweep?" "Oh!" said the broom, "Titty's dead, and Tatty weeps, and the stool hops, and so I sweep." "Then," said the door, "I'll jar," so the door jarred.

Then said the window, "Door, why do you jar?" "Oh!" said the door, "Titty's dead, and Tatty weeps, and the stool hops, and the broom sweeps, and so I jar."

Then said the window, "I'll creak," so the window creaked. Now there was an old form outside the house, and when the window creaked, the form said, "Window, why do you creak?" "Oh!" said the window, "Titty's dead, and Tatty weeps, and the stool hops, and the broom sweeps, the door jars, and so I creak."

"Then," said the old form, "I'll run around the house," then the old form ran around the house. Now there was a fine large walnut-tree growing by the cottage, and the tree said to the form, "Form, why do you run around the house?" "Oh!" said the form, "Titty's dead, and Tatty weeps, and the stool hops, and the broom sweeps, the door jars, and the window creaks, and so I run around the house."

"Then," said the walnut-tree, "I'll shed my leaves," so the walnut-tree shed all its beautiful green leaves. Now there was a little bird perched on one of the boughs of the tree, and when all the leaves fell, it said, "Walnut-tree, why do you shed your leaves?" "Oh!" said the tree, "Titty's dead, and Tatty weeps, the stool hops, and the brooom sweeps, the door jars, and the window creaks, the old form runs around the house, and so I shed my leaves."

"Then," said the little bird, "I'll moult all my feathers," so he moulted all his pretty feathers. Now there was a little girl walking below, carrying a jug of milk for her brothers' and sisters' supper, and when she saw the poor little bird moult all its feathers, she said;

238

"Little bird, why do you moult all your feathers?" "Oh!" said the little bird, "Titty's dead, and Tatty weeps, the stool hops, and the broom sweeps, the door jars, and the window creaks, the old form runs around the house, the walnut-tree sheds its leaves, and so I moult all my feathers."

"Then," said the little girl, "I'll spill the milk," so she dropped the pitcher and spilled the milk. Now there was an old man just by on the top of a ladder thatching a rick, and when he saw the little girl spill the milk, he said, "Little girl, what do you mean by spilling the milk?—your little brothers and sisters must go without their supper." Then said the little girl, "Titty's dead, Tatty weeps, the stool hops, and the broom sweeps, the door jars, and the window creaks, the old form runs around the house, the walnut-tree sheds all its leaves, the little bird moults all its feathers, and so I spill the milk."

"Oh!" said the old man, "then I'll tumble off the ladder and break my neck," so he tumbled off the ladder and broke his neck; and when the old man broke his neck, the great walnut-tree fell down with a crash, and upset the old form and house, and the house falling knocked the window out, and the window knocked the door down, and the door upset the broom, and the broom upset the stool, and poor little Tatty Mouse was buried beneath the ruins.

THE WISE MEN OF GOTHAM

Of Buying Sheep

here were two men of Gotham, and one of them was going to market to Nottingham to buy sheep, and the other came from the market, and they both met together upon Nottingham bridge.

"Where are you going?" said the one who came from Nottingham.

"Marry," said he that was going to Nottingham, "I am going to buy sheep."

"Buy sheep?" said the other. "And which way will you bring them home?"

"Marry," said the other, "I will bring them over this bridge."

"By Robin Hood," said he that came from Nottingham, "but thou shalt not."

"By Maid Marion," said he that was going thither, "but I will."

"You will not," said the one.

"I will."

Then they beat their staves against the ground one against the other, as if there had been a hundred sheep between them.

"Hold in," said one; "beware lest my sheep leap over the bridge."

"I care not," said the other; "they shall not come this way."

"But they shall," said the other.

Then the other said, "If that thou make much to do, I will put my fingers in thy mouth."

"Will you?" said the other.

Now, as they were at their contention, another man of Gotham came from the market with a sack of meal upon a horse, and seeing and hearing his neighbors at strife about sheep, though there were none between them, said, "Ah, fools! will you ever learn wisdom? Help me, and lay my sack upon my shoulders."

They did so, and he went to the side of the bridge, unloosened the mouth of the sack, and shook all his meal out into the river.

"Now, neighbors," he said, "how much meal is there in my sack?"

"Marry," said they," there is none at all."

"Now, by my faith," said he, "even as much wit as is in your two heads to stir up strife about a thing you have not."

Which was the wisest of these three persons? Judge yourself.

Of Hedging a Cuckoo

Once upon a time the men of Gotham would have kept the Cuckoo so that she might sing all the year, and in the midst of their town they made a hedge round in compass and they got a Cuckoo, and put her into it, and said, "Sing there all through the year, or thou shalt have neither meat nor water." The Cuckoo, as soon as she perceived herself within the hedge, flew away. "A vengeance on her!" said they. "We did not make our hedge high enough."

Of Sending Cheeses

There was a man of Gotham who went to the market at Nottingham to sell cheese, and as he was going down the hill to Nottingham bridge, one of his cheeses fell out of his wallet and rolled down the hill. "Ah, gaffer," said the fellow, "can you run to market alone? I will send one after another after you." Then he laid down his wallet and took out the cheeses, and rolled them down the hill. Some went into one bush; and some went into another.

"I charge you all to meet me near the marketplace"; and when the fellow came to the market to meet his cheeses, he stayed there till the market was nearly done: Then he went about to inquire of his friends and neighbors, and other men, if they did see his cheeses come to the market.

"Who should bring them?" said one of the market men.

"Marry, themselves," said the fellow; "they know the way well enough."

He said, "A vengeance on them all. I did fear, to see them run so fast, that they would run beyond the market. I am now fully persuaded that they must be now almost at York." Whereupon he forthwith hired a horse to ride to York, to seek his cheeses where they were not, but to this day no man can tell him of his cheeses.

Of Drowning Eels

When Good Friday came, the men of Gotham cast their heads together what to do with their white herrings, their red herrings, their sprats, and other salt fish. One consulted with the other, and agreed that such fish should be cast into their pond (which was in the middle of the town), that they might breed again the next year, and every man that had salt fish left cast them into the pool.

"I have many white herrings," said one.

"I have many sprats," said another.

"I have many red herrings," said the other.

"I have much salt fish. Let all go into the pond or pool, and we shall fare like lords next year."

At the beginning of next year following the men drew near the pond to have their fish, and there was nothing but a great eel. "Ah," said they all, "a mischief on this eel, for he has eaten up all our fish."

"What shall we do to him?" said one of the others.

"Kill him," said one.

"Chop him into pieces," said another.

"Not so," said another; "let us drown him."

"Be it so," said all. And they went to another pond, and cast the eel into the pond. "Lie there and shift for yourself, for no help thou shalt have from us"; and they left the eel to drown.

Of Sending Rent

Once on a time the men of Gotham had forgotten to pay their landlord. One said to the other, "Tomorrow is our pay-day, and what shall we find to send our money to our landlord?"

The one said, "This day I have caught a hare, and he shall carry it, for he is light of foot."

"Be it so," said all; "he shall have a letter and a purse to put our money in, and we shall direct him the right way." So when the letters were written and the money put in a purse, they tied it round the hare's neck saying, "First you go to Lancaster, then thou must go to Loughborough, and Newarke is our landlord, and commend us to him and there is his dues."

The hare, as soon as he was out of their hands, ran on along the country way. Some cried, "Thou must go to Lancaster first."

"Let the hare alone," said another; "he can tell a nearer way than the best of us all. Let him go."

Another said, "It is a subtle hare, let her alone; she will not keep the highway for fear of dogs."

Of Counting

On a certain time there were twelve men of Gotham who went fishing, and some went into the water and some stayed on dry ground; and, as they were coming back, one of them said, "We have ventured much this day wading; I pray to God that none of us that did come from home be drowned."

"Marry," said one, "let us see about that. Twelve of us came out," and every man did count eleven, and the twelfth man did never count himself.

"Alas!" said one to another, "one of us is drowned." They went back to the brook where they had been fishing, and looked up and down for him that was drowned, and made great lamentation. A courtier came riding by, and he did ask what they were seeking, and why they were so sorrowful. "Oh," said they, "this day we came to fish in this brook, and there were twelve of us, and one is drowned."

"Why," said the courtier, "count me how many of you there be," and one counted eleven and did not count himself. "Well" said the courtier, "what will you give me if I find the twelfth man?"

"Sir," said they, "all the money we have."

"Give me the money," said the courtier; and he began with the first, and gave him a whack over the shoulders that he groaned, and said, "There is one," and he served all of them that they groaned; but when he came to the last he gave him a good blow, saying, "Here is the twelfth man."

"God bless you on your heart," said all the company; "you have found our neighbor."

JACK AND THE BEANSTALK

Jack lives with his mother, and they are very poor. Until one day Jack goes out to sell their cow and comes back with five magical beans. The beans are the key to their fortune.

 here was once upon a time a poor widow who had an only son named Jack, and a cow named Milky-white. And all they had to live on was the milk the cow gave every morning, which they carried to the market and sold. But one morning Milky-white gave no milk, and they didn't know what to do.

"What shall we do, what shall we do?" said the widow, wringing her hands.

"Cheer up, mother, I'll go and work somewhere," said Jack.

"We've tried that before, and nobody would take you," said his mother; "we must sell Milky-white and with the money start a shop, or something."

"All right, mother," says Jack; "it's market-day today, and I'll soon sell Milky-white, and then we'll see what we can do."

So he took the cow's halter in his hand, and off he started. He hadn't gone far when he met a funny-looking old man, who said to him: "Good morning, Jack."

"Good morning to you," said Jack, and wondered how he knew his name.

"Well, Jack, and where are you off to?" said the man.

"I'm going to market to sell our cow there."

"Oh, you look the proper sort of chap to sell cows," said the man; "I wonder if you know how many beans make five."

"Two in each hand and one in your mouth," says Jack, as sharp as a needle.

"Right you are," says the man, "and here they are, the very beans themselves," he went on, pulling out of his pocket a number of strange-looking beans. "As you are so sharp," says he, "I don't mind doing a swap with you—your cow for these beans."

"Go along," says Jack; "wouldn't you like it?"

"Ah! you don't know what these beans are," said the man, "If you plant them overnight, by morning they grow right up to the sky."

"Really?" said Jack; "you don't say so."

"Yes, that is so, and if it doesn't turn out to be true you can have your cow back."

"Right," says Jack, and hands him over Milky-white's halter and pockets the beans.

Back goes Jack home, and as he hadn't gone very far it wasn't dusk by the time he got to his door.

"Back already, Jack?" said his mother; "I see you haven't got Milky-white, so you've sold her. How much did you get for her?"

"You'll never guess, mother," says Jack.

"No, you don't say so. Good boy! Five pounds, ten, fifteen, no, it can't be twenty."

"I told you you couldn't guess. What do you say to these beans; they're magical, plant them overnight and—"

"What!" says Jack's mother, "have you been such a fool, such a dolt, such an idiot, as to give away Milky-white, the best milker in the parish, and prime beef to boot, for a set of paltry beans? Take that! Take that! Take that! And as for your precious beans, here they go out of the window. And now off with you to bed. Not a sup shall you drink, and not a bit shall you swallow this very night."

So Jack went upstairs to his little room in the attic, and sad and sorry he was, to be sure, as much for his mother's sake, as for the loss of his supper.

At last he dropped off to sleep.

When he woke up, the room looked so funny. The sun was shining into part of it, and yet all the rest was quite dark and shady. So Jack jumped up and dressed himself and went to the window. And what do you think he saw? Why, the beans his mother had thrown out of the window into the garden had sprung up into a big beanstalk which went up and up and up till it reached the sky. So the man spoke truth after all.

The beanstalk grew up quite close past Jack's window, so all he had to do was to open it and give a jump on to the beanstalk which ran up just like a big ladder. So Jack climbed, and he climbed and he climbed and he climbed and he climbed and he climbed and he climbed till at last he reached the sky. And when he got there he found a long broad road going as straight as a dart. So he walked along and he walked along and he walked along till he came to a great big tall house, and on the doorstep there was a great big tall woman.

"Good morning, mom," says Jack, quite polite-like. "Could you be so kind as to give me some breakfast?" For he hadn't had anything to eat, you know, the night before and was as hungry as a hunter.

"It's breakfast you want, is it?" says the great big tall woman, "it's breakfast you'll be if you don't move off from here. My man is an ogre and there's nothing he likes better than boys broiled on toast. You'd better be moving on or he'll be coming."

"Goodness gracious me! It's my old man," said the ogre's wife, "what on earth shall I do? Come along quick and jump in here." And she bundled Jack into the oven just as the ogre came in.

He was a big one, to be sure. At his belt he had three calves strung up by the heels, and he unhooked them and threw them down on the table and said, "Here, wife, broil me a couple of these for breakfast. Ah! what's this I smell?

> *"Fee-fi-fo-fum,*
> *I smell the blood of an Englishman,*
> *Be he alive, or be he dead,*
> *I'll have his bones to grind my bread."*

"Nonsense, dear," said his wife, "you're dreaming. Or perhaps you smell the scraps of that little boy you liked so much for yesterday's dinner. Here, you go and have a wash and tidy up and by the time you come back your breakfast'll be ready for you."

So off the ogre went, and Jack was just going to jump out of the oven and run away when the woman told him not. "Wait till he's asleep," says she; "he always has a doze after breakfast."

Well, the ogre had his breakfast, and after that he goes to a big chest and takes out a couple of bags of gold, and down he sits and counts till at last his head began to nod and he began to snore till the whole house shook again.

Then Jack crept out on tiptoe from his oven, and as he was passing the ogre he took one of the bags of gold under his arm, and off he pelters till he came to the beanstalk, and then he threw down the bag of gold, which, of course, fell into his mother's garden, and then he climbed down and climbed down till at last he got home and told his mother and showed her the gold and said: "Well mother, wasn't I right about the beans? They are really magical, you see."

So they lived on the bag of gold for some time, but at last they came to the end of it, and Jack made up his mind to try his luck once more at the top of the beanstalk. So one fine morning he rose up early, and got on to the beanstalk and he climbed and he climbed and he climbed and he climbed and he climbed and he climbed till at last he came out on to the road again and up to the great tall house he had been to before. There, sure enough, was the great tall woman a-standing on the doorstep.

"Good morning, mom," says Jack, as bold as brass, "could you be so good as to give me something to eat?"

"Go away, my boy," said the big tall woman, "or else my man will eat you up for breakfast. But aren't you the youngster who came here once before? Do you know, that every day my man missed one of his bags of gold."

"That's strange, mum," said Jack, "I dare say I could tell you something about that, but I'm so hungry I can't speak till I've had something to eat."

Well, the big tall woman was so curious that she took him in and gave him something to eat. But he had scarcely begun munching it as slowly as he could when thump! thump! they heard the giant's footstep, and his wife hid Jack away in the oven.

All happened as it did before. In came the ogre as he did before, said, "Fee-fi-fo-fum," and had his breakfast of three broiled oxen. Then he said, "Wife, bring me the hen that lays the golden eggs." So she brought it, and the ogre said, "Lay," and it laid an egg all of gold. And then the ogre began to nod his head, and to snore till the house shook.

Then Jack crept out of the oven on tiptoe and caught hold of the golden hen, and was off before you could say "Jack Robinson." But this time the hen gave a cackle which woke the ogre, and just as Jack got out of the house he heard him calling, "Wife, wife, what have you done with my golden hen?"

And the wife said, "Why, my dear?"

But that was all Jack heard, for he rushed off to the beanstalk and climbed down like a house on fire. And when he got home he showed his mother the wonderful hen, and said "Lay" to it; and it laid a golden egg every time he said "Lay."

Well, Jack was not happy, and wanted to try again. So, he rose in the morning and climbed to the top. But this time he knew better than to go straight to the ogre's house. And when he got near it, he waited behind a bush till he saw the ogre's wife come out with a pail to get some water, and then he crept into the house and got into the copper. He hadn't been there long when he heard thump! thump! thump! as before, and in came the ogre and his wife.

"Fee-fi-fo-fum, I smell the blood of an Englishman," cried out the ogre. "I smell him, wife, I smell him."

"Do you, my dearie?" says the ogre's wife. "Then, if it's that little rogue that stole your gold and the hen that laid the golden eggs he's sure to have got into the oven." And they both rushed to the oven. But Jack wasn't here, luckily, and the ogre's wife said, "There you are again with your fee-fi-fo-fum. Why, of course, it's the boy you caught last night that I've just broiled for your breakfast. How forgetful I am, and how careless you are not to know the difference between live and dead after all these years."

So the ogre sat down to the breakfast and ate it, but every now and then he would mutter, "Well, I could have sworn—" and he'd get up and search the larder and the cupboards and everything, only, luckily, he didn't think of the copper.

After breakfast was over, the ogre called out, "Wife, wife, bring me my golden harp." So she brought it and put it on the table before him. Then he said, "Sing!" and the golden harp sang most beautifully. And it went on singing till the ogre fell asleep, and commenced to snore like thunder.

Then Jack lifted up the copper-lid very quietly and got down like a mouse and crept on hands and knees till he came to the table, when up he crawled, caught hold of the golden harp and dashed with it towards the door. But the harp called out quite loud, "Master! Master!" and the ogre woke up just in time to see Jack running off with his harp.

Jack ran as fast as he could, and the ogre came rushing after. When the ogre got to the beanstalk, he saw Jack disappear and begin climbing down. Well, the ogre didn't like trusting himself to such a ladder, and he stood and waited, so Jack got another start. But just then the harp cried out, "Master! Master!" and the ogre swung himself down on to the beanstalk, which shook with his weight. Down climbs Jack, and after him climbed the ogre. By this time Jack had climbed down and climbed down and climbed down till he was very nearly home. So he called out, "Mother! Mother! Bring me an axe, bring me an axe." And his mother came rushing out with the axe in her hand, but when she came to the beanstalk she stood stock still with fright, for there she saw the ogre with his legs just through the clouds.

But Jack jumped down and got hold of the axe and gave a chop at the beanstalk which cut it half in two. The ogre felt the beanstalk shake and quiver, so he stopped to see what was the matter. Then Jack gave another chop with the axe, and the beanstalk was cut in two and began to topple over. Then the ogre fell down and broke his crown, and the beanstalk came toppling after.

Then Jack showed his mother his golden harp, and what with showing that and selling the golden eggs, Jack and his mother became very rich, and he married a great princess, and they lived happily ever after.

Jacobs, Joseph, ed. *English Fairytales*. New York: Knopf, 1993.

THREE BILLY GOATS GRUFF

ASBJORNSEN & MOE

Here is an old tale, less than ten minutes reading time, but important nonetheless. This brief story leaves us with a deep and poignant message.

 Once upon a time there were three billy goats, who went up the hillside to make themselves fat, and the name of all three was "Gruff."

On the way up was a bridge over a brook; and under the bridge lived a great, ugly Troll, with eyes as big as saucers, and a nose as long as your arm.

First of all came the youngest Billy Goat Gruff to cross the bridge.

Trip trap! trip trap! went the bridge. "Who's that tripping over my bridge?" roared the Troll.

"Oh, it is only I, the Tiniest Billy Goat Gruff; and I'm going up the hillside to make myself fat," said the billy goat, with such a small voice.

"Now I'm coming to gobble you up," said the Troll.

"Oh, no, pray don't take me! I'm too little," said the billy goat. "Wait a bit till the next Billy Goat Gruff comes; he's much bigger."

"Well, be off with you!" said the Troll.

A little while after came the Second Billy Goat Gruff to cross the bridge.

Trip trap! trip trap! trip trap! went the bridge.

"Who's that tripping over my bridge?" roared the Troll.

"Oh, it's only the Second Billy Goat Gruff; and I'm going up the hillside to make myself fat," said the billy goat, who hadn't such a small voice.

"Now I'm coming to gobble you up," said the Troll.

"Oh, no, don't take me! Wait a little till the Big Billy Goat Gruff comes; he's much bigger."

"Very well, be off with you!" said the Troll.

But just then came the Big Billy Goat Gruff.

Trip trap! trip trap! trip trap! went the bridge, for the billy goat was so heavy that the bridge creaked under him.

"Who's that tramping over my bridge?" roared the Troll.

"It's I, the Big Billy Goat Gruff," said the billy goat, who had an ugly, hoarse voice of his own.

"Now I'm coming to gobble you up," roared the Troll.

> *"Well, come along! I've got two spears,*
> *And I'll poke your eyeballs out at your ears;*
> *I've got besides two curling-stones,*
> *And I'll crush you to bits, body and bones."*

That was what the big billy goat said; and so he flew at the Troll, and poked his eyes out with his horns, and crushed him to bits, body and bones, and tossed him out into the stream, and after that he went up to the hillside. There the billy goats got so fat they were scarce able to walk home again; and if the fat hadn't fallen off them, why, they're still fat; and so—

> *"Snip, snap, snout,*
> *This tale's told out."*

A Child's Books of Stories. New York: Random House, 1986.

THE PRINCESS WHO COULD NOT CRY

Kathleen Adams & Frances Elizabeth Atchinson

The princess who could not cry laughed at everything even if it wasn't appropriate. Her parents searched far and wide for someone who could make their daughter cry once, to break the spell under which she languished.

There was once a little princess who could not cry.

That wouldn't have mattered so very much, but the trouble was that she laughed at everything, often on the most unsuitable occasions, and this was an extremely vexing and awkward habit, especially for a princess.

Her parents were very troubled about it, and they called in a wise old fairy in order to get her advice. She went into the matter thoroughly, and finally told them that if the princess could only once be made to cry, the spell would be broken for ever and she would thenceforward be just like other people.

This wasn't particularly helpful, but it gave them some hope, and they immediately set about the task of making the princess weep. Of course it was a rather difficult matter, because naturally they didn't want her to be really miserable, and they hardly knew how to begin. Finally they offered a reward of five hundred crowns to anybody who should succeed in making their daughter cry without doing her any harm.

Wise men came from all over the kingdom to see what they could do, and many things were tried, but all to no purpose.

One of them suggested that she should be shut up in a room by herself and fed on bread and water for a whole week. The queen thought this very cruel, but the king persuaded her to try it. She insisted, however, that at any rate it should be bread and milk. But every time they came to bring the princess her basin of bread and milk they found her laughing, and at the end of the week she was still as cheerful as ever.

"Look," she said, "my feet have grown so thin that I can't keep my slippers on." And she kicked her foot into the air and sent her slipper flying across the room, and laughed to see the scandalized face of the butler.

But her mother burst into tears. "My poor little lamb," she said, "they shall not treat you so any longer." And she rushed into the kitchen and ordered soup and chicken and pink jelly to be sent up to the princess for her next meal.

249

Another wise man came who said that for six months he had been practicing pulling the most awful faces and making the most terrible noises imaginable, in order to be able to cure the princess. Children, he said, were so frightened by him that they had to be carried shrieking and howling from the room, and even grown-up people were so terrified that they wept aloud. He requested that he might be left alone with the princess but the queen waited outside the door and listened.

She trembled with anxiety as she stood there, for the noises the wise man made were so blood-curdling that she could hardly bear to hear them herself, and it seemed dreadful that her child should be left alone to endure such a trial. But in a few minutes she heard peals of laughter coming from inside the room, and presently the wise man opened the door. He was quite done up, and blue in the face, with the efforts he had been making. "It's no use," he said rather crossly. "No use at all," and went away looking much annoyed.

The princess came running out to her mother.

"Oh, he was a funny man," she said. "Can't he come and do it again?'

Another wise man suggested that all her favorite toys should be broken up. But when he went into the nursery and began smashing her beautiful dolls and playthings, the princess clapped her hands and jumped about and laughed more heartily than ever.

"What fun, what fun," she said, and she too began throwing the things about. So that plan had to be given up also.

Other wise men came, but as many of their suggestions were cruel and unkind ones, naturally the king and queen would not hear of them, and at last they began to fear that nothing could be done.

Now, in a small village on the borders of the king's great park, there lived a widow with her little daughter Marigold.

They were very poor, and the mother earned what she could by doing odd jobs of washing, sewing, or cleaning for her neighbors. But she fell ill, and poor Marigold was in great trouble, for she had no money to buy comforts for her mother.

Their little savings had to go for food to keep them alive, and every day these grew less and less.

Marigold knew all about the little princess at the castle. She had often heard speak of her, and had even seen her sometimes riding about the roads on her white pony. And one day as she was cooking the midday meal an idea came into her head.

As soon as dinner was over, she put on her hat and cloak and told her mother that she was going up to the king's palace to see if she could make the princess cry and so earn the five hundred crowns.

Her mother did her best to persuade her not to go.

"How can you hope to succeed," she said, "when so many clever people have tried and failed? You are my own dear little Marigold, but it is useless for you to attempt such a task. Give it up, my child."

But Marigold was determined, and when her mother saw this she said no more, but lay and watched her rather sadly as she set bravely off for the castle with her little basket over her arm.

When Marigold came to the castle gates she felt frightened. The gates were so big and she was so small. But she thought of her mother and of the five hundred crowns which would buy her everything she needed, and she stood on tiptoe on the top step and pulled the bell handle so hard that she was quite frightened at the noise it made.

A very grand footman opened the door, and when he saw Marigold standing there in her woolen frock and cloak with her little basket, he said, "Back entrance!" in a loud, cross voice, and shut the door in her face.

So she went round to the back entrance. This time the door was opened by a red-faced kitchen-maid. "We've no dripping to give away today," she said, and she was about to shut the door.

But the queen happened to be in the kitchen giving her orders for the day, and she saw Marigold through the window. She came to the window and called to her.

"What is it, my child?" she asked, for Marigold stood there looking the picture of unhappiness.

"I've come to make the princess cry, please, your majesty," she said, and made a curtsey, for the queen looked very magnificent with her crown on her head and her lovely ermine train held up over her arm to keep it off the kitchen floor.

When the queen heard what Marigold had come for, she smiled and shook her head, for how could a little country girl hope to do what so many wise men had been unable to accomplish? But Marigold was so earnest and so sure that she could make the princess cry that at last the queen promised to let her attempt it.

"You won't hurt her?" she said. But she smiled as she said it. Marigold had such a kind little face; she did not look as if she could hurt any one.

She was taken to the princess's apartments, and the queen went with her into the nursery and introduced her to the princess and explained why she had come.

The princess was delighted to see a nice little rosy-cheeked girl instead of the dull old men who so often came to visit her. The queen shut the door and left them alone together.

By this time the news of the little village girl who had come to make the princess cry, had spread all over the palace; and presently a whole crowd of people were standing anxiously waiting outside the nursery door.

"It's such nonsense," whispered the ladies-in-waiting to the court pages. "Do you think she knows how to make a correct curtsey?"

At last the king and queen could stand the suspense no longer. They quietly opened the door and peeped in. And what do you think they saw? The princess, standing at the table in the middle of the room with Marigold's basket in front of her, busily peeling onions as hard as she could go, while the tears streamed down her face all the while. She was crying at last!

The king and queen rushed in and clasped her in their arms, onions and all. The ladies-in-waiting stood with their perfumed handkerchiefs pressed to their noses, the pages tittered, and the cook, who was standing at the bottom of the stairs, muttered to himself when he heard the news, "Well, I could have done that," while the Prime Minister rushed about the room with his wig on one side and shook everybody violently by the hand, exclaiming, "Wonderful wonderful! And so simple! We must get out a proclamation at once. Where are my spectacles? Where is my pen?"

And so the princess was cured, and from that time she became like everybody else and cried when she was unhappy and laughed when she was glad, though I am pleased to say that she always laughed a great deal more than she cried. ·

As for Marigold, she got her five hundred crowns, of course and was able to give her mother everything she needed, so that she was soon quite well. The king and queen were most grateful, and often invited her up to play with their little daughter, and loaded her with presents.

Because she was so sweet and modest, she didn't get spoiled, but grew up charming, kind, and beautiful. I did hear that in the end she married a king's son and that they had an onion for their crest, but I'm not sure at all about that.

THE STUPID PRINCESS

KATHLEEN ADAMS & FRANCES ELIZABETH ATCHINSON

The Fairy Ire vows to get revenge against the young king of Peronia who rejects her marriage proposal and marries a mortal woman (a princess) instead. She places a spell on the king and queen's son. The Fairy Diamantine says that, "true love shall banish enchantment," assuring them that in time all will be well.

nce upon a time the proud Fairy Ire resolved to marry, but not after the custom of her race. "My husband," said she, "shall be no magician; he shall be a mortal man, and he shall be royal."

She was a fastidious Fairy, and sought far and wide until at last she found the young king of Peronia, and to him she offered her heart and her dower of gifts.

"I thank you, Madame," said he; "but I prefer a human wife, and tomorrow I am to marry the most charming Princess on earth."

The Fairy Ire made no answer but disappeared, muttering words of which the king heard only one: "Revenge."

At that he was greatly alarmed, but a friend of his family, the good Fairy Diamantine, said, "Do not be troubled; Ire can do you no harm for I will protect you."

So the king was satisfied and married the lovely Princess; but directly something unforeseen happened in Fairyland, and Diamantine thought, "It is too late to tell them that Ire is chosen Queen of the Fairies and that now she may do what evil she pleases."

So she said nothing, and the King and Queen were happy as birds, and when the little Prince Feradir was born life was all sunshine.

But one day as they were standing together by the Baby's cradle the Queen exclaimed, "He is surely an angel. I fear he may fly away."

Then a voice close to her ear hissed, "Your angel shall be such a monster that you will wish him to fly away."

The Queen was paralyzed and King knew that this was the Fairy Ire's revenge. They called for Diamantine who hastened to the palace.

"Things could be worse," said she. "The dear child shall be the wisest king that has ever ruled, and may make wise the one he most loves—" here she paused and then added in a slow, meditative way, "and surely at last true love shall banish enchantment."

From that time the little Prince changed. His cherub face became ugly beyond description. Whether he laughed or cried, so frightful was he that the children who were brought to be his playmates fled away shrieking, and could never be coaxed to return.

Years passed and he grew to be a wise and brave man, gracious and gentle; nevertheless when the King, his father, died the people said, "This hobgoblin shall never reign over us. We will have another ruler," and their will was law, for they had the right to choose.

Feradir resigned the crown with slight regret.

"In Nature and books I shall find happiness," he said.

But that the Prince should find happiness was not the intention of the Fairy Ire.

"He shall be the most disappointed and wretched of men. I will see to that," said she.

Now the malicious Fairy had a godson named Charmant whom she loved and watched over like a mother.

"Charmant is handsome and he shall not suffer because he is stupid," said she.

So she stole from a foreign land the little Princess Astra, who was a marvel of beauty.

"Never will she object to Charmant," said the Fairy, "for she has not the mind of a chicken."

The children grew up together, and at sixteen neither one could read, but Astra was beauty itself, which precisely suited the Fairy Ire, for she had another object in view besides getting a wife for Charmant.

"Now we will visit Prince Feradir and add a drop to his cup of happiness," she muttered, as she laid Astra's portrait upon Feradir's desk.

All happened as she knew it would. The Prince lost his heart.

"I must discover who this is and where she is," he said to himself, and he had no difficulty in doing so, for the good Fairy Diamantine gladly told him all he wished to know, and added, "I am Astra's governess; I will walk with her in the Palace garden and there you may see her."

But when Astra saw the Prince she threw her arms around Diamantine's neck, screaming, "What is that? What is that? Take it away, take it away."

Feradir tried to speak while she was not looking, but it was useless for she would not hear. At that moment the Fairy Ire appeared, and said with a mocking smile, "Pray remain with us, Prince, for then you can listen to Astra though she will not listen to you."

Feradir hesitated, then thought:

"Why should I heed this disagreeable Fairy?"

He remained, but when he heard Astra and Charmant chattering together like two magpies, "She is an idiot," thought he. "I will go back and forget her—But ah! She is so beautiful! So beautiful!" And he sighed deeply.

When he bade farewell to the good Fairy Diamantine, she said with decision, "You are not to go away, Prince, for I know how to make Astra love you."

"I thank you, Madame," replied Feradir, "I am in no haste to marry. I shall never part with Astra's picture. It is always charming for it is always silent."

"Do not be disdainful," answered the Fairy; "the happiness of your life depends upon your marrying Astra."

"Then, Madame," said the Prince, "I assure you that my life will never be a happy one, for rather than spend it with an imbecile, I would marry a woman uglier than myself—were such a Being possible."

"You amuse me," said the good Fairy, "and now I will say that you have it in your power to bestow wisdom upon her whom you love. By one wish you may transform Astra into the most intellectual woman in the world; and then she will be the most perfect, for she has the kindest of hearts."

"I shall make my own misery," thought Feradir, "for when she sees me she will hate me, but I will sacrifice myself."

Then Diamantine smiled, for she had read his thought.

Now the Fairy held in her hand a silver chain and a Chain of Pearl.

"Here," she said, "are the Links of Progress. They will transport you to the Rock of Eternal Snow, down whose side trickles a rill. There, fill this Shell of Pearl, and make your one and only wish."

As the Prince took the Chain and the Shell, all around faded away, and again all around became new and strange. He was in the Underworld where, in a vaulted hall, lay heaps of shining metals, and where countless little Beings—Dwarfs and Gnomes—were hurrying to and fro like swarms of busy bees.

Then, as two Dwarves bearing on their shoulders heavy bars of iron staggered by, one whispered, "Beware! The Rill is not here," and he murmured, "We were men, but we filled our flasks and were bewitched."

They passed on, and the Prince heard a strange, sweet song that drew him irresistibly where a rivulet sparkled down a hillside, and where the songstress sat combing her long green hair with a golden comb.

As he approached she said, "Welcome, Prince of Peronia! Quickly fill your Shell of Pearl."

"Not yet nor here will I fill my Shell of Pearl," answered Feradir, and he made as though he would have ascended the hill.

Springing to her feet and letting fall her golden comb, the Songstress caught from the ground a hidden bow. It was strung and pointing the arrow at the Prince, she commanded, "Fill now your Shell of Pearl or die."

"Neither yet nor here will I fill my Shell of Pearl," replied the Prince.

There was a flash of light and Feradir saw the wicked face of the Fairy Ire glaring under the green tresses of the Water Witch.

It was but a glimpse, for he found himself in a meadow, blossoming with asphodel, and in the presence of a group of grave and stately women. As he bowed before them the eldest, moving slowly forward, said, "Welcome, Prince of Pretoria. We are your friends, and we keep for you a wife on whom we have bestowed wondrous gifts, and to yourself we will restore the face and form which you have lost. See."

And before Feradir arose two figures, the one a crowned Queen of incomparable beauty, the other a King—a man such as he had dreamed of but had never seen.

Without speaking he turned away, but suddenly thought, "That Queen is like Astra and he would have looked again; but the vision was gone, and he stood by the Rock of Eternal Snow, where the Rill trickled down like a reflection of the silver Chain. There he filled his Shell of Pearl and lifting it high, said, "I wish for Astra a mind to match her face."

Now at that same moment Astra, who was entertaining herself with colored beads, said in a low startled tone to Diamantine, "Something has happened! I seem to be in a new world! I feel ashamed of myself and my ways! I want my books!"

"Why should you want those?" asked Diamantine. "In two days you are to marry Charmant, and then you will have no governess and may amuse yourself with toys."

"I want no toys," exclaimed Astra, "and why must I marry Charmant? He is stupid! So stupid! How is it that I have never known it?"

"It is because you were like him," answered Diamantine; "but here he is." And Charmant entered calling for Astra.

"Come with me," he said; "and see me shoot at the mark. I am rid of my tutor and in two days I shall burn all my books."

He went out, but Astra did not follow him as usual. She only said decidedly, "Never will I be his wife! Prince Feradir is ugly, but what is beauty? An illness may destroy it, and then what is left where there is no mind? I wish I might marry the prince."

"I am glad you are so reasonable," replied Diamantine; "but conceal your feelings from Ire, or both you and the Prince are lost."

Now, from midnight until sunrise the Fairy Ire slept; and as soon as the clock struck the magic slumber-hour Diamantine led Astra into the Palace garden where stood Prince Feradir.

And what was his joy to behold not the Astra whom he had left, but the Queen whom he had seen in the meadow, and to know that his one wish had made her what she was! While Astra, listening to him, forgot his ugliness, and when Diamantine told her what she owed to him, she exclaimed, "Never can I pay my debt."

"You can pay it now," replied the Fairy, "for you can give Feradir as much beauty as he has given you mind."

"Oh, no," cried Astra; "I will not have him changed. I love him as he is. He is good and wise and that is enough for me."

"This choice, dear child, is the seal of your happiness," said Diamantine, taking both Astra's hands in her own. "You have been led by your heart and the Fairy Ire has no more power over you, nor over the people of Peronia, for the glamour which she cast over them is dispelled and they are calling for their King."

And so it was that never had been seen in Peronia splendor so dazzling nor ever had been joy so heartfelt as at the wedding of Feradir and Astra, when the vision of the meadow was realized and the people saw the beautiful crowned Queen, and the King who had regained his own face and form.

INCREDIBLE JOURNEYS

THE WIZARD OF OZ

L. FRANK BAUM

Dorothy awakes after a tornado to find that she and her house have landed with a bump in the curious land of the Munchkins—strange little people who are at least as old as her uncle, but no bigger than she. They welcome her as a hero, but as kind as the Munchkins are, Dorothy wants only to return home to Kansas.

Chapter II THE COUNCIL WITH THE MUNCHKINS

She was awakened by a shock so sudden and severe that if Dorothy had not been lying on the soft bed she might have been hurt. As it was, the jar made her catch her breath and wonder what had happened; and Toto put his cold little nose into her face and whined dismally. Dorothy sat up and noticed that the house was not moving; nor was it dark, for the bright sunshine came in at the window, flooding the little room. She sprang from her bed and with Toto at her heels ran and opened the door.

The little girl gave a cry of amazement and looked about her, her eyes growing bigger and bigger at the wonderful sights she saw.

The cyclone had set the house down, very gently—for a cyclone—in the midst of a country of marvelous beauty. There were lovely patches of green all about, with stately trees bearing rich and luscious fruits. Banks of gorgeous flowers were on every hand, and birds with rare and brilliant plumage sang and fluttered in the trees and bushes. A little way off was a small brook, rushing and sparkling along between green banks, and murmuring in a voice very grateful to a little girl who had lived so long on the dry, gray prairies.

While she stood looking eagerly at the strange and beautiful sights, she noticed coming toward her a group of the queerest people she had ever seen. They were not as big as the grown folk she had always been used to; but neither were they very small. In fact, they seemed about as tall as Dorothy, who was a well-grown child for her age, although they were, so far as looks go, many years older.

Three were men and one a woman, and all were oddly dressed. They wore round hats that rose to a small point a foot above their heads, with little bells around the brims that tinkled sweetly as the moved. The hats of the men were blue; the little woman's hat was white, and she wore a white gown that hung in plaits from her shoulders; over it were sprinkled little stars that glistened in the sun like diamonds. The men were dressed in blue, of the same shade as their hats, and wore well–polished boots with a deep roll of blue at the tops. The men, Dorothy thought, were about as old as Uncle Henry, for two of them had beards. But the little woman was doubtless much older: her face was covered with wrinkles, her hair was nearly white, and she walked rather stiffly.

When these people drew near the house where Dorothy was standing in the doorway, they paused and whispered among themselves, as if afraid to come farther. But the little old woman walked up to Dorothy, made a low bow and said, in a sweet voice:

"You are welcome, most noble Sorceress, to the land of the Munchkins. We are so grateful to you for having killed the wicked Witch of the East, and for setting our people free from bondage."

Dorothy listened to this speech with wonder. What could the little woman possibly mean by calling her a sorceress, and saying she had killed the wicked Witch of the East? Dorothy was an innocent, harmless little girl, who had been carried by a cyclone many miles from home; and she had never killed anything in all her life.

But the little woman evidently expected her to answer; so Dorothy said, with hesitation, "You are very kind; but there must be some mistake. I have not killed anything."

"Your house did, anyway," replied the little old woman, with a laugh; "and that is the same thing. See!" she continued, pointing to the corner of the house; "there are her two toes, still sticking out from under a block of wood."

Dorothy looked and gave a little cry of fright. There, indeed, just under the corner of the great beam the house rested on, two feet were sticking out, shod in silver shoes with pointed toes.

"Oh, dear! oh, dear!" cried Dorothy, clasping her hands together in dismay; "the house must have fallen on her. What ever shall we do?"

"There is nothing to be done," said the little woman calmly.

"But who was she?" asked Dorothy.

"She was the wicked Witch of the East, as I said," answered the little woman. "She has held all the Munchkins in bondage for many years, making them slave for her night and day. Now they are all set free, and are grateful to you for the favor."

"Who are the Munchkins?" enquired Dorothy.

"They are the people who live in this land of the East, where the wicked Witch ruled."

"Are you a Munchkin?" asked Dorothy.

"No, but I am their friend, although I live in the land of the North. When they saw the Witch of the East was dead, the Munchkins sent a swift messenger to me, and I came at once. I am the Witch of the North."

"Oh, gracious!" cried Dorothy; "are you a real witch?"

"Yes, indeed"; answered the little woman. "But I am a good witch, and the people love me. I am not as powerful as the wicked Witch was who ruled here, or I should have set the people free myself."

"But I thought all witches were wicked," said the girl, who was half frightened at facing a real witch.

"Oh, no; that is a great mistake. There were only four witches in all the Land of Oz, and two of them, those who live in the North and the South, are good witches. I know this is true, for I am one of them myself, and cannot be mistaken. Those who dwelt in the East and the West were, indeed, wicked witches; but now that you have killed one of them, there is but one wicked Witch in all the Land of Oz—the one who lives in the West."

"But," said Dorothy, after a moment's thought, "Aunt Em has told me that the witches were all dead—years and years ago."

"Who is Aunt Em?" inqired the old woman.

"She is my aunt who lives in Kansas, where I came from."

The Witch of the North seemed to think for a time, with her head bowed and her eyes upon the ground. Then she looked up and said, "I do not know where Kansas is, for I have never heard that country mentioned before. But tell me, is it a civilized country?"

"Oh, yes," replied Dorothy.

"Then that accounts for it. In the civilized countries I believe there are no witches left; nor wizards, nor sorceresses, nor magicians. But, you see, the Land of Oz has never been civilized, for we are cut off from all the rest of the world. Therefore we still have witches and wizards amongst us."

"Who are the wizards?" asked Dorothy.

"Oz himself is the Great Wizard," answered the Witch, sinking her voice to a whisper. "He is more powerful than all the rest of us together. He lives in the City of Emeralds."

Dorothy was going to ask another question, but just then the Munchkins, who had been standing silently by, gave a loud shout and pointed to the corner of the house where the Wicked witch had been lying.

"What is it?" asked the little old woman; and looked, and began to laugh. The feet of the dead Witch had disappeared entirely and nothing was left but the silver shoes.

"She was so old," explained the Witch of the North, "that she dried up quickly in the sun. That is the end of her. But the silver shoes are yours, and you shall have them to wear." She reached down and picked up the shoes, and after shaking the dust out of them handed them to Dorothy.

"The Witch of the East was proud of those silver shoes," said one of the Munchkins; "and there is some charm connected with them; but what it is we never know."

Dorothy carried the shoes into the house and placed them on the table. Then she came out again to the Munchkins and said, "I am anxious to get back to my aunt and uncle, for I am sure they will worry about me. Can you help my find my way?"

The Munchkins and the Witch first looked at one another, and then at Dorothy, and then shook their heads.

"At the East, not far from here," said one, "there is a great desert, and none could live to cross it."

"It is the same at the South," said another, "for I have been there and seen it. The South is the country of the Quadlings."

"I am told," said the third man, "that it is the same at the West. And that country, where the Winkies live, is ruled by the wicked Witch of the West, who would make you her slave if you passed her way."

"The North is my home," said the old lady, "and at its edge is the same great desert that surrounds this land of Oz. I'm afraid, my dear, you will have to live with us."

Dorothy began to sob at this, for she felt lonely among all these strange people. Her tears seemed to grieve the kind-hearted Munchkins, for they immediately took out their handkerchiefs and began to weep also. As for the little old woman, she took off her cap and balanced the point on the end of her nose, while she counted "one, two, three," in a solemn voice. At once the cap changed to a slate, on which was written in big, white chalk marks:

LET DOROTHY GO TO THE CITY OF EMERALDS.

The little old woman took the slate from her nose, and, having read the words on it, asked, "Is your name Dorothy, my dear?"

"Yes," answered the child, looking up and drying her tears.

"Then you must go to the City of Emeralds. Perhaps Oz will help you."

"Where is this City?" asked Dorothy.

"It is exactly in the center of the country, and is ruled by Oz, the Great Wizard I told you of."

"Is he a good man?" inquired the girl, anxiously.

"He is a good Wizard. Whether he is a man or not I cannot tell, for I have never seen him."

"How can I get there?" asked Dorothy.

"You must walk. It is a long journey, through a country that is sometimes pleasant and sometimes dark and terrible. However, I will use all the magic arts I know of to keep you from harm."

"Won't you go with me?" pleaded the girl, who had begun to look upon the little old woman as her only friend.

"No, I cannot do that," she replied; "but I will give you my kiss, and no one will dare injure a person who has been kissed by the Witch of the North."

She came close to Dorothy and kissed her gently on the forehead. Where her lips touched the girl they left a round, shining mark, as Dorothy found out soon after.

"The road to the City of Emeralds is paved with yellow brick," said the Witch; "so you cannot miss it. When you get to Oz do not be afraid of him, but tell your story and ask him to help you. Good-bye, my dear."

The three Munchkins bowed low to her and wished her a pleasant journey, after which they walked away through the trees. The Witch gave Dorothy a friendly little nod, whirled around on her left heel three times, and straightaway disappeared, much to the surprise of little Toto, who barked loudly when she had gone, because he had been afraid even to growl while she stood by.

But Dorothy, knowing her to be a witch, had expected her to disappear in just that way, and was not surprised in the least.

In this chapter, Dorothy continues her journey to the City of Emeralds in the hopes that the Wizard of Oz might help her get home to Kansas. She has picked up three new friends along the way to help her in her journey—the Tin Woodman, the Cowardly Lion, and the Scarecrow. Dorothy is lucky to have met them, for the trip turns out to be a hazardous one, full of adventures for all.

Chapter VII THE DEADLY POPPY FIELD

ur little party of travelers awakened next morning refreshed and full of hope, and Dorothy breakfasted like a princess off peaches and plums from the trees beside the river.

Behind them was the dark forest they had passed safely through, although they had suffered many discouragements; but before them was a lovely, sunny country that seemed to beckon them to the Emerald City.

To be sure, the broad river now cut them off from this beautiful land; but the raft was nearly done, and after the Tin Woodman had cut a few more logs and fastened them together with wooden pins, they were ready to start. Dorothy sat down in the middle of the raft and held Toto in her arms. When the Cowardly Lion stepped upon the raft it tipped badly, for he was big and heavy; but the Scarecrow and the Tin Woodman stood upon the other end to steady it, and they had long poles in their hands to push the raft through the water.

They got along quite well at first, but when they reached the middle of the river the swift current swept the raft down stream, farther and farther away from the road of yellow brick; and the water grew so deep that the long poles would not touch the bottom.

"This is bad," said the Tin Woodman, "for if we cannot get to the land we shall be carried into the country of the wicked Witch of the West, and she will enchant us and make us her slaves."

"And then I should get no brains," said the Scarecrow.

"And I should get no courage," said the Cowardly Lion.

"And I should get no heart," said the Tin Woodman.

"And I should never get back to Kansas," said Dorothy.

"We must certainly get to the Emerald City if we can," the Scarecrow continued, and he pushed so hard on his long pole that it stuck fast in the mud at the bottom of the river, and before he could pull it out again, or let go, the raft was swept away and the poor Scarecrow was left clinging to the pole in the middle of the river.

"Good bye!" he called after them, and they were very sorry to leave him; indeed, the Tin Woodman began to cry, but fortunately remembered that he might rust, and so dried his tears on Dorothy's apron.

Of course this was bad thing for the Scarecrow.

"I am worse off than when I first met Dorothy," he thought. "Then, I was stuck on a pole in a cornfield, where I could make believe scare the crows, at any rate; but surely there is no use for a Scarecrow stuck on a pole in the middle of a river. I am afraid I shall never have any brains, after all!"

Down the stream the raft floated, and the poor Scarecrow was left far behind. Then the Lion said: "Something must be done to save us. I think I can swim to the shore and pull the raft after me, if you will only hold fast to the tip of my tail."

So he sprang into the water and the Tin Woodman caught fast hold of his tail, then the Lion began to swim with all his might toward the shore. It was hard work, although he was so big; but by and by they were drawn out of the current, and then Dorothy took the Tin Woodman's long pole and helped push the raft to the land.

They were all tired out when they reached the shore at last and stepped off upon the pretty green grass, and they also knew that the stream had carried them a long ways past the road of yellow brick that led to the Emerald City.

"What shall we do now?" asked the Tin Woodman, as the Lion lay down on the grass to let the sun dry him.

"We must get back to the road, in some way," said Dorothy.

"The best plan will be to walk along the river bank until we come to the road again," remarked the Lion.

So, when they were rested, Dorothy picked up her basket and they started along the grassy bank, back to the road from which the river had carried them. It was a lovely country, with plenty of flowers and fruit trees and sunshine to cheer them, and had they not felt so sorry for the poor Scarecrow they could have been very happy.

They walked along as fast as they could, Dorothy only stopping once to pick a beautiful flower; and after a time the Tin Woodman cried out:

"Look!"

Then they all looked at the river and saw the Scarecrow perched upon his pole in the middle of the water, looking lonely and sad.

"What can we do to save him?" asked Dorothy.

The Lion and the Woodman both shook their heads, for they did not know. So they sat down upon the bank and gazed wistfully at the Scarecrow until a Stork flew by, which, seeing them, stopped to rest at the water's edge.

"Who are you, and where are you going?" asked the Stork.

"I am Dorothy," answered the girl; "and these are my friends, the Tin Woodman and the Cowardly Lion; and we are going to the Emerald City."

"This isn't the road," said the Stork, as she twisted her long neck and looked sharply at the queer party.

"I know it," returned Dorothy, "but we have lost the Scarecrow, and are wondering how we shall get him again."

"Where is he?" asked the Stork.

"Over there in the river," answered the girl.

"If he wasn't so big and heavy I would get him for you," remarked the Stork.

"He isn't heavy a bit," said Dorothy, eagerly, "for he is stuffed with straw; and if you will bring him back to us we shall thank you ever and ever so much."

"Well, I'll try," said the Stork, "but if I find he is too heavy to carry I shall have to drop him in the river again."

So the big bird flew into the air and over the water till she came to where the Scarecrow was perched upon his pole. Then the Stork with her great claws grabbed the Scarecrow by the arm and carried him up into the air and back to the bank, where Dorothy and the Lion and the Tin Woodman and Toto were sitting.

When the Scarecrow found himself among his friends again he was so happy that he hugged them all, even the Lion and Toto; and as they walked along he sang "To-de-ri-de-oh!" at every step, he felt so gay.

Baum, L. Frank. *The Wizard of Oz*. New York: Books of Wonder, 1987.
Other Editions:
——. *The Wizard of Oz*. New York: Scholastic, 1993.
——. *The Wizard of Oz*. New York: Putnam, (Illustrated Junior Library) 1994.

THE SECRET GARDEN

FRANCES HODGSON BURNETT

Mary Lennox is sent from India to live in her wealthy uncle's mansion on the moors of Yorkshire, in England. Mary arrives in England orphaned, spoiled, and lonely. Her only two friends are Martha, a young, maid and a robin, who leads her to an intriguing key buried in the ground near the garden.

THE ROBIN WHO SHOWED THE WAY

he looked at the key quite a long time. She turned it over and over, and thought about it. As I have said before, she was not a child who had been trained to ask permission or consult her elders about things. All she thought about the key was that if it was the key to the closed garden, and she could find out where the door was, she could perhaps open it and see what was inside the walls, and what had happened to the old rose-trees. It was because it had been shut up so long that she wanted to see it. It seemed as if it must be different from other places and that something strange must have happened to it during ten years. Besides that, if she liked it she could go into it every day and shut the door behind her, and she could make up some play of her own and play it quite alone, because nobody would ever know where she was, but would think the door was still locked and the key buried in the earth. The thought of that pleased her very much.

Living, as it were, all by herself in a house with a hundred mysteriously closed rooms, and having nothing whatever to do to amuse herself, had set her inactive brain to working and was actually awakening her imagination. There is no doubt that the fresh, strong, pure air from the moor had a great deal to do with it. Just as it had given her an appetite, and fighting with the wind had stirred her blood, so the same things had stirred her mind. In India she had always been too hot and languid and weak to care much about anything, but in this place she was beginning to care and to want to do new things. Already she felt less "contrary," though she did not know why.

She put the key in her pocket and walked up and down her walk. No one but herself ever seemed to come there, so she could walk slowly and look at the wall, or, rather, at the ivy growing on it. The ivy was the baffling thing. Howsoever carefully she looked she could see nothing but thickly growing, glossy, dark-green leaves. She was very much disappointed. Something of her contrariness came back to her as she paced the walk and looked over it at the tree-tops inside. It seemed so silly, she said to herself, to be near it and not be able to get in. She took the key in her pocket when she went back to the house, and she made up her mind that she would always carry it with her when she went out, so that if she ever should find the hidden door she would be ready.

Mrs. Medlock had allowed Martha to sleep all night at the cottage, but she was back at her work in the morning with cheeks redder than ever and in the best of spirits.

"I got up at four o'clock" she said. "Eh! it was pretty on the' moor with th' birds gettin' up an' th' rabbits scamperin' about an' th' sun risin'. I didn't walk all th' way. A man gave me a ride in his cart an' I did enjoy myself."

She was full of stories of the delights of her day out. Her mother had been glad to see her and they had got the baking and washing all out of the way. She had even made each of the children a dough-cake with a bit of brown sugar in it.

"I had' em all pipin' hot when they came in from playin' on th' moor. An' th' cottage all smelt o' nice, clean hot bakin' an' there was a good fire, an' they just shouted for joy. Our Dickon he said our cottage was good enough for a king."

In the evening they had all sat round the fire, and Martha and her mother had sewed patches on torn clothes and mended stockings and Martha had told them about the little girl who had come back from India and who had been waited on all her life by what Martha called "blacks" until she didn't know how to put on her own stockings.

"Eh! they did like to hear about you," said Martha. "They wanted to know all about th' blacks an' about th' ship you came in. I couldn't tell' em enough."

Mary reflected a little.

"I'll tell you a great deal more before your next day out," she said, " so that you will have more to talk about. I dare say they would like to hear about riding on elephants and camels, and about the officers going to hunt tigers."

"My word!" cried delighted Martha. It would set' em clean off their heads. Would tha' really do that, Miss? It would be same as a wild beast show like we heard they had in York once."

"India is quite different from Yorkshire," Mary said slowly, as she thought the matter over. "I never thought of that. Did Dickon and your mother like to hear you talk about me?"

"Why, our Dickon's eyes nearly started out o' his head, they got that round," answered Martha. "But mother, she was put out about your seemin' to be all by yourself like. She said, 'Hasn't Mr. Craven got no governess for her, nor no nurse?' and I said, 'No, he hasn't, though Mrs. Medlock says he will when he thinks of it, but she says he mayn't think of it for two or three years.'"

"I don't want a governess," said Mary sharply.

"But mother says you ought to be learnin' your book by this time an' you ought to yourself, in a big place like that, wanderin' about all alone, an' no mother. You do your best to cheer her up,' she says, an' I said I would."

Mary gave her a long, steady look.

"You do cheer me up," she said. "I like to hear you talk."

Presently Martha went out of the room and came back with something held in her hands under her apron.

"What does tha' think," she said, with a cheerful grin. "I've brought thee a present."

"A present!" exclaimed Mistress Mary. How could a cottage full of 14 hungry people give anyone a present!

"A man was drivin' across the moor peddlin'," Martha explained. "An' he stopped his cart at our door. He had pots an' pans an' odds an' ends, but mother had no money to buy anythin'. Just as he was goin' away our 'Lizabeth Ellen called out, 'Mother, he's got skippin'-ropes with red an' blue handles.' An' mother she calls out quite sudden, 'Here, stop, mister! How much are they?' An' he says 'Tuppence,' an' mother she began fumblin' in her pocket an' she says to me, 'Martha, tha's brought me thy wages like a good lass, an' I've got four places to put every penny, but I'm just goin' to take tuppence out of it to buy that child a skippin'-rope,' an' she bought one an' here it is."

She brought it out from under her apron and exhibited it quite proudly. It was a strong, slender rope with a striped red and blue handle at each end, but Mary Lennox had never seen a skipping-rope before. She gazed at it with a mystified expression.

"What is it for?" she asked curiously.

"For!" cried out Martha. "Does tha' mean that they've not got skippin'-ropes in India, for all they've got elephants and tigers and camels! No wonder most of 'em's black. This is what it's for; just watch me."

And she ran into the middle of the room and, taking a handle in each hand, began to skip, and skip, and skip, while Mary turned in her chair to stare at her, and the queer faces in the old portraits seemed to stare at her, too, and wonder what on earth this common little cottager had the impudence to be doing under their very noses. But Martha did not even see them. The interest and curiosity in Mistress Mary's face delighted her, and she went on skipping and counted as she skipped until she had reached a hundred.

"I could skip longer than that," she said when she stopped. "I've skipped as much as 500 when I was 12, but I wasn't as fat then as I am now, an' I was in practice."

Mary got up from her chair beginning to feel excited herself.

"It looks nice," she said. "Your mother is a kind woman. Do you think I could ever skip like that?"

"You just try it," urged Martha, handing her the skipping-rope. "You can't skip a hundred at first, but if you practice you'll mount up. That's what mother said. She says, 'Nothin' will do her more good than skippin' rope. It's th' sensiblest toy a child can have. Let her play out in th' fresh air skippin' an' it'll stretch her legs an' arms an' give her some strength in 'em.'"

It was plain that there was not a great deal of strength in Mistress Mary's arms and legs when she first began to skip. She was not very clever at it, but she liked it so much that she did not want to stop.

"Put on tha' things and run an' skip out o' doors," said Martha. "Mother said I must tell you to keep out o' doors as much as you could, even when it rains a bit, so as tha' wrap up warm."

Mary put on her coat and hat and took her skipping-rope over her arm. She opened the door to go out, and then suddenly thought of something and turned back rather slowly.

"Martha," she said, "they were your wages. It was your twopence really. Thank you." She said it stiffly because she was not used to thanking people or noticing that they did things for her. "Thank you," she said, and held out her hand because she did not know what else to do.

Martha gave her hand a clumsy little shake, as if she was not accustomed to this sort of thing either. Then she laughed.

"Eh! tha' art a queer, old-womanish thing," she said. "If tha'd been our 'Lizabeth Ellen tha'd have given me a kiss."

Mary looked stiffer than ever.

"Do you want me to kiss you?"

Martha laughed again.

"Nay, not me," she answered. "If tha' was different, p'raps tha'd want to thysel'. But tha' isn't. Run off outside an' play with thy rope."

Mistress Mary felt a little awkward as she went out of the room. Yorkshire people seemed strange, and Martha was always rather a puzzle to her. At first she had disliked her very much, but now she did not.

The skipping-rope was a wonderful thing. She counted and skipped, and skipped and counted, until her cheeks were quite red, and she was more interested than she had ever been since she was born. The sun was shining and a little wind was blowing—not a rough wind, but one which came in delightful little gusts and brought a fresh scent of newly turned earth with it. She skipped round the fountain garden, and up one walk and down another. She skipped at last into the kitchen-garden and saw Ben Weatherstaff digging and talking to his robin, which was hopping about him. She skipped down the walk toward him and he lifted his head and looked at her with a curious expression. She had wondered if he would notice her. She wanted him to see her skip.

"Well!" he exclaimed. "Upon my word! P'raps tha' art a young 'un, after all, an' p'raps tha's got child's blood in thy veins instead of sour buttermilk. Tha's skipped red into thy cheeks as sure as my name's Ben Weatherstaff. I wouldn't have believed tha' could do it."

"I never skipped before," Mary said. "I'm just beginning. I can only go up to 20."

"Tha' keep on," said Ben. "Tha' shapes well enough at it for a young 'un that's lived with heathen. Just see how he's watchin' thee," jerking his head toward the robin. "He followed after thee yesterday. He'll be at it again today. He'll be bound to find out what th' skippin'-rope is. He's never seen one. Eh!" shaking his head at the bird, "Tha' curiosity will be th' death of thee sometime if tha' doesn't look sharp."

Mary skipped round all the gardens and round the orchard, resting every few minutes. At length she went to her own special walk and made up her mind to try if she could skip the whole length of it. It was a good long skip and she began slowly, but before she had gone halfway down the path she was so hot and breathless that she was obliged to stop. She did not mind much, because she had already counted up to 30. She stopped with a laugh of pleasure, and there, lo and behold, was the robin swaying on a long branch of ivy. He had followed her and he greeted her with a chirp. As Mary had skipped toward him she felt something heavy in her pocket strike against her at each jump, and when she saw the robin she laughed again.

"You showed me where the key was yesterday," she said. "You ought to show me the door today; but I don't believe you know!"

The robin flew from his swinging spray of ivy on to the top of the wall and he opened his beak and sang a loud, lovely trill, merely to show off. Nothing in the world is quite as adorably lovely as a robin when he shows off—and they are nearly always doing it.

Mary Lennox had heard a great deal about Magic in her Ayah's stories, and she always said that what happened almost at that moment was Magic.

One of the nice little gusts of wind rushed down the walk, and it was a stronger one than the rest. It was strong enough to wave the branches of the trees, and it was more than strong enough to sway the trailing sprays of untrimmed ivy hanging from the wall. Mary had stepped close to the robin, and suddenly the gust of wind swung aside some loose ivy trails, and more suddenly still she jumped toward it and caught it in her hand. This she did because she had been covered by the leaves hanging over it. It was the knob of a door.

She put her hands under the leaves and began to pull and push them aside. Thick as the ivy hung, it nearly all was a loose and swinging curtain, though some had crept over wood and iron. Mary's heart began to thump and her hands to shake a little in her delight and excitement. The robin kept singing and twittering away and tilting his head on one side, as if he were as excited as she was. What was this under her hands which was square and made of iron and which her fingers found a hole in?

It was the lock of the door which had been closed ten years and she put her hand in her pocket, drew out the key, and found it fitted the keyhole. She put the key in and turned it. It took two hands to do it, but it did turn.

And then she took a long breath and looked behind her up the long walk to see if any one was coming. No one was coming. No one ever did come, it seemed, and she took another long breath, because she could not help it, and she held back the swinging curtain of ivy and pushed back the door which opened slowly—slowly.

Then she slipped through it, and shut it behind her, and stood with her back against it, looking about her and breathing quite fast with excitement, and wonder, and delight.

She was standing inside the secret garden.

THE STRANGEST HOUSE

t was the sweetest, most mysterious-looking place any one could imagine. The high walls which shut it in were covered with the leafless stems of climbing roses which were so thick that they were matted together. Mary Lennox knew they were roses because she had seen a great many roses in India. All the ground was covered with grass of a wintry brown and out of it grew clumps of bushes which were surely rose-bushes if they were alive. There were numbers of standard roses which had so spread their branches that they were like little trees. There were other trees in the garden, and one of the things which made the place look strangest and loveliest was that climbing roses had run all over them and swung down long tendrils which made light swaying curtains, and here and there they had caught at each other or at a far-reaching branch and had crept from one tree to another and made lovely bridges of themselves. There were neither leaves nor roses on them now and Mary did not know whether they were dead or alive, but their thin gray or brown branches and sprays looked like a sort of hazy mantle spreading over everything, walls, and trees, and even brown grass, where they had fallen from their fastenings and run along the ground. It was this hazy tangle from tree to tree which made it all look so mysterious. Mary had thought it must be different from other gardens which had not been left all by themselves so long; and indeed it was different from any other place she had ever seen in her life.

"How still it is!" she whispered. "How still!"

Then she waited a moment and listened at the stillness. The robin, who had flown to his treetop, was still as all the rest. He did not even flutter his wings; he sat without stirring, and looked at Mary.

"No wonder it is still," she whispered again. "I am the first person who has spoken in here for ten years."

She moved away from the door, stepping as softly as if she were afraid of awakening some one. She was glad that there was grass under her feet and that her steps made no sounds. She walked under one of the fairy-like gray arches between the trees and looked up at the sprays and tendrils which formed them.

"I wonder if they are all quite dead," she said. "Is it all a quite dead garden? I wish it wasn't."

If she had been Ben Weatherstaff she could have told whether the wood was alive by looking at it, but she could only see that there were only gray or brown sprays and branches and none showed any signs of even a tiny leaf-bud anywhere.

But she was inside the wonderful garden and she could come through the door under the ivy any time and she felt as if she had found a world all her own.

The sun was shining inside the four walls and the high arch of blue sky over this particular piece of Misselthwaite seemed even more brilliant and soft than it was over the moor. The robin flew down from his tree-top and hopped about or flew after her from one bush to another. He chirped a good deal and had a very busy air, as if he were showing her things. Everything was strange and silent and she seemed to be hundreds of miles away from any one, but somehow she did no feel lonely at all. All that troubled her was her wish that she knew whether all the roses were dead, or if perhaps some of them had lived and might put out leaves and buds as the weather got warmer. She did not want it to be a quite dead, dead garden. If it were a quite alive garden, how wonderful it should be, and what thousands of roses would grow on every side!

Her skipping-rope had hung over her arm when she came in and after she had walked about for a while she thought she'd skip around the whole garden, stopping when she wanted to look at things. There seemed to have been grass paths here and there, and in one or two corners there were alcoves of evergreen with stone seats or tall moss-covered flower urns in them.

As she came near the second of these alcoves she stopped skipping. There had once been a flowerbed in it, and she thought she saw something sticking out of the black earth—some sharp little pale green points. She remembered what Ben Weatherstaff had said and she knelt down to look at them.

"Yes, they are tiny growing things and they might be crocuses or snowdrops or daffodils," she whispered.

She bent very close to them, and sniffed the fresh scent of the damp earth. She liked it very much.

"Perhaps there are some other ones coming up in other places," she said. "I will go all over the garden and look."

She did not skip, but walked. She went slowly and kept her eyes on the ground. She looked in the old border beds and among the grass, and after she had gone around, trying to miss nothing, she had found ever so many more sharp, pale green points, and she had become quite excited again.

"It isn't a quite dead garden," she cried out softly to herself. "Even if the roses are dead, there are other things alive."

She did not know anything about gardening, but the grass seemed so thick in some places where the green points were pushing their way through that she thought they did not seem to have room enough to grow. She searched about until she found a rather sharp piece of wood and knelt down and dug and weeded out the weeds and grass until she made nice little clear places around them.

"Now they look as if they could breathe," she said, after she had finished with the first ones. "I am going to do ever so many more. I'll do all I can see. If I haven't time today I can come tomorrow."

She went from place to place, and dug and weeded, and enjoyed herself so immensely that she was led on from bed to bed and into the grass under the trees. The exercise made her so warm that she first threw her coat off, and then her hat, and without knowing it she was smiling down on to the grass and the pale green points all the time.

The robin was tremendously busy. He was very much pleased to see gardening begun on his own estate. He had often wondered at Ben Weatherstaff. Where gardening is done all sorts of delightful things to eat are turned up with the soil. Now here was this new kind of creature who was not half Ben's size and yet had had the sense to come into his garden and begin at once.

Mistress Mary worked in her garden until it was time to go to her midday dinner. In fact, she was rather late in remembering, and when she put on her coat and hat, and picked up her skipping-rope, she could not believe that she had been working two or three hours. She had been actually happy all the time; and dozens of the tiny, pale green points were to be seen in cleared places, looking twice as cheerful as they had looked before, when the grass and weeds had been smothering them.

"I shall come back this afternoon," she said, looking all around at her new kingdom, and speaking to the trees and the rose-bushes as if they heard her.

Then she ran lightly across the grass, pushed open the slow old door and slipped through it under the ivy. She had such red cheeks and such bright eyes and ate such a dinner that Martha was delighted.

"Two pieces o' meat an' two helps o' rice puddin'!" she said. "Eh! mother will be pleased when I tell her what th' skippin'-rope's done for thee."

In the course of her digging with her pointed stick Mistress Mary had found herself digging up a sort of white root rather like an onion. She had put it back in its place and patted the earth carefully down on it and just now she wondered if Martha could tell her what it was.

"Martha," she said, "what are those white roots that look like onions?"

"They're bulbs," answered Martha. "Lots o' spring flowers grow from 'em. Th' very little ones are snowdrops an' crocuses an' th' big ones are narcissus an' jonquils an' daffy-downdillys. Th' biggest of all is lilies an' purple flags. Eh! they are nice. Dickon's got a whole lot of 'em planted in our bit o' garden."

"Does Dickon know all about them?" asked Mary, a new idea taking possession of her.

"Our Dickon can make a flower grow out of a brick walk. Mother says he just whispers things out o' th' ground."

"Do bulbs live a long time? Would they live years and years if no one helped them?" inquired Mary anxiously.

"They're things as helps themselves," said Martha. "That's why poor folk can afford to have 'em. If you don't trouble 'em, most of 'em'll work away underground for a lifetime an' spread out an' have little 'uns. There's a place in th' park woods here where there's snowdrops by thousands. They're the prettiest sight in Yorkshire when th' spring comes. No one knows when they was first planted."

"I wish the spring was here now," said Mary. "I want to see all the things that grow in England."

Burnett, Frances H. *The Secret Garden*. New York: HarperCollins, Harper Trophy, 1987.
    Other Editions:
      ——. *The Secret Garden*. New York: Knopf, 1993.
      ——. *The Secret Garden*. New York: Penguin, Puffin Books, 1994.

ALICE IN WONDERLAND

LEWIS CARROLL

Alice is having an average, dull day sitting with her sister outside on a bank. That is, until she sees a white rabbit hustling by her—taking a watch out of its waistcoat pocket! Thinking this a very curious sight, she follows the rabbit down a rabbit-hole, plummeting past cupboards and book-shelves. Thus begins a day full of zany adventures. Alice encounters some very odd creatures, she shrinks and grows, and she has some very peculiar conversations with some very peculiar animals—and cards even! Here she comes across the house of the March Hare. It has chimneys shaped like ears, and a roof thatched with fur.

Chapter VII A MAD TEA-PARTY

here was a table set out under a tree in front of the house, and the March Hare and the Hatter were having tea at it: a Dormouse was sitting between them, fast asleep, and the other two were using it as a cushion, resting their elbows on it, and talking over its head. "Very uncomfortable for the Dormouse," thought Alice; "only as it's asleep, I suppose it doesn't mind."

The table was a large one, but the three were all crowded together at one corner of it. "No room! No room!" they cried out when they saw Alice coming.

"There's plenty of room!" said Alice indignantly, and she sat down in a large arm-chair at one end of the table.

"Have some wine," the March Hare said in an encouraging tone.

Alice looked all around the table, but there was nothing on it but tea. "I don't see any wine," she remarked.

"There isn't any," said the March Hare.

"Then it wasn't very civil of you to offer it," said Alice angrily.

"It wasn't very civil of you to sit down without being invited," said the March Hare.

"I didn't know it was your table," said Alice, "It's laid for a great many more than three."

"Your hair wants cutting," said the Hatter. He had been looking at Alice for some time with great curiosity, and this was his first speech.

"You should learn not to make personal remarks," Alice said with some severity, "it's very rude."

The Hatter opened his eyes very wide on hearing this; but all he said was, "Why is a raven like a writing-desk?"

"Come, we shall have some fun now!" thought Alice. "I'm glad they've begun asking riddles—I believe I can guess that," she added aloud.

"Do you mean that you think you can find out the answer to it?" said the March Hare.

"Exactly so," said Alice.

"Then you should say what you mean," the March Hare went on.

"I do," Alice hastily replied; "at least—at least I mean what I say—that's the same thing, you know."

"Not the same thing a bit!" said the Hatter. "Why, you might just as well say that 'I see what I eat' is the same thing as 'I eat what I see'!"

"You might just as well say," added the March Hare, "that 'I like what I get' is the same thing as 'I get what I like'!"

"You might just as well say," added the Dormouse, which seemed to be talking in its sleep, "that 'I breathe when I sleep' is the same thing as 'I sleep when I breathe'!"

"It is the same thing with you," said the Hatter, and here the conversation dropped, and the party sat silent for a minute, while Alice thought over all she could remember about ravens and writing-desks, which wasn't much.

The Hatter was the first to break the silence. "What day of the month is it?" he said, turning to Alice, he had taken his watch out of his pocket, and was looking at it uneasily, shaking it every now and then, and holding it to his ear.

Alice considered a little, and then said, "The fourth."

"Two days wrong!" sighed the Hatter. "I told you butter wouldn't suit the works!" he added, looking angrily at the March Hare.

"It was the best butter," the March Hare meekly replied.

"Yes, but some crumbs must have got in as well," the Hatter grumbled; "you shouldn't have put it in with the bread-knife."

The March Hare took the watch and looked at it gloomily; then he dipped it into his cup of tea, and looked at it again; but he could think of nothing better to say than his first remark, "It was the best butter, you know."

Alice had been looking over his shoulder with some curiosity. "What a funny watch!" she remarked. "It tells the day of the month, and doesn't tell what o'clock it is!"

"Why should it?" muttered the Hatter. "Does your watch tell you what year it is?"

"Of course not," Alice replied very readily; "but that's because it stays the same year for such a long time together."

"Which is just the case with mine," said the Hatter.

Alice felt dreadfully puzzled. The Hatter's remark seemed to her to have no sort of meaning in it, and yet it was certainly English. "I don't quite understand you," she said, as politely as she could.

"The Dormouse is asleep again," said the Hatter, and he poured a little hot tea upon its nose.

The Dormouse shook its head impatiently, and said, without opening its eyes, "Of course, of course; just what I was going to remark myself."

"Have you guessed the riddle yet?" the Hatter said, turning to Alice again.

"No, I give it up," Alice replied. "What's the answer?"

"I haven't the slightest idea," said the Hatter.

"Nor I," said the March Hare.

Alice sighed wearily. "I think you might do something better with the time," she said, "than wasting it in asking riddles that have no answers."

"If you knew Time as well as I do," said the Hatter, "you wouldn't talk about wasting it. It's him."

"I don't know what you mean," said Alice.

"Of course you don't!" the Hatter said, tossing his head contemptuously. "I dare say you never even spoke to Time!"

"Perhaps not," Alice cautiously replied; "but I know I have to beat time when I learn music."

"Ah! That accounts for it," said the Hatter. "He won't stand beating. Now, if you only kept on good terms with him, he'd do almost anything you liked with the clock. For instance, suppose it were nine o'clock in the morning, just time to begin lessons; you'd only have to whisper a hint to Time, and round goes the clock in a twinkling! Half-past one, time for dinner!"

("I only wish it was," the March Hare said to itself in a whisper.)

"That would be grand, certainly," said Alice thoughtfully; "but then—I shouldn't be hungry for it, you know."

"Not at first, perhaps," said the Hatter; "but you could keep it to half-past one as long as you liked."

"Is that the way you manage?" Alice asked.

The Hatter shook his head mournfully. "Not I!" he replied. "We quarreled last March—just before he went mad, you know"— pointing with his teaspoon at the March Hare, —"it was at the great concert given by the Queen of Hearts, and I had to sing

Twinkle, twinkle, little bat!

How I wonder what you're at!

You know the song, perhaps?"

"I've heard something like it," said Alice.

"It goes on, you know," the Hatter continued, "in this way—

Up above the world you fly,
Like a tea-tray in the sky.
Twinkle, twinkle——"

Here the Dormouse shook itself, and began singing in its sleep "Twinkle, twinkle, twinkly, twinkle—" and went on so long that they had to pinch it to make it stop.

"Well, I'd hardly finished the first verse," said the Hatter, "when the Queen bawled out 'He's murdering the time! Off with his head!'"

"How dreadfully savage!" exclaimed Alice.

"And ever since that," the Hatter went on in a mournful tone, "he won't do a thing I ask! It's always six o'clock now."

A bright idea came into Alice's head. "Is that the reason so many tea-things are put out here?" she asked.

"Yes, that's it," said the Hatter with a sigh; "it's always tea-time, and we've no time to wash the things between whiles."

"Then you keep moving around, I suppose?" said Alice.

"Exactly so," said the Hatter, "as the things get used up."

"But what happens when you come to the beginning again?" Alice ventured to ask.

"Suppose we change the subject," the March Hare interrupted, yawning. "I'm getting tired of this. I vote the young lady tells us a story."

"I'm afraid I don't know one," said Alice, rather alarmed at the proposal.

"Then the Dormouse shall!" they both cried. "Wake up, Dormouse!" And they pinched it on both sides at once.

The Dormouse slowly opened its eyes. "I wasn't asleep," it said in a hoarse, feeble voice, "I heard every word you fellows were saying."

"Tell us a story!" said the March Hare.

"Yes, please do!" pleaded Alice.

"And be quick about it," added the Hatter, "or you'll be asleep again before it's done."

"Once upon a time there were three little sisters," the Dormouse began in a great hurry; "and their names were Elsie, Lacie, and Tillie; and they lived at the bottom of a well—"

"What did they live on?" said Alice, who always took a great interest in questions of eating and drinking.

"They lived on a treacle," said the Dormouse, after thinking a minute or two.

"They couldn't have done that, you know," Alice gently remarked. "They'd have been ill."

"So, they were," said the Dormouse, "very ill."

Alice tried a little to fancy herself what such an extraordinary way of living would be like, but it puzzled her too much, so she went on: "But why did they live at the bottom of a well?"

"Take some more tea," the March Hare said to Alice, very earnestly.

"I've had nothing yet," Alice replied in an offended tone, "so I can't take more."

"You mean you can't take less," said the Hatter, "it's very easy to take more than nothing."

"Nobody asked your opinion," said Alice.

"Who's making personal remarks now?" the Hatter asked triumphantly.

Alice did not quite know what to say to this, so she helped herself to some tea and bread-and-butter, and then turned to the Dormouse, and repeated her question. "Why did they live at the bottom of a well?"

The Dormouse again took a minute or two to think about it, and then said, "It was a treacle-well."

"There's no such thing!" Alice was beginning very angrily, but the Hatter and the March Hare went "Sh! Sh!" and the Dormouse sulkily remarked, "If you can't be civil, you'd better finish the story for yourself."

"No, please go on!" Alice said very humbly. "I won't interrupt you again. I dare say there may be one."

"One, indeed!" said the Dormouse indignantly. However, he consented to go on. "And so these three little sisters—they were learning to draw, you know—"

"What did they draw?" said Alice, quite forgetting her promise.

"Treacle," said the Dormouse, without considering at all, this time.

"I want a clean cup," interrupted the Hatter; "let's all move one place on."

He moved on as he spoke, and the Dormouse followed him: the March Hare moved into the Dormouse's place, and Alice rather unwillingly took the place of the March Hare. The Hatter was the only one who got any advantage from the change; and Alice was a good deal worse off than before, as the March Hare had just upset the milk-jug into his plate.

Alice did not wish to offend the Dormouse again, so she began very cautiously: "But I don't understand. Where did they draw the treacle from?"

"You can draw water out of a water-well," said the Hatter; "so I should think you could draw treacle out of a treacle-well—eh, stupid?"

"But they were in the well," Alice said to the Dormouse, not choosing to notice this last remark.

"Of course they were," said the Dormouse; "well in."

This answer so confused poor Alice, that she let the Dormouse go on for some time without interrupting it.

"They were learning to draw," the Dormouse went on, yawning and rubbing its eyes, for it was getting very sleepy; "and they drew all manner of things—everything that begins with an M—"

"Why with an M?" said Alice.

"Why not?" said the March Hare.

Alice was silent.

The Dormouse had closed its eyes by this time, and was going off into a doze; but, on being pinched by the Hatter, it woke up again with a little shriek, and went on: "—that begins with an M, such as mouse-traps, and the moon, and memory, and muchness—you know you say things are 'much of a muchness'—did you ever see such a thing as a drawing of a muchness!"

"Really, now you ask me," said Alice, very much confused, "I don't think—"

"Then you shouldn't talk," said the Hatter. This piece of rudeness was more than Alice could bear: she got up in great disgust, and walked off; the Dormouse fell asleep instantly, and neither of the others took the least notice of her going, though she looked back once or twice, half hoping that they would call after her. The last time she saw them, they were trying to put the Dormouse into the teapot.

"At any rate I'll never go there again!" said Alice, as she picked her way through the wood. "It's the stupidest tea-party I ever was at in all my life!"

Just as she said this, she noticed that one of the trees had a door leading right into it. "That's very curious!" she thought. "But everything's curious today. I think I may as well go in at once." And in she went.

Once more she found herself in the long hall, and close to the little glass table. "Now, I'll manage better this time," she said to herself, and began by taking the little golden key, and unlocking the door that led into the garden. Then she set to work nibbling at the mushroom (she had kept a piece of it in her pocket) till she was about a foot high: then she walked down the little passage, and then—she found herself at last in the beautiful garden, among the bright flower-beds and the cool fountains.

Carroll, Lewis. *Alice in Wonderland*. New York: Dell, 1992.
    Other Editions:
    ——. *Alice in Wonderland*. New York: Norton, 1992.

CHARLIE AND THE CHOCOLATE FACTORY

ROALD DAHL

Charlie Bucket has won a ticket to visit Willy Wonka's famous chocolate factory. Only five children are allowed inside. Violet Beauregarde is one of them. She decides to sample one of Wonka's inventions during the tour of his factory—but she doesn't count on the amazing consequences. They all learn a lesson about greed—and bad habits—from Willy and his assistants, the Oompa-Loompas.

Chapter 21 GOOD-BYE, VIOLET

y dear sir!" cried Mr. Wonka, "when I start selling this gum in the shops it will change everything! It will be the end of all kitchens and all cooking! There will be no more marketing to do! No more buying of meat and groceries! There will be no knives and forks at mealtimes! No plates! No washing up! No garbage! No mess! Just a little strip of Wonka's magic chewing gum—and that's all you'll ever need at breakfast, lunch, and supper! This piece of gum I've just made happens to be tomato soup, roast beef, and blueberry pie, but you can have almost anything you want!"

"What do you mean, it's tomato soup, roast beef, and blueberry pie?" said Violet Beauregarde.

"If you were to start chewing it," said Mr. Wonka, "then that is exactly what you would get on the menu. It's absolutely amazing! You can actually feel the food going down your throat and into your tummy! And you can taste it perfectly! And it fills you up! It satisfies you! It's terrific!"

"It's utterly impossible," said Veruca Salt.

"Just so long as it's gum," shouted Violet Beauregarde, "just so long as it's a piece of gum and I can chew it, then that's for me!" And quickly she took her own world-record piece of chewing gum out of her mouth and stuck it behind her left ear. "Come on, Mr. Wonka," she said, "hand over this magic gum of yours and we'll see if the thing works."

"Now, Violet," said Mrs. Beauregarde, her mother; "don't let's do anything silly, Violet."

"I want the gum!" Violet said obstinately. "What's so silly?"

"I would rather you didn't take it, Mr. Wonka told her gently. "You see, I haven't got it quite right yet. There are still one or two things . . ."

"Oh, to heck with that!" said Violet, and suddenly, before Mr. Wonka could stop her, she shot out a fat hand and grabbed the stick of gum out of the little drawer and popped it in her mouth. At once, her huge well-trained jaws started chewing away on it like a pair of tongs.

"Don't!" said Mr. Wonka.

"Fabulous!" shouted Violet. "It's tomato soup! It's hot and creamy and delicious! I can feel it running down my throat!"

"Stop!" said Mr. Wonka. "The gum isn't ready yet! It's not right!"

"Of course it's right!" said Violet. "It's working beautifully! Oh my, what lovely soup this is!"

"Spit it out!" said Mr. Wonka.

"It's changing!" shouted Violet, chewing and grinning both at the same time. "The second course is coming up! It's roast beef! It's tender and juicy! Oh boy, what a flavor! The baked potato is marvelous, too! It's got a crispy skin and it's all filled with butter inside!"

"But how in-teresting, violet," said Mrs. Beauregarde. "You are a clever girl."

"Keep chewing, kiddo!" said Mrs. Beauregarde. "Keep right on chewing, baby! This is a great day for the Beauregardes! Our little girl is the first person in the world to have a chewing-gum meal!"

Everybody was watching Violet Beauregarde as she stood there chewing this extraordinary gum. Little Charlie Bucket was staring at her absolutely spellbound, watching her huge rubbery lips as they pressed and unpressed with the chewing, and Grandpa Joe stood beside him, gaping at the girl. Mr. Wonka was wringing his hands and saying, "No, no, no, no, no! It isn't ready for eating! It isn't right! You mustn't do it!"

"Blueberry pie and cream!" shouted Violet. "Here it comes! Oh my, it's perfect! It's beautiful! It's . . . it's exactly as though I'm swallowing it! It's as though I'm chewing and swallowing great big spoonfuls of the most marvelous blueberry pie in the world!"

"Good heavens, girl," shrieked Mrs. Beauregarde suddenly, staring at Violet, "what's happening to your nose!"

"Oh, be quiet, mother, and let me finish!" said Violet.

"It's turning blue!" screamed Mrs. Beauregarde. "Your nose is turning blue as a blueberry!"

"Your mother is right!" shouted Mr. Beauregarde. "Your whole nose has gone purple!"

"What do you mean?" said Violet, still chewing away.

"Your cheeks!" screamed Mrs. Beauregarde. "They're turning blue as well! So is your chin! Your whole face is turning blue!"

"Spit that gum out at once!" ordered Mr. Beauregarde.

"Mercy! Save us!" yelled Mrs. Beauregarde. "The girl's going blue and purple all over!

Even her hair is changing color! Violet, you're turning violet, Violet! What is happening to you!"

"I told you I hadn't got it quite right," sighed Mr. Wonka, shaking his head sadly.

"I'll say you haven't!" cried Mrs. Beauregarde. "Just look at the girl now!"

Everybody was staring at Violet. And what a terrible peculiar sight she was! Her face and hands and legs and neck, in fact the skin all over her body, as well as her great big mop of curly hair, had turned a brilliant, purplish-blue, the color of blueberry juice!

"It always goes wrong when we come to the dessert," sighed Mr. Wonka. "It's the blueberry pie that does it. But I'll get it right one day, you wait and see."

"Violet," screamed Mrs. Beauregarde again, "you're swelling up!"

"I feel sick," Violet said.

"You're swelling up!" screamed Mrs. Beauregarde again.

"I feel most peculiar!" gasped Violet.

"I'm not surprised!" said Mr. Beauregarde.

"Great heavens, girl!" screeched Mrs. Beauregarde. "You're blowing up like a balloon!"

"Like a blueberry," said Mr. Wonka.

"Call me a doctor!" shouted Mr. Beauregarde.

"Prick her with a pin!" said one of the fathers.

"Save her!" cried Mrs. Beauregarde, wringing her hands.

But there was no saving her now. Her body was swelling up and changing shape at such a rate that within a minute it had turned into nothing less than an enormous round blue

ball—a gigantic blueberry, in fact—and all that remained of Violet Beauregarde herself was a tiny pair of legs and a tiny pair of arms sticking out of the great round fruit and a little head on top.

"It always happens like that," sighed Mr. Wonka. "I've tried it twenty times in the Testing Room on twenty Oompa-Loompas, and every one of them finished up as a blueberry. It's most annoying. I just can't understand it."

"But I don't want a blueberry for a daughter!" yelled Mrs. Beauregarde. "Put her back to what she was this instant!"

Mr. Wonka clicked his fingers, and ten Oompa-Loompas appeared immediately at his side.

"Roll Miss Beauregarde into the boat," he said to them, "and take her along to the Juicing Room at once."

"The Juicing Room?" cried Mrs. Beauregarde. "What are they going to do to her there?"

"Squeeze her," said Mr. Wonka. "We've got to squeeze the juice out of her immediately. After that, we'll just have to see how she comes out. But don't worry, my dear Mrs. Beauregarde. We'll get her repaired if it's the last thing we do. I am sorry about it all, I really am . . ."

Already the ten Oompa-Loompas were rolling the enormous blueberry across the floor of the Inventing Room toward the door that led to the chocolate river where the boat was waiting. Mr. and Mrs. Beauregarde hurried after them. The rest of the party, including little Charlie Bucket and Grandpa Joe, stood absolutely still and watched them go.

"Listen!" whispered Charlie. "Listen, Grandpa! The Oompa-Loompas in the boat outside are starting to sing!"

The voices, one hundred of them singing together, came loud and clear into the room:

"Dear friends we surely all agree
There's almost nothing worse to see
Than some repulsive little bum
Who's always chewing chewing gum.
(It's very near as bad as those
Who sit around and pick the nose)
So please believe us when we say
That chewing gum will never pay;
This sticky habit's bound to send
The chewer to a sticky end.
Did any of you ever know
A person called Miss Bigelow?
This dreadful woman saw no wrong
In chewing, chewing all day long.
She chewed while bathing in the tub,

She chewed while dancing at her club,
She chewed in church and on the bus;
It really was quite ludicrous!
And when she couldn't find her gum
She'd chew up the linoleum,
Or anything that happened near—
A pair of boots, the postman's ear,
Or other people's underclothes,
And once she chewed her boyfriend's nose.
She went on chewing till, at last,
Her chewing muscles grew so vast
That from her face her giant chin
Stuck out just like a violin.
For years and years she chewed away,
Consuming fifty packs a day,
Until one summer's eve, alas,
A horrid business came to pass.
Miss Bigelow went late to bed,
For half an hour she lay and read,
Chewing and chewing all the while
Like some great clockwork crocodile.
At last, she put her gum away
Upon a special little tray,
And settled back and went to sleep—
(She managed this by counting sheep)
But now, how strange! Although she slept,
Those massive jaws of hers still kept
On chewing, chewing through the night,
Even with nothing there to bite.
They were, you see, in such a groove
They positively had to move.
And very grim it was to hear
In pitchy darkness, loud and clear,
This sleeping woman's great big trap
Opening and shutting, snap-snap-snap!
Faster and faster, chop-chop-chop,
The noise went on, it wouldn't stop.
Until at last her jaws decide
To pause and open extra wide,

And with the most tremendous chew
They bit the lady's tongue in two.
Thereafter, just from chewing gum,
Miss Bigelow was always dumb,
And spent her life shut up in some
Disgusting sanatorium.
And that is why we'll try so hard
To save Miss Violet Beauregarde
From suffering an equal fate.
She's still quite young, It's not too late,
Provided she survives the cure.
We hope she does. We can't be sure."

Dahl, Roald. *Charlie and the Chocolate Factory.* New York: Penguin, Puffin Books, 1973.
   Other Editions:
   ——. *Charlie and the Chocolate Factory.* New York: Buccaneer Books, 1992.
   ——. *Charlie and the Chocolate Factory.* New York: Penguin, Puffin Books, 1988.

THE RETURN OF
THE TWELVES

Pauline Clarke

Max has found twelve old wooden soldiers in the attic of an English farmhouse into which his family has just moved. Here is what happens when his parents leave him alone with his new treasures.

Chapter 2   THE PATRIARCH

ax waited until he heard the motor-car doors slam, and the engine purr and sing. Then he did, in fact, race down to his own room, and lean out of the window, in time to see the number-plate of the Land Rover disappear out of the yard. For a minute he felt sorry and lonely.

Then he went quietly up the attic stairs again, and looked through the keyhole.

The wooden soldiers stood exactly as he had seen them when Jane interrupted. They had not moved a tenth of an inch. They were as dead as ninepins. They had frozen again. Max sighed, enraged. This would be a sell, if he had prevented himself going with the others for nothing.

All the same, he did not give up hope. He had seen them move twice now, and what you saw, you believed. (Max also believed many things he did not see, like everyone else.) The gob-stopper was becoming more manageable now, and as he knelt there, Max turned it over and over in his mouth. Suddenly, he crunched it all up with determination and impatience. He decided to go in.

He wandered around the attic, pretending to be busy looking at things, but all the while keeping half a cautious eye upon them. It felt to him as if they were keeping cautious eyes on him. It was like two cats, casually looking away from each other, but really each wondering if the other were going to pounce.

It seemed much more than a week that they had been here. It had seemed a lovely house to come to, and as if it were theirs at once and always had been. He remembered the time they first came up here, to the attic, carrying the stool, the boat, and the drum.

Mrs. Morley had said: "Now, we won't banish Great-grandpa's Ashanti things forever, but as I don't know quite where they're going, will you take them carefully up to the attic, please?"

Philip, Jane, and Max were only too eager to explore the attic. Philip had seized the heavy, carved wooden stool with its curved seat, Jane had clasped the curious-shaped, skin-covered, oblong drum to her chest, and Max had taken the carved model canoe. Their great-grandfather had been a missionary on the Gold Coast of West Africa. He had gone up the Niger further than any other missionary before him, no doubt in just such a boat, he had talked to kings who thought it was quite all right to kill people for sacrifices, he had seen the pits where they threw them and huts that were full of skulls.

Max now came to the stool, sat down upon its curve which fitted the sitter so comfortably, and looked squarely at the soldiers. On just such a stool, their mother had often told them, were crowned the kings of Ashanti. She had been told by Grandma, who was the daughter of the missionary.

Max had stayed behind that first time, to explore thoroughly. He had stamped around the attic, just as he had seen the surveyor do, jumping on boards and tapping walls. He had been rewarded by finding the loose board near the window. Max never left things half explored. He got his knife, levered up the board, and found the dirty, torn roll of rag in which were the old soldiers. Twelve of them.

"After all," said Max aloud, "I did rescue you from a living death."

He thought this was a fine expression, he had read it in some book lately. Although they were so old and knocked about, it was exciting and mysterious to find them hidden, and to wonder who had hidden them. Added to this, when he brought them to show the family, his mother had said:

"Max! How interesting. Do take care of them, because I should think they're really old, they ought to be in a museum."

"How old, Mummy? How old, Daddy?" Max said, clutching them in his two hands.

"Careful, they look a bit frail," his father had said. And he took one, and scrutinized it. "Not much face left, or paint. He's got a sort of high, black cap on. I should think they're Napoleonic, or rather, Wellington, being English. From what you can see of their clothes."

"Well, how old, Daddy?" Max persisted.

"Well over a hundred years, if I'm right, Max. Take care of them, do, I don't know that you ought to be allowed to play with them."

"But I found them," Max exploded. And of course, because they were admired and valued, Max had quickly become devoted to them. Jane said they were shabby, and Philip said they were worm-eaten (which was not true, it was only because he had not found them himself). But Max adored them. One or two still had a round, flat stand with two holes in it for the feet to go into. They were not all the same size, some were taller than others, and although their faces were blurred and rubbed, you could still tell that each was different. Mrs. Morley said this was delightful because it proved they were hand-made, each carved with his own face. Max agreed.

But all this was as nothing to the time, two days ago, when he had set them out on the attic floor and, lying on his tummy, had beat with his fingers on the Ashanti drum, so that they could march to it. Before Max's startled eyes, one, a tallish fellow, at once picked out by his sly, birdlike alertness, hopped and twirled into life at the sound of the drum. He threw his tiny arms in the air as if he were glad to feel life again, he skipped along the ranks, punching some in the jaw, tweaking the noses of others, and tripping the feet of the most stolid. Then he found his place in line again and the whole lot stood to surprised attention and took at least ten tiny steps forward over the boards.

When Max half started to his feet in excitement, they stopped. Frozen, like a toad which freezes when you meet him crossing the lawn. Even the lively fellow froze.

Then, today, he had heard their tiny noises and seen them at it. Before Jane had come and spoiled everything.

So now he knew he must be gentle and careful and not do sudden things. Max was a persistent boy, and patient for his age (which is not a patient age), so he just sat there on the Ashanti stool, wondering if an Ashanti king had been crowned on it, and with his hands on his thin knees. He could wait as long as they could. They would trust him sooner or later. Surely they knew he loved them? . . . If he were an Ashanti king, the first person he would sacrifice would be Anthony Gore. He knew that it was wrong to do human sacrifices, but then if he were an Ashanti king in those old days, he would not know this, so it would be all right. He supposed. When they knew better, they stopped doing it. Max wondered if they missed it very much.

Max sighed and tried smiling at the soldiers. Then he tapped with two fingers on the drum which stood beside him, the rhythm of a song. He started to sing it, almost in a whisper, so as not to frighten them:

> *Oh, the brave old Duke of York,*
> *He had ten thousand men;*
> *He marched them up to the top of the hill*
> *And he marched them down again.*

It was the only marching song he could think of, about old soldiers.

> *And when they were up, they were up,*
> *And when they were down, they were down,*
> *And when they were only halfway up,*
> *They were neither up nor down . . .*

. . . piped Max, very quietly, soft as a pin. To his joy, the soldiers broke ranks and clustered all together in a little band. Again he heard that faint crackling, whisking sound which was their talk. He was not surprised this time, because he had been expecting it. He kept still.

One of them turned away from the rest and came boldly over the attic floor to Max. Behind him, prancing from side to side as if to urge him on, came the lively soldier Max had first seen move. He gave the other a good push at the last, but he seemed to be a stately and dignified character and did not lose his balance. Then they all bowed low from the waist, and the one in front lifted his arms and waggled his head.

"Now, does he want me to pick him up?" Max wondered. Dare he? Would it frighten them?

He gently put out his hand, leaned down, and grasped the dignified little soldier by the waist. No bigger than that lizard he picked up the other day on the moor. The fellow waved his arms, but did not struggle.

Max brought him up to his face. He perhaps wanted to say something. He held him near to his ear. There was a crackle. Max closed his eyes and listened very hard, holding his breath. The crackle came again, in more of a pattern. Max brought him a bit nearer. The third time, he could hear and understand.

"Are you one of the Genii?" said the creature.

Now Max had read the Arabian Nights, he know all about the Genii, those spirits who preside over a person's destiny all his life. If these soldiers wanted him to be a Genii to them, he did not mind. So he said:

"Yes," very solemnly and quietly. He was surprised to hear a sudden faint sprinkle of sound like rice falling on the floor. It was the soldiers, clapping.

"I am Butter Crashey," said the small fellow he was holding. Max did not know what to say to this. Should he say how do you do? Or, I like you very much? Or, how old are you? Or, where did you come from? None seemed quite right, and the last two seemed rude, so he said:

"I like your name. How did you get it?"

"I fell, long ago, into the butter," said his friend.

"I thought you must have," said Max.

"I am the patriarch of the Twelves," he went on, "and my age is one hundred and forty." Max had a vague idea that if a person were very old, it was proper to congratulate him. So he said:

"Good for you." Then he thought this sounded not old-fashioned enough, so he added: "Allow me to congratulate you upon being full of years and wisdom."

This was the way Philip sometimes spoke. Max felt pleased with it, and so, it was clear, did Butter Crashey. He bent his head to receive the compliment. Now that he was alive, his face had become sharp and detailed. Max looked at all the others, and saw that the same was true of them. The jaunty soldier seemed to have particularly piercing eyes, and he pulled a face as Max looked. Max was delighted.

"Under your protection," announced Butter Crashey next, "we propose to make a journey of discovery, as we once set forth under the four Genii to carve out a kingdom amongst the Ashanti."

"That is a very good idea," said Max, who was longing to see the soldiers moving about downstairs. He put the patriarch gently down with the rest, and went to the attic door. He opened it and stood to one side. The twelve soldiers formed into a column, marched toward the door, and out onto the landing.

Clarke, Pauline. *The Return of the Twelves*. New York: Dell, 1986.

A CHRISTMAS CAROL

Charles Dickens

Scrooge's favorite expression is "Bah humbug!" He works and counts his money and wants to be left alone. And while the Christmas season brings out the best in most people, Scrooge wants no part of it.

Chapter One MARLEY'S GHOST

h! but he was a tight-fisted hand at the grindstone, Scrooge! a squeezing, wrenching, grasping, scraping, clutching, covetous old sinner! hard and sharp as flint, from which no steel had ever struck out generous fire, secret, and self-contained, and solitary as an oyster. The cold within him froze his old features, nipped his pointed nose, shriveled his cheek, stiffened his gait, made his eyes red, his thin lips blue, and spoke out shrewdly in his grating voice. A frosty rime was on his head, and on his eyebrows, and his wiry chin. He carried his own low temperature always about with him; he iced his office in the dog-days; and didn't thaw it one degree at Christmas.

External heat and cold had little influence on Scrooge. No warmth could warm, no wintry weather chill him. No wind that blew was bitterer than he, no falling snow was more intent upon its purpose, no pelting rain less open to entreaty. Foul weather didn't know where to have him. The heaviest rain, and snow, and hail, and sleet, could boast of the advantage over him in only one respect. They often "came down" handsomely, and Scrooge never did.

Nobody ever stopped him in the street to say, with gladsome looks, "My dear Scrooge, how are you? When will you come to see me?" No beggars implored him to bestow a trifle, no children asked him what it was o'clock, no man or woman ever once in all his life inquired the way to such and such a place, of Scrooge. Even the blind men's dogs appeared to know him; and, when they saw him coming on, would tug their owners into doorways and up courts; and then would wag their tails as though they said, "No eye at all is better than an evil eye, dark master!"

But what did Scrooge care? It was the very thing he liked. To edge his way along the crowded paths of life, warning all human sympathy to keep its distance, was what the knowing ones call "nuts" to Scrooge.

Once upon a time—of all the good days in the year, on Christmas Eve—old Scrooge sat busy in his counting-house. It was cold, bleak, biting weather, foggy withal, and he could hear the people in the court outside go wheezing up and down, beating their hands upon their breasts, and stamping their feet upon the pavement stones to warm them. The city clocks had only just gone three, but it was quite dark already—it had not been light all day—and candles were flaring in the windows of the neighboring offices, like ruddy smears upon the palpable brown air. The fog came pouring in at every chink and keyhole, and was so dense without, that, although the court was of the narrowest, the houses opposite were mere phantoms. To see the dingy cloud come drooping down, obscuring everything, one might have thought that Nature lived hard by, and was brewing on a large scale.

The door of Scrooge's counting-house was open, that he might keep his eye upon his clerk, who, in a dismal little cell beyond, a sort of tank, was copying letters. Scrooge had a very small fire, but the clerk's fire was so very much smaller that it looked like one coal. But he couldn't replenish it, for Scrooge kept the coal-box in his own room; and so surely as the clerk came in with the shovel, the master predicted that it would be necessary for them to part. Wherefore the clerk put on his white comforter, and tried to warm himself at the candle; in which effort, not being a man of a strong imagination, he failed.

"A merry Christmas, uncle! God save you!" cried a cheerful voice. It was the voice of Scrooge's nephew, who came upon him so quickly that this was the first intimation he had of his approach.

"Bah!" said Scrooge. "Humbug!"

He had so heated himself with rapid walking in the fog and frost, this nephew of Scrooge's, that he was all in a glow; his face was ruddy and handsome; his eyes sparkled, and his breath smoked again.

"Christmas a humbug, uncle!" said Scrooge's nephew. "You don't mean that, I am sure?"

"I do," said Scrooge. "Merry Christmas! What right have you to be merry? What reason have you to be merry? You're poor enough."

"Come, then," returned the nephew gaily. "What right have you to be dismal? What reason have you to be morose? You're rich enough."

Scrooge, having no better answer ready on the spur of the moment, said, "Bah!" again; and followed it up with "Humbug!"

"Don't be cross, uncle!" said the nephew.

"What else can I be," returned the uncle, "when I live in such a world of fools as this? Merry Christmas! Out upon merry Christmas! What's Christmas-time to you but a time for paying bills without money; a time for finding yourself a year older, and not an hour richer; a time for balancing your books, and having every item in 'em through a round dozen of months presented dead against you? If I could work my will," said Scrooge indignantly, "every idiot who goes about with 'Merry Christmas' on his lips should be boiled with his own pudding, and buried with a stake of holly through his heart. He should!"

"Uncle!" pleaded the nephew.

"Nephew!" returned the uncle sternly, "keep Christmas in your own way, and let me keep it in mine."

"Keep it!" repeated Scrooge's nephew. "But you don't keep it."

"Let me leave it alone, then," said Scrooge. "Much good may it do you! Much good it has ever done you!"

"There are many things from which I might have derived good by which I have not profited, I dare say," returned the nephew, "Christmas among the rest. But I am sure I have always thought of Christmas-time, when it has come round—apart from the veneration due to its sacred name and origin, if anything belonging to it can be apart from that—as a good time; a kind, forgiving, charitable, pleasant time; the only time I know of, in the long calendar of the year, when men and women seem by one consent to open their shut-up hearts freely, and to think of people below them as if they really were fellow-passengers to the grave, and not another race of creatures bound on other journeys. And therefore, uncle, although it has never put a scrap of gold or silver in my pocket, I believe that it has done me good and will do me good; and I say, God bless it!"

The clerk in the tank involuntarily applauded. Becoming immediately sensible of the impropriety, he poked the fire, and extinguished the last frail spark forever.

"Let me hear another sound from you," said Scrooge, "and you'll keep your Christmas losing your situation! You're quite a powerful speaker, sir," he added, turning to his nephew. "I wonder you don't go into Parliament."

"Don't be angry, uncle. Come! Dine with us tomorrow."

Scrooge said that he would see him—yes, indeed, he did. He went the whole length of the expression, and said that he would see him in that extremity first.

"But why?" cried Scrooge's nephew. "Why?"

"Why did you get married?" said Scrooge.

"Because I fell in love."

"Because you fell in love!" growled Scrooge, as if that were the only one thing in the world more ridiculous than a merry Christmas. "Good afternoon!"

"Nay, uncle, but you never came to see me before that happened. Why give it as a reason for not coming now?"

"Good afternoon," said Scrooge.

"I want nothing from you; I ask nothing of you; why cannot we be friends?"

"Good afternoon!" said Scrooge.

"I am sorry, with all my heart, to find you so resolute. We have never had any quarrel, to which I have been a party. But I have made the trial in homage to Christmas, and I'll keep my Christmas humor to the last. So a merry Christmas, uncle!"

"Good afternoon," said Scrooge.

"And a happy New Year!"

"Good afternoon!" said Scrooge.

His nephew left the room without an angry word, notwithstanding. He stopped at the outer door to bestow the greetings of the season on the clerk, who, cold as he was, was warmer than Scrooge, for he returned them cordially.

"There's another fellow," muttered Scrooge, who overheard him; "my clerk, with 15 shillings a week, and a wife and family, talking about a merry Christmas. I'll retire to Bedlam!

This lunatic, in letting Scrooge's nephew out, had let two other people in. They were portly gentlemen, pleasant to behold, and now stood with their hats off, in Scrooge's office. They had books and papers in their hands, and bowed to him.

"Scrooge and Marley's, I believe," said one of the gentlemen, referring to his list. "Have I the pleasure of addressing Mr. Scrooge, or Mr. Marley?"

"Mr. Marley has been dead these seven years," Scrooge replied. "He died seven years ago, this very night."

We have no doubt his liberality is well represented by his surviving partner," said the gentleman, presenting his credentials.

It certainly was; for they had been two kindred spirits. At the ominous word "liberality," Scrooge frowned, and shook his head, and handed the credentials back.

"At this festive season of the year, Mr. Scrooge," said the gentleman, taking up a pen, "it is more than usually desirable that we should make some slight provision for the poor and destitute, who suffer greatly at the present time. Many thousands are in want of common necessaries; hundreds of thousands are in want of common comforts, sir."

"Are there no prisons?" asked Scrooge.

"Plenty of prisons," said the gentleman, laying down the pen again.

"And the Union workhouses?" demanded Scrooge. "Are they still in operation?"

"They are. Still," returned the gentleman, "I wish I could say they were not."

"The treadmill and the Poor Law are in full vigor, then?" said Scrooge.

"Both very busy, sir."

"Oh! I was afraid, from what you said at first that something had occurred to stop them in their useful course," said Scrooge. "I'm very glad to hear it."

"Under the impression that they scarcely furnish Christian cheer of mind or body to the multitude," returned the gentleman, "a few of us are endeavoring to raise a fund to buy the poor some meat and drink, and means of warmth. We choose this time, because it is a time, of all others, when Want is keenly felt, and Abundance rejoices. What shall I put you down for?"

"Nothing!" Scrooge replied.

"You wish to be anonymous?"

"I wish to be left alone," said Scrooge. "Since you ask me what I wish, gentlemen, that is my answer. I don't make merry myself at Christmas, and I can't afford to make idle people merry. I help to support the establishments I have mentioned—they cost enough; and those who are badly off must go there."

"Many can't go there; and many would rather die."

"If they would rather die," said Scrooge, "they had better do it, and decrease the surplus population. Besides—excuse me—I don't know that."

"But you might know it," observed the gentleman.

"It's not my business," Scrooge returned. "It's enough for a man to understand his own business, and not to interfere with other people's. Mine occupies me constantly. Good afternoon, gentlemen!"

Chapter Three THE SECOND OF THE THREE SPIRITS

Scrooge's "Bah-humbug" attitude towards Christmas makes him the perfect target for the three Spirits of Christmas: Past, Present, and Future. Here the Ghost of Christmas Present comes to teach Scrooge a lesson.

aking in the middle of a prodigiously tough snore, and sitting up in bed to get his thoughts together, Scrooge had no occasion to be told that the bell was again upon the stroke of One. He felt that he was restored to consciousness in the right nick of time, for the especial purpose of holding a conference with the second messenger despatched to him through Jacob Marley's intervention. But, finding that he turned uncomfortably cold when he began to wonder which of his curtains this new specter would draw back, he put them every one aside with his own hands, and, lying down again, established a sharp lookout all around the bed. For he wished to challenge the Spirit on the moment of its appearance, and did not wish to be taken by surprise, and made nervous.

Gentlemen of the free-and-easy sort, who plume themselves on being acquainted with a move or two, and being usually equal to the time of day, express the wide range of their capacity for adventure by observing that they are good for anything from pitch-and-toss to manslaughter; between which opposite extremes, no doubt, there lies a tolerably wide and comprehensive range of subjects. Without venturing for Scrooge quite as hardily as this, I don't mind calling on you to believe that he was ready for a broad field of strange appearances, and that nothing between a baby and a rhinoceros would have astonished him very much.

Now, being prepared for almost anything, he was not by any means prepared for nothing; and, consequently, when the bell struck One, and no shape appeared, he was taken with a violent fit of trembling. Five minutes, ten minutes, a quarter of an hour went by, yet nothing came. All this time he lay upon his bed, the very core and center of a blaze of ruddy light, which streamed upon it when the clock proclaimed the hour; and which, being only light, was more alarming than a dozen ghosts, as he was powerless to make out what it meant, and was sometimes apprehensive that he might be at that very moment an interesting case of spontaneous combustion, without having the consolation of knowing it. At last, however, he began to think—as you or I would have thought at first; for it is always the person not in the predicament who knows what ought to have been done in it, and I would unquestionably have done it too—at last, I say, he began to think that the source and secret of this ghostly light might be in the adjoining room, from whence, on further tracing it, it seemed to shine. This idea taking full possession of his mind, he got up softly, and shuffled in his slippers to the door.

The moment Scrooge's hand was on the lock, a strange voice called him by name, and bade him enter. He obeyed.

It was his own room. There was no doubt about that. But it had undergone a surprising transformation. The walls and ceiling were so hung with living green that it looked a perfect grove; from every part of which bright, gleaming berries glistened. The crisp leaves of holly, mistletoe, and ivy reflected back the light, as if so many little mirrors had been scattered there, and such a mighty blaze went roaring up the chimney, as that dull petrification of a hearth had never known in Scrooge's time. Heaped up on the floor, to form a kind of throne, were turkeys, geese, game, poultry, brawn, great joints of meat, sucking-pigs, long wreaths of sausages, mince-pies, plum-puddings, barrels of oysters, red-hot chestnuts, cherry-cheeked apples, juicy oranges, luscious pears, immense twelfth-cakes, and seething bowls of punch, that made the chamber dim with their delicious steam. In easy state upon this couch, there sat a jolly Giant, glorious to see who bore a glowing torch, in shape not unlike Plenty's horn, and held it up, high up, to shed its light on Scrooge, as he came peeping round the door.

"Come in!" exclaimed the Ghost—"come in! and know me better, man!"

Scrooge entered timidly, and hung his head before this Spirit. He was not the dogged Scrooge he had been and though the Spirit's eyes were clear and kind, he did not like to meet them.

"I am the Ghost of Christmas Present," said the Spirit. "Look upon me!"

Scrooge reverently did so. It was clothed in one simple, deep-green robe, or mantle, bordered with white fur. This garment hung so loosely on the figure that its capacious breast was bare, as if disdaining to be warded or concealed by any artifice. Its feet, observable beneath the ample folds of the garment, were also bare, and on its head it wore no other covering than a holly wreath, set here and there with shining icicles. Its dark-brown curls were long and free, free as its genial face, its sparkling eye, its open hand, its cheery voice, its unconstrained demeanor, and its joyful air. Girded round its middle was an antique scabbard, but no sword was in it, and the ancient sheath was eaten up with rust.

"You have never seen the like of me before!" exclaimed the Spirit.

"Never," Scrooge made answer to it.

"Have never walked forth with the younger members of my family, meaning (for I am very young) my elder brothers born in these later years?" pursued the Phantom.

"I don't think I have," said Scrooge. "I am afraid I have not. Have you had many brothers, Spirit?"

"More than eighteen hundred," said the Ghost.

"A tremendous family to provide for," muttered Scrooge.

The Ghost of Christmas Present rose.

"Spirit," said Scrooge submissively, "conduct me where you will. I went forth last night on compulsion, and I learned a lesson which is working now. Tonight, if you have aught to teach me, let me profit by it."

"Touch my robe!"

Scrooge did as he was told, and held it fast.

Holly, mistletoe, red berries, ivy, turkeys, geese, game, poultry, brawn, meat, pigs, sausages, oysters, pies, puddings, fruit, and punch, all vanished instantly. So did the room, the fire, the ruddy glow, the hour of the night, and they stood in the city streets on Christmas morning, where (for the weather was severe) the people made a rough, but brisk and not unpleasant kind of music, in scraping the snow from the pavement in front of their dwelling, and from the tops of their houses, whence it was mad delight to the boys to see it come plumping down to the road below, and splitting into artificial little snow-storms.

The house-fronts looked black enough, and the windows blacker, contrasting with the smooth white sheet of snow upon the roofs, and with the dirtier snow upon the ground which last deposit had been plowed up in deep furrows by the heavy wheels of carts and wagons, furrows that crossed and recrossed each other hundreds of times where the great streets branched off, and made intricate channels, hard to trace, in the thick yellow mud and icy water. The sky was gloomy, and the shortest streets were choked up with a dingy mist, half thawed. half frozen, whose heavier particles descended in a shower of sooty atoms, as if all the chimneys in Great Britain had, by one consent, caught fire, and were blazing away to their dear hearts' content.

For the people who were shoveling away on the housetops were jovial and full of glee, calling out to one another and laughing heartily. The poulterers' shops were still half open, and the fruiterers' were radiant in their glory. There were great, round, pot-bellied baskets of chestnuts, shaped like the waistcoats of jolly old gentlemen, lolling at the doors, and tumbling out into the street. There were ruddy, brown-faced, broad-girthed Spanish onions, shining in the fatness of their growth like Spanish friars. There were pears and apples, clustered high in blooming pyramids; there were bunches of grapes, made to dangle from conspicuous hooks, that people's mouths might water gratis as they passed; and squab and swarthy, setting off the yellow of the oranges and lemons, and, in the great compactness of their juicy persons, urgently entreating and beseeching to be carried home in paper bags and eaten after dinner.

But soon the steeples called good people all to church and chapel, and away they came, flocking through the streets in their best clothes, and with their gayest faces. And at the same time people emerged carrying their dinners to the bakers' shops. The sight of these poor revelers appeared to interest the Spirit very much, for he stood, with Scrooge behind him, in a bakers' doorway, and, taking off the covers as their bearers passed, sprinkled incense on their dinners from his torch. And it was a very uncommon kind of torch, for once or twice when there were angry words between some dinner-carriers who had jostled each other, he shed a few drops of water on them from it, and their good humor was restored directly. For they said, it was a shame to quarrel upon Christmas Day. And so it was! God love it, so it was!

In time the bells ceased, and the bakers were shut up, and yet there was a genial shadowing forth of all these dinners, and the progress of their cooking, in the thawed blotch of wet above each baker's oven, where the pavement smoked as if its stones were cooking too.

"Is there a peculiar flavor in what you sprinkle from your torch?" asked Scrooge.

"There is. My own."

"Would it apply to any kind of dinner on this day?" asked Scrooge.

"To any kindly given. To a poor one most."

"Why to a poor one most?" asked Scrooge.

"Because he needs it most."

"Spirit," said Scrooge, after a moment's thought, "I wonder you, of all beings in the many worlds about us, should desire to cramp these people's opportunities of innocent enjoyment."

"I!" cried the Spirit.

"You seek to close these places on the Seventh Day," said Scrooge. "And it comes to the same thing."

"I seek!" exclaimed the Spirit.

"Forgive me if I am wrong. It has been done in your name, or at least in that of your family," said Scrooge.

"There are some upon this earth of yours," returned the Spirit, "who claim to know us, and who do their deeds of passion, pride, ill will, hatred, envy, bigotry, and selfishness in our name, who are as strange to us, and all out kith and kin, as if they never lived. Remember that, and charge their doings on themselves, not us."

Scrooge promised that he would and they went on, invisible, as they had been before, into the suburbs of the town. It was a remarkable quality of the Ghost (which Scrooge had observed at the baker's), that notwithstanding his gigantic size, he could accomodate himself to any place with ease, and that he stood beneath a low roof quite as gracefully, and like a supernatural creature, as it was possible he could have done in any lofty hall.

And perhaps it was the pleasure the good Spirit had in showing off this power of his, or else it was his own kind, generous, hearty nature, and his sympathy with all poor men, that led him straight to Scrooge's clerk's; for there he went, and took Scrooge with him, holding to his robe and on the threshold of the door the Spirit smiled, and stopped to bless Bob Cratchit's dwelling with the sprinklings of his torch.

Much they saw, and far they went, and many homes they visited, but always with a happy end. The Spirit stood beside sick-beds, and they were cheerful; on foreign lands, and they were lose at home; by struggling men, and they were patient in their greater hope; by poverty, and it was rich. In almshouse, hospital, and jail, in misery's every refuge, where vain man in his little brief authority had not made fast the door, and barred the Spirit out, he left his blessing, and taught Scrooge his precepts.

It was a long night, if it were only a night, but Scrooge had his doubts of this, because Christmas holidays appeared to be condensed into the space of time they passed together. It was strange, too, that while Scrooge remained unaltered in his outward form, the Ghost grew older, clearly older. Scrooge had observed this change but never spoke of it, until they left a children's Twelfth Night party, when, looking at the Spirit as they stood together in an open place, he noticed that its hair was gray.

"Are spirits' lives so short?" asked Scrooge.

"My life upon this globe is very brief," replied the Ghost. "It ends tonight."

"Tonight!" cried Scrooge.

"Tonight at midnight. Hark. The time is drawing near."

The chimes were ringing the three quarters past eleven at that moment.

"Forgive me if I am not justified in what I ask," said Scrooge, looking intently at the Spirit's robe, "but I see something strange, and not belonging to yourself, protruding from your skirts."

From the foldings of its robe, it brought two children, wretched, abject, frightful, hideous, miserable. they knelt down at his feet, and clung upon the outside of its garment. They were a boy and a girl. Yellow, meager, ragged, scowling, and wolfish.

Scrooge started back appalled. Having shown to him in this way, he tried to say they were fine children, but the words choked themselves, rather than be parties to a lie of such enormous magnitude.

"Spirit! are they yours?" Scrooge could say no more.

"They are Man's," said the Spirit, looking down upon them. "And they cling to me, appealing from their fathers. This boy is ignorance. This girl is Want. Beware of them both, and all of their degree, but most of all beware this boy, for on his brow I see that written which is Doom, unless the writing be erased. Deny it!" cried the Spirit, stretching out his hand toward the city. "Slander those who tell it ye! Admit it for your factious purposes, and make it worse! And bide the end!"

"Have they no refuge or resource?" cried Scrooge.

"Are there no prisons?" said the Spirit, turning on him for the last time with his own words. "Are there no workhouses?"

The bell struck twelve.

Scrooge looked about him for the Ghost, and saw it not. As the last stroke ceased to vibrate, he remembered the prediction of old Jacob Marley, and lifting up his eyes, beheld a solemn Phantom, draped and hooded, coming, like a mist along the ground, toward him.

Dickens, Charles. *A Christmas Carol.* New York: Penguin, Puffin Books, 1984.
    Other Editions:
    ——. *A Christmas Carol.* New York: Random House, 1994.
    Dickens, Charles., et al. *Christmas Carol & Other Victorian Fairytales.* New York: Bantam, 1985.

THE WITCH FAMILY

ELEANOR ESTES

Amy and Clarissa love to draw witches so much that they create a whole witch family—Wicked Old Witch, Little Witch Girl, and Weeny Witch. The witch family lives on a desolate glass hill where Amy says the Wicked Old Witch must remain—with the exception of Halloween, of course. Find out what happens on Halloween night when Little Girl Witch disobeys Old Witch and flies on her broomstick in search of Amy and Clarissa.

Chapter 15 THE REAL WITCH AND THE PRETEND WITCH

This is what happened. Little Witch Girl saw Amy, but she did not recognize her in her witch costume. She had been looking for the two girls, Amy and Clarissa, one in a pink dress and the other in a blue dress—the way they were the two other times she had seen them. Who could know that Amy was behind that awful witch mask? Little Witch Girl thought Amy must be another real little witch girl, like herself, out on her saturnalia. So, she brought her broomstick down, landing neatly on the sidewalk beside the make-believe little witch, Amy.

Amy's heart beat more wildly than ever. She, of course, had recognized the little witch girl the moment she had seen her. She ought to. She had drawn her often enough. "Hi!" she said shyly.

The minute the real little witch girl heard Amy's voice, she recognized her too. She said. "Hi!" back. She was happy to have located Amy so quickly and to know that real girls dress up like witches on Halloween. "I didn't recognize you at first," she said apologetically. "I thought you always wore pink."

"That's all right," said Amy reassuringly. "If you had a pink dress on instead of your witch clothes, I might not have recognized you."

For a moment the two witches, real and pretend, surveyed each other silently. Then Amy said, "I wasn't sure that Old Witch would let you come."

"She didn't," said the little witch girl. "I just came."

"And Weeny Witchie?"

"She is with the little mermaid."

"Oh, yes, of course," said Amy.

"Would you like to fly on my broomstick?" asked the little witch girl. "I have learned the abracadabra that will make it go for you. We just learned it in school."

Amy was overcome with joy. Ever since she had seen Little Witch Girl soaring up and down the street, she had longed to try to fly the broomstick. "Oh, yes," she said. "Thank you." Amy had often dreamed that she could fly. And although flying on a broomstick is not as important as plain flying, with only arms and legs to make you go, as in dreams, still it is quite important, she thought.

So, the real little witch girl got off the broomstick, and the pretend little witch got on. Little Witch Girl gave her broomstick a magic pat, the way one pats a pony, and she said, "tcl, tcl." Amy was half scared and half delighted as the broomstick began to bump along the brick sidewalk, under the ginkgo trees. She was sure it left the ground.

This left the real little witch girl standing alone in the light of the lamp, without her broomstick but with her little Tommy cat in her arms. And at this moment the other children of the trick-or-treat expedition came trooping out of the little gray house, their bags more bulging than ever. Of course, they mistook the real little witch girl for Amy.

"Amy!" said Clarissa. "Where were you? Where did you find that cat? Go on in. Take your bag. The lady is waiting for you." And she pushed the little witch girl, whom she thought was Amy, up the steps to the red door of the little gray house, which was still wide open. The lady of the house, a very friendly lady who liked children and who did not keep their kites or balls or anything and who had baked brownies for this occasion, stood in the doorway, beckoning to the little witch girl.

She said she wanted to see this little witch girl close to try and guess who she was. So far, she had not been able to guess who anyone was, which shows how wonderful their costumes must have been, for she knew all the children well and sometimes told them stories.

"Now, let me see," said this lady who did not confiscate balls. "Could this be . . . possibly be . . . Amy?"

The real little Halloween witch shook her head. But she said nothing lest a Halloween croak escape.

"I know you just must be Amy by your hair," said the nice lady, and she gave the little witch girl a red apple. Little Witch Girl forgot to keep silent and she croaked, "Cr-cr-cr," happily. She did not intend to put poison in one half the apple or to do anything wicked with it, even though this was Halloween. She was just going to eat it. It smelled good, being a Winesap. She took a bite, and "cr-cr-cr," she croaked happily at the juicy morsel.

"Why, Amy darling! Or whoever you are! You must have a terrible cold. Don't stay out too late. And tell your mother to rub your throat with Baume bengée when you get home."

Then she ushered the little witch girl out and closed the door, and she never found out that she had entertained a real live little witch girl in her house.

So then, while Amy was off on the broomstick, trying to get it in front of the moon, Little Witch Girl had the fun of going from house to house and getting the candies and apples and cookies, popcorn too, that were meant for Amy, the pretend witch of Garden Lane.

The real little witch girl was afraid of Christopher Knapp, the red devil, and shrank inside her cloak when he came too close to her. She was also frightened of the big pretend black cat, for Polly Knapp, swept away with enthusiasm at being a cat, kept coming at the little witch girl with her big paws thinking, of course, this was Amy.

And Little Witch Girl was absolutely terrified of a group of little imps, ghouls, tigers, and lions who were tricking and treating with their plainclothes ordinary mothers. These mothers were hiding behind trees, trying to look as though they were not there but keeping careful watch over their tiny ones. They thought the tiny ones wanted to think that they were motherless for the Halloween fun. But some of these two-year-olds were scared of themselves and one, a tiger, said "Wah-h-h-h" when he saw the real little witch's face up close. Having had enough of being motherless, he fled, and his mother took him home. "There's another witch!" he screamed catching sight of Amy on the broomstick. His mother put him right to bed.

Amy was having a wonderful time with the broomstick, but she felt it really needed another little pat of magic to make it go higher. She wanted to get it in front of the moon. So, she turned it around and want back to the lamppost where she had left the real little witch taking care of her trick-or-treat bag. She was going to ask Little Witch Girl to rub more magic onto the broomstick.

At this moment the children came trooping out of a house across the street from the little gray one. They were congregating again under the lamplight to decide where to go next, just as Amy came along on the broomstick. What a shame that none of the children, not even Clarissa, saw her flying! But Clarissa did see that there was one more witch here than there had been before.

"Look, Amy!" she exclaimed, tugging at the cloak of the real little witch whom she still thought was Amy despite the unusual sound of her voice. "Who's this witch?" She became all mixed-up when the new little witch girl dismounted from her broomstick and stood right beside the real little witch girl whom Clarissa thought was Amy.

These two witch girls, the real one and the pretend one, stood side by side, and no one could tell one from the other. They both had long blond hair, exactly the same and the color of moonlight.

"Amy," said Clarissa to the wrong witch again. "Who is this new witch? Who do you think this new witch is that came up on a broomstick? Do you think it is Mary Maloney from up on Starr Street? Or maybe Sally Trout? And where did you get that cute cat?"

The two little witch girls, the real one and the pretend one, looked at each other and laughed. At first Amy had not understood why Clarissa called the other little witch Amy when she was Amy herself. She thought anyone would know she was Amy! "She's probably gone into the houses with them," thought Amy, catching on still more. It was not surprising for the other children to get mixed-up! But for her best friend, Clarissa, to get mixed-up was too funny! Think of all the pictures that she and Clarissa had drawn of Little Witch Girl. And still Clarissa did not recognize the true witch! Think of the birthday party, too, the witch girl's birthday party!

"Oh, well," said Amy, excusing her. "After all. It is Halloween. Anybody can get mixed-up on Halloween."

"This girl," she said slowly and solemnly to Clarissa, "is real Little Witch Girl that we draw all the time."

Clarissa looked from one to the other in utter confusion. Then she said hastily, "Why, yes, of course," for she certainly recognized Amy's voice and, for the moment at least, knew that Amy was Amy.

"Please rub some more magic on that broomstick," Amy asked the real little witch girl.

Little Witch Girl shook her head. "Not in front of all the children. It doesn't work well unless we are alone."

"Later?" asked Amy.

"Maybe," said Little Witch Girl.

Polly and Christopher Knapp eyed the new witch girl (Amy) and the other witch girl (real one) suspiciously. They did not know one from the other until Amy spoke and they recognized her voice. Then they decided to be rude to the stranger witch girl who they had thought was Amy and whom they had let come into houses with them on their street on

Halloween. They would pull her hair, for one thing. "You can't have that bag," said Christopher. "That's Amy's."

They had decided that this other witch was a girl from a different school, not their school. They decided she must be Mary Maloney or Sally Trout from Starr Street, both of whom had long blond hair like Amy's, unless this hair was a Halloween wig. They pulled it to see. No, it was not a wig, for it did not come off. But it crackled electrically, giving them a slight shock, so they decided to leave the new little witch girl alone. They had heard that Mary Maloney was rather a rough girl, and the shock confirmed the rumor. Anyway, they still kept getting her and Amy mixed-up, and they would not want to pull the hair of Amy by mistake and get scolded by their mother who always said, "Don't pull Amy's hair!"

So, they contented themselves with singing, "Mary Maloney is full of baloney." But suddenly they stopped. There came the sound of a great whrirra-whirra. The moon darkened over. "Heh-heh! Ha-ha! He-he!" The harsh laugh of the great old Halloween witch could be heard. Wind whistled. Branches of the great ginkgo trees bent low. The little make-believe hobgoblins, frightened and excited, darted hither and thither and looked real. Newspapers flew up the street and wound around the children's legs. Happily terrified, they all raced for Amy's house, where they had agreed to wind up the expedition. And in this way trick-or-treat ended for the year.

Estes, Eleanor. *The Witch Family.* New York: Harcourt Brace & Company, Odyssey, 1990.

PADDLE-TO-THE-SEA

HOLLING CLANCY HOLLING

"Please put me back in the water, I am Paddle-to-the-Sea." These are the words carved into the bottom of a one-foot-long wooden canoe fashioned by an Indian boy living in the Canadian wilderness. And thus begins an adventurous journey from Lake Superior to the Atlantic Ocean.

1. HOW PADDLE-TO-THE-SEA CAME TO BE

he Canadian wilderness was white with snow. From Lake Superior northward the evergreen trees wore hoods and coats of white. A heavy blanket of cloud hung low across the hills. There was no sound. Nothing moved. Even a thread of gray smoke stood up like a pole, keeping the sky from falling in a log cabin in the valley.

Then far off a sound began, grew louder, louder—and swept overhead in a wild cackle of honks and cries. "Geese!" cried the Indian boy standing in the door of the cabin. "They come back too soon. I must hurry to finish my Paddle Person!"

He returned to his bear robe by the fire where he had sat for many days whittling a piece of pine. Now he worked on in silence. He bent over the fire to melt lead in an iron spoon, and poured it out to cool and harden in a hollow of the wood. He fastened a piece of tin to one end of the carving. Then he brought out the oil paints and worked carefully with a brush.

Satisfied at last, the boy sat back on his heels. Before him lay a canoe one foot long. It looked like his father's big birchbark loaded with packs and supplies for a journey. Underneath was a tin rudder to keep it headed forward, and a lump of lead for ballast. This would keep the canoe low in the water, and turn it right-side-up after an upset. An Indian figure knelt just back of the middle, grasping a paddle. And along the bottom were carved these words:

"Please put me back in the water, I am Paddle-to-the-Sea."

2. LONG RIVER REACHING TO THE SEA

Next day the Indian boy climbed the hill back of his home. His snowshoes wide as shovels sank into the drifts at every step. When he reached the top he took from his coat the canoe he had made. He then set it in the snow facing southward where, far away, a river cut an icy path through the forest.

"Now I will tell you something!" said the boy to the figure in the canoe. "I have learned in school that when snow in our Nipigon country melts, the water flows to that river. The river flows into the Great Lakes, the biggest lakes in the world. They are set like bowls on a gentle slope. The water from our river flows into the top one, drops into the next, and on to the others. Then it makes a river again, a river that flows to the Big Salt Water.

"I made you, Paddle Person, because I had a dream. A little wooden man smiled at me. He sat in a canoe on a snowbank on this hill. Now the dream has begun to come true. The Sun Spirit will look down at the snow. The snow will melt and the water will run downhill to the river, on down to the Great Lakes, down again and on at last to the sea. You will go with the water and you will have adventures that I would like to have. But I cannot go with you because I have to help my father with the traps.

"The time has come for you to sit on this snowbank and wait for the Sun Spirit to set you free. Then you will be a real Paddle Person, a real Paddle-to-the-Sea."

3. PADDLE STARTS ON HIS JOURNEY

At night wood mice crept over the little canoe. White owls swooped low just to look at it. Rabbits hopped near. Two wolves came to sniff at Paddle; then a wolverine and a weasel.

Each morning when the boy went to make certain that Paddle was safe, he found the tracks in the snow. But he knew that Paddle could not be eaten because he was only painted wood.

All this time the world was changing. The air grew warmer, the birch twigs swelled with new buds. A moose pawed the snow beside a log, uncovering green moss and arbutus like tiny stars. And then, one morning, the gray clouds drifted from the sky. The sun burst out warm and bright above the hills, and under its glare the snow blankets drooped on the fir trees. Everywhere the snow was melting. There was a steady tap-tap-tap of fat drops falling.

The snowbank began to settle under Paddle. Next morning it had split wide open. Across a narrow, deep canyon in the snow, the canoe made a little bridge. But hour by hour it tipped farther forward.

The boy came running over the slippery ground. He was just in time to see the canoe slide down into rushing water. It sank and came to the surface upside down. Then it righted itself and the watching boy saw it plunge forward, leaping on the crest of a brook that dashed downhill.

"Ho!" he called. "You have started on your journey! Good-bye, Paddle-to-the-Sea!"

4. BROOK AND BEAVER POND

The canoe rushed down a snowy canyon with steep sides. The busy brook backed it, pushed it forward, rolled it under, sent it on, and, finally, dropped it into the quiet water of a pond.

Beavers had made this pond by building a dam of logs and sticks plastered with mud. To do this they had gnawed down trees. The stumps of the trees showed here and there along the banks. In the middle of the pond, the beavers built their home, an island of sticks with an underwater entrance, safe from enemies. Inside on a shelf above water level, the nest of soft rushes would always be warm and dry. An old beaver crept out of the water, sleek and dripping, to sit on the roof and scratch himself in the sun. A buck deer waded in the shallows. He had only one antler and the weight of it made him walk with his head turned aside. he swung the antler hard against a stump. It came off easily and dropped into the mud. He shook his head and bounded off into the forest, glad to be free of the weight. By fall he would grow a new set of weapons. A mink dived off a melting snowbank and came up with a fish. A muskrat swam past the drifting canoe and disappeared in the dead rushes. A skunk met a porcupine on a log. Each looked disgusted, turned about, and waddled solemnly away.

The flooding pond burst through a corner of the beaver dam that afternoon. Old leaves, with Paddle in the midst of them, pushed through the gap. Paddle-to-the-Sea was free. The little canoe rushed on with the brook, on toward the river.

5 . BREAKUP OF THE RIVER

On a warm day, perhaps the very day that the snow had melted and started Paddle on his journey, the breakup of the river had come. All through the winter the river had lain frozen. Wild animals had used it as and ice trail. Lumberjacks had used it as a road for takiing their horses and tractors to the logging camps in the forest. But they had not hauled their logs to the sawmill this way. Instead they piled them up along the frozen banks waiting for the river to carry them when the spring breakup came.

And now it had come. Hundreds of brooks and streams had been flooding the river under its ice. The water, pushing from beneath, forced the ice upward. The banks shook as in an earthquake. Up and down the river the glass pavement cracked all over. The cracks split open. Blocks of ice began to move downstream—faster and faster. A foaming river roared through the forest where the frozen trail had been.

Paddle's canoe tumbled along with the brook until, with one last leap, it shot into the middle of the mad current of the river. The ice and the lumberman's logs crushed on every side. Escaping again and again, Paddle raced on. The river rounded a bend. Logs and ice ahead plunged out of sight without warning. Paddle, too, plunged forward, through mist, over the falls.

He was still bottom-side-up in the water when a log rushed over the falls behind him, striking the canoe such a hard blow that it was wedged in a crack of the shaggy bark. And when the log raced away it carried Paddle-to-the-Sea with it, upside down, under water.

6. PADDLE MEETS A SAWMILL

Paddle's log was four feet thick. Timbers and ice crashed against it, but it floated so low in the water that the canoe, held snugly underneath, was well out of danger. Hours went by, days passed. In time the river widened into a bay dotted with islands, the ice disappeared, and the rivermen in spiked boots leaped from log to log prodding them with long pike-poles toward the sawmill.

The mill, a mass of red buildings on stilts above the river bank, opened its mouth wide in the main building. From the mouth ran the log chute, a giant tongue, licking into the water. A heavy chain of spikes moved up the center of the chute, turned over a wheel and returned to the river, an endless belt called a bull-chain. Rivermen pushed the logs onto the spikes which carried them up the chute into the open mouth. A buzzing noise which sometimes became a shriek came from inside the mill. The great saws were at work.

The spikes dug into Paddle's log. The great tree rolled over, bringing Paddle upright and dripping out of the water into the sunlight. The rivermen shouted with surprise as Paddle rode his log up the bull-chain. At the top he was heaved through the door, onto a carrier that looked like a flatcar. Ahead the saw, an endless belt of thin steel, raced so fast its teeth were a blur. Paddle's log was being pushed nearer and nearer to the hungry saw.

Holling, Holling C. *Paddle to the Sea*. New York: Houghton Mifflin, 1960.
Other Editions:
——. *Paddle to the Sea*. New York: Houghton Mifflin, 1980.

A WRINKLE IN TIME

MADELEINE L'ENGLE

Meg Murry and her younger brother, Charles Wallace, desperately miss their scientist father, who has mysteriously disappeared. The mystery, however, slowly unravels when they meet three peculiar women—one constantly quotes famous people, another speaks in vibrations—who tell them that "there is such a thing as a tesseract," or a wrinkle in time! The two children and Meg's schoolmate, Calvin, are whisked away by these outlandish strangers, named Mrs. Whatsit, Mrs. Who, and Mrs. Which, to a new place, or dimension, where they begin their valiant rescue of their father.

Chapter Four THE BLACK THING

The trees were lashed into a violent frenzy. Meg screamed and clutched at Calvin, and Mrs. Which's authoritative voice called out, "Qquiett, chilldd!"

Did a shadow fall across the moon or did the moon simply go out, extinguished as abruptly and completely as a candle? There was still the sound of leaves, a terrified, terrifying rushing. All light was gone. Darkness was complete. Suddenly the wind was gone, and all sound. Meg felt that Calvin was being torn from her. When she reached for him her fingers touched nothing

She screamed out, "Charles!" and whether it was to help him or for him to help her, she did not know. The word was flung back down her throat and she choked on it.

She was completely alone.

She had lost the protection of Calvin's hand. Charles was nowhere, either to save or to turn to. She was alone in a fragment of nothingness. No light, no sound, no feeling. Where was her body? She tried to move in her panic, but there was nothing to move. Just as light and sound had vanished, she was gone, too. The corporeal Meg simply was not.

Then she felt her limbs again. Her legs and arms were tingling faintly, as though they had been asleep. She blinked her eyes rapidly, but though she herself was somehow back, nothing else was. It was not as simple as darkness, or absence of light. Darkness has a tangible quality; it can be moved through and felt; in darkness you can bark your shins; the world of things still exists around you. She was lost in a horrifying void.

It was the same way with the silence. This was more than silence. A deaf person can feel vibrations. Here there was nothing to feel.

Suddenly she was aware of her heart beating rapidly within the cage of her ribs. Had it stopped before? What had made it start again? The tingling in her arms and legs grew stronger, and suddenly she felt movement. This movement, she felt, must be the turning of the Earth, rotating on its axis, traveling its elliptic course about the Sun. And this feeling of moving with the earth was somewhat like the feeling of being in the ocean, out in the ocean beyond this rising and falling of the breakers, lying on the moving water, pulsing gently with the swells, and feeling the gentle, inexorable tug of the Moon.

I am asleep; I am dreaming, she thought. I'm having a nightmare. I want to wake up. Let me wake up.

"Well!" Charles Wallace's voice said. "That was quite a trip! I do think you might have warned us."

Light began to pulse and quiver. Meg blinked and shoved shakily at her glasses and there was Charles Wallace standing indignantly in front of her, his hands on his hips. "Meg!" he shouted. "Calvin! Where are you?"

She saw Charles, she heard him, but she could not go to him. She could not shove through the strange, trembling light to meet him.

Calvin's voice came as though it were pushing through a cloud. "Well, just give me time, will you? I'm older than you are."

Meg gasped. It wasn't that Calvin wasn't there and then that he was. It wasn't that part of him came first and then the rest of him followed, like a hand and then an arm, an eye and then a nose. It was a sort of shimmering, a looking at Calvin through water, through smoke, through fire, and then there he was, solid and reassuring.

"Meg!" Charles Wallace's voice came. "Meg! Calvin, where's Meg?"

"I'm right here," she tried to say, but her voice seemed to be caught at its source.

"Meg!" Calvin cried, and he turned around, looking about wildly.

"Mrs. Which, you haven't left Meg behind, have you?" Charles Wallace shouted.

"If you've hurt Meg, any of you—" Calvin started, but suddenly Meg felt a violent thrust through a wall of glass.

"Oh, there you are!" Charles Wallace said, and rushed over to her and hugged her.

"But where am I?" Meg asked breathlessly, relieved to hear that her voice was now coming out of her in more or less a normal way.

She looked around rather wildly. They were standing in a sunlit field, and the air about them was moving with the delicious fragrance that comes only on the rarest of spring days when the sun's touch is gentle and the apple blossoms are just beginning to unfold. She pushed her glasses up on her nose to reassure herself that what she was seeing was real.

They had left the silver glint of a biting autumn evening; and now around them everything was golden with light. The grasses of the field were a tender new green, and scattered about were tiny, multicolored flowers. Meg turned slowly to face a mountain reaching so high into the sky that its peak was lost in a crown of puffy white clouds. From the trees at the base of the mountain came a sudden singing of birds. There was an air of such ineffable peace and joy all around her that her heart's wild thumping slowed.

310

"When shall we three meet again,
In thunder, lightning, or in rain,"

came Mrs. Who's voice. Suddenly the three of them were there, Mrs. Whatsit with her pink stole askew; Mrs. Who with her spectacles gleaming; and Mrs. Which still little more than a shimmer. Delicate, multicolored butterflies were fluttering about them, as though in greeting.

Mrs. Whatsit and Mrs. Who began to giggle, and they giggled until it seemed that, whatever their private joke was, they would fall down laughing, too. It became vaguely darker and more solid; and then there appeared a figure in a black robe and a black peaked hat, beady eyes, a beaked nose, and long gray hair; one bony claw clutched a broomstick.

"Wwell, jusstt ttoo kkeepp yyou girrlls happpy," the strange voice said, and Mrs. Whatsit and Mrs. Who fell into each other's arms in gales of laughter.

"If you ladies have had your fun I think you should tell Calvin and Meg a little more about all this," Charles Wallace said coldly. "You scared Meg half out of her wits, whisking her off this way without any warning."

"*Finxerunt animi, raro et perpauca loquentis,*" Mrs. Who intoned. "Horace. To action little, less to words inclined."

"Mrs. Who, I wish you'd stop quoting!" Charles Wallace sounded very annoyed.

Mrs. Whatsit adjusted her stole. "But she finds it so difficult to verbalize, Charles dear. It helps her if she can quote instead of working out words of her own."

"Anndd wee mussttn'tt looose ourr sensses of hummorr," Mrs. Which said. "Thee onnlly wway ttoo ccope withh ssometthingg ddeadly sseriouss iss tto ttry ttoo trreatt itt a llittle lligghtly."

"But that's going to be hard for Meg," Mrs. Whatsit said. "It's going to be hard for her to realize that we are serious."

"What about me?" Calvin asked.

"The life of your father isn't at stake," Mrs. Whatsit told him.

"What about Charles Wallace, then?"

Mrs. Whatsit's unoiled-door-hinge voice was warm with affection and pride. "Charles Wallace knows. Charles Wallace knows that it's far more than just the life of his father. Charles Wallace knows what's at stake."

"But remember," Mrs. Who said, "Nothing is hopeless; we must hope for everything."

"Where are we now, and how did we get here?" Calvin asked.

"Uriel, the third planet of the star Malak in the spiral nebula Messier 101."

"This I'm supposed to believe?" Calvin asked indignantly.

"Aas yyou llike," Mrs. Which said coldly.

For some reason Meg felt that Mrs. Which, despite her looks and ephemeral broomstick, was someone in whom one could put complete trust. "It doesn't seem any more peculiar than anything else that's happened."

"Well, then, someone just tell me how we got here!" Calvin's voice was still angry and his freckles seemed to stand out on his face. "Even traveling at the speed of light it would take us years and years to get here."

"Oh, we don't travel at the speed of anything," Mrs. Whatsit explained earnestly. "We tesser. Or you might say, we wrinkle."

"Clear as mud," Calvin said.

Tesser, Meg thought. Could that have anything to do with Mother's tesseract?

She was about to ask when Mrs. Which started to speak, and one did not interrupt when Mrs. Which was speaking. "Mrs. Whatsit iss yyoungg andd nnaive."

"She keeps thinking she can explain things in words," Mrs. Who said. "*Qui plus sait, plus se tait.* French, you know. The more a man knows, the less he talks."

"But she has to use words for Meg and Calvin," Charles reminded Mrs. Who. "If you brought them along, they have a right to know what's going on."

Meg went up to Mrs. Which. In the intensity of her question she had forgotten all about the tesseract. "Is my father here?"

Mrs. Which shook her head. "Nnott heeere, Megg. Llet Mrs. Whatsit expllainn. Shee isss yyoungg annd thee llanguage of worrds iss eeasierr fforr hherr thann itt iss ffor Mrs. Whoo andd mee."

"We stopped here," Mrs. Whatsit explained, "more or less to catch our breath. And to give you a chance to know what you're up against."

"But what about Father?" Meg asked. "Is he all right?"

"For the moment, love, yes. He's one of the reasons we're here. But you see, he's only one."

"Well, where is he? Please take me to him!"

"We can't, not yet," Charles said. "You have to be patient, Meg."

"But I'm not patient!" Meg cried passionately. "I've never been patient!"

Mrs. Who's glasses shone at her gently. "If you want to help your father then you must learn patience. *Vitam impendere vero.* To stake one's life for the truth. That is what we must do."

"That is what your father is doing." Mrs. Whatsit nodded, her voice, like Mrs. Who's, very serious, very solemn. Then she smiled her radiant smile. "Now! Why don't you three children wander around and Charles can explain things a little. You're perfectly safe on Uriel. That's why we stopped here to rest."

"But aren't you coming with us?" Meg asked fearfully.

There was silence for a moment. Then Mrs. Which raised her authoritative hand. "Sshoww themm," she said to Mrs. Whatsit, and at something in her voice Meg felt prickles of apprehension.

"Now?" Mrs. Whatsit asked, her creaky voice rising to a squeak. Whatever it was Mrs. Which wanted them to see, it was something that made Mrs. Whatsit uncomfortable, too.

"Nnoww," Mrs. Which said. "Tthey mmay aas welll knoww."

"Should—should I change?" Mrs. Whatsit asked.

"Bbetter."

"I hope it won't upset the children too much," Mrs. Whatsit murmured, as though to herself.

"Should I change, too?" Mrs. Who asked. "Oh, but I've had fun in these clothes. But I'll have to admit Mrs. Whatsit is the best at it. *Das Werk lobt den Meister.* German. The work proves the craftsman. Shall I transform now, too?"

Mrs. Which shook her head. "Nnott yett. Nnott heere. Yyou mmay wwaitt."

"Now, don't be frightened, loves," Mrs. Whatsit said. Her plump little body began to shimmer, to quiver, to shift. The wild colors of her clothes became muted, whitened. The pudding-bag shape stretched, lengthened, merged. And suddenly before the children was a creature more beautiful than any Meg had even imagined, and the beauty lay in far more than the outward description. Outwardly Mrs. Whatsit was surely no longer a Mrs. Whatsit. She was a marble white body with powerful flanks, something like a horse but at the same time completely unlike a horse, for from the magnificently modeled back sprang a nobly formed torso, arms, and a head resembling a man's, but a man with a perfection of dignity and virtue, and exaltation of joy such as Meg had never before seen. No, she thought, it's not like a Greek centaur. Not in the least.

From the shoulders slowly a pair of wings unfolded, wings made of rainbows, of light upon water, of poetry.

Calvin fell to his knees.

L'Engle, Madeleine. *A Wrinkle in Time*. New York: Dell Yearling, 1973.

CHRONICLES OF NARNIA: THE MAGICIAN'S NEPHEW

C. S. LEWIS

Digory lives in a big old house with a bedridden Mother, an aunt, and a mad uncle. He's told never to go up to his mad uncle's study. However, one day, Digory and his friend Polly explore the attic and find themselves in Uncle Andrew's study by accident. Polly puts on one of Andrew's magic rings and vanishes into thin air. It's up to Digory to rescue her.

Chapter Two DIGORY AND HIS UNCLE

It was so sudden, and so horribly unlike anything that had ever happened to Digory even in a nightmare, that he let out a scream. Instantly, Uncle Andrew's hand was over his mouth. "None of that!" he hissed in Digory's ear. "If you start making a noise your Mother'll hear it. And you know what a fright might do to her."

As Digory said afterward, the horrible meanness of getting at a chap in that way almost made him sick. But of course he didn't scream again.

"That's better," said Uncle Andrew. "Perhaps you couldn't help it. It is a shock when you first see someone vanish. Why, it gave even me a turn when the guinea-pig did it the other night."

"Was that when you yelled?" asked Digory.

"Oh, you heard that, did you? I hope you haven't been spying on me?"

"No, I haven't," said Digory indignantly. "But what's happened to Polly?"

"Congratulate me, my dear boy," said Uncle Andrew, rubbing his hands. "My experiment has succeeded. The little girl's gone—vanished—right out of the world."

"What have you done to her?"

"Sent her to—well—to another place."

"What do you mean?" asked Digory.

Uncle Andrew sat down and said, "Well, I'll tell you all about it. Have you ever heard of old Mrs. Lefay?"

"Wasn't she a great-aunt or something?" said Digory.

"Not exactly," said Uncle Andrew. "She was my godmother. That's her, there, on the wall."

Digory looked and saw a faded photograph: it showed the face of an old woman in a bonnet. And he could now remember that he had once seen a photo of the same face in an old drawer, at home, in the country. He had asked his mother who it was and Mother had not seemed to want to talk about the subject much. It was not at all a nice face, Digory thought, though of course with those early photographs one could never really tell.

"Was there—wasn't there—something wrong about her, Uncle Andrew?" he said.

"Well," said Uncle Andrew with a chuckle, "It depends what you call wrong. People are so narrow-minded. She certainly got very queer in later life. Did very unwise things. That was why they shut her up."

"In an asylum, do you mean?"

"Oh no, no, no," said Uncle Andrew in a shocked voice. "Nothing of that sort. Only in prison."

"I say!" said Digory. "What had she done?"

"Ah, poor woman," said Uncle Andrew. "She had been very unwise. There were a good many different things. We needn't go into all that. She was always very kind to me."

"But look here, what has all this got to do with Polly? I do wish you'd—"

"All in good time, my boy," said Uncle Andrew. "They let old Mrs. Lefay out before she died and I was one of the very few people whom she would allow to see her in her last illness. She had got to dislike ordinary, ignorant people, you understand. I do myself. But she and I were interested in the same sort of things. It was only a few days before her death that she told me to go to an old bureau in her house and open a secret drawer and bring her a little box that I would find there. The moment I picked up that box I could tell by the pricking in my fingers that I held some great secret in my hands. She gave it to me and made me promise that as soon as she was dead I would burn it, unopened, with certain ceremonies. That promise I did not keep."

"Well, then, it was jolly rotten of you," said Digory.

"Rotten?" said Uncle Andrew with a puzzled look. "Oh, I see. You mean that little boys ought to keep their promises. Very true: most right and proper, I'm sure, and I'm very glad you have been taught to do it. But of course you must understand that rules of that sort, however excellent they may be for little boys—and servants—and women—and even people in general, can't possibly be expected to apply to profound students and great thinkers and sages. No, Digory. Men like me, who possess hidden wisdom, are freed from common rules just as we are cut off from common pleasures. Ours, my boy, is a high and lonely destiny."

As he said this he sighed and looked so grave and noble and mysterious that for a second Digory really thought he was saying something rather fine. But then he remembered the ugly look he had seen on his Uncle's face the moment before Polly had vanished; and all at once he saw through Uncle Andrew's grand words. "All it means," he said to himself, "is that he thinks he can do anything he likes to get anything he wants."

"Of course," said Uncle Andrew, "I didn't dare to open the box for a long time, for I knew it might contain something highly dangerous. For my godmother was a very remarkable woman. The truth is, she was one of the last mortals in this country who had fairy blood in her. (She said there had been two others in her time. One was a duchess and the other was a charwoman.) In fact, Digory, you are now talking to the last man (possibly) who really had a fairy godmother. There! That'll be something for you to remember when you are an old man yourself."

"I bet she was a bad fairy," thought Digory; and added out loud, "But what about Polly?"

"How you do harp on that!" said Uncle Andrew. "As if that was what mattered! My first task was of course to study the box itself. It was very ancient. And I knew enough even then to know that it wasn't Greek, or Old Egyptian, or Babylonian, or Hittite, or Chinese. It was older than any of those nations. Ah—that was a great day when I at last found out the truth. The box was Atlantean; it came from the lost island of Atlantis. That meant it was centuries older than any of the stone-age things they dig up in Europe. And it wasn't a rough, crude thing like them either. For in the very dawn of time Atlantis was already a great city with palaces and temples and learned men."

He paused for a moment as if he expected Digory to say something. But Digory was disliking his Uncle more every minute, so he said nothing.

"Meanwhile," continued Uncle Andrew, "I was learning a good deal in other ways (it wouldn't be proper to explain them to a child) about Magic in general. That meant that I came to have a fair idea what sort of things might be in the box. By various tests I narrowed down the possibilities. I had to get to know some—well, some devilish queer people, and go through some very disagreeable experiences. That was what turned my head gray. One doesn't become a magician for nothing. My health broke down in the end. But I got better. And at last I actually knew."

Although there was not really the least chance of anyone overhearing them, he leaned forward and almost whispered as he said:

"The Atlantean box contained something that had been brought from another world when our world was only just beginning."

"What?" asked Digory, who was now interested in spite of himself.

"Only dust," said Uncle Andrew. "Fine, dry dust. Nothing much to look at. Not much to show for a lifetime of toil, you might say. Ah, but when I looked at that dust (I took jolly good care not to touch it) and thought that every grain had once been in another world—I don't mean another planet, you know; they're part of our world and you could get to them if you went far enough—but a really Other World—another Nature—another universe—somewhere you would never reach even if you traveled through the space of this universe forever and ever—a world that could be reached only by Magic—Well!" Here Uncle Andrew rubbed his hands till his knuckles cracked like fireworks.

"I knew," he went on, "that if only you could get it into the right form, that dust would draw you back to the place it had come from. But the difficulty was to get it into the right form. My earlier experiments were all failures. I tried them on guinea-pigs. Some of them only died. Some exploded like little bombs—"

"It was a jolly cruel thing to do," said Digory who had once had a guinea-pig of his own.

"How do you keep getting off the point!" said Uncle Andrew "That's what the creatures were for. I'd bought them myself. Let me see—where was I? Ah yes. At last I succeeded in making the rings: the yellow rings. But now a new difficulty arose. I was pretty sure, now, that a yellow ring would send any creature that touched it into the Other Place. But what would be the good of that if I couldn't get them back to tell me what they had found there?"

"And what about them?" said Digory. "A nice mess they'd be in if they couldn't get back!"

"You will keep on looking at everything from the wrong point of view," said Uncle Andrew with a look of impatience. "Can't you understand that the thing is a great experiment? The whole point of sending anyone into the Other Place is that I want to find out what it's like."

"Well why didn't you go yourself then?"

Digory had hardly ever seen anyone look so surprised and offended as his Uncle did at this simple question. "Me? Me?" he exclaimed. "The boy must be mad! A man at my time of life, and in my state of health, to risk the shock and the dangers of being flung suddenly into a different universe? I never heard anything so preposterous in my life! Do you realize what you're saying? Think what Another World means—you might meet anything—anything."

"And I suppose you've sent Polly into it then," said Digory. His cheeks were flaming with anger now. "And all I can say," he added, "even if you are my uncle—is that you've behaved like a coward, sending a girl to a place you're afraid to go to yourself."

"Silence, sir!" said Uncle Andrew, bringing his hand down on the table. "I will not be talked to like that by a little dirty schoolboy. You don't understand. I am the great scholar, the magician, the adept, who is doing the experiment. Of course I need subjects to do it on. Bless my soul, you'll be telling me next that I ought to have asked the guinea-pigs' permission before I used them! No great wisdom can be reached without sacrifice. But the idea of my going myself is ridiculous. It's like asking a general to fight as a common soldier. Supposing I got killed, what would become my life's work?"

"Oh, do stop jawing," said Digory. "Are you going to bring Polly back?"

"I was going to tell you, when you so rudely interrupted me," said Uncle Andrew, "that I did at last find out a way of doing the return journey. The green rings draw you back."

"But Polly hasn't got a green ring."

"No," said Uncle Andrew with a cruel smile.

"Then she can't get back," shouted Digory. "And it's exactly the same as if you'd murdered her."

"She can get back," said Uncle Andrew, "if someone else will go after her, wearing a yellow ring himself and taking two green rings, one to bring himself back and one to bring her back."

And now of course Digory saw the trap in which he was caught; and he stared at Uncle Andrew, saying nothing, with his mouth wide open. His cheeks had gone very pale.

"I hope," said Uncle Andrew presently in a very high and mighty voice, just as if he were a perfect uncle who had given one a handsome tip and some good advice, "I hope, Digory, you are not given to showing the white feather. I should be very sorry to think that anyone of our family had not enough honor and chivalry to go to the aid of—er—a lady in distress."

"Oh shut up!" said Digory. "If you had any honor and all that, you'd be going yourself. But I know you won't. All right. I see I've got to go. But you are a beast. I suppose you planned the whole thing, so that she'd go without knowing it and then I'd have to go after her."

"Of course," said Uncle Andrew with his hateful smile.

Lewis, C.S., *The Chronicles of Narnia: The Magician's Nephew*. New York: HarperCollins Publishers, Inc., Harper Trophy, 1994.

INSPIRED BY HISTORY

LITTLE WOMEN

LITTLE MEN

CHEAPER BY THE DOZEN

POLLYANNA

THE PUSHCART WAR

ROBIN HOOD

THE STORY OF MACBETH

MUCH ADO ABOUT NOTHING

JOHNNY TREMAIN

REBECCA OF SUNNYBROOK FARM

HEIDI

LITTLE WOMEN

Louisa May Alcott

The March family is very close and so when Jo March's short story wins first place in a contest and is published, her parents and three sisters, Meg, Beth, and Amy, are ecstatic.

Chapter 27 LITERARY LESSONS

ortune suddenly smiled upon Jo, and dropped a good-luck penny in her path. Not a golden penny, exactly, but I doubt if half a million would have given more real happiness than did the little sum that came to her in this wise.

Every few weeks she would shut herself up in her room, put on her scribbling suit, and "fall into a vortex," as she expressed it, writing away at her novel with all her heart and soul, for till that was finished she could find no peace. Her "scribbling suit" consisted of a black woolen pinafore on which she could wipe her pen at will, and a cap of the same material, adorned with a cheerful red bow, into which she bundled her hair when the decks were cleared for action. This cap was a beacon to the inquiring eyes of her family, who during these periods kept their distance, merely popping in their heads semi-occasionally, to ask, with interest, "Does genius burn, Jo?" They did not always venture even to ask this question, but took an observation of the cap, and judged accordingly. If this expressive article of dress was drawn low upon the forehead, it was a sign that hard work was going on; in exciting moments it was pushed rakishly askew; and when despair seized the author it was plucked wholly off, and cast upon the floor. At such times the intruder silently withdrew; and not until the red bow was seen gayly erect upon the gifted brow, did any one dare address Jo.

She did not think herself a genius by any means; but when the writing fit came on, she gave herself up to it with entire abandon, and led a blissful life, unconscious of want, care, or bad weather, while she sat safe and happy in an imaginary world, full of friends almost as real and dear to her as any in the flesh. Sleep forsook her eyes, meals stood untasted, day and night were all too short to enjoy the happiness which blessed her only at such times, and made these hours worth living, even if they bore no other fruit. The divine afflatus usually lasted a week or two, and then she emerged from her "vortex," hungry, sleepy, cross, or despondent.

She was just recovering from one of these attacks when she was prevailed upon to escort Miss Crocker to a lecture, and in return for her virtue was rewarded with a new idea.

It was a People's Course, the lecture on the Pyramids, and Jo rather wondered at the choice of such a subject for such an audience, but took it for granted that some great social evil would be remedied or some great want supplied by unfolding the glories of the Pharaohs to an audience whose thoughts were busy with the price of coal and flour, and whose lives were spent in trying to solve harder riddles than that of the Sphinx.

They were early; and while Miss Crocker set the heel of her stocking, Jo amused herself by examining the faces of the people who occupied the seat with them. On her left were two matrons, with massive foreheads, and bonnets to match, discussing Woman's Rights and making tatting. Beyond sat a pair of humble lovers, artlessly holding each other by the hand, a sombre spinster eating peppermints out of a paper bag, and an old gentleman taking his preparatory nap behind a yellow bandanna. On her right, her only neighbor was a studious-looking lad absorbed in a newspaper.

It was a pictorial sheet, and Jo examined the work of art nearest her, idly wondering what unfortuitous concatenation of circumstances needed the melodramatic illustration of an Indian in full war costume, tumbling over a precipice with a wolf at this throat, while two infuriated young gentlemen, with unnaturally small feet and big eyes, were stabbing each other close by, and a dishevelled female was flying away in the background with her mouth wide open. Pausing to turn a page, the lad saw her looking, and, with boyish good-nature, offered half his paper, saying bluntly, "Want to read it? That's a first-rate story."

Jo accepted it with a smile, for she had never outgrown her liking for lads, and soon found herself involved in the usual labyrinth of love, mystery, and murder, for the story belonged to that class of light literature in which the passions have a holiday, and when the author's invention fails, a grand catastrophe clears the stage of one half the dramatis personae, leaving the other half to exult over their downfall.

"Prime, isn't it?" asked the boy, as her eye went down the last paragraph of her portion.

"I think you and I could do as well as that if we tried," returned Jo, amused at this admiration of the trash.

"I should think I was a pretty lucky chap if I could. She makes a good living out of such stories, they say"; and he pointed to the name of Mrs. S.L.A.N.G. Northbury, under the title of the tale.

"Do you know her?" asked Jo, with sudden interest.

"No; but I read all her pieces, and I know a fellow who works in the office where this paper is printed."

"Do you say she makes a good living out of stories like this?" and Jo looked more respectfully at the agitated group and thickly sprinkled exclamation points that adorned the page.

"Guess she does! She knows just what folks like, and gets paid well for writing it."

Here the lecture began, but Jo heard very little of it, for while Professor Sands was prosing away about Belzoni, Cheops, Scarabei, and hieroglyphics, she was covertly taking down the address of the paper, and boldly resolving to try for the hundred-dollar prize offered in its columns for a sensational story. By the time the lecture ended and the audience awoke, she had built up a splendid fortune for herself (not the first founded upon paper), and was already deep in the concoction of her story, being unable to decide whether the duel should come before the elopement or after the murder.

She said nothing of her plan at home, but fell to work next day, much to the disquiet of her mother, who always looked a little anxious when "genius took to burning." Jo had never tried this style before, contenting herself with very mild romances for the "Spread Eagle." Her theatrical experience and miscellaneous reading were of service now, for they gave her some idea of dramatic effect, and supplied plot, language, and costumes. Her story was as full of desperation and despair as her limited acquaintance with those uncomfortable emotions enabled her to make it, and, having located it in Lisbon, she wound up with an earthquake, as a striking and appropriate dénouement. The manuscript was privately dispatched, accompanied by a note, modestly saying that if the tale didn't get the prize, which writer hardly dared expect, she would be very glad to receive any sum it might be considered worth.

Six weeks is a long time to wait, and a still longer time for a girl to keep a secret; but Jo did both, and was just beginning to give up all hope of ever seeing her manuscript again, when a letter arrived which almost took her breath away; for on opening it, a check for a hundred dollars fell into her lap. For a minute she stared at it as if it had been a snake, then she read her letter and began to cry. If the amiable gentleman who wrote that kindly note could have known what intense happiness he was giving a fellow-creature, I think he would devote his leisure hours, if he has any to that amusement; for Jo valued the letter more than the money, because it was encouraging; and after years of effort it was so pleasant to find that she had learned to do something, though it was only to write a sensation story.

A prouder young woman was seldom seen than she, when, having composed herself, she electrified the family by appearing before them with the letter in one hand, the check in the other, announcing that she had won the prize. Of course there was a great jubilee, and when the story came every one read and praised it; though after her father had told her that the language was good, the romance fresh and hearty, and the tragedy quite thrilling, he shook his head, and said in his unworldly way—

"You can do better than this, Jo. Aim at the highest, and never mind the money."

"I think the money is the best part of it. What will you do with such a fortune?" asked Amy, regarding the magic slip of paper with a reverential eye.

"Send Beth and mother to the seaside for a month or two," answered Jo promptly.

"Oh, how splendid! No, I can't do it, dear, it would be so selfish," cried Beth, who had clapped her thin hands, and taken a long breath, as if pining for fresh ocean-breezes; then stopped herself, and motioned away the check which her sister waved before her.

"Ah, but you shall go, I've set my heart on it; that's what I tried for, and that's why I

succeeded. I never get on when I think of myself alone, so it will help me to work for you, don't you see? Besides, Marmee needs the change, and she won't leave you, so you must go. Won't it be fun to see you come home plump and rosy again? Hurray for Dr. Jo, who always cures her patients!"

To the seaside they went, after much discussion; and though Beth didn't come home as plump and rosy as could be desired, she was much better, while Mrs. March declared she felt ten years younger; so Jo was satisfied with the investment of her prize money and fell to work with a cheery spirit, bent on earning more of those delightful checks. She did earn several that year, and began to feel herself a power in the house; for by the magic of a pen, her "rubbish" turned into comforts for them all. "The Duke's Daughter" paid the butcher's bill, "A Phantom Hand" put down a new carpet, and the "Curse of the Coventrys" proved the blessing of the Marches in the way of groceries and gowns.

Wealth is certainly a most desirable thing, but poverty has its sunny side, and one of the sweet uses of adversity is the genuine satisfaction which comes from hearty work of head or hand; and to the inspiration of necessity, we owe half the wise, beautiful, and useful blessings of the world. Jo enjoyed a taste of this satisfaction, and ceased to envy richer girls, taking great comfort in the knowledge that she could supply her own wants, and need ask no one for a penny.

Little notice was taken of her stories, but they found a market; and, encouraged by this fact, she resolved to make a bold stroke for fame and fortune. Having copied her novel for the fourth time, read it to all her confidential friends, and submitted it with fear and trembling to three publishers, she at last disposed of it, on condition that she would cut it down one third, and omit all the parts which she particularly admired.

"Now I must either bundle it back into my tin-kitchen to mould, pay for printing it myself, or chop it up to suit purchasers, and get what I can for it. Fame is a very good thing to have in the house, but cash is more convenient; so I wish to take the sense of the meeting on this important subject," said Jo, calling a family council.

"Don't spoil your book, my girl, for there is more in it than you know, and the idea is well worked out. Let it wait and ripen," was her father's advice; and he practiced as he preached, having waited patiently thirty years for fruit of his own to ripen, and being in no haste to gather it, even now, when it was sweet and mellow.

Alcott, Louisa May. *Little Women*. New York: Barnes & Noble Books, 1994.

LITTLE MEN

LOUISA MAY ALCOTT

Nat is a twelve-year-old orphaned street violinist who comes to Plumfield, a school run by Mr. and Mrs. Bhaer, and finds, for the first time in his life, a benevolent home.

Chapter One LIFE AT PLUMFIELD WITH JOE'S BOYS

n the room on the left a long supper-table was seen, set forth with great pitchers of new milk, piles of brown and white bread, and perfect stacks of the shiny gingerbread so dear to boyish souls. A flavor of toast was in the air, also suggestions of baked apples, very tantalizing to one hungry little nose and stomach.

The hall, however, presented the most inviting prospect of all, for a brisk game of tag was going on in the upper entry. One landing was devoted to marbles, the other to checkers, while the stairs were occupied by a boy reading, a girl singing lullaby to her doll, two puppies, a kitten, and a constant succession of small boys sliding down the bannisters, to the great detriment of their clothes, and danger to their limbs.

So absorbed did Nat become in this exciting race, that he ventured farther and farther out of his corner; and when one very lively boy came down so swiftly that he could not stop himself, but fell off the bannisters, with a crash that would have broken any head but one rendered nearly as hard as a cannon-ball by eleven years of constant bumping, Nat forgot himself, and ran up to the fallen rider, expecting to find him half-dead. The boy, however, only winked rapidly for a second, then lay calmly looking up at the new face with a surprised "Hullo!"

"Hullo!" returned Nat, not knowing what else to say, and thinking that form of reply both brief and easy.

"Are you a new boy?" asked the recumbent youth, without stirring.

"Don't know yet."

"What's your name?"

"Nat Blake."

"Mine's Tommy Bangs; come up and have a go, will you?" and Tommy got upon his legs like one suddenly remembering the duties of hospitality.

"Guess I won't, till I see whether I'm going to stay or not," returned Nat, feeling the desire to stay increase every moment.

"I say, Demi, here's a new one. Come and see to him"; and the lively Thomas returned to his sport with unabated relish.

At his call, the boy reading on the stairs looked up with a pair of big brown eyes, and after an instant's pause, as if a little shy, he put the book under his arm, and came soberly down to greet the new-comer, who found something very attractive in the pleasant face of this slender, mild-eyed boy.

"Have you seen Aunt Jo?" he asked, as if that was some sort of important ceremony.

"I haven't seen anybody yet but you boys; I'm waiting," answered Nat.

"Did Uncle Laurie send you?" proceeded Demi, politely, but gravely.

"Mr. Laurence did."

"He is Uncle Laurie; and he always sends nice boys."

Nat looked gratified at the remark, and smiled, in a way that made his thin face very pleasant. He did not know what to say next, so the two stood staring at one another in friendly silence, till the little girl came up with her doll in her arms, she was very like Demi, only not so tall, and had a rounder, rosier face, and blue eyes.

"This is my sister Daisy," announced Demi, as if presenting a rare and precious creature.

The children nodded to one another; and the little girl's face dimpled with pleasure, as she said, affably, "I hope you'll stay. We have such good times here; don't we, Demi?"

"Of course, we do; that's what Aunt Jo has Plumfield for."

"It seems a very nice place indeed," observed Nat, feeling that he must respond to these amiable young persons.

"It's the nicest place in the world; isn't it Demi?" said Daisy, who evidently regarded her brother as authority on all subjects.

"No; I think Greenland, where the icebergs and seals are, is more interesting. But I'm fond of Plumfield, and it is a very nice place to be in," returned Demi, who was interested just now in a book on Greenland. He was about to offer to show Nat the pictures and explain them, when the servant returned, saying, with a nod toward the parlor-door—

"All right; you are to stop."

"I'm glad; now come to Aunt Jo." And Daisy took him by the hand with a pretty protecting air, which made Nat feel at home at once.

Demi returned to his beloved book, while his sister led the new-comer into a back room, where a stout gentleman was frolicking with two little boys on the sofa, and a thin lady was just finishing the letter which she seemed to have been re-reading.

"Here he is, Aunty!" cried Daisy.

"So this is my new boy? I am glad to see you, my dear, and hope you'll be happy here," said the lady, drawing him to her, and stroking back the hair from his forehead with a kind hand and a motherly look, which made Nat's lonely little heart yearn toward her.

She was not at all handsome, but she had a merry sort of face, that never seemed to have forgotten certain childish ways and looks, any more than her voice and manner had;

and these things, hard to describe but very plain to see and feel, made her a genial, comfortable kind of person, easy to get on with, and generally "jolly," as boys would say. She saw the little tremble of Nat's lips as she smoothed his hair, and her keen eyes grew softer, but she only drew the shabby figure nearer and said, laughing—

"I am Mother Bhaer, that gentleman is Father Bhaer, and these are the two little Bhaers. Come here, boys, and see Nat." The three wrestlers obeyed at once; and the stout man, with a chubby child on each shoulder, came up to welcome the new boy. Rob and Teddy merely grinned at him, but Mr. Bhaer shook hands, and pointing to a low chair near the fire, said, in a cordial voice—

"There is a place all ready for thee, my son; sit down and dry thy wet feet at once."

"Wet? So they are! My dear, off with your shoes this minute, and I'll have some dry things ready for you in a jiffy," cried Mrs. Bhaer, bustling about so energetically that Nat found himself in the cozy little chair, with dry socks and warm slippers on his feet, before he would have had time to say Jack Robinson, if he had wanted to try. He said, "Thank you, ma'am" instead; and said it so gratefully that Mrs. Bhaer's eyes grew soft again, and she said something merry, because she felt so tender, which was a way she had.

"These are Tommy Bang's slippers; but he never will remember to put them on in the house; so he shall not have them. They are too big; but that's all the better; you can't run away from us so fast as if they fitted."

"I don't what to run away, ma'am." And Nat spread his grimy little hands before the comfortable blaze, with a long sigh of satisfaction.

"That's good! Now I am going to toast you well, and try to get rid of that ugly cough. How long have you had it, dear?" asked Mrs. Bhaer, as she rummaged in her big basket for a strip of flannel.

"All winter. I got cold, and it wouldn't get better, somehow."

"No wonder, living in that damp cellar with hardly a rag to his poor dear back!" said Mrs. Bhaer, in a low tone to her husband, who was looking at the boy with a skillful pair of eyes, that marked the thin temples and feverish lips, as well as the hoarse voice and frequent fits of coughing that shook the bent shoulders under the patched jacket.

"Robin, my man, trot up to Nursey, and tell her to give thee the coughbottle and the liniment," said Mr. Bhaer, after his eyes had exchanged telegrams with his wife's.

Nat looked a little anxious at the preparations, but forgot his fears, in a hearty laugh, when Mrs. Bhaer whispered to him, with a droll look—

"Hear my rogue Teddy try to cough. The syrup I'm giving you has honey in it; and he wants some."

Little Ted was red in the face with his exertions by the time the bottle came, and was allowed to suck the spoon, after Nat had manfully taken a dose, and had the bit of flannel put about his throat.

These first steps toward a cure were hardly completed, when a great bell rang, and a loud tramping through the hall announced supper. Bashful Nat quaked at the thought of meeting many strange boys, but Mrs. Bhaer held out her hand to him, and Rob said, patronizingly, "Don't be afraid; I'll take care of you."

Twelve boys, six on a side, stood behind their chairs, prancing with impatience to begin, while the tall flute-playing youth was trying to curb their ardor. But no one sat down, till Mrs. Bhaer was in her place behind the teapot, with Teddy on her left, and Nat on her right.

"This is our new boy, Nat Blake. After supper you can say, 'How do you do?' Gently, boys, gently."

As she spoke every one stared at Nat, and then whisked into their seats, trying to be orderly, and failing utterly. The Bhaers did their best to have the lads behave well at meal times, and generally succeeded pretty well, for their rules were few and sensible, and the boys, knowing that they tried to make things easy and happy, did their best to obey. But there are times when hungry boys cannot be repressed without real cruelty, and Saturday evening, after a half-holiday, was one of those times.

"Dear little souls, do let them have one day in which they can howl and racket and frolic, to their hearts' content. A holiday isn't a holiday without plenty of freedom and fun; and they shall have full swing once a week," Mrs. Bhaer used to say, when prim people wondered why banister-sliding, pillow-fights, and all manner of jovial games were allowed under the once decorous roof of Plumfield.

It did seem at times as if the aforesaid roof was in danger of flying off; but it never did, for a word from Father Bhaer could at any time produce a lull, and the lads had learned that liberty must not be abused. So, in spite of many dark predictions, the school flourished, and manners and morals were insinuated, without the pupils exactly knowing how it was done.

Alcott, Louisa May. *Little Men.* New York: Random House, 1991.

CHEAPER BY THE DOZEN

Frank B. Gilbreth, Jr. and
Ernestine Gilbreth Carey

The dozen red-headed children in the Gilbreth family make for a guaranteed onslaught of rollicking adventures—especially when faced with their inimitable father, whose quest for efficiency and innovation is relentless. This portion of their true-life memoir takes place on their annual excursion to Nantucket Island in Massachusetts.

Chapter 11   NANTUCKET

We spent our summers at Nantucket, Massachusetts, where Dad bought two lighthouses, which had been abandoned by the government, and a ramshackle cottage, which looked as if it had been abandoned by Coxey's Army. Dad had the lighthouses moved so that they flanked the cottage. He and Mother used one of them as an office and den. The other served as a bedroom for three of the children.

He named the cottage The Shoe, in honor of Mother, who, he said, reminded him of the old woman who lived in one. The cottage and lighthouses were situated on a flat stretch of land between the fashionable Cliff and the Bathing Beach. Besides our place, there was only one other house in the vicinity. This belonged to an artist couple named Whitney. But after our first summer at Nantucket, the Whitneys had their house jacked up, placed on rollers, and moved a mile away to a vacant lot near the tip of Brant Point. After that, we had the strip of land all to ourselves.

Customarily, en route from Montclair to Nantucket, we spent the night in a hotel in New London, Connecticut. Dad knew the hotel manager and all of the men at desk, and they used to exchange loud and good-natured insults for the benefit of the crowds that followed us in from the street.

"Oh, Lord, look what's coming," the manager called when we entered the door. And then to an assistant, "Alert the fire department and the house detective. It's the Gilbreths. And take that cigar-cutter off the counter and lock it in the safe."

"Do you still have that dangerous guillotine?" Dad grinned. "I know you'll be disappointed to hear that the finger grew in just as good as new. Show the man your finger, Ernestine."

Ernestine held up the little finger of her right hand. On a previous visit, she had pushed it inquisitively into the cigar cutter, and had lost about an eighth of an inch of it. She had bled considerably on a rug, while Dad tried to fashion a tourniquet and roared inquiries about whether there was a doctor in the house.

"Tell me," Dad remarked as he picked up a pen to register in the big book, "do my Irishmen come cheaper by the dozen?"

"Irishmen! If I were wearing a sheet, you'd call them Arabs. How many of them are there, anyway? Last year, when I went to make out your bill, you claimed there were only seven. I can count at least a dozen of them now."

"It's quite possible there may have been some additions since then," Dad conceded.

"Front, boy. Front, boy. Front, boy. Front, boy. You four boys show Mr. and Mrs. Gilbreth and their seven—or so—Irishmen to 503, 504, 505, 506, and 507. And mind you take good care of them, too."

When we first started going to Nantucket, which is off the tip of Cape Cod, automobiles weren't allowed on the island, and we'd leave the Pierce Arrow in a garage at New Bedford, Massachusetts. Later, when the automobile ban was lifted, we'd take the car with us on the Gay Head or the Sankaty, the steamers which plied between the mainland and the island. Dad had a frightening time backing the automobile up the gangplank. Mother insisted that we get out of the car and stand clear. Then she'd beg Dad to put on a life preserver.

"I know you and it are going into the water one of these days," she warned.

"Doesn't anybody, even my wife, have confidence in my driving?" he would moan. Then on a more practical note, "Besides, I can swim."

The biggest problem, on the boat and in the car, was Martha's two canaries, which she had won for making the best recitation in Sunday school. All of us, except Dad, were fond of them. Dad called one of them Shut Up and the other You Heard Me. He said they smelled so much that they ruined his whole trip, and were the only creatures on earth with voices louder than his children. Tom Grieves, the handyman, who had to clean up the cage, named the birds Peter Soil and Maggie Mess. Mother wouldn't let us use those full names, she said they were "Eskimo." (Eskimo was Mother's description of anything that was off-color, revolting, or evil-minded.) We called the birds simply Peter and Maggie.

On one trip, Fred was holding the cage on the stern of the ship, while Dad backed the car aboard. Somehow, the wire door popped open and the birds escaped. They flew to a piling on the dock, and then to a roof of a warehouse. When Dad, with the car finally stowed away, appeared on deck, three of the younger children were sobbing. They made so much noise that the captain heard them and came off the bridge.

"What's the trouble now, Mr. Gilbreth?" he asked.

"Nothing," said Dad, who saw a chance to put 30 miles between himself and the canaries. "You can shove off at any time captain."

331

"No one tells me when to shove off until I'm ready to shove off," the captain announced stubbornly. He leaned over Fred. "What's the matter, son?"

"Peter and Maggie," bawled Fred. "They've gone over the rail."

"My God," the captain blanched. "I've been afraid this would happen ever since you Gilbreths started coming to Nantucket."

"Peter and Maggie aren't Gilbreths," Dad said irritatedly. "Why don't you just forget about the whole thing and shove off?"

The captain leaned over Fred again. "Peter and Maggie who? Speak up, boy!"

Fred stopped crying. "I'm not allowed to tell you their last names," he said. "Mother says they're Eskimo."

The captain was bewildered. "I wish someone would make sense," he complained. "You say Peter and Maggie, the Eskimos, have disappeared over the rail?"

Fred nodded. Dad pointed to the empty cage. "Two canaries," Dad shouted, "known as Peter and Maggie and by other aliases, have flown the coop. No matter. We wouldn't think of delaying you further."

"Where did they fly to, sonny?"

Fred pointed to the roof of the warehouse. The captain sighed.

"I can't stand to see children cry," he said. He walked back to the bridge and started giving orders.

Four crew members, armed with crab nets, climbed to the roof of the warehouse. While passengers shouted encouragements from the rail, the men chased the birds across the roof, back to the dock, onto the rigging of the ship, and back to the warehouse again. Finally Peter and Maggie disappeared altogether, and the captain had to give up.

"I'm sorry, Mr. Gilbreth," he said. "I guess we'll have to shove off without your canaries."

"You've been too kind already," Dad beamed.

Dad felt good for the rest of the trip, and even managed to convince Martha of the wisdom of throwing the empty, but still smelly, bird cage over the side of the ship.

The next day, after we settled in our cottage, a cardboard box arrived from the captain. It was addressed to Fred, and it had holes punched in the top.

"You don't have to tell me what's in it," Dad said glumly. "I've got a nose." He reached in his wallet and handed Martha a bill. "Take this and go down to the village and buy another cage. And after this, I hope you'll be more careful of your belongings."

Dad had promised before we came to Nantucket that there would be no formal studying—no language records and no schoolbooks. He kept his promise, although we found he was always teaching us things informally, when our backs were turned.

For instance, there was the matter of the Morse code.

"I have a way to teach you the code without any studying," he announced one day at lunch.

We said we didn't want to learn the code, that we didn't want to learn anything until school started in the fall.

"There's no studying," said Dad, "and the ones who learn it first will get rewards. The ones who don't learn it are going to wish they had."

After lunch, he got a small paint brush and a can of black enamel, and locked himself in the lavatory, where he painted the alphabet in code on the wall.

For the next three days Dad was busy with his paint brush, writing code over the whitewash in every room in The Shoe. On the ceiling in the dormitory bedrooms, he wrote the alphabet together with key words, whose accents were a reminder of the code for the various letters. It went like this: A, dot-dash, a-BOUT; B, dash-dot-dot-dot, BOIS-ter-ous-ly; C, dash-dot-dash-dot, CARE-less CHILD-ren; D, dash-dot-dot, DAN-ger-ous, etc.

When you lay on your back, dozing, the words kept going through your head, and you'd find yourself saying, "DAN-ger-ous, dash-dot-dot, DAN-ger-ous."

He painted secret messages in code on the walls of the front porch and dining room.

"What do they say, Daddy?" we asked him.

"Many things," he replied mysteriously. "Many secret things and many things of great humor."

We went into the bedrooms and copied the code alphabet on pieces of paper. Then, referring to the paper, we started translating Dad's messages. He went right on painting, as if he were paying no attention to us, but he didn't miss a word.

"Lord, what awful puns," said Anne. "And this, I presume, is meant to fit into the category of 'things of great humor.' Listen to this one: 'Bee it ever so bumble there's no place like comb.'"

"And we're stung," Ern moaned. "We're not going to be satisfied until we translate them all. I see dash-dot-dash-dot, and I hear myself repeating CARE-less CHILD-ren. What's this one say?"

We figured it out: "When igorots is bliss, 'tis folly to be white." And another, by courtesy of Mr. Irvin S. Cobb, "Eat, drink and be merry for tomorrow you may diet." And still another, which Mother made Dad paint out, "Two maggots were fighting in dead Ernest."

"That one is Eskimo," said Mother. "I won't have it in my dining room, even in Morse code."

"All right, boss," Dad grinned sheepishly. "I'll paint over it. It's already served its purpose, anyway."

Every day or so after that, Dad would leave a piece of paper, containing a Morse code message, on the dining room table. Translated, it might read something like this: "The first one who figures out this secret message should look in the right hand pocket of my linen knickers, hanging on a hook in my room. Daddy." Or: "Hurry up before someone beats you to it, and look in the bottom left drawer of the sewing machine."

In the knickers' pocket and in the drawer would be some sort of reward—a Hershey bar, a quarter, a receipt entitling the bearer to one chocolate ice cream soda at Coffin's Drug Store, payable by Dad on demand.

Some of the Morse code notes were false alarms. "Hello, Live Bait. This one is on the house. No reward. But there may be a reward next time. When you finish reading this, dash off like mad so the next fellow will think you are on some hot clue. Then he'll read it, too, and you won't be the only one who got fooled. Daddy."

As Dad had planned, we all knew the Morse code fairly well within a few weeks. Well enough, in fact, so that we could tap out messages to each other by bouncing the tip of a fork on a butter plate. When a dozen or so persons all attempt to broadcast in this manner, and all of us preferred sending to receiving, the accumulation is loud and nerve-shattering. A present-day equivalent might be reproduced if the sound-effects man on Gangbusters and Walter Winchell should go on the air simultaneously, before a battery of powerful amplifiers.

Gilbreth, Frank L. and Gilbreth Carey, Ernestine. *Cheaper by the Dozen*. New York: Bantam, Starfire, 1984.

POLLYANNA

ELEANOR H. PORTER

Pollyanna is alone in the world but she has a giant imagination. When she goes to stay with her cold aunt and is given the tiny attic room as a welcome, she realizes what her new life is going to be like. But then she sees the tree outside her window.

Chapter 4 THE LITTLE ATTIC ROOM

iss Polly Harrington did not rise to meet her niece. She looked up from her book, it is true, as Nancy and the little girl appeared in the sitting room doorway, and she held out a hand with duty written large on every coldly extended finger.

"How do you do, Pollyanna? I—" She had no chance to say more. Pollyanna had fairly flown across the room and flung herself into her aunt's scandalized, unyielding lap.

"Oh, Aunt Polly, Aunt Polly, I don't know how to be glad enough that you let me come to live with you," she was sobbing. "You don't know how perfectly lovely it is to have you and Nancy and all this after you've had just the Ladies' Aid!"

"Very likely—though I've not had the pleasure of the Ladies' Aid's acquaintance," rejoined Miss Polly stiffly, trying to unclasp the small, clinging fingers and turning frowning eyes on Nancy in the doorway. "Nancy, that will do. You may go. Pollyanna, be good enough, please, to stand erect in a proper manner. I don't know yet what you look like."

Pollyanna drew back at once, laughing a little hysterically.

"No, I suppose you don't—but you see I'm not very much to look at anyway, on account of the freckles. Oh, and I ought to explain about the red gingham and the black velvet basque with white spots on the elbows. I told Nancy how Father said—"

"Yes; well, never mind now what your father said," interrupted Miss Polly crisply. "You had a trunk, I presume?"

"Oh, yes, indeed, Aunt Polly. I've got a beautiful trunk that the Ladies' Aid gave me. I haven't got so very much in it—of my own, I mean. The barrels haven't had many clothes for little girls in them lately. But here were all Father's books, and Mrs. White said she thought I ought to have those. You see Father—"

"Pollyanna," interrupted her aunt again sharply, "there is one thing that might just as well be understood right away at once. And that is, I do not care to have you keep talking of your father to me."

The little girl drew in her breath tremulously.

"Why, Aunt Polly, you—you mean . . ." She hesitated, and her aunt filled the pause.

"We will go upstairs to your room. Your trunk is already there, I presume. I told Timothy to take it up—if you had one. You may follow me, Pollyanna."

Without speaking Pollyanna turned and followed her aunt from the room. Her eyes were brimming with tears, but her chin was bravely high.

After all, I—I reckon I'm glad she doesn't want to talk about Father, Pollyanna was thinking. It'll be easier, maybe—if I don't talk about him. Probably, anyhow, that is why she told me not to talk about him. And Pollyanna, convinced anew of her aunt's "kindness," blinked off the tears and looked eagerly about her.

She was on the stairway now. Just ahead her aunt's black silk skirt rustled luxuriously. Behind her an open door allowed a glimpse of soft-tinted rugs and satin-covered chairs. Beneath her feet a marvelous carpet was like green moss to the tread. On every side the gilt of picture frames or the glint of sunshine through the filmy mesh of lace curtains flashed in her eyes.

"Oh, Aunt Polly, Aunt Polly," breathed the little girl rapturously, "what a perfectly lovely, lovely house! How awfully glad you must be you're so rich!"

"Pollyanna!" ejaculated her aunt, turning sharply about as she reached the head of the stairs. "I'm surprised at you—making a speech like that to me!"

"Why, Aunt Polly, aren't you?" queried Pollyanna in frank wonder.

"Certainly not, Pollyanna. I hope I could not so far forget myself as to be sinfully proud of any gift the Lord has seen fit to bestow upon me," declared the lady, "certainly not of riches!"

Miss Polly turned and walked down the hall toward the attic stairway door. She was glad, now, that she had put the child in the attic room. Her idea at first had been to get her niece as far away as possible from herself, and at the same time place her where her childish heedlessness would not destroy valuable furnishings. Now—with this evident strain of vanity showing thus early—it was all the more fortunate that the room planned for her was plain and sensible, thought Miss Polly.

Eagerly Pollyanna's small feet pattered behind her aunt. Still more eagerly her big blue eyes tried to look in all directions at once, that no thing of beauty or interest in this wonderful house might be passed unseen. Most eagerly of all her mind turned to the wondrously exciting problem about to be solved: behind which of all these fascinating doors was waiting now her room—the dear, beautiful room full of curtains, rugs, and pictures that was to be her very own? Then, abruptly, her aunt opened a door and ascended another stairway.

There was little to be seen here. A bare wall rose on either side. A the top of the stairs wide reaches of shadowy space led to far corners where the roof came almost down to the floor, and where were stacked innumerable trunks and boxes. It was hot and stifling too. Unconsciously Pollyanna lifted her head higher—it seemed so hard to breathe. Then she saw that her aunt had thrown open a door at the right.

"There, Pollyanna, here is your room, and your trunk is here, I see. Have you your key?"

Pollyanna nodded dumbly. Her eyes were a little wide and frightened.

Her aunt frowned.

"When I ask a question, Pollyanna, I prefer that you should answer aloud—not merely with your head."

"Yes, Aunt Polly."

"Thank you; that is better. I believe you have everything that you need here," she added, glancing at the well-filled towel rack and water pitcher. "I will send Nancy up to help you unpack. Supper is at six o'clock," she finished as she left the room and swept downstairs.

For a moment after she had gone Pollyanna stood quite still, looking after her. Then she turned her wide eyes to the bare wall, the bare floor, the bare windows. She turned them last to the little trunk that had stood not so long before in her own little room in the faraway Western home. The next moment she stumbled blindly toward it and fell on her knees at its side, covering her face with her hands.

Nancy found her there when she came up a few minutes later.

"There, there, you poor lamb," she crooned, dropping to the floor and drawing the little girl into her arms. "I was just a-fearin' I'd find you like this, like this."

Pollyanna shook her head.

"But I'm bad and wicked, Nancy—awful wicked," she sobbed. "I just can't make myself understand that God and the angels needed my father more than I did."

"No more they did neither," declared Nancy, stoutly.

"Ohh—Nancy!" The burning horror in Pollyanna's eyes dried the tears.

Nancy gave a shamefaced smile and rubbed her own eyes vigorously.

"There, there, child, I didn't mean it, of course," she cried briskly. "Come, let's have your key and we'll get inside this trunk and take out your dresses in no time, no time."

Somewhat tearfully Pollyanna produced the key.

"There aren't very many there, anyway," she faltered.

"Then they're all the sooner unpacked," declared Nancy.

Pollyanna gave a sudden radiant smile.

"That's so! I can be glad of that, can't I?" she cried.

Nancy stared.

"Why, of—course," she answered a little uncertainly.

Nancy's capable hands made short work of unpacking the books, the patched undergarments, and the few pitifully unattractive dresses. Pollyanna, smiling bravely now, flew about, hanging the dresses in the closet, stacking the books on the table, and putting away the undergarments in the bureau drawers.

"I'm sure it—it's going to be a very nice room. Don't you think so?" she stammered after a while.

There was no answer. Nancy was very busy, apparently, with her head in the trunk. Pollyanna, staring at the bureau, gazed a little wistfully at the bare wall above.

And I can be glad there isn't any looking glass here, too, 'cause where there isn't any glass I can't see my freckles."

Nancy made a sudden queer little sound with her mouth—but when Pollyanna turned, her head was in the trunk again. At one of the windows, a few minutes later, Pollyanna gave a glad cry and clapped her hands joyously.

"Oh, Nancy, I hadn't seen this before," she breathed. "Look—way off there, with those trees and the houses and that lovely church spire, and the river shining just like silver. Why, Nancy, there doesn't anybody need any pictures with that to look at. Oh, I'm so glad now she let me have this room!"

To Pollyanna's surprise and dismay Nancy burst into tears. Pollyanna hurriedly crossed to her side.

"Why, Nancy, Nancy—what is it?" she cried; then, fearfully: "This wasn't—your room, was it?"

"My room!" stormed Nancy hotly, choking back the tears. "If you ain't a little angel straight from heaven, and if some folks don't eat dirt before—Oh, land! There's her bell!" After which amazing speech Nancy sprang to her feet, dashed out of the room, and went clattering down the stairs.

Left alone, Pollyanna went back to her "picture," as she mentally designated the beautiful view from the window. After a time she touched the sash tentatively. It seemed as if no longer could she endure the stifling heat. To her joy the sash moved under her fingers. The next moment the window was wide open, and Pollyanna was leaning far out, drinking in the fresh, sweet air.

She ran then to the other window. That, too, soon flew up under her eager hands. A big fly swept past her nose and buzzed noisily about the room. Then another came, and another, but Pollyanna paid no heed. Pollyanna had made a wonderful discovery—against this window a huge tree flung great branches. To Pollyanna they looked like arms out-stretched, inviting her.

Porter, Eleanor. *Pollyanna*. New York: Bantam, 1990.

THE PUSHCART WAR

JEAN MERRILL

The streets of New York City were jam-packed with huge trucks that blocked traffic and bullied anything in their way, so the pushcart peddlers decided to go to war against the trucks. They thought of an ingenious secret weapon—pea shooters that shoot peas with pins in them, to pop truck tires. Here is the story of the day when the Pea Shooter Campaign began, Mr. Jerusalem struggled with his conscience, and he finally triumphed over Louie Livergreen's Leaping Lema truck.

Chapter XXII THE PEA SHOOTER CAMPAIGN—PHASE I

t took a week for the pushcart peddlers to prepare for their attack. Maxie Hammerman kept his shop open 24 hours a day, and the peddlers in teams of 20 men took turns putting the pins in peas. Carlos made all 509 shooters himself. He cut them from a roll of yellow plastic tubing that a storekeeper had given him for taking away his cartons for 10 years at no charge.

At last, everything was ready. The attack was set for the morning of March 23rd. The evening before, the peddlers all reported to Maxie Hammerman's shop to collect their shooters and 24 rounds of ammunition each.

General Anna outlined the plan of battle. Everyone was to go to the location where he usually did business. He was to wait until 10:00 a.m., when the morning traffic would be well under way. At 10:00 sharp, he was to fire at the tires of the any trucks that came in range.

Frank the Flower had wanted Wanda Gambling to fire the opening shot from in front of the Empire State Building, but General Anna felt that this would attract too much attention.

"Where there is a movie star," said General Anna, "there is a crowd. We do not want the trucks to know what is hitting them."

So the Pea Shooter Campaign began in quite an ordinary way. Between 10:05 a.m. and 10:10 a.m. on March 23rd, 97 truck drivers in different parts of the city discovered that they had flat tires. Not one of the drivers knew what had hit him.

Ninety-seven hits (out of some five hundred pea-pins that were fired in the opening attack) is, according to the Amateur Weapons Association, a very good average, especially as many of the peddlers had never handled a pea shooter before. And there were a few, like Mr. Jerusalem, who had grave doubts about the whole idea.

Mr. Jerusalem's heart was not in the attack. Though he had voted with the other peddlers to fight the trucks, fighting of any sort went against his nature. Mr. Jerusalem's performance on the first morning of the Pea Shooter Campaign is, therefore, of special interest.

At the time of the Pushcart War, Mr. Jerusalem was already an old man. No one knew exactly how old. He was held in great respect by the other pushcart peddlers, because his cart was not only his business, but it was also his home.

Unlike the other peddlers, Mr. Jerusalem did not have a room where he went to sleep or cook his meals. Instead he had a small frying pan, a cup, and a tin plate which he hung neatly from the underside of his cart. He had a charcoal burner built into one corner of the cart so that he could cook for himself whenever he felt like a hot meal.

Mr Jerusalem's favorite joke was: "Some people go out to dinner on special occasions. I eat out all the time." This was true. Mr. Jerusalem was often to be seen sitting on a curb eating a plate of beans or turnips that he had cooked himself.

At night Mr. Jerusalem dropped canvas sheets over the sides of his cart so that there was a sort of tent underneath the cart. Then he would park the cart under a tree or in a vacant lot, crawl under the cart, roll up in a quilt, and go to sleep. In the summer he often did not bother with the canvas sheets, but slept alongside the cart so that he could see the stars. He was usually the first peddler on the streets in the morning.

Mr. Jerusalem had lived this way for 50 or 60 years, and he had never picked a fight with anyone. His motto was: "I live the way I want. You don't bother me. And I won't bother you."

Having lived by this motto for so long, Mr. Jerusalem was not happy about the Pea Shooter Campaign. To be sure, he had a great deal more at stake than the other peddlers. In his case, it was not only his business, but his home that was in danger as long as the

trucks continued to attack the pushcarts. Still it went against his deepest convictions to cause another man trouble.

"There are not troubles enough in the world?" he had asked himself as he had worked alongside the other peddlers, putting pins in the peas. "Why should I make more?"

Mr. Jerusalem was still asking himself this question as he set off down Delancey Street on the morning of March 23rd. Like the other peddlers, Mr. Jerusalem was fully armed, although no one walking down the street would have noticed.

Anyone glancing at Mr. Jerusalem would have taken the yellow plastic straw sticking from his coat pocket for a yellow pencil. And no one would have taken any notice at all of the two dozen peas with a pin stuck carefully through the center of each, which Mr. Jerusalem had pinned to the sleeve of his jacket.

Or, even if someone had noticed, he would have supposed that Mr. Jerusalem had 24 tiny sleeve buttons on his jacket. Mr. Jerusalem's clothes never looked like anyone else's anyway. He picked them up here and there, secondhand, and he had his own style of wearing them.

"A sleeveful of ammunition!" Mr. Jerusalem muttered to himself, as he set off on the morning of March 23rd to pick up a secondhand popcorn machine that he had arranged to buy. "Who would believe it?

"A man my age—going to war!" Mr. Jerusalem shook his head sadly. "I can hardly believe it myself.

341

"Fighting in the streets!" he continued. "A man of peace for 80 years is walking fully armed down Delancey Street. A man who does not care for fighting."

"It is not only that I do not care for fighting," he went on.

"Naturally, I do not care for fighting," he admitted. "But it is also that fighting a 10-ton truck with a pea shooter is a little crazy. I do not think it will work."

"But what else can we do?" he asked himself.

He could not think of anything else. "So I will fight," he said. "If I have to," he added.

All the same, Mr. Jerusalem was relieved when at 10:00, the hour the attack was to begin, there was no truck parked within a hundred feet of his cart. Mr. Jerusalem did not think he could hit the tire of a moving truck.

"Would General Anna want me to waste the ammunition?" he asked himself. "Or Maxie Hammerman? Or Miss Wanda Gambling who has been so kind as to pay for one ton of pins? Not to mention the peas."

When Mr. Jerusalem arrived at the candy store where he was to pick up the popcorn machine, he parked his cart. He was just starting into the store, when someone shouted at him.

Mr. Jerusalem looked around and saw a Leaping Lema. The driver of the Leaping Lema was trying to back into a space in front of Mr. Jerusalem's cart. The truck was loaded with new glass-and-chromium popcorn machines.

Now if there was any kind of truck that Mr. Jerusalem did not like, it was a Leaping Lema. The reason for this was that Mr. Jerusalem had known Louie Livergreen's father.

Louie's father had been, before his death, one of the most-respected pushcart peddlers in the secondhand-clothes line. Mr. Jerusalem had often made a cup of tea on his charcoal burner for Solomon Livergreen when he and Solomon were working on the same street.

Mr. Jerusalem should have been glad that Solomon's son was a big success—people said Louie Livergreen now owned 100 big trucks. But Mr. Jerusalem held it against Louie Livergreen that from the day Louie had got his first truck, he had never come to see his father again. So every time Mr. Jerusalem saw a Leaping Lema on the streets, he thought, "They are breaking up family life."

As he watched the Leaping Lema backing into the curb on the first day of the Pea Shooter Campaign, Mr. Jerusalem wondered what his old friend Solomon Livergreen would have thought of the Pushcart War. Would Solomon, he wondered, have shot at a truck belonging to his own son, Louie Livergreen? And what would Solomon have wished his old friend Mr. Jerusalem to do?

"Shoot if you have to." That is what Solomon Livergreen would say, Mr. Jerusalem said to himself.

Mr. Jerusalem's conversation with Solomon Livergreen was interrupted by the driver of the Leaping Lema.

"Hey, Bud," shouted the driver. "Stop talking to yourself and move the baby buggy!" The driver was Little Miltie, a driver mentioned in the diary of Joey Kafflis.

Mr. Jerusalem frowned. It was bad enough that Little Miltie, a man one half the age of Mr. Jerusalem and not as tall, should call Mr. Jerusalem "Bud." But that Little Miltie should call Mr. Jerusalem's cart, which was also his home, a "baby buggy"—this was unnecessarily rude. However, Mr. Jerusalem answered courteously.

"I will only be a minute," he said.

"I can't wait a minute," said Little Miltie. "I got to deliver a popcorn machine."

"Well," said Mr. Jerusalem, "I have to pick up a popcorn machine. And until I pick up this secondhand popcorn machine, there will be no room in the store for a new machine such as you wish to deliver." And he turned to go about his business.

But as Mr. Jerusalem started into the candy store, Little Miltie raced his motor. Mr. Jerusalem hesitated. He remembered what had happened to Morris the Florist. He glanced over his shoulder.

"I'm backing up, Bud," Little Miltie said.

Mr. Jerusalem sighed and walked back to move his cart to the other side of the street. Little Miltie grinned. "That's a good boy, Buster."

Mr. Jerusalem did not reply, but as Little Miltie was backing into the place Mr. Jerusalem had left, the old peddler took out his pea shooter. He looked at it doubtfully.

"A man my age—with a pea shooter!" he sighed. "Such a craziness on Delancey Street." However, he inserted one of the pea-pins, took careful aim—and fired.

For a moment nothing happened. Mr. Jerusalem felt foolish. "All right, I admit it," he said. "We are all crazy."

Mr. Jerusalem was about to drop his pea shooter in the gutter when he heard a slight hissing sound—the sound of air escaping from a tire.

"Or perhaps not so crazy," said Mr. Jerusalem.

He put the pea shooter back in this pocket and went to collect the popcorn machine. When he came out of the candy store, one of Little Miltie's rear tires was quite flat. Little Miltie was stamping up and down in the street and speaking even more rudely to the tire than he had spoken to Mr. Jerusalem.

"What is the matter?" asked Mr. Jerusalem. "The Leaping Lema is not leaping so good? A little trouble maybe?"

But Little Miltie was too angry to reply.

"Believe me, Solomon," he continued, as he roped the popcorn machine onto his cart, "to cause a little trouble now and then is maybe good for a man."

"But, Solomon," he asked as he set off down Delancey Street, "who would have thought a man of my age would be such a good shot?

"Naturally, it pays to use high-quality pin," he added.

Although Mr. Jerusalem knew where he could get a good price for the secondhand popcorn machine, he was now in no hurry to get there. He paused to look over every truck that had stopped for a traffic light or had pulled up to a curb to make a delivery.

Mr. Jerusalem chose his targets very carefully, and to his astonishment he hit four more trucks before he ran out of ammunition. At 2:30 in the afternoon, he headed back to Marie Hammerman's for more pea-pins. He still had not got around to selling his popcorn machine.

Merrill, Jean. *The Pushcart War*. New York: Dell Yearling, 1987.
    Other editions:
    ——. *The Pushcart War*, New York: HarperCollins, HarperCollins Children's Books, 1992.

ROBIN HOOD

Retold by Louis Rhead

The dashing character of Robin Hood, the benevolent outlaw who gathered together a band of "merry men" to steal from the rich and give to the poor, has been beloved by generations. Is he based on a real, historical figure, or just the stuff of legend? We're not really sure. Louis Rhead, an Englishman working at the turn of the century, created a compelling version of this hero. The first of the two stories collected here recounts the first meeting of Robin and one of his staunchest friends. The second tale reveals Robin in a prankish mood: Fearing himself bested by Little John for cleverness, he sets out to commit mischief on a scale large enough to prove that he is still king of the forest.

ROBIN HOOD FIGHTS LITTLE JOHN

obin said to his jolly bowmen, "This day I mean to fare forth to seek adventures. Mayhap I shall find some tall knight or fat abbot with an overfull purse."

Picking out a few followers, he said to the rest, "Pray, tarry, my merry men, in this our grove, and see that ye heed well my call, for should I be hard bestead I will sound three blasts on my horn, and then ye shall know that I am in dire need. So come to help me with all speed."

So saying, he wended his way with those he had chosen, to the outskirts of Sherwood Forest. At last they came to a meadow hard by a village, through which flowed a stream, little but deep.

"Bide here, my lads," quoth Robin, "behind these trees, while I go forth to meet yon tall fellow whom I see stalking forth this way."

So Robin started toward a long, narrow bridge made of a huge, flattened tree-trunk that spanned the brook. Now it chanced that both he and the stranger set foot upon the bridge at the same instant. They eyed each other up and down, and Robin said to himself, "This tall, lusty blade would be a proper man for our band, for he stands nigh seven foot high, and hath a mighty frame." Then, to test if the fellow's valor were equal to his height, bold Robin sturdily stood and said, "Get off the bridge and give way. Dost thou not see there's no room for both to cross?"

"Get off thyself, thou saucy knave, or I'll baste thy hide with my staff," the stranger replied.

Then Robin drew from his quiver a long, straight shaft and fitted it to his bow-string.

"Thou pratest like an ass," quoth he. "Ere thou couldst strike me one blow I could send this goose-winged shaft through thy heart."

"None but a base coward would shoot at my breast while I have naught but a staff in my hand to reach thee."

At this Robin lowered his bow and thrust the shaft back into the quiver. "I scorn thee," he said, "as I do the name of a coward, and to prove that I fear thee not let me lay by my long-bow and choose a tough staff of ground-oak from yonder thicket. Then here upon this narrow bridge we will fight, and whosoever shall be doused in the brook shall own himself beaten."

The tall stranger replied, "That suits me full well to a dot, and here will I abide till thou comest."

Then bold Robin strode off to the thicket, where he cut and trimmed a trusty, knotted six-foot staff. Sooth to say, the more he looked upon the stranger the less he relished coming to blows with him, for he thought he had never seen a sturdier knave. None the less, he stepped upon the bridge and began to flourish his staff above his head right bravely. With watchful eyes and careful tread both stepped forward till they met in the middle.

In a trice, Robin gave the stranger a crack on his broad neck that made his bones ring like stones in a tin can; but he was as tough as he was big, and he said naught but, "One good turn deserves another." With that, he whirled his great staff faster and faster, bringing it down on Robin's guard with such a rain of blows that one would think twenty men were at it. Both played so rapidly and the blows were so deftly struck that neither one after half an hour's battle seemed to gain a whit. Robin tried all his skill in parrying and feinting, but he could do no more than give the stranger a whack on his ribs and shoulder which only made him grunt. As he began to grow weary the other laid on the faster, so that Robin's jacket smoked with many a thwack and he felt as if he were on fire.

At last he got a crack on the crown that caused the blood to flow down his cheek, but he only fought the more fiercely and pressed on so hard that the stranger slipped and nigh fell over. But he regained his footing, and with a furious onslaught he brought his staff down with such tremendous force that he smashed Robin's staff into smithers and topped him with a great splash full on his back into the brook.

"Prithee, good fellow, where art thou now?" quoth the stranger.

"Good faith, in the flood," quoth Robin, "and floating along with the tide."

Thereupon he waded the stream and pulled himself up on the bank by an overhanging branch. He sat him down, wet to the skin, and laughingly cried, "My brave soul, thou hast won the bout, and I'll no longer fight with thee." So saying, he set his horn to his lips and blew a loud blast, whereat the stout yeomen came running forth from behind the trees.

"Oh, what is the matter, good master?" they cried. "Thou art as wet as a drown'd rat."

"Matter or no matter," quoth Robin, "yon tall fellow hath in fighting tumbled me into the brook."

"Seize him, comrades, for in the brook he shall likewise go to cool his hot spirit," said one.

"Nay, nay, forbear," cried Robin, "he is a stout fellow. They shall do thee no harm, my tall friend. These bowmen are my followers, with three-score-and-nine others, and if thou wilt, my jolly blade, thou shalt join us and be my good right-hand man. Three good suits of Lincoln green shalt thou have each year and a full share in all we take. We'll teach thee to shoot the fat fallow deer, and thou shalt eat sweet venison steak whene'er thou wilt, washing down with foaming ale. What saist thou, sweet chuck?"

The stranger replied, "Here is my hand on't, and with my whole heart will I serve so bold a leader, for no man living doubteth that I, John Little, can play my part with the best. But on one condition will I join your band."

"And what may that be?" quoth Robin.

"It is that ye show me an archer who can mend a shot I shall shoot with stout long-bow and arrow."

"Well, thou shalt shoot," quoth Robin, "and we will mend thy shot if we may." So saying, he went and cut a willow wand about the thickness of a man's thumb and, peeling off the skin, set it up before a tree fivescore paces away. "Now," quoth he, "do thou choose a bow to thy liking from among all my men, and let us see thy skill."

"That I will, blithely," quoth John. Choosing the stoutest bow and straightest arrow he could find among a group lying on the sward, he took most careful aim, pulling the arching bow to its utmost stretch. The arrow flew, and lodged with its point right through the wand. "A brave shot!" cried the archers all.

"Canst thou mend that, bold outlaw?" asked John.

"I cannot mend the shot, but I'll notch thy shaft in twain." So saying, Robin took his bow, put on a new string, and chose a perfect, straight arrow with gray goose feathers truly tied. Then, bending the great bow, he let fly the shaft. For a moment the archers watched, breathless; then, with shouts of glee, they saw the stranger's arrow split fairly in twain.

"Enough," quoth John. "Never before have I seen so true an eye guide a shaft. Now I know an archer fit to serve."

All cried out that he had said well, and then in right merry mood they started back to their forest home, there to feast and christen their new comrade.

"What name shall we call this pretty sweet babe?"

A bald-headed yeoman, offering to act the part of priest, answered, "This infant," quoth he, "was called John Little, but that name we shall change anon. Henceforth, wherever he goes, not John Little but Little John shall he be called."

The liquor was then poured over John's head, trickling down his face; and so they baptized him. With shouts of laughter that made the forest ring, in which Little John Merrily joined, the christening came to an end with sweet song and jocund jest.

Then Robin took Little John to the treasure chamber and gave him a suit of Lincoln green and a great bow of yew.

ROBIN TRIES HIS HAND SELLING MEATS

ittle John had been getting the better of the Sheriff quite regularly, and, while Robin Hood owned that his right-hand man was craftier than he had thought, he resolved that he would not be outdone, but would himself show the Sheriff a thing or two. Robin and his band had no hatred against the Sheriff, nor, for that matter, against anyone else, much cause as they had to be bitter against the world, for they were all outlawed men. What they did was done in a spirit of jovial frolic and fun. It is certain that they never did any foul misdeed. They robbed the rich, who robbed others, that they might live and have means to help the poor and needy. In those cruel old days, when might seemed to make right, few were so kind and honest as Robin Hood and his merry men. Robin himself often went to mass at the little church on the outskirts of the forest, where he was welcomed because of his many lavish gifts. For he loved the humble and sincere churchmen even as he hated the purse-proud and selfish.

It fell upon a day that Robin started off alone through the forest singing a blithesome song. He had not gone far when he chanced to meet a jolly butcher, who likewise was singing merrily as he rode through the wood among the leaves so green. The butcher bestrode a fine mare, and swinging from behind on each side hung two great silk bags full of meat he was taking to Nottingham market to sell.

"Good morrow, my fine fellow," quoth jolly Robin. "Tell me what gods thou hast in thy panniers, for I have a mind for thy company and would fain know thy trade and where thou dost dwell."

"Truly, a butcher am I, and to Nottingham do I go to sell my meats. But what is it to thee where I do dwell? Tel me thy name."

"My name is Robin Hood, and in Sherwood do I dwell."

Then in a trembling voice the butcher said, "I cry your mercy, good Robin, for I fear that name. Have mercy on me and mind; let me go on my way."

"Nay, jolly butcher," quoth Robin, "fear nothing, for I will do thee no harm. Come, tell me, what is the price of thy meat and of they mare, for, by the mass, be it never so dear, I fain would be a butcher."

"I will soon tell thee," quoth the butcher. Then he looked straight before him and for a space seemed lost in thought. At last he said, "Good Robin, I like thee well and would not offend thee. Therefore thou shalt have my meats, and eke my bonny mare, for four marks, though the price be beggarly."

"Get down from they horse," quoth Robin, "and come, count out the money from my bag. Right gladly do I pay thy price, for I long to be a butcher for a day, and I warrant I shall sell my wares first of them all at the market."

When the butcher had seen the money counted aright he snugly packed it away in a little bag in his pouch, well content with his bargain; and Robin, mounting the horse, jogged off to Nottingham market. First of all, he got from the officers of the guild a market-stand, for which he paid a small fee. Then he put on the butcher's apron, cap, and jacket, cleaned off the stand, got out all the legs and shoulders of mutton and veal, sharpened his knives, and was soon busy with cleaver and saw, cutting up pieces to make the best display in the market.

All the other butchers looked askance at Robin because he was a stranger and seemed ignorant of the ways and sly tricks of the trade. However, when all was set out to the best advantage, he began to cry out in a loud voice, "Come hither, good people, come and buy, buy, buy. I sell good meat cheap, and cheap meat good. Pay no heed to the other butchers, for they sell naught but bone and skin. Be not backward good wives, good maids, good widows, and good spinsters; come up, come up and buy. I sell as much meat for one penny as you will get from the other butchers for three pennies. I will cut away all the fat and sell you the lean. An' it please you, good dames, I will strip away all the bones and sell naught but flesh. As for the bones, ye shall take them home to your dogs. Six pounds of good fresh meat, with never a bone, for one penny!"

So lustily did Robin cry his wares that soon a throng of dames and lasses pressed about his stand, while scarce a soul came near the booths of the other butchers. Ere long his trade was so brisk that he had no need to shout. Then, when a pretty lass asked the price of a piece of meat, he would answer, "Naught, but one kiss from thy pretty lips." Thus the handsome young butcher got many a kiss, which gladdened him more than silver coins. Long before the market closed Robin was clean sold out, and the others were full wroth because they had not thriven that day. They talked with one another, saying, "Surely he is some prodigal, that hath sold his father's land and now wastes the money in selling meat at so low a price." Said one, "Perhaps his is a man of much store and cattle. We had best be friendly with him." So several of them stepped up to Robin, saying, "Come, brother, we be all of one trade, and the Butchers' Guild is to dine with the Sheriff. Wilt thou join us in the feast?"

"Ay, marry, that will I," quoth merry Robin. "I will go with my true brethren as fast as I can hie."

So they all marched off together to the Sheriff's house. The Sheriff had been told of this wonderful butcher who could afford to sell as much meat for a penny as the others did for three pennies, so he made up his mind to place Robin beside him as the honored guest, thinking to lure the young spendthrift into some bad bargain.

While the butchers were drinking at Robin's expense they smiled and nudged one another and talked in whispers. "This is a mad blade," said one of them; "a wise one saves, and a fool spends." The Sheriff whispered to his left-hand neighbor, "His father hath left him lands which he hath sold for silver and gold, and now means to be rid of its cares." Then he said to himself, "'Twere a good deed to help him in so worthy a purpose."

"Good fellow," quoth he to Robin, "hast thou any horned beasts to sell unto me?"

"Yea, good master Sheriff, that I have—some 200, as well a 100 acres of good land, an it please you to see it. And I will make as good a bargain of it to you as my father did make to me."

"What is the price thou askest, my good fellow, for the two hundred horned beasts? For if the price be within reason, I warrant I shall find one who will buy."

"The price to thee noble Sheriff, shall be small enough. 'Tis but 200 pounds."

"Ay," thought the Sheriff, "but one quarter of their true worth. I must go to see these same horned beasts before it chance he change his price. By my faith good fellow," he said aloud, "I fain would look upon thy 200 horned beasts."

"That is easily done," quoth Robin, "for they are not far to seek."

So when the feast was ended the Sheriff had his palfrey saddled, put 200 pounds in gold in his pouch, and made ready to go with the spendthrift butcher. Robin saddled his mare, and away they rode to the forest of merry Sherwood.

As they were passing through the leafy woods the Sheriff crossed himself, saying, "God save us this day from that naughty varlet, Robin Hood!"

"Amen, so be it," said jolly Robin, who was leading deeper and deeper into the forest.

When they had gone a little farther, bold Robin chanced to spy 100 head of good red deer that came tripping along full nigh their path. "Look you," quote he, "how like you my horned beasts, good master Sheriff? Are they not fat and fair to see?"

Then the Sheriff was wroth and fearful. He trembled in his boots, for a sad thought of a sudden flashed through his brain. Quoth he, "I tell you, good fellow, I would I were gone from this forest, for I like not thy company nor thy fat beasts."

"Tarry but a moment, Sir Sheriff," quoth Robin, and, putting his horn to his mouth, he blew three blasts, whereat Little John and all his company came running.

"What is thy will, my good master?" cried Little John.

"I have brought hither," laughed jolly Robin, "the Sheriff of Nottingham this day to dine with three."

"Then, by Saint Swithin, he is right welcome to me, and I hope he will honestly pay for the feast, for I know he has gold. I can smell it in his pouch and I warrant if it be well counted there will be enough to serve us with wine to drink a whole year."

Then Little John lovingly grasped the Sheriff round the waist and drew him down from his palfrey. Taking his mantle gently from his back, he laid it on the ground. The proud Sheriff stood still and doleful while Robin opened his pouch and jingled out the 200 pounds in golden coins into the mantle. Little John carefully picked up the golden pieces and deftly cast the cloak again upon the Sheriff's back, then set him upon his dapple-gray palfrey, saying, "Adieu, good Sheriff, I wish thee a safe journey home."

Robin took the bridle-rein and led the palfrey to the edge of the forest, where he bade the Sheriff God-speed.

"Commend me to your lady wife at home," quoth he, "and tell her that Robin Hood found much profit in the butcher's trade in fair Nottingham town this day." So Robin went away laughing to his bower.

Robin Hood. Retold by Louis Rhead. New York: Random House, 1988.
Other Editions:
Ingle, Annie., ed. *Robin Hood.* New York: Random House, Random Books Young
Readers, 1993.
Creswick, Paul., *Robin Hood.* New York: Macmillan, Macmillan Children's Group, 1984.

THE STORY OF MACBETH

WILLIAM SHAKESPEARE
AS TOLD BY CHARLES AND MARY LAMB

William Shakespeare is regarded as perhaps the finest writer in the English language. His 37 dramas include tragedies, comedies, and historical plays. Macbeth, *published in 1623, is a tragic play about the life of a nobleman named Macbeth, a thane, who became king of Scotland.*

In the early 1800s Charles and Mary Lamb wove Shakespeare's plays into stories. This section of Macbeth *portrays the dark events leading up to a bloody act that will change Macbeth's life forever.*

hen Duncan the Meek reigned king of Scotland, there lived a great thane, or lord, called Macbeth. This Macbeth was a near kinsman to the king, and held in high esteem after defeating a rebel army.

The two Scottish generals, Macbeth and Banquo, returning victorious from this great battle, were stopped by the strange appearance of three figures, like women, except that they had beards, and their withered skins and wild attire made them not look like any earthly creatures. Macbeth first addressed them, when they, seemingly offended, laid each one her choppy finger upon her skinny lips, in token of silence: and the first of them saluted Macbeth with the title of thane of Glamis. The general was not a little startled to find himself known by such creatures; but how much more, when the second of them followed up that salute by giving him the title of thane of Cawdor, to which honor he had no pretensions! And again the third bid him, "All hail! King that shall be hereafter!" Such a prophetic greeting might well amaze him, who knew that while the king's sons lived he could not hope to succeed to the throne. Then turning to Banquo, they pronounced him, in a sort of riddling terms, to be lesser than Macbeth and greater! Not so happy, yet much happier! And predicted he shall never reign, but his sons will be Kings in Scotland. They then turned into air and vanished; by which the generals knew to be the weird sisters, or witches.

While they stood pondering on the strangeness of this adventure, there arrived certain messengers from the king, who were empowered by him to confer upon Macbeth the dignity of thane of Cawdor. An event so miraculously corresponding with the prediction of the witches astonished Macbeth, and he stood wrapt in amazement, unable to make reply to the messengers: and in that point of time swelling hopes arose in his mind, that the prediction of the third witch might in like manner have its accomplishment, and that he should one day reign king in Scotland.

Turning to Banquo, he said, "Do you not hope that your children shall be kings, when what the witches promised to me has so wonderfully come to pass?" "That hope," answered the general, "might enkindle you to aim at the throne; but often times these ministers of darkness tell us truths in little things to betray us into deeds of greatest consequence."

But the wicked suggestions of the witches had sunk too deep into the mind of Macbeth to allow him to attend to the warnings of the good Banquo. From that time he bent all his thoughts on how to compass the throne of Scotland.

Macbeth had a wife, to whom he communicated the strange prediction of the weird sisters, and its partial accomplishment. She was a bad, ambitious woman, and so as her husband and herself could arrive at greatness, she cared not by what means. She spurred on the reluctant purpose of Macbeth, who felt compunction at the thought of blood, and did not cease to represent the murder of the king as a step absolutely necessary to the fulfillment of the flattering prophecy.

The King and his sons, Malcolm and Donalbain, came to honor Macbeth. The king, being tired with his journey, went early to bed. He had been unusually pleased with his reception, and had made presents, before he retired, to his principal officers; and among the rest had sent a rich diamond to Lady Macbeth, greeting her by the name of his most kind hostess.

Now was the middle of the night, when over half the world nature seems dead, and wicked dreams abuse men's minds asleep, and none but the wolf and the murderer is abroad. This was the time when Lady Macbeth waked to plot the murder of the king. She would not have undertaken a deed so abhorrent to her sex, but that she feared her husband's nature, that it was too full of the milk of human kindness, to do a contrived murder. So with her own hands armed with a dagger, she approached the king's bed; having taken care to ply the grooms of his chamber so with wine that they slept intoxicated, and careless of their charge. There lay Duncan, in a sound sleep after the fatigues of his journey, and as she viewed him earnestly, there was something in his face, as he slept, which resembled her own father; and she had not the courage to proceed.

She returned to confer with her husband. His resolution had begun to stagger. He considered that there were strong reasons against the deed. In the first place, he was not only a subject but a near kinsman to the king; and he had been his host and entertainer that day, whose duty by the laws of hospitality it was to shut the door against his murderers, not bear the knife himself. Then he considered how just and merciful a king this Duncan had been. Besides, by the favors of the king, Macbeth stood high in the opinion of all sorts of men, and how would those honors be stained by the reputation of so foul a murder!

In these conflicts of the mind Lady Macbeth found her husband, inclining to the better part, and resolving to proceed no further. But she being a woman not easily shaken from her evil purpose, began to implore him about: how easy the deed was; how soon it would be over; and how the action of one short night would give to all their nights and days to come a sovereign sway and royalty! Then she threw contempt on his change of purpose, and accused him of fickleness and cowardice; and declared that she had given suck, and knew how tender it was to love the babe that milked her, but she would, while it was smiling in her face, have plucked it from her breast, and dashed its brains out, if she had so sworn to do it, so he had sworn to perform that murder. Then she added, how practicable it was to lay the guilt of the deed upon the drunken, sleepy grooms. And with the valor of her tongue she so chastised his sluggish resolutions, that he once more summoned up courage to the bloody business.

So, taking the dagger in his hand, he softly stole in the dark room where Duncan lay; and as he went, he thought he saw another dagger in the air, with the handle toward him, and on the blade and at the point of it drops of blood; but when he tried to grasp at it, it was nothing but air, a mere phantasm proceeding from his own hot and oppressed brain and the business he had in hand.

Getting rid of this fear, he entered the king's room, whom he dispatched with one stroke of his dagger. Just as he had done the murder, one of his grooms, who slept in the chamber, laughed in his sleep, and the other cried, "Murder!" which woke them both: but they said a short prayer; one of them said, "God bless us!" and the other answered, "Amen"; and addressed themselves to sleep again. Macbeth, who stood listening to them, tried to say, "Amen" when the fellow said "God bless us!" but, though he had most need of a blessing, the word stuck in his throat, and he could not pronounce it.

Again he thought he heard a voice which cried, "Sleep no more; Macbeth doth murder sleep, the innocent sleep, that nourishes life." Still it cried, "Sleep no more" to all the house. "Glamis hath murdered sleep, and therefore Cawdor shall sleep no more, Macbeth shall sleep no more."

Lamb, Charles and Mary. *Tales from Shakespeare*. New York: Random House, 1986.

MUCH ADO ABOUT NOTHING

WILLIAM SHAKESPEARE
AS TOLD BY CHARLES AND MARY LAMB

There lived in the palace at Messina two ladies whose names were Hero and Beatrice. Hero was the daughter, and Beatrice the niece of Leonato, the governor of Messina. Beatrice was of a lively temper, and loved to divert her cousin Hero, who was of a more serious disposition, with her sprightly sallies.

Passing through Messina on their return from a war that was just ended, were Don Pedro, the Prince of Arragon, and his friend Claudio, who was a lord of Florence; and with them came the wild and witty Benedick, and he was a lord of Padua.

These strangers had been at Messina before, and the hospitable governor introduced them to his daughter and his niece as their old friends and aquaintance.

The modest lady Hero was silent before the noble guests; and while Claudio was attentively observing the improvement which time had made in her beauty, the prince was highly amused with listening to the humorous dialogue between Benedick and Beatrice; and he said in a whisper to Leonato, "This is a pleasant-spirited young lady. She were an excellent wife for Benedick." Contrary to Leonato's feeling, the prince did not give up the idea of matching these two keen wits together.

When the prince returned with Claudio from the palace, he found that Benedick and Beatrice were not the only ones to marry; for Claudio spoke in such terms of Hero, as made the prince guess at what was passing in his heart. The Prince asked Claudio, "Do you affect Hero?" To this question Claudio replied, "O my lord, when I was last at Messina, I looked upon her with a soldier's eye, that liked, but had no leisure for loving; but now, in this happy time of peace, I have soft and delicate thoughts, all prompting me how fair young Hero is, reminding me that I liked her before I went to the wars." Claudio's confession of his love for Hero was so wrought upon the prince that he lost no time in soliciting the consent of Leonato to accept of Claudio for a son-in-law.

Claudio was to wait but a few days before he was to be married to his fair lady; yet he complained of the interval being tedious, as indeed most young men in such a position are impatient. So as a kind of merry pastime, they devised to invent some artful scheme to make Benedick and Beatrice fall in love with each other. Claudio entered with great satisfaction into this whim of the prince, and Leonato promised them his assistance, and even Hero said she would do any modest office to help her cousin to a good husband.

The device the prince invented was, that the gentleman should make Benedick believe that Beatrice was in love with him, and that Hero should make Beatrice believe that Benedick was in love with her.

The prince, Leonato, and Claudio began their operations first, and, watching an opportunity when Benedick was quietly seated reading in an arbor, the Prince and his assistants took their station among the trees behind the arbor, so near that Benedick could not choose but to hear all they said; and after some careless talk, the prince said, "Come hither, Leonato. What was it you told me the other day—that your niece Beatrice was in love with sign or Benedick? I did never think that lady would have loved any man."

"No, nor I either, my lord," answered Leonato. "It is most wonderful that she should dote on Benedick, whom she in all outward behavior seemed ever to dislike." Claudio confirmed all this, by saying that Hero had told him Beatrice was so in love with Benedick that she would certainly die of grief, if he could not be brought to love her; which Leonato and Claudio seemed to agree was impossible, he having always been such a railer against all fair ladies, and in particular against Beatrice.

Benedick had been listening with great eagerness to this conversation; and he said to himself when he heard Beatrice loved him, "Is it possible? Sits the wind in that corner?" And when they were gone, he began to reason in this manner with himself. "This can be no trick! they were very serious, and they have the truth from Hero, and seem to pity the lady. Love me! Why, it must be requited! I did never think to marry. But when I said I should die a bachelor, I did not think I should live to be married. They say the lady is virtuous and fair. She is so. And wise in everything but in loving me. Why this is no great argument of her folly." Beatrice now approached him and said with her usual tartness, "Against my will I am sent to bid you come in to dinner." Benedick, who never felt disposed to speak so politely to her before, replied, "Fair Beatrice, I thank you for your pains": and when Beatrice, after two or three more rude speeches, left him, Benedick thought he observed a concealed meaning of kindness under the uncivil words she uttered. The gentleman being thus caught in the net they had spread for him, it was now Hero's turn to play her part with Beatrice; and for this purpose she sent for Ursula and Margaret, two gentlewomen who attended upon her, and she said to Margaret, "Good Margaret, run to the parlor; there you will find my cousin Beatrice talking with the prince and Claudio. Whisper in her ear, that I and Ursula are walking in the orchard, and that our discourse is all of her. Bid her steal into that pleasant arbor."

Hero, then taking Ursula with her into the orchard, said to her, "Now, Ursula, when Beatrice comes, we will walk up and down this alley, and our talk must be only of Benedick, and when I name him, let it be your part to praise him highly. My talk to you must be how Benedick is in love with Beatrice." They then began; Hero saying, as if in answer to something which Ursula had said, "No, truly, Ursula. She is too disdainful; her spirits are as coy as wild birds of the rock." "But are you sure," said Ursula, "that Benedick loves Beatrice so entirely?" Hero replied, "So says the prince, and my lord Claudio, and they entreated me to acquaint her with it; but I persuaded them, if they loved Benedick, never to let Beatrice know of it." "Certainly," replied Ursula, "it were not good she knew his love, lest she made sport of it." "He hath an excellent good name," said Hero; "indeed he is the first man in Italy, always excepting my dear Claudio." And now, Hero giving her attendant a hint that it was time to change the discourse, Ursula said, "And when are you to be married, madam?" Hero then told her, that she was to be married to Claudio the next day, and desired she would go in with her, and look at some new attire, as she wished to consult with her on what she would wear on the morrow. Beatrice, who had been listening with breathless eagerness to this dialogue, when they went away, exclaimed, "What fire is in my ears? Can this be true? Farewell contempt, and scorn and maiden pride, adieu! Benedick, love on! I will requite you, taming my wild heart to your loving hand."

It must have been a pleasant sight to see these old enemies converted into new and loving friends; and to behold their first meeting after being cheated into mutual liking by the merry artifice of the good-humored prince. But a sad reverse in the fortunes of Hero must now be thought of. The morrow, which was to have been her wedding day, brought sorrow on the heart of Hero and her good father Leonato.

The prince had a half-brother, who came from the wars along with hime to Messina. This brother (his name was Don John) was a meloncholy, discontented man. He hated the prince, his brother, and he hated Claudio, because he was the prince's friend, and determined to prevent Claudio's marriage wih Hero, only for the malicious pleasure of making Claudio and the prince unhappy. To effect his wicked purpose, he employed one Borachio, a man as bad as himself, with who he encouraged with the offer of a great reward. Thus Borachio paid his court to Margaret, Hero's attendant; and Don John, knowing this, prevailed upon him to make Margaret promise to talk with him from her lady's chamber-window that night, after Hero was asleep, and also to dress herself in Hero's clothes, the better to deceive Claudio into the belief that it was Hero; for that was the end he meant to compass by his wicked plot.

Don John went to the prince and Claudio, and told them that Hero was an imprudent lady, and that she talked with men from her chamber-window at midnight. Now this was the evening before the wedding, and he offered to take them that night, where they should themselves hear Hero discoursing with a man from her window; and they consented to go along with him, and Claudio said, "If I see anything tonight why I should not marry her, tomorrow in the congregation, where I intended to wed her, there will I shame her." The prince also said, "And as I assisted you to obtain her, I will join you to disgrace her."

When Don John brought them near Hero's chamber that night, they saw Borachio standing under the window, and they saw Margaret looking out of Hero's window, and heard her talking with Borachio; and Margaret being dressed in the same clothes they had seen Hero wear, the prince and Claudio believed it was the lady Hero herself.

Nothing could equal the anger of Claudio, when he had made (as he thought) this discovery. All his love for the innocent Hero was at once converted into hatred, and he resolved to expose her in church, as he had said he would, the next day; and the prince agreed to this, thinking no punishment could be too severe for the naughty lady, who talked with a man from her window the very night before she was going to be married to the noble Claudio.

The next day when they were all met to celebrate the marriage, and Claudio and Hero were standing before the priest, Claudio, in the most passionate language, proclaimed the guilt of the blameless Hero, who, amazed at the strange words he uttered, said meekly,

"Is my lord well, that he does speak so wide?"

Leonato, in the utmost horror, said to the prince,

"My lord, why speak not you?" "Why should I speak?" said the prince, "I stand dishonored, that have gone about to link my dear friend to an unworthy woman. Leonato, upon my honor, myself, my brother, and this grieved Claudio, did see and hear her last night at midnight talk with a man at her chamber-window."

Benedick, in astonishment at what he had heard, said, "This looks not like a nuptial."

"True, O God!" replied the heart-struck Hero; and then this hapless lady sunk down in a fainting fit, to all appearance dead. The prince and Claudio left the church, without staying to see if Hero would recover.

When Hero recovered from the swoon into which she had fallen, the friar said to her, "Lady, what man is he you are accused of?" Hero replied, "They know that do accuse me; I know of none," then turning to Leonato, she said, "O my father, if you can prove that any man has ever conversed with me at hours unmeet, or that I yesternight changed words with any creature, refuse me, hate me, torture me to death."

"There is," said the friar, "some strange misunderstanding in the prince and Claudio," and then he counseled Leonato, that he should report that Hero was dead. "What shall become of this?" said Leonato; "what will this do?" The friar replied, "This report of her death shall change slander into pity: that is some good; but that is not all the good I hope for. When Claudio shall hear she died upon hearing his words, the idea of her life shall sweetly creep into his imagination. Then shall he mourn, if ever love had interest in his heart, and wished he had not so accused her."

The kind friar then led Leonato and Hero away to comfort and console them, and Beatrice and Benedick remained alone. Benedick was the first who spoke, and he said, "Lady Beatrice, have you wept all this while?" "Yea, and I will weep a while longer," said Beatrice. "Surely," said Benedick, "I do believe your fair cousin is wronged." "Ah!" said Beatrice, "how much might that man deserve of me who would right her!" Benedick then said, "Is there any way to show such friendship? I do love nothing in the world as well as you; is not that strange?" "It were as possible," said Beatrice, "for me to say I loved nothing in the world so well as you." "By my sword," said Benedick, "you love me, and I protest I love you. Come bid me do anything for you." "Kill Claudio," said Beatrice. "Ha! not for the wide world," said

Benedick; for he loved his friend Claudio, and he believed he had been imposed upon. "Is not Claudio a villain that has slandered, scorned, and dishonored my cousin?" said Beatrice, "O that I were a man!" "Hear me Beatrice!" said Benedick. But Beatrice would hear nothing in Claudio's defense; and she continued to urge on Benedick to revenge her cousin's wrongs: and she said, "Talk with a man out of the window; a proper saying! Sweet Hero! She is wronged; she is slandered; she is undone." "Think you on your soul, that Claudio has wronged Hero?" asked Benedick. "Yea," answered Beatrice; "as sure as I have a thought, or a soul." "Enough," said Benedick; "I am engaged; I will challenge him. I will kiss your hand, and so leave you. By this hand, Claudio shall render me a dear account! As you hear from me, so think of me. Go, comfort your cousin."

While Beatrice was thus powerfully pleading with Benedick, and working his gallant temper be the spirit of her angry words to engage in the cause of Hero, and fight even with his dear friend Claudio, Leonato was challenging the prince and Claudio to answer with their swords the injury they had done his child, who, affirmed, had died for grief. And now came Benedick, and he also challenged Claudio to answer with his sword the injury he had done to Hero; and Claudio and the prince said to each other, "Beatrice has set him on to do this."

While the prince and Claudio were yet talking of the challenge of Benedick, Borachio was brought before the prince. He had been overheard talking with one of his companions of the mischief he had been employed by Don John to do.

Borachio made a full confession to the prince in Claudio's hearing, and no doubt remained on their minds of the innocence of Hero. If doubt had remained, it must have been removed by the flight of Don John, who, finding his villainies were detected, fled from Messina to avoid the just anger of his brother.

The heart of Claudio was sorely grieved, when he found he had falsely accused Hero, who, he thought, died upon hearing his cruel words. Claudio implored forgiveness of Leonato for the injury he had done to his child.

The penance Leonato enjoined him was, to marry the next morning a cousin of Hero's, who, he said, was now his heir, and in person very like Hero.

When morning came, at the sight of the second nuptial Leonato presented to Claudio his promised bride; and she wore a mask, that Claudio might not discover her face. And Claudio said to the lady in the mask, "Give me your hand, before this holy friar; I am your husband, if you will marry me." "And when I lived I was your other wife," said this unknown lady; and taking off her mask, she proved to be no niece, but Leonato's very daughter, the lady Hero herself. We may be sure that this proved a most agreeable surprise to Claudio, who thought her dead, so that he could scarcely for joy believe his eyes: and the prince, who was equally amazed at what he saw, exclaimed, "Is not this Hero, Hero that was dead?" Leonato replied, "She died, my lord, but while her slander lived." The friar promised them an explanation of this seeming miracle after the ceremony was ended; and was proceeding to marry them, when he was interrrupted by Benedick, who desired to be married at the same time to Beatrice. Beatrice making some demur to this match, and Benedick challenging her with her love for him, which he had learned from Hero, a pleasant explanation took place; and they found that they had both been tricked into a belief of love, which had never existed and had become lovers in truth by the power of a false jest. Benedick swore to Beatrice that he took her but for pity, and because he heard she was dying of love for him; and Beatrice protested the same. So these two mad wits were reconciled, and made a match of it, after Claudio and Hero were married; and to complete the history, Don John, the contriver of the villainy, was taken in his flight, and brought back to Messina; and a brave punishment it was to this gloomy discontented man, to see the joy and feastings which, by the disappointment of his plots, took place at the palace in Messina.

Lamb, Charles and Mary. *Tales from Shakespeare*. New York: Random House, 1986.

JOHNNY TREMAIN

ESTHER FORBES

A story filled with danger and excitement drawn from real-life events, Johnny Tremain *takes place in turbulent Boston, just before the Revolutionary War. Johnny, a young apprentice silversmith, is caught up in the plots and plans of John Hancock, Paul Revere, Samuel Adams, and the like. Little does he realize that their actions will set in motion the Boston Tea Party, the Battle of Lexington—and ultimately, the precious freedom of the United States of America.*

VI. SALT-WATER TEA

n Sundays the boys might relax a little, breakfast when they pleased, only they must turn up clean and shining in time to go to church with Aunt and Uncle and listen to the inflammatory Reverend Sam Cooper. Doctor Cooper was putting more politics than gospel into his sermons that fall, and more fear of "taxation with representation" than God into his congregation.

England had, by the fall of 1773, gone far in adjusting the grievances of her American colonies. But she insisted upon a small tax on tea. Little money would be collected by this tax. It worked no hardship on the people's pocketbooks: only three-pence per pound. The stubborn colonists, who were insisting they would not be taxed unless they could vote for the men who taxed them, would hardly realize that the tax had been paid by the East India Company in London before the tea was shipped over here. After all, thought Parliament, the Americans were yokels and farmers—not political thinkers. And the East India tea, even after that tax was paid, would be better and cheaper than any the Americans ever had had. Weren't the Americans, after all human beings? Wouldn't they care more for their pocketbooks than their principles?

Shivering—for the last week in November was bitterly cold—Johnny built up the fire in the attic. From the back window he could see that the roofs of the African Queen were white with frost.

A sharp rat-tat on the shop door below woke Rab.

"What time's it?" he grumbled, as people do who think they are disturbed too early Sunday morning.

"Seven and past. I'll see what's up."

It was Sam Adams himself. When either cold or excited, his palsy increased. His head and hands were shaking. But his strong, seamed face, which always looked cheerful, today looked radiant. Sam Adams was so pleased that Johnny, a little naively, thought he must have word that Parliament had backed down again. The expected tea ships had not sailed.

"Look you, Johnny. I know it's Lord's Day, but there's a placard I must have printed and posted secretly tonight. The Sons of Liberty will take care of the posting, but Mr. Lorne must see to the printing. Could you run across and ask him to step over? And Rab—where's he?"

Rab was coming down the ladder.

"What's up?" said Rab sleepily.

"The first of the tea ships, the Dartmouth, is entering the harbor. She'll be at Castle Island by nightfall."

"So they dared send them?"

"Yes."

"And the first has come?"

"Yes. God give us strength to resist. That tea cannot be allowed to land."

When Johnny got back with Mr. Lorne, Rab had Mr. Adams's text in his hands, reading it as a printer reads, thinking first of spacing and capitals, not of the meaning.

"I can set that in no time. Two hundred copies? They'll be fairly dry by nightfall."

"Ah, Mr. Lorne," said Adams, shaking hands, "without you printers, the cause of liberty would be lost forever."

"Without you"—Mr. Lorne's voice shook with emotion—"there would not have been any belief in liberty to lose. I will, as always, do anything—everything you wish."

"I got word before dawn. It's the Dartmouth and she will be as far as Castle Island by nightfall. If that tea is landed—if that tax is paid—everything is lost. The selectmen will meet all day today and I am calling a mass meeting for tomorrow. This is the placard I will put up."

He took it from Rab's hands and read:

Friends! Brethren! Countrymen! That worst of Plagues, the detested

T E A

*shipped for this Port by the East India Company is now arrived in the Harbor:
the hour of destruction, of manly opposition to the
machinations of Tyranny, stares you in the Face; Every Friend to his
Country, to Himself, and to Posterity, is now called upon to meet at
Faneuil Hall, at nine o'clock this day, at which time the bells will ring
to make united and successful resistance to this last, worst, and most
destructive measure of Administration . . .
Boston, Nov. 29, 1773.*

Then he said quietly, "Up to the last moment—up to the 11th hour, we will beg the Governor's permission for the ships return to London with their cargo. We have 20 days."

Johnny knew that by law any cargo that was not unloaded within 20 days might be seized by the custom-house and sold at auction.

"Mr. Lorne, needless to say, the Observers will meet tonight. There are private decisions to be made before the mass meeting tomorrow at nine."

Johnny pricked up his ears. Ever since he had come to Mr. Lorne's (and Rab said he might be trusted with anything—possibly with men's lives) he had now and then summoned the members of the Observers' Club. They were so close to treason they kept no list of members. Rab made Johnny memorize the 22 names. They met in Rab and Johnny's attic.

"Johnny," said Mr. Lorne, anxious and overanxious to please Mr. Adams, "start right out."

"No sir, if you please. Noon will be better. That will give the members time to get home from church. And as usual, Johnny, make no stir. Simply say, 'Mr. So-and-so owes eight shillings for his newspaper.'"

Johnny nodded. That meant the meeting would be tonight at eight o'clock. If he said one pound eight shillings, it would mean the next night at eight. Two pounds, three and six would mean the day after at three-thirty. It gave him a feeling of excitement and pleasure to be even on the fringes of great, secret, dangerous events.

Forbes, Esther. *Johnny Tremain*. New York: Bantam, 1987.

REBECCA OF SUNNYBROOK FARM

KATE DOUGLAS WIGGIN

Rebecca—a wide-eyed, sprightly, and intelligent girl—is sent from her family's farm to live with her two strict aunts, Miranda and Jane. She brings vitality, mischief, and poetry to their household, and to the whole town, as well! Here, we witness Rebecca's effect on her schoolmate, Samuel "Seesaw" Simpson, and on her intrigued young teacher.

Chapter V WISDOM'S WAYS

amuel Simpson was generally called Seesaw because of his difficulty in making up his mind. Whether it were a question of fact, of spelling, or of date, of going swimming or fishing, of choosing a book in the Sunday-school library or a stick of candy at the village store, he had no sooner determined on one plan of action than his wish fondly reverted to the opposite one. Seesaw was pale, flaxen-haired, blue-eyed, round-shouldered, and given to stammering when nervous. Perhaps because of his very weakness, Rebecca's decision of character had a fascination for him, and although she snubbed him to the verge of madness, he could never keep his eyes away from her. When, having obtained permission, she walked to the water-pail in the corner and drank from the dipper, unseen forces dragged Seesaw from his seat to go and drink after her. It was not only that there was something akin to association and intimacy in drinking next, but there was the fearful joy of meeting her in transit, and receiving a cold and disdainful look from her wonderful eyes.

On a certain warm day in summer, Rebecca's thirst exceeded the bounds of propriety. When she asked a third time for permission to quench it at the common fountain Miss Dearborn nodded yes, but lifted her eyebrows unpleasantly as Rebecca neared the desk. As she replaced the dipper Seesaw promptly raised his hand, and Miss Dearborn indicated a weary affirmative.

"What is the matter with you, Rebecca?" she asked.

"I had salt mackerel for breakfast," answered Rebecca.

There seemed nothing humorous about this reply, which was merely the statement of a fact, but an irrepressible titter ran through the school. Miss Dearborn did not enjoy jokes neither made nor understood by herself, and her face flushed.

"I think you had better stand by the pail for five minutes, Rebecca; it may help you to control your thirst."

Rebecca's heart fluttered. She had to stand in the corner by the water-pail and be stared at by all the scholars. She unconsciously made a gesture of angry dissent and moved a step nearer her seat, but was arrested by Miss Dearborn's command in a still firmer voice.

"Stand by the pail, Rebecca! Samuel, how many times have you asked for water today?"

"This is the f-f-fourth."

"Don't touch the dipper, please. The school has done nothing but drink this afternoon; it has had no time whatever to study. I suppose you had something salty for breakfast, Samuel?" queried Miss Dearborn with sarcasm.

"I had m-m-mackerel, j-just like Reb-b-becca." (Irrepressible giggles by the school.)

"I judged so. Stand by the other side of the pail, Samuel."

Rebecca's head was bowed with shame and wrath. Life looked too black a thing to be endured. The punishment was bad enough, but to be coupled in correction with Seesaw Simpson was beyond human endurance.

Singing was the last exercise in the afternoon, and Minnie Smellie chose "Shall we Gather at the River?" It was a baleful choice and seemed to hold some secret and subtle association with the situation and general progress of events; or at any rate there was apparently some obscure reason for the energy and vim with which the scholars shouted the choral invitation again and again:

> *Shall we gather at the river—*
> *The beautiful, the beautiful river?*

Miss Dearborn stole a look at Rebecca's bent head and was frightened.

"You may go to your seat, Rebecca," said Miss Dearborn at the end of the first song. "Samuel, stay where you are till the close of school. And let me tell you, scholars, that I asked Rebecca to stand by the pail only to break up this habit of incessant drinking, which is nothing but empty-mindedness and desire to walk to and fro over the floor. Every time Rebecca has asked for a drink today the whole school has gone to the pail one after another. She is really thirsty, and I dare say I ought to have punished you for following her example, not her for setting it. What shall we sing now, Alice?"

"'The Old Oaken Bucket,' please."

"Think of something dry, Alice, and change the subject. Yes, 'The Star-Spangled Banner,' if you like, or anything else."

Rebecca sank into her seat and pulled the singing-book from her desk. Miss Dearborn's public explanation had shifted some of the weight from her heart, and she felt a trifle raised in her self-esteem.

Under cover of the general relaxation of singing, votive offerings of respectful sympathy began to make their appearance at her shrine. Living Perkins, who could not sing, dropped

365

a piece of maple sugar in her lap as he passed her on his way to the blackboard to draw the map of Maine. Alice Robinson rolled a perfectly new slate pencil over the floor with her foot until it reached Rebecca's place, while her seat-mate, Emma Jane, had made up a little mound of paper balls and labelled them "Bullets for you know who."

Altogether existence grew brighter, and when she was left alone with the teacher for her grammar lesson she had nearly recovered her equanimity, which was more than Miss Dearborn had. The last clattering foot had echoed through the hall, Seesaw's backward glance of penitence had been met and answered defiantly by one of cold disdain.

"Rebecca, I am afraid I punished you more than I meant," said Miss Dearborn, who was only 18 herself, and in her year of teaching at country schools had never encountered a child like Rebecca.

"I hadn't missed a question this whole day, nor whispered either," quavered the culprit; "and I don't think I ought to be shamed just for drinking."

"You started all the others, or it seemed as if you did. Whatever you do they all do, whether you laugh, or miss, or write notes, or ask to leave the room, or drink; and it must be stopped."

"Sam Simpson is a copycat!" stormed Rebecca. "I wouldn't have minded standing in the corner alone—that is, not so very much; but I couldn't bear standing with him."

"I saw that you couldn't, and that's the reason I told you to take your seat, and left him in the corner. Remember that you are a stranger in the place, and they take notice of what you do, so you must be careful. Now let's have our conjugations. Give me the verb 'to be,' potential mood, past-perfect tense."

"I might have been.
Thou mightst have been.
He might have been.
We might have been.
You might have been.
They might have been."

"Give me an example, please."

"I might have been glad.
Thou mightst have been glad.
He, she, or it might have been glad."

"'He' or 'she' might have been glad because they are masculine and feminine, but could 'it' have been glad?" asked Miss Dearborn, who was very fond of splitting hairs.

"Why not?" asked Rebecca.

"Because 'it' is neuter gender."

"Couldn't we say, 'The kitten might have been glad if it had known it was not going to be drowned'?"

"Ye—es," Miss Dearborn answered hesitatingly, never very sure of herself under Rebecca's fire; "but though we often speak of a baby, a chicken, or a kitten as 'it,' they are really masculine or feminine gender, not neuter."

Rebecca reflected a long moment and then asked, "Is a hollyhock neuter?"

"Oh yes, of course it is, Rebecca."

"Well, couldn't we say, 'The hollyhock might have been glad to see the rain, but there was a weak little hollyhock bud growing out of its stalk, and it was afraid that there might be hurt by the storm; so the big hollyhock was kind of afraid, instead of being real glad'?"

Miss Dearborn looked puzzled as she answered, "Of course, Rebecca, hollyhocks could not be sorry, or glad, or afraid, really."

"We can't tell, I s'pose," replied the child; "but I think they are, anyway. Now what shall I say?"

"The subjunctive mood, past-perfect tense of the verb 'to know'."

> *"If I had known.*
> *If thou hadst known.*
> *If he had known.*
> *If we had known.*
> *If you had known.*
> *If they had known.*

"Oh, it is the saddest tense!" sighed Rebecca, with a little break in her voice; "nothing but ifs, ifs, ifs! And it makes you feel that if they had known, things might have been better!"

Miss Dearborn had not thought of it before, but on reflection she believed the subjunctive mood was a "sad" one, and "if" rather a sorry "part of speech."

"Give me some examples of the subjunctive, Rebecca, and that will do for this afternoon," she said.

"If I had not loved mackerel, I should not have been thirsty," said Rebecca with an April smile, as she closed her grammar. "If thou hadst loved me truly, thou wouldst not have stood me up in the corner. If Samuel had not loved wickedness, he would not have followed me to the water-pail."

"And if Rebecca had loved the rules of the school, she would have controlled her thirst," finished Miss Dearborn with a kiss, and the two parted friends.

Wiggin, Kate Douglas. *Rebecca of Sunnybrook Farm.* New York: Signet Classic, 1991.

HEIDI

Johanna Spyri

The story of Heidi was written in 1880. It is about a five-year-old orphan who is brought to live with her grandfather on a remote mountain in the Swiss Alps. We now visit Heidi in the Alps soon after she joins her grandfather on his farm and they are fixing her a bed on a loft in his house.

et us go down then, as we both think alike," said the old man, and he followed the child down the ladder. Then he went up to the hearth, pushed the big kettle aside, and drew forward the little one that was hanging on the chain, and seating himself on the round-topped, three-legged stool before the fire, blew it up into a clear bright flame. The kettle soon began to boil, and meanwhile the old man held a large piece of cheese on a long iron fork over the fire. Heidi watched all that was going on with eager curiosity. Suddenly some new idea seemed to come into her head. Presently the grandfather got up and came to the table with a jug and the cheese, and there he saw it already tidily set.

"Ah, that's right," said the grandfather, "I am glad to see that you have some ideas of your own," and as he spoke he laid the toasted cheese on a layer of bread, "but there is still something missing."

Heidi looked at the jug that was steaming away invitingly, and ran quickly back to the cupboard. She returned with two glasses and the bowl and put them down on the table.

"Good! I see you know how to set about things; but what will you do for a seat?" The grandfather himself was sitting on the only chair in the room. Heidi flew to the hearth, and dragging the three-legged stool up to the table, sat herself down upon it.

"Well, you have managed to find a seat for yourself, I see, only a rather low one I am afraid," said the grandfather, "but you would not be tall enough to reach the table even if you sat in my chair; the first thing now, however, is to have something to eat, so come along."

With that he stood up, filled the bowl with milk, got a slice of bread, and placing it on the chair, pushed it in front of Heidi on her little three-legged stool, so that she now had a table to herself. After which he went and sat down on the corner of the table and began his own meal. Heidi lifted the bowl with both hands and drank without pause till it was empty, for the thirst of her long hot journey had returned upon her.

"Was the milk nice?" asked her grandfather.

"I never drank anything so good before," answered Heidi.

"Then you must have some more," and the old man filled her bowl again to the brim and set it before the child, who was now hungrily beginning her bread, having first spread it with the cheese, which after being toasted was soft as butter; the two together tasted deliciously, and the child looked the picture of content as she sat eating, and at intervals taking further draughts of the milk. The meal being over, the grandfather went outside to put the goat-shed in order, and Heidi watched with interest as he first swept it out, and then put the fresh straw for goats to sleep upon. Then he went to the little well-shed and cut some long round sticks, and a small round board; in this he bored some holes and stuck the sticks into them, and there, as if by magic, there was a three-legged stool just like her grandfather's, only higher. Heidi stood and looked at it, speechless with astonishment.

"What do you think that is?" asked her grandfather.

"It's my stool, I know, because it is such a high one; and it was made all of a minute," said the child, still lost in wonder and admiration.

"She understands what she sees, her eyes are in the right place," remarked the grandfather to himself.

And so the time passed happily on till evening. Then the wind began to roar louder than ever through the old fir trees; Heidi listened with delight to the sound, and it filled her heart so full of gladness that she skipped and danced round the old trees. The grandfather stood and watched her from the shed.

Suddenly a shrill whistle was heard. Heidi paused in her dancing, and the grandfather came out. Down from the heights above the goats came springing one after another, with Peter in their midst. Heidi sprang forward with a cry of joy and rushed among the flock, greeting first one and then another of her old friends of the morning. As they neared the huts the goats stood still, and then two of their number, two beautiful slender animals, one white and one brown, ran forward to where the grandfather was standing and began licking his hands, for he was holding a little salt which he always had ready for his goats on their return home. Peter disappeared with the remainder of his flock. Heidi tenderly stroked the two goats in turn, running first to one side of them and then the other, and jumping about in her glee at the pretty little animals. "Are they ours, grandfather? Are they both ours? Are you going to put them in the shed? Will they always stay with us?"

Heidi's questions came tumbling out one after the other, so that her grandfather had only time to answer each of them with "Yes, yes." When the goats had finished licking up the salt her grandfather told her to go and fetch her bowl and the bread.

Heidi obeyed and was soon back again. The grandfather milked the white goat and filled her basin, and then breaking off a piece of bread, "Now eat your supper," he said, "and then go up to bed. Cousin Dete left another little bundle for you with a nightgown and other small things in it, which you will find at the bottom of the cupboard if you want them. I must go and shut up the goats, so be off and sleep well."

"Good night, grandfather! Good night. What are their names, grandfather, what are their names?" she called out as she ran after his retreating figure and the goats.

"The white one is named Little Swan, and the brown one Little Bear," he answered.

"Good night, Little Swan, good night, Little Bear!" she called again at the top of her voice, for they were already inside the shed. Then she sat down on the sheet and began to eat and drink, but the wind was so strong that it almost blew her away; so she made haste and finished her supper and then went indoors and climbed up to her bed, where she was soon lying as sweetly and soundly asleep as any young princess on her couch of silk.

Not long after, and while it was still twilight, the grandfather also went to bed, for he was up every morning at sunrise, and the sun came climbing up over the mountains at a very early hour during these summer months. The wind grew so tempestuous during the night, and blew in such gusts against the walls, that the hut trembled and the old beams groaned and creaked. It came howling and wailing down the chimney like voices of those in pain, and it raged with such fury among the old fir trees that here and there a branch was snapped and fell. In the middle of the night the old man got up. "The child will be frightened," he murmered half aloud. He mounted the ladder and went and stood by the child's bed.

Outside the moon was struggling with the dark, fast-driving clouds, which at one moment left it clear and shining, and the next swept over it, and all again was dark. Just now the moonlight was falling through the round window straight on to Heidi's bed. She lay under the heavy coverlid, her cheeks rosy with sleep, her head peacefully resting on her little round arm, with a happy expression on her baby face as if dreaming of something pleasant. The old man stood looking down on the sleeping child until the moon again disappeared behind the clouds and he could see no more, then he went back to bed.

Spyri, Johanna. *Heidi*. Stamford: Longmeadow Press, 1986.

FANTASTIC CREATURES

THE ANIMAL FAMILY

RANDALL JARRELL

This is the last story written by the acclaimed American poet, Randall Jarrell, before his death in 1965. It tells of an irresistible family made up of a hunter, a mermaid, a bear, a lynx, and a boy.

n a little while they forgot that they had ever lived without the boy. Things would remind them, of course. "It feels strange to make them so small," the mermaid would say as she made the boy shoes and shirts and trousers of the softest, whitest deerskin, all covered with shell-patterns of birds and flowers. (She said about clothes, "I can see they're right for him.") And she made a deerskin cap, and then sewed so many bluejay feathers on it that you couldn't tell it was made of deerskin; the boy's head was one blaze of blue.

The hunter made the boy four arrows and a bow as good as his own, only smaller. The boy wore them, but he was still too young to shoot with them, except when the hunter held his hands on the bow and bowstring. The hunter made him a little bed, covered it with the skin of a mountain lion, hung the bow and arrows over it, and every night put him in it together with his toys: the ball, and a fur bear, and a wooden lynx, and the hunter's necklace—so as not to hurt the mermaid's feelings, it was only lent to the boy—and the carvings of the hunter's father and mother. Sometimes the real lynx would come in the middle of the night, and in the morning when the boy awoke, the lynx would be there, curled at the bottom of the bed; the boy would reach down and stroke his head, and the lynx would yawn and give a sleepy purr. But the bear was too big for the bed; when he lay down by it his head went up past its head and his feet down past its foot.

The mermaid and the hunter and the boy went to the beach almost as much as the mermaid and the hunter had gone in the old days. The boy loved the sand and shells and little shallow waves that splashed in over his legs and stomach. Sometimes the hunter, with the boy in his arms, would wade out to where the big waves were, and as some great, green, white-headed wave hung over them, about to break, it would seem to the boy that there was nothing in the world strong enough to save them—then the hunter would thrust himself up powerfully, the wave would burst around them in a smother of white, salt, blinding foam, the boy would gasp and shut his eyes, and when he opened them he and the hunter stood there alone, the wave was over.

In the little pool at the side of the river, the mermaid taught the boy to swim "the way

I do, but with legs." Before long swimming was as natural to him as walking, just as hearing the mermaid's stories, saying the mermaid's words were as natural to him as hearing the hunter's stories and saying the hunter's words. "He talks like one of the sea people," the mermaid said proudly. "Whatever he says has that watery sound."

The hunter gasped in his best Dolphin: "Help me! Help me to the beach!" and asked the mermaid whether it had a watery sound. The mermaid said, pointing: "You say it the way your father would. Whatever you say has that—that walnut sound."

"Live and live let," the hunter replied amicably. This was the way the mermaid had remembered "Live and let live," and the hunter hadn't corrected her, at first out of politeness and then because her way made better sense to him. Of course the mermaid had no idea that he was repeating her proverb, not his own.

Sometimes they would tell the boy how the lynx had come for them and led them to him, and how they had found him pressed up against the bear, fast asleep; once or twice they took him to the little marker the hunter had put over the mother's grave. But except for one or two confused, uneasy dreams, all the boy's memories were memories of the mermaid and the hunter; he knew that the hunter was his father and the mermaid his mother and had always been. (The two of them were different from him, different from each other, but aren't a boy's father and mother always different from him, different from each other? The difference between the hunter and the mermaid was no greater, to the boy, than the difference between his father's short hair and trousers, his mother's long hair and skirts, is to any child.) The boy felt, "They're always telling me the lynx found me!" But he would smile at his father and mother and pretend the lynx had found him.

One day the hunter smiled back and said, "You must think you've lived with us always." The boy didn't know whether to say yes or no, and gave a laugh of confused joy, so that the mermaid smiled and said, "Yes, you think you've lived with us always."

The boy's heart beat faster, but he said, "No, the lynx found me." And this got to be a game of theirs. Because he knew it wasn't so, the boy enjoyed saying the lynx had found him; and the hunter and the mermaid enjoyed saying that the boy had lived with them always, because of—because of many things.

The boy went to sleep before the hunter and the mermaid and woke up before them; sometimes he and the lynx were the only things awake in the house. The boy would sit up in his bed and look around at the hunter asleep under the bearskin, the mermaid asleep on top of it, the bear snoring by the fireplace, the hunter's bows and his own bow, the skins and shells and hunting horn, the blue-flowered, deer-hooved figurehead over the door, and there was not one thing there that, to the boy, was strange.

One night an hour or two after he'd gone to sleep, the sound of the rain waked him, and he heard his mother saying to his father: "He's so good and so clever, but he does grow slowly. I don't understand it. Remember how fast the bear grew? And the lynx."

The hunter didn't answer for a moment: he must have been remembering his own childhood. "I don't know," he said. "I don't think we grow as fast as they do. It seems to me I was a boy a long time—a long time."

The mermaid went on: "He's so different from our little ones. He's better than they are—they are bad little things—and he's a lot more interesting. He thinks of the queerest things."

"He does?"

"I should say so. He makes up under-sea stories he tells me. This morning he told me that when he grows up he's going to make a bow and arrow you can shoot under water, and marry one of the sea people and live with her at the bottom of the ocean."

"That's not so queer," the hunter retorted. "I've often thought of doing that myself."

The mermaid said blandly: "You think of the queerest things."

Next morning when the boy remembered hearing them, he didn't know whether or not it had been a dream. The part about growing slowly was important to him: he'd always lived with the mermaid and the hunter, he reasoned, and the bear and the lynx had come later and grown faster, that was why they were bigger. He liked having heard his father's "It seems to me I was a boy a long time"—it seemed to him that he had been a boy a long time.

The days went by for him, all different and all the same. The boy was happy, and yet he didn't know that he was happy, exactly: he couldn't remember having been unhappy. If one day as he played at the edge of the forest some talking bird had flown down and asked him: "Do you like your life?" he would not have known what to say, but would have asked the bird: Can you not like it?"

Jarrell, Randall. *The Animal Family.* New York: Pantheon Books, 1965.

THE HOBBIT

J.R.R. Tolkien

Bilbo Baggins was a well-to-do hobbit who lived a very comfortable, quiet life until Gandalf, the great wizard, asked him to help recover a large treasure of gold from the much feared dragon, Smaug.

CHAPTER ONE

he music began all at once, so sudden and sweet that Bilbo forgot everything else, and was swept away into dark lands under strange moons, far over The Water and very far from his hobbit-hole under The Hill.

The dark came into the room from the little window that opened in the side of The Hill; the firelight flickered—it was April—and still they played on. And suddenly first one and then another began to sing as they played, deep-throated singing of the dwarves in the deep places of their ancient homes; and this is like a fragment of their song without their music.

Far over the misty mountains cold
To dungeons deep and caverns old
We must away ere break of day
To seek the pale enchanted gold.

The dwarves of yore made mighty spells,
while the hammers fell like ringing bells
In places deep, where dark things sleep,
In hollow halls beneath the fells.

For ancient king and elvish lord
There many a gleaming golden hoard
They shaped and wrought, and light they caught
To hide in gems on hilt of sword.

On silver necklaces they strung
The flowering stars, on crowns they hung
The dragon-fire, in twisted wire
They meshed the light of moon and sun.

Far over the misty mountains cold
To dungeons deep and caverns old
We must away, ere break of day,
To claim our long-forgotten gold.

Goblets they carved there for themselves
and harps of gold; where no man delves
There lay they long, and many a song
Was sung unheard by men or elves.

The pines were roaring on the height,
The winds were moaning in the night.
The fire was red, it flaming spread;
The trees like torches blazed with light.

The bells were ringing in the dale
And men looked up with faces pale;
The dragon's ire more fierce than fire
Laid low their towers and houses frail.

The mountain smoked beneath the moon;
The dwarves, they heard the tramp of doom.
They fled their hall to dying fall
Beneath his feet, beneath the moon.

Far over the misty mountains grim
To dungeons deep and caverns dim
We must away, ere break of day,
To win our harps and gold from him!

As they sang, the hobbit felt the love of beautiful things made by hands and by cunning and by magic moving through him, a fierce and jealous love, the desire of the hearts of dwarves. Then something Tookish woke up inside him, and he wished to go and see the great mountains, and hear the pine-trees and the waterfalls, and explore the caves, and wear a sword instead of a walking-stick. He looked out of the window. The stars were out in a dark sky above the trees. He thought of the jewels of the dwarves shining in dark caverns. Suddenly in the wood beyond The Water a flame leapt up—probably somebody lighting a wood-fire—and he thought of plundering dragons settling on his quiet Hill and kindling it all to flames. He shuddered; and very quickly he was plain Mr. Baggins of Bag-end, Under-Hill, again.

He got up trembling. He had less than half a mind to fetch the lamp, and more than half a mind to pretend to, and go and hide behind the beer barrels in the cellar, and not come out again until all the dwarves had gone away. Suddenly he found that the music and the singing had stopped, and they were all looking at him with eyes shining in the dark.

"Where are you going?" said Thorin, in a tone that seemed to show that he guessed both halves of the hobbit's mind.

"What about a little light?" said Bilbo apologetically.

"We like the dark," said the dwarves. "Dark for dark business! There are many hours before dawn."

"Of course!" said Bilbo, and sat down in a hurry. He missed the stool and sat in the fender, knocking over the poker and shovel with a crash.

"Hush!" said Gandalf. "Let Thorin speak!" And this is how Thorin began.

"Gandalf, dwarves and Mr. Baggins! We are not together in this house of our friend and fellow conspirator, this most excellent and audacious hobbit—may the hair on his toes never fall out! all praise to his wine and ale!—" He paused for breath and for a polite remark from the hobbit, but the compliments were quite lost on poor Bilbo Baggins, who was wagging his mouth in protest at being called audacious and worst of all fellow conspirator, though no noise came out, he was so flummoxed. So Thorin went on:

"We are met to discuss our plans, our ways, means, policy and devices. We shall soon before the break of day start on our long journey, a journey from which some of us, or perhaps all of us (except our friend and counselor, the ingenious wizard Gandalf) may never return. It is a solemn moment. Our object is, I take it, well known to us all. To the estimable Mr. Baggins, and perhaps to one or two of our younger dwarves (I think I should be right in naming Kili and Fili, for instance), the exact situation at the moment may require a little brief explanation—"

This was Thorin's style. He was an important dwarf. If he had been allowed, he would probably have gone on like this until he was out of breath, without telling any one there anything that was not known already. But he was rudely interrupted. Poor Bilbo couldn't bear it any longer. At may never return he began to feel a a shriek coming up inside, and very soon it burst out like the whistle of an engine coming out of a tunnel. All the dwarves sprang up knocking over the table. Gandalf struck a blue light on the end of his magic staff, and in its firework glare the poor little hobbit could be seen kneeling on the hearth-rug, shaking like a jelly that was melting. Then he fell flat on the floor, and kept on calling out, "Struck by lightning, struck by lightning!" over and over again; and that was all they could get out of him for a long time. So they took him and laid him out of the way on the drawing-room sofa with a drink at his elbow, and they went back to their dark business.

"Excitable little fellow," said Gandalf, as they sat down again. "Gets funny queer fits, but he is one of the best, one of the best—as fierce as a dragon in a pinch."

If you have ever seen a dragon in a pinch, you will realize that was only poetical exaggeration applied to any hobbit, even to Old Took's great-grand uncle Bullroarer, who was so huge (for a hobbit) that he could ride a horse. He charged the ranks of goblins of Mount Gram in the Battle of the Green fields, and knocked their king Golfimbul's head clean off with a wooden club. It sailed a hundred yards through the air and went down a rabbit-hole, and in this way the battle was won and the game of Golf invented at the same moment.

In the meanwhile, however, bullroarer's gentler descendant was reviving in the drawing-room. After a while and a drink he crept nervously to the door of the parlor. This is what he heard, Gloin speaking: "Humph!" (or some snort more or less like that). "Will he do, do you think? It is all very well for Gandalf to talk about this hobbit being fierce, but one shriek like that in a moment of excitement would be enough to wake the dragon and all his relatives, and kill the lot of us. I think it sounded more like fright than excitement! In fact, if it had not been for the sign on the door, I should have been sure we had come to the wrong house. As soon as I clapped eyes on the little fellow bobbing and puffing on the mat, I had my doubts. He looks more like a grocer than a burglar!"

Then Mr. Baggins turned the handle and went in. The Took side had won. He suddenly felt he would go without bed and breakfast to be thought fierce. As for little fellow bobbing on the mat, it almost made him really fierce. Many a time afterwards the Baggins part regretted what he did now, and he said to himself: "Bilbo, you were a fool; you walked right in and put your foot in it."

"Pardon me," he said, "if I have overheard words that you were saying. I don't pretend to understand what you are talking about, or your reference to burglars, but I think I am right in believing" (this is what he called being on his dignity) "that you think I am no good. I will show you. I have no signs on my door—it was painted a week ago—and I am quite sure you have come to the wrong house. As soon as I saw your funny faces on my door-step, I had my doubts. But treat it as the right one. Tell what you want done, and I will try it, if I have to walk from here to the East of the East and fight the wild Were-worms in the last Desert. I had a great-great-great-grand uncle once, Bullroarer Took, and—"

"Yes, yes, but that was long ago," said Gloin. "I was talking about you. And I assure you there is a mark on this door—the usual one in the trade, or used to be. Burglar wants a good job, plenty of Excitement and Reasonable Reward, that's how it is usually read. You can say expert Treasure-hunter instead of Burglar if you like. Some of them do. It's all the same to us. Gandalf told us that there was a man of the sort in these parts looking for a job at once, and that he had arranged for a meeting here this Wednesday tea-time."

Tolkien, J.R.R. *The Hobbit.* New York: Ballantine Books, 1993.

CHARLOTTE'S WEB

E. B. WHITE

Charlotte's Web tells the story of a friendship between a spider named Charlotte and a pig named Wilbur. Wilbur is facing the fate of most farm pigs—slaughter. Charlotte, devastated by this prospect, thinks of ways to prove to everyone that Wilbur is indeed special and should not be made into bacon. Here is one of Charlotte's more inventive plans.

CHAPTER 13

 ar into the night, while the other creatures slept, Charlotte worked on her web. First she ripped out a few of the orb lines near the center. She left the radial lines alone, as they were needed for support. As she worked, her eight legs were a great help to her. So were her teeth. She loved to weave and she was an expert at it. When she was finished ripping things out, her web looked something like this:

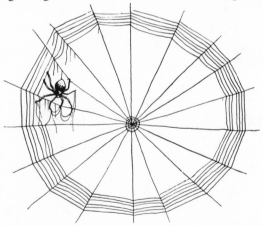

A spider can produce several kinds of thread. She uses a dry, tough thread for foundation lines, and she uses a sticky thread for snare lines—the ones that catch and hold insects. Charlotte decided to use her dry thread for writing the new message.

"If I write the word 'Terrific' with sticky thread," she thought, "every bug that comes along will get stuck in it and spoil the effect."

"Now let's see, the first letter is T."

Charlotte climbed to a point at the top of the left-hand side of the web. Swinging her spinnerets into position, she attached her thread and then dropped down. As she dropped, her spinning tubes went into action and she let out thread. At the bottom, she attached the thread. This formed the upright part of the letter T. Charlotte was not satisfied, however. She climbed up and made another attachment, right next to the first. Then she carried the line down, so that she had a double line instead of a single line. "It will show up better if I make the whole thing with double lines."

She climbed back up, moved over about an inch to the left, touched her spinnerets to the web, and then carried a line across to the right, forming the top of the T. She repeated this, making it double. Her eight legs were very busy helping.

"Now for the E!"

Charlotte got so interested in her work, she began to talk to herself, as though to cheer herself on. If you had been sitting quietly in the barn cellar that evening, you would have heard something like this:

"Now for the R! Up we go! Attach! Descend! Pay out line! Whoa! Attach! Good! Up you go! Repeat! O.K.! Easy, keep those lines together! Now, then, out and down for the leg of the R! Pay out line! Whoa! Attach! Ascend! Repeat! Good girl!"

And so, talking to herself, the spider worked at her difficult task. When it was completed, she felt hungry. She ate a small bug that she had been saving. Then she slept.

Next morning, Wilbur arose and stood beneath the web. He breathed the morning air into his lungs. Drops of dew, catching the sun, made the web stand out clearly. When Lurvy arrived with breakfast, there was the handsome pig, and over him, woven neatly in block letters, was the word TERRIFIC. Another miracle.

Lurvy rushed and called Mr. Zuckerman. Mr. Zuckerman rushed and called Mrs. Zuckerman. Mrs. Zuckerman ran to the phone and called the Arables. The Arables climbed into their truck and hurried over. Everybody stood at the pigpen and stared at the web and read the word, over and over, while Wilbur, who really felt terrific, stood quietly swelling out his chest and swinging his snout from side to side.

"Terrific!" breathed Zuckerman in joyful admiration. "Edith, you better phone the reporter on the *Weekly Chronicle* and tell him what has happened. He will want to know about this. He may want to bring a photographer. There isn't a pig in the whole state that is as terrific as our pig."

The news spread. People who had journeyed to see Wilbur when he was "some pig" came back again to see him now that he was "terrific."

That afternoon, when Mr. Zuckerman went to milk the cows and clean out the tie-ups, he was still thinking about what a wondrous pig he owned.

"Lurvy!" he called. "There is to be no more cow manure thrown down into that pigpen. I have a terrific pig. I want that pig to have clean, bright straw every day for his bedding. Understand?"

"Yes, sir," said Lurvy.

"Furthermore," said Mr. Zuckerman, "I want you to start building a crate for Wilbur. I have decided to take the pig to the County Fair on September sixth. Make the crate large and paint it green with gold letters!"

"What will the letters say?" asked Lurvy

"They should say Zuckerman's Famous Pig."

Lurvy picked up a pitchfork and walked away to get some clean straw. Having such an important pig was going to mean plenty of extra work, he could see that.

Below the apple orchard, at the end of a path, was the dump where Mr. Zuckerman threw all sorts of trash and stuff that nobody wanted any more. Here, in a small clearing hidden by young alders and wild raspberry bushes, was an astonishing pile of old bottles and empty tin cans and dirty rags and bits of metal and broken bottles and broken hinges and broken springs and dead batteries and last month's magazines and old discarded dishmops and tattered overalls and rusty spikes and leaky pails and forgotten stoppers and useless junk of all kinds, including a wrong-size crank for a broken ice-cream freezer.

Templeton knew the dump and liked it. There were good hiding places there—excellent cover for a rat. And there was usually a tin can with food still clinging to the inside.

Templeton was down there now, rummaging around. When he returned to the barn, he carried in his mouth an advertisement he had torn from a crumpled magazine.

"How's this?" he asked, showing the ad to Charlotte. "It says 'Crunchy.' Crunchy would be a good word to write in your web."

"Just the wrong idea," replied Charlotte. "Couldn't be worse. We don't want Zuckerman to think Wilbur is crunchy. He might start thinking about crisp crunchy bacon and tasty ham. That would put ideas into his head. We must advertise Wilbur's noble qualities, not his tastiness. Go get another word, please, Templeton."

The rat looked disgusted. But he sneaked away to the dump and was back in a while with a strip of cotton cloth. "How's this?" he asked. "It's a label off an old shirt."

Charlotte examined the label. It said PRE-SHRUNK.

"I'm sorry, Templeton," she said "but Pre-shrunk is out of the question. We want Zuckerman to think Wilbur is nicely filled out, not all shrunk up. I'll have to ask you to try again."

"What do you think I am, a messenger boy?" grumbled the rat. "I'm not going to spend all my time chasing down to the dump after advertising material."

"Just once more—please!" said Charlotte.

"I'll tell you what I'll do," said Templeton. "I know where there's a package of soap flakes in the woodshed. It has writing on it. I'll bring you a piece of the package."

He climbed the rope that hung on the wall and disappeared through a hole in the ceiling. When he came back he had a strip of blue-and-white cardboard in his teeth.

"There!" he said, triumphantly. "How's that?"

Charlotte read the words: "With New Radiant Action."

"What does it mean?" asked Charlotte, who had never used any soap flakes in her life.

"How should I know?" said Templeton. "You asked for words and I brought them. I suppose the next thing you'll want me to fetch is a dictionary."

Together they studied the soap ad. "'With new radiant action,'" repeated Charlotte, slowly. "Wilbur!" she called.

Wilbur who was asleep in the straw, jumped up.

"Run around!" commanded Charlotte. "I want to see you in action, to see if you are radiant."

Wilbur raced to the end of his yard.

"Now back again, faster!" said Charlotte.

Wilbur jumped as high as he could.

"Keep your knees straight and touch the ground with your ears!" called Charlotte.

Wilbur obeyed.

"Do a back flip with a half twist in it!" cried Charlotte.

Wilbur went over backwards, writhing and twisting as he went.

"O.K., Wilbur," said Charlotte. "You can go back to sleep. O.K., Templeton, the soap ad will do, I guess. I'm not sure Wilbur's action is exactly radiant, but it's interesting."

"Actually," said Wilbur, "I feel radiant."

"Do you?" said Charlotte. looking at him with affection. "Well, you're a good little pig, and radiant you shall be. I'm in this thing pretty deep now—I might as well go the limit."

Tired from his romp, Wilbur lay down in the clean straw. He closed his eyes. The straw seemed scratchy—not as comfortable as the cow manure. Wilbur sighed. It had been a busy day—his first day of being terrific. Dozens of people had visited his yard during the afternoon, and he had to stand and pose, looking as terrific as he could. Now he was tired. Fern had arrived and seated herself quietly on her stool in the corner.

"Tell me a story, Charlotte!" said Wilbur, as he lay waiting for sleep to come. "Tell me a story!"

So Charlotte, although she, too, was tired, did what Wilbur wanted.

"Once upon a time," she began, "I had a beautiful cousin who managed to build her web across a small stream. One day a tiny fish leaped into the air and got tangled in the web. My cousin was very much surprised, of course. The fish was thrashing wildly. My cousin hardly dared tackle it. But she did. She swooped down and threw great masses of wrapping material around the fish and fought bravely to capture it."

"Did she succeed?" asked Wilbur.

"It was a never-to-be-forgotten battle," said Charlotte. "There was the fish, caught only by one fin, its tail wildly thrashing and shining in the sun. There was the web, sagging dangerously under the weight of the fish."

"How much did the fish weigh?" asked Wilbur eagerly.

"I don't know," said Charlotte. "There was my cousin, slipping in, dodging out, beaten mercilessly over the head by the wildly thrashing fish, dancing in, dancing out, throwing her threads and fighting hard. First she threw a left around the tail. The fish lashed back. Then a left to the tail and a right, and another right to the fin. Then a hard left to the head, while the web swayed and stretched."

"Then what happened?" asked Wilbur.

"Nothing," said Charlotte. "The fish lost the fight. My cousin wrapped it up so tight it couldn't budge."

"Then what happened?" asked Wilbur.

"Nothing," said Charlotte. "My cousin kept the fish for a while, and then when she got good and ready, she ate it."

"Tell me another story!" begged Wilbur.

So Charlotte told him about another cousin of his who was an aeronaut.

"What is an aeronaut? asked Wilbur.

"A balloonist," said Charlotte. "My cousin used to stand on her head and let out enough thread to form a balloon. Then she'd let go and be lifted into the air and carried upward on the warm wind."

"Is that true?" asked Wilbur. "Or are you just making it up?"

"It's true," replied Charlotte. "I have some very remarkable cousins. And now, Wilbur, it's time you went to sleep."

"Sing something!" begged Wilbur, closing his eyes.

So Charlotte sang a lullaby, while crickets chirped in the grass and the barn grew dark. This was the song she sang.

> *"Sleep, sleep, my love, my only,*
> *Deep, deep, in the dung and the dark;*
> *Be not afraid and be not lonely!*
> *This is the hour when frogs and thrushes*
> *Praise the world from the woods and the rushes.*
> *Rest from care, my one and only,*
> *Deep in the dung and the dark!"*

But Wilbur was already asleep. When the song ended, Fern got up and went home.

White, E.B. *Charlotte's Web*. New York: HarperCollins, Harper Trophy, 1980.
  Other editions:
    ——. *Charlotte's Web*. New York: HarperCollins, Harper Perennial Books, 1990.
    ——. Boxed Set. Including *Charlotte's Web; The Trumpet of the Swan; Stuart Little*. New York: HarperCollins, Harper Trophy, 1974.

STUART LITTLE

E. B. WHITE

Stuart Little is a mouse who lives with the Frederick C. Little family. The Littles' cat, Snowball, is not very fond of Stuart. One morning, Stuart accidentally gets rolled up in one of the living-room window shades and Snowball mischievously decides to hide Stuart's hat and cane. So when Mr. and Mrs. Little and George, Stuart's brother, wake up, they fear the worst.

Chapter III WASHING UP

Stuart was an early riser: he was almost always the first person up in the morning. He liked the feeling of being the first one stirring; he enjoyed the quiet rooms with the books standing still on the shelves, the pale light coming in through the windows, and the fresh smell of day. In wintertime it would be quite dark when he climbed from his bed made out of the cigarette box, and he sometimes shivered with cold as he stood in his nightgown doing his exercises. (Stuart touched his toes ten times every morning to keep himself in good condition. He had seen his brother George do it, and George had explained that it kept the stomach muscles firm and was a fine abdominal thing to do.)

After exercising, Stuart would slip on his handsome wool wrapper, tie the cord tightly around his waist, and start for the bathroom, creeping silently through the long, dark hall past his mother's and father's room, past the hall closet where the carpet sweeper was kept, past George's room, and along by the head of the stairs till he got to the bathroom.

Of course, the bathroom would be dark, too, but Stuart's father had thoughtfully tied a long string to the pull-chain of the light. The string reached clear to the floor. By grasping it as high up as he could and throwing his whole weight on it, Stuart was able to turn on the light. Swinging on the string this way, with his long bathrobe trailing around his ankles, he looked like a little old friar pulling the bellrope in an abbey.

To get to the washbasin, Stuart had to climb a tiny rope ladder which his father had fixed for him. George had promised to build Stuart a small special washbasin only one inch high and with a little rubber tube through which water would flow; but George was always saying that he was going to build something and then forgetting about it. Stuart just went ahead and climbed the rope ladder to the family washbasin every morning to wash his face and hands and brush his teeth. Mrs. Little had provided him with a doll's washcloth, and a doll's comb—which he used for combing his whiskers. He carried these things in his bathrobe pocket, and when he reached the rope of the ladder he took them out, laid them neatly in a row, and set about the task of turning the water on. For such a small fellow, turning the water on was quite a problem. He had discussed it with father one day after making several unsuccessful attempts.

"I can get up onto the faucet all right," he explained, "but I can't seem to turn it on, because I have nothing to brace my feet against."

"Yes, I know," his father replied, "that's the whole trouble."

George, who always listened to conversations whenever he could, said that in his opinion they ought to construct a brace for Stuart; and with that he got out some boards, a saw, a hammer, a screwdriver, a brad-awl, and some nails, and started to make a terrific fuss in the bathroom, building what he said was going to be a brace for Stuart. But he soon became interested in something else and disappeared, leaving the tools lying around all over the bathroom floor.

Stuart, after examining this mess, turned to his father again. "Maybe I could pound the faucet with something and turn it on that way," he said.

So Stuart's father provided him with a very small, light hammer made of wood; and Stuart found that by swinging it three times around his head and letting it come down with a crash against the handle of the faucet, he could start a thin stream of water flowing—enough to brush his teeth in, anyway, and moisten his washcloth. So every morning, after climbing to the basin, he would seize his hammer and pound the faucet, and the other members of the household, dozing in their beds, would hear the bright sharp plink plink plink of Stuart's hammer, like a faraway blacksmith, telling them that day had come and that Stuart was trying to brush his teeth.

Chapter IV EXERCISE

ne fine morning in the month of May, when Stuart was three years old, he arose early as was his custom, washed and dressed himself, took his hat and cane, and went downstairs into the living room to see what was doing. Nobody was around but Snowbell, the white cat belonging to Mrs. Little. Snowbell was another early riser, and this morning he was lying on the rug in the middle of the room, thinking about the days when he was just a kitten.

"Good morning," said Stuart.

"Hello," replied Snowbell, sharply. "You're up early, aren't you?"

Stuart looked at his watch. "Yes," he said, "it's only five minutes past six, but I felt good and I thought I'd come down and get a little exercise."

"I should think you'd get all the exercise you want up there in the bathroom, banging around, waking all the rest of us up trying to get that water started so you can brush your teeth. Your teeth aren't really big enough to brush anyway. Want to see a good set? Look at mine!" Snowbell opened his mouth and showed two rows of gleaming white teeth, sharp as needles.

"Very nice," said Stuart. "But mine are all right, too, even though they're small. As for exercise, I take all I can get. I bet my stomach muscles are firmer than yours."

"I bet they're not," said the cat.

"I bet they are," said Stuart. "They're like iron bands."

"I bet they're not," said the cat.

Stuart glanced around the room to see what he could do to prove to Snowbell what good stomach muscles he had. He spied the window shade on the east window, with its shade cord and ring, like a trapeze, and it gave him an idea. Climbing to the window sill he took off his hat and laid down his cane.

"You can't do this," he said to the cat. And he ran and jumped onto the ring, the way acrobats do in a circus, meaning to pull himself up.

A surprising thing happened. Stuart had taken such a hard jump that it started the shade: with a loud snap the shade flew up clear to the top of the window, dragging Stuart along with it and rolling him up inside, so that he couldn't budge.

"Holy mackerel!" said Snowbell, who was almost as surprised as Stuart Little. "I guess that will teach him to show off his muscles."

"Help! Let me out!" cried Stuart, who was frightened and bruised inside the rolled-up shade, and who could hardly breathe. But his voice was so weak that nobody heard. Snowbell just chuckled. He was not fond of Stuart and it didn't bother him at all that Stuart was all wrapped up in a window shade, crying and hurt and unable to get out.

Instead of running upstairs and telling Mr. and Mrs. Little about the accident, Snowbell did a very curious thing. He glanced around to see if anybody was looking, then he leapt softly to the window sill, picked up Stuart's hat and cane in his mouth, carried them to the pantry and laid them down at the entrance to the mousehole.

When Mrs. Little came down later and found them there, she gave a shrill scream which brought everybody on the run.

"It's happened," she cried.

"What has?" asked her husband.

"Stuart's down the mousehole."

Chapter V RESCUED

George was in favor of ripping up the pantry floor. He ran and got his hammer, his screw driver, and an ice pick.

"I'll have this old floor up in double-quick time," he said, inserting his screwdriver under the edge of the first board and giving a good vigorous pry.

"We will not rip up this floor till we have had a good search," announced Mr. Little. "That's final, George! You can put that hammer away where you got it."

"Oh, all right," said George. "I see that nobody in this house cares anything about Stuart but me."

Mrs. Little began to cry. "My poor dear little son!" she said. "I know he'll get wedged somewhere."

"Just because you can't travel comfortably in a mousehole doesn't mean that it isn't a perfectly suitable place for Stuart," said Mr. Little. "Just don't get yourself all worked up."

"Maybe we ought to lower some food to him," suggested George. "That's what the State Police did when a man got stuck in a cave." George darted into the kitchen and came running back with a dish of applesauce. "We can pour some of this in, and it will run down to where he is." George spooned out a bit of the applesauce and started to poke it into the hole.

"Stop that!" bellowed Mr. Little. "George, will you kindly let me handle this situation? Put that applesauce away immediately!"

Mr. Little glared fiercely at George.

"I was just trying to help my own brother," said George, shaking his head as he carried the sauce back to the kitchen.

"Let's all call to Stuart," suggested Mrs. Little. "It is quite possible that the mousehole branches and twists about, and that he has lost his way."

"Very well," said Mr. Little. "I will count three, then we will all call, then we will all keep perfectly quiet for three seconds, listening for the answer." He took out his watch.

Mr. and Mrs. Little and George got down on their hands and knees and put their mouths as close as possible to the mousehole. Then they all kept perfectly still for three seconds.

Stuart, from his cramped position inside the rolled-up shade, heard them yelling in the pantry and called back, "Here I am!" But he had such a weak voice and was so far inside the shade that the other members of the family did not hear his answering cry.

"Again!" said Mr. Little. "One, two, three—Stooooo-art!"

It was no use. No answer was heard. Mrs Little went up to her bedroom, lay down, and sobbed. Mr. Little went to the telephone and called up the Bureau of Missing Persons, but when the man asked for a description of Stuart and was told that he was only two inches high, he hung up in disgust. George, meantime, went down to the cellar and hunted around to see if he could find the other entrance to the mousehole. He moved a great many trunks, suitcases, flower pots, baskets, boxes, and broken chairs from one end of the cellar to the other in order to get at the section of wall which he thought was likeliest, but found no hole. He did, however, come across an old discarded rowing machine of Mr. Little's, and becoming interested in this, carried it upstairs with some difficulty and spent the rest of the morning rowing.

When lunchtime came (everybody had forgotten about breakfast) all three sat down to a lamb stew which Mrs. Little had prepared, but it was a sad meal, each one trying not to stare at the small empty chair which Stuart always occupied, right next to Mrs. Little's glass of water. No one could eat, so great was the sorrow. George ate a bit of dessert but nothing else. When lunch was over Mrs. Little broke out crying again, and said she thought Stuart must be dead. "Nonsense, nonsense!" growled Mr. Little.

"If he is dead," said George, "we ought to pull down the shades all through the house." And he raced to the windows and began pulling down the shades.

"George!" shouted Mr. Little in an exasperated tone. "If you don't stop acting in an idiotic fashion, I will have to punish you. We are having enough trouble today without having to cope with your foolishness."

But George had already run into the living room and had begun to darken it, to show his respect for the dead. He pulled a cord and out dropped Stuart onto the window sill.

"Well, for the love of Pete," said George. "Look who's here, Mom!"

"It's about time somebody pulled down that shade," remarked Stuart. "That's all I can say." He was quite weak and hungry.

Mrs. Little was so overjoyed to see him that she kept right on crying. Of course, everybody wanted to know how it had happened.

"It was simply an accident that might happen to anybody," said Stuart. "As for my hat and cane being found at the entrance to the mousehole, you can draw your own conclusions."

White, E.B. *Stuart Little*. New York: HarperCollins, 1973.
    Other Editions:
        ——. Boxed Set. Including *Charlotte's Web; The Trumpet of the Swan; Stuart Little*. New York: HarperCollins, 1975.
        ——. *Stuart Little*. New York: HarperCollins, Harper Perennial Books, 1990.

TALES OF
BEATRIX POTTER

BEATRIX POTTER

Beatrix Potter, born in 1866 in London, wrote lively tales of the busy world of little creatures. These stories are about determined rabbits, quick-witted mice, and bothersome gardeners. The cast of characters in the following tales include Peter Rabbit; his nieces and nephews, The Flopsy Bunnies; and Tom Kitten and his siblings.

THE TALE OF PETER RABBIT

 nce upon a time there were four little Rabbits, and their names were Flopsy, Mopsy, Cotton-tail, and Peter. They lived with their Mother in a sand-bank, underneath the root of a very big fir-tree.

"Now, my dears," said old Mrs. Rabbit one morning, "you may go into the fields or down the lane, but don't go into Mr. McGregor's garden; your Father had an accident there; he was put in a pie by Mrs. McGregor. Now run along, and don't get into mischief. I am going out."

Then old Mrs. Rabbit took a basket and her umbrella, and went through the wood to the baker's. She bought a loaf of brown bread and five currant buns. Flopsy, Mopsy, and Cotton-tail, who were good little bunnies, went down the lane to gather blackberries. But Peter, who was very naughty, ran straight away to Mr. McGregor's garden, and squeezed under the gate!

First he ate some lettuces and some French beans; and then he ate some radishes; and then, feeling rather sick, he went to look for some parsley. But round the end of a cucumber frame, whom should he meet but Mr. McGregor!

Mr. McGregor was on his hands and knees planting out young cabbages, but he jumped up and ran after Peter, waving a rake and calling out, "Stop thief!"

Peter was most dreadfully frightened; he rushed all over the garden, for he had forgotten the way back to the gate. He lost one of his shoes among the cabbages, and the other shoe amongst the potatoes.

After losing them, he ran on four legs and went faster, so that I think he might have got away altogether if he had not unfortunately run into a gooseberry net, and got caught by the large buttons on his jacket. It was a blue jacket with brass buttons, quite new.

Peter gave himself up for lost, and shed big tears; but his sobs were overheard by some friendly sparrows, who flew to him in great excitment, and implored him to exert himself.

Mr. McGregor came up with a sieve, which he intended to pop upon the top of Peter; but Peter wriggled out just in time, leaving his jacket behind. And rushed into the toolshed, and jumped into a can. It would have been a beautiful thing to hide in, if it had not had so much water in it.

Mr. McGregor was quite sure that Peter, was somewhere in the toolshed, perhaps hidden underneath a flower-pot. He began to turn them over carefully, looking under each. Presently Peter sneezed—"Kertyschoo!" Mr. McGregor was after him in no time, and tried to put his foot upon Peter, who jumped out of a window, upsetting three plants. The window was too small for Mr. McGregor, and he was tired of running after Peter. He went back to his work.

Peter sat down to rest; he was out of breath and trembling with fright, and he had not the least idea which way to go. Also he was very damp with sitting in that can. After a time he began to wander about, going lippity—lippity—not very fast, and looking all around. He found a door in a wall; but it was locked, and there was no room for a fat little rabbit to squeeze underneath. An old mouse was running in and out over the stone doorstep, carrying peas and beans to her family in the wood. Peter asked her the way to the gate, but she had such a large pea in her mouth that she could not answer. She only shook her head at him. Peter began to cry.

He went back towards the toolshed, but suddenly, quite close to him, he heard the noise of a hoe—scratch, scratch, scritch. Peter scuttered underneath the bushes. But presently, as nothing happened, he came out, and climbed upon a wheelbarrow, and peeped over. The first thing he saw was Mr. McGregor hoeing onions. His back was turned towards Peter, and beyond him was the gate! Peter got down very quietly off the wheelbarrow, and started running as fast as he could go, along a straight walk behind some black-current bushes.

Mr. McGregor caught sight of him at the corner, but Peter did not care. He slipped underneath the gate, and was safe at last in the wood outside the garden. Mr. McGregor hung up the little jacket and the shoes for a scare-crow to frighten the blackbirds.

Peter never stopped running or looked behind him till he got home to the big fir-tree. He was so tired that he flopped down upon the nice soft sand on the floor of the rabbit-hole, and shut his eyes. His mother was busy cooking; she wondered what he had done with his clothes. It was the second little jacket and pair of shoes that Peter had lost in a fortnight!

I am sorry to say that Peter was not very well during the evening. His mother put him to bed, and made some camomile tea; and she gave a dose of it to Peter!

"One tablespoonful to be taken at bedtime!"

But Flopsy, Mopsy, and Cotton-tail had bread and milk and blackberries for supper.

394

THE TALE OF THE FLOPSY BUNNIES

I t is said that the effect of eating too much lettuce is "soporific." I have never felt sleepy after eating lettuces; but then I am not a rabbit. They certainly had a very soporific effect upon the Flopsy Bunnies!

When Benjamin Bunny grew up, he married his cousin Flopsy. They had a large family, and they were very improvident and cheerful. I do not remember the separate names of their children; they were generally called the "Flopsy Bunnies." As there was not always quite enough to eat—Benjamin used to borrow cabbages from Flopsy's brother, Peter Rabbit, who kept a nursery garden. Sometimes Peter Rabbit had no cabbages to spare. When this happened, the Flopsy Bunnies went across the field to a rubbish heap, in the ditch outside Mr. McGregor's garden.

Mr. McGregor's rubbish heap was a mixture. There were jam pots and paper bags, and mountains of chopped grass from the mowing machine (which always tasted oily), and some rotten vegetable marrows and an old boot or two. One day—oh joy!—there were a quantity of overgrown lettuces, which had "shot" into flower. The Flopsy Bunnies simply stuffed lettuces. By degrees, one after another, they were overcome with slumber, and lay down in the mown grass.

Benjamin was not so much overcome as his children. Before going to sleep he was sufficiently wide awake to put a paper bag over his head to keep off the flies. The little Flopsy Bunnies slept delightfully in the warm sun. From the lawn beyond the garden came

the distant clacketty sound of the mowing machine. The blue-bottles buzzed about the wall, and a little old mouse picked over the rubbish among the jam pots. (I can tell you her name, she was called Thomasina Tittlemouse, a woodmouse with a long tail.) She rustled across the paper bag, and awakened Benjamin Bunny. The mouse apologized profusely, and said that she knew Peter Rabbit.

While she and Benjamin were talking, close under the wall, they heard a heavy tread above their heads; and suddenly Mr. McGregor emptied out a sackful of lawn mowings right upon the sack of sleeping Flopsy Bunnies! Benjamin shrank down under his paper bag. The mouse hid in the jam pot.

The little rabbits smiled sweetly in their sleep under the shower of grass; they did not awake because the lettuces had been so soporific. They dreamt that their mother Flopsy was tucking them up in a hay bed.

Mr. McGregor looked down after emptying his sack. He saw some funny little brown tips of ears sticking up through the lawn mowings. He stared at them for some time. Presently a fly settled on one of them and it moved. Mr. McGregor climbed down on to the rubbish heap—

"One, two, three, four! five! six leetle rabbits!" said he as he dropped them into his sack. The Flopsy Bunnies dreamt that their mother was turning them over in bed. They stirred a little in their sleep, but still they did not wake up. Mr. McGregor tied up the sack and left it on the wall. He went to put away the mowing machine.

While he was gone, Mrs. Flopsy Bunny (who had remained at home) came across the field. She looked suspiciously at the sack and wondered where everybody was. Then the mouse came out of her jam pot, and Benjamin took the paper bag off his head, and they told the doleful tale. Benjamin and Flopsy were in despair, they could not undo the string. But Mrs. Tittlemouse was a resourceful person. She nibbled a hole in the bottom corner of the sack. The little rabbits were pulled out and pinched to wake them. Their parents stuffed the empty sack with three rotten vegetable marrows, an old blacking brush and two decayed turnips.

Then they all hid under a bush and watched for Mr. McGregor. Mr. McGregor came back and picked up the sack, and carried it off. He carried it hanging down, as if it were rather heavy. The Flopsy Bunnies followed at a safe distance. They watched him go into his house. And then they crept up to the window to listen.

Mr. McGregor threw down the sack on the floor in a way that would have been extremely painful to the Flopsy Bunnies, if they had happened to have been inside it.

They could hear him drag his chair on the flags, and chuckle—

"One, two, three, four, five, six leetle rabbits!" said Mr. McGregor.

"Eh? What's that? What have they been spoiling now? enquired Mrs. McGregor.

"One, two, three, four, five, six leetle fat rabbits!" repeated Mr. McGregor, counting on his fingers—"one, two, three—"

"Don't you be silly: What do you mean, you silly old man?"

"In the sack! One, two, three, four, five, six!" replied Mr. McGregor.

(The youngest Flopsy Bunny got upon the windowsill.)

Mrs. McGregor took hold of the sack and felt it. She said she could feel six, bit they must be old rabbits, becuse they were so hard and all different shapes.

"Not fit to eat; but the skins will do fine to line my old cloak."

"Line your old cloak?" shouted Mr. McGregor—"I shall sell them to buy myself baccy!"

"Rabbit tobacco! I shall skin them and cut off their heads."

Mrs. McGregor untied the sack and put her hand inside. When she felt the vegetables she became very very angry. She said that Mr. McGregor had "done it a purpose." And Mr. McGregor was very angry too. One of the rotten marrows came flying through the kitchen window, and hit the youngest Flopsy Bunny. It was rather hurt. Then Benjamin and Flopsy thought that it was time to go home. So Mr. McGregor did not get his tobacco, and Mrs. McGregor did not get her rabbit skins.

But next Christmas Thomasina Tittlemouse got a present of enough rabbit wool to make herself a cloak and a hood, and a handsome muff and a pair of warm mittens.

THE TALE OF TOM KITTEN

nce upon a time there were three little kittens, and their names were Mittens, Tom Kitten, and Moppet. They had dear little fur coats of their own; and they tumbled about the doorstep and played in the dust.

But one day their mother—Mrs. Tabitha Twitchit—expected friends to tea; so she fetched the kittens indoors, to wash and dress them, before the fine company arrived. First she scrubbed their faces. Then she brushed their fur. Then she combed their tails and whiskers. Tom was very naughty, and he scratched.

Mrs. Tabitha dressed Moppet and Mittens in clean pinafores and tuckers; and then she took all sorts of elegant uncomfortable clothes out of a chest of drawers, in order to dress up her son Thomas. Tom Kitten was very fat, and he had grown; several buttons burst off. His mother sewed them on again.

When the three kittens were ready, Mrs. Tabitha unwisely turned them out into the garden, to be out of the way while she made hot buttered toast.

"Now keep your frocks clean, children! You must walk on your hind legs. Keep away from the dirty ash-pit, and from Sally Henny Penny, and from the pigsty and the Puddle-ducks."

Moppet and Mittens walked down the garden path unsteadily. Presently they trod upon their pinafores and fell on their noses. When they stood up there were several green smears!

"Let us climb up the rockery and sit on the garden wall," said Moppet.

They turned their pinafores back to front and went up with a skip and a jump; Moppet's white tucker fell down into the road. Tom Kitten was quite unable to jump when walking upon his hind legs in his trousers. He came up the rockery by degrees, breaking the ferns and shedding buttons right and left. He was all in pieces when he reached the top of the wall.

Moppet and Mittens tried to pull him together; his hat fell off, and the rest of his buttons burst. While they were in difficulties, there was a pit pat, paddle pat! and the three Puddle-ducks came along the hard high road, marching one behind the other and doing the goose step—pit, pat, paddle pat! pit pat, waddle pat!

They stopped and stood in a row and stared up at the kittens. They had very small eyes and looked surprised. The two duck-birds, Rebeccah and Jemima Puddle-duck, picked up the hat and tucker and put them on.

Mittens laughed so that she fell off the wall. Moppet and Tom descended after her; the pinafores and all the rest of Tom's clothes came off on the way down.

"Come! Mr. Drake Puddle-duck," said Moppet. "Come and help us dress him! Come buttom up Tom!"

Mr. Drake Puddle-duck advanced in a slow sideways manner and picked up the various articles. But he put them on himself! They fitted him even worse than Tom Kitten.

"It's a very fine morning!" said Mr. Drake Puddle-duck.

And he and Jemima and Rebeccah Puddle-duck set off up the road, keeping step—pit pat, paddle pat! pit pat, waddle pat! Then Tabitha Twitchit came down to the garden and found her kittens on the wall with no clothes on. She pulled them off the wall, smacked them, and took them back to the house.

"My friends will arrive in a minute, and you are not fit to be seen; I am affronted," said Mrs. Tabitha Twitchit.

She sent them upstairs; and I am sorry to say she told her friends that they were in bed with the measles—which was not true. Quite the contrary; they were not in bed: not in the least.

Somehow there were very extraordinary noises overheard, which disturbed the dignity and repose of the tea party. And I think that some day I shall have to make another, larger book, to tell you more about Tom Kitten!

As for the Puddle-ducks—they went into a pond. The clothes all came off directly, because there were no buttons. And Mr. Drake Puddle-duck, and Jemima and Rebeccah, have been looking for them ever since.

Potter, Beatrix. *Peter Rabbit.* New York: Random House, 1984.
> Other editions:
>> ——. *Peter Rabbit and Eleven Other Favorite Tales.* Adapted by Pat Stewart. New York: Dover, 1994.

ACKNOWLEDGMENTS

From *Tales of a Fourth Grade Nothing* by Judy Blume. Copyright © 1972 by Judy Blume. Illustrations copyright © 1972 by E.P. Dutton. Used by permission of Dutton Children's Books, a division of Penguin Books USA Inc.

From *The Return of the Twelves* by Pauline Clarke. Copyright © 1962 by Pauline Clarke. Used by permission of Dell Books, a division of Bantam Doubleday Dell Publishing Group, Inc.

For *The Return of the Twelves* United Kingdom and Canadian rights granted by Curtis Brown Group on behalf of Mrs. Peter Hunter Blair.

Excerpt from Ch. 3, from *Ramona Forever* by Beverly Cleary. Copyright © 1984 by Beverly Cleary. Used by permission of Morrow Jr. Books, a division of William Morrow and Company, Inc.

"Good-bye Violet" from *Charlie and the Chocolate Factory* by Roald Dahl, illustrated by Joseph Schindelman. Copyright © 1964 by Roald Dahl. Copyright renewed 1992 by Roald Dahl and Alfred A. Knopf, Inc.

"The Real Witch and the Pretend Witch" from *The Witch Family*, copyright © 1960 and renewed 1988 by Eleanor Estes, reprinted by permission of Harcourt Brace & Company.

"The Storm" from *The Black Stallion* by Walter Farley. Copyright © 1941 and renewed 1969 by Walter Farley. Reprinted by permission of Random House, Inc.

Excerpt from "Nantucket" from *Cheaper By the Dozen* by Frank Gilbreth, Jr. and Ernestine Gilbreth Carey. Copyright © 1948, 1963 by Frank Gilbreth, Jr. and Ernestine Gilbreth Carey. Reprinted by permission of HarperCollins Publishers, Inc.

Excerpt from *Old Yeller* by Fred Gipson. Copyright © 1956 by Fred Gipson. Copyright renewed. Reprinted by permission of HarperCollins Publishers, Inc.

Excerpt from *Paddle-To-The-Sea*. Copyright © 1941, renewed 1969 by Holling Clancy Holling. Reprinted by permission of Houghton Mifflin Co. All rights reserved.

Excerpt from *Animal Family* by Randall Jarell. Copyright © 1965 by Randall Jarrell. Reprinted with permission of HarperCollins Publishers, Inc.

Excerpt from *From the Mixed-Up Files of Mrs. Basil E. Frankweiler* reprinted with the permission of Atheneum Books for young Readers, an imprint of Simon & Schuster Children's Publishing Division from *From the Mixed-Up Files of Mrs. Basil E. Frankweiler* by E.L. Konigsburg. Copyright © 1967 E.L. Konigsburg.

Excerpt from "The Black Thing" from *A Wrinkle in Time* by Madeleine L'Engle. Copyright ©1962 and renewed © 1990 by Crosswicks Ltd. Reprinted by permission of Farrar, Straus & Giroux, Inc.

Excerpt from "Digory and His Uncle," from *The Chronicles of Narnia, Book One: The Magician's Nephew* by C.S. Lewis. Copyright © 1955 by C. S. Lewis. Used by permission of HarperCollins Publishers.

"Pippi Plays Tag with Some Policemen, Ch. 3," from *Pippi Longstocking* by Astrid Lindgren, translated by Florence Lamborn. Translation copyright 1950 by the Viking Press, Inc., renewed © 1978 by Viking Penguin Inc. Used by permission of Viking Penguin, a division of Penguin Books USA Inc.

"Illustrations" by Louis S. Glanzman, from *Pippi Longstocking* by Astrid Lindgren, translated by Florence Lamborn. Translation copyright 1950 by the Viking Press, Inc., renewed © 1978 by Viking Penguin Inc. Used by permission of Viking Penguin, a division of Penguin Books USA Inc.

"The Doughnuts," from *Homer Price* by Robert McCloskey. Copyright 1943, renewed © 1971 by Robert McCloskey. Used by permission Viking Penguin, a division of Penguin Books USA Inc.

Unabridged text of Chapter XII "The Pea Shooter Campaign— Phase 1" from *The Pushcart War* by Jean Merrill. Text copyright © 1964 by Jean Merrill. Illustrations copyright © 1964 by Ronni Solbert. Selection reprinted by permission of HarperCollins Publishers.

Excerpt from *Harris and Me: A Summer Remembered,* copyright © 1993 by Gary Paulsen, reprinted by permission of Harcourt Brace & Company.

From *Summer of the Monkeys* by Woodrow Wilson Rawls. Copyright © 1976 by Woodrow Wilson Rawls. Used by permission of Doubleday, a division of Bantam Doubleday Dell Publishing Group, Inc.

"The Case of the Headless Runner," from *Encyclopedia Brown Shows the Way* by Donald J. Sobol. Copyright © 1972 by Donald J. Sobol; Copyright © 1972 by Thomas Nelson. Used by permission of Lodestar Books, an affiliate of Dutton Children's Books, a division of Penguin USA Inc.

Excerpt from *The Little Prince* by Antoine de Saint-Exupéry, copyright 1943 and renewed 1971 by Harcourt Brace & Company, reprinted by permission of the publisher.

Excerpt from *The Hobbit.* Copyright © 1966 by J.R.R. Tolkien. Reprinted by permission of Houghton Mifflin Co. All rights reserved.

Unabridged text and illustrations of Chapter 13, "Good Progress" from *Charlotte's Web* by E.B. White. Copyright 1952 by E.B. White renewed © 1980 by E.B. White. Selection reprinted by permission of HarperCollins Publishers.

Unabridged text of Chapters 3, 4, and 5 from *Stuart Little* by E.B. White. Copyright 1945 by E.B. White. Text Copyright renewed © 1973 by E.B. White. Selection reprinted by permission of HarperCollins Publishers.

Excerpt from Chapter 19 from *Little House on the Prairie* by Laura Ingalls Wilder. Text Copyright 1935 by Laura Ingalls Wilder, Copyright © renewed 1963 by Roger L. Macbride. Selection reprinted by permission of HarperCollins Publishers.